An Inspector Calls

THE GRAPHIC NOVEL
J. B. Priestley

QUICK TEXT VERSION

Script Adaptation: Jason Cobley
American English Adaptation: Joe Sutliff Sanders
Linework: Will Volley
Coloring: Alejandro Sanchez
Lettering: Jim Campbell
Design & Layout: Jo Wheeler,
Jenny Placentino & Carl Andrews
Editor in Chief: Clive Bryant

An Inspector Calls: The Graphic Novel
Quick Text Version
J. B. Priestley

First US edition

Published by: Classical Comics Ltd
with the permission of The Estate of J. B. Priestley
for which the publisher extends their sincere thanks.

Play first published by William Heinemann Ltd 1947.

All rights whatsoever in this play are strictly reserved and applications for performances,
etc., should be made in advance by professional companies to United Agents,
12-26 Lexington Street, London WIF OLE and by amateur companies to
Samuel French Ltd, 52 Fitzroy Street, London WIT 5JR.

Acknowledgments: Every effort has been made to trace copyright holders of
material reproduced in this book. Any rights not acknowledged here will be
acknowledged in subsequent editions if notice is given to Classical Comics Ltd.

All enquiries should be addressed to:
Classical Comics Ltd
PO Box 7280
Litchborough
Towcester
NN12 9AR
United Kingdom

info@classicalcomics.com
www.classicalcomics.com

ISBN: 978-1-907127-24-3

Printed in the USA

This book is printed by CG Book Printers using environmentally safe inks, on paper from
responsible sources. This material can be disposed of by recycling, incineration for energy
recovery, composting and biodegradation.

The rights of Jason Cobley, Joe Sutliff Sanders, Will Volley, Alejandro Sanchez and Jim Campbell
to be identified as the artists of this adaptation have been asserted in accordance with
the Copyright, Designs and Patents Act 1988 sections 77 and 78.

Contents

An Inspector Calls

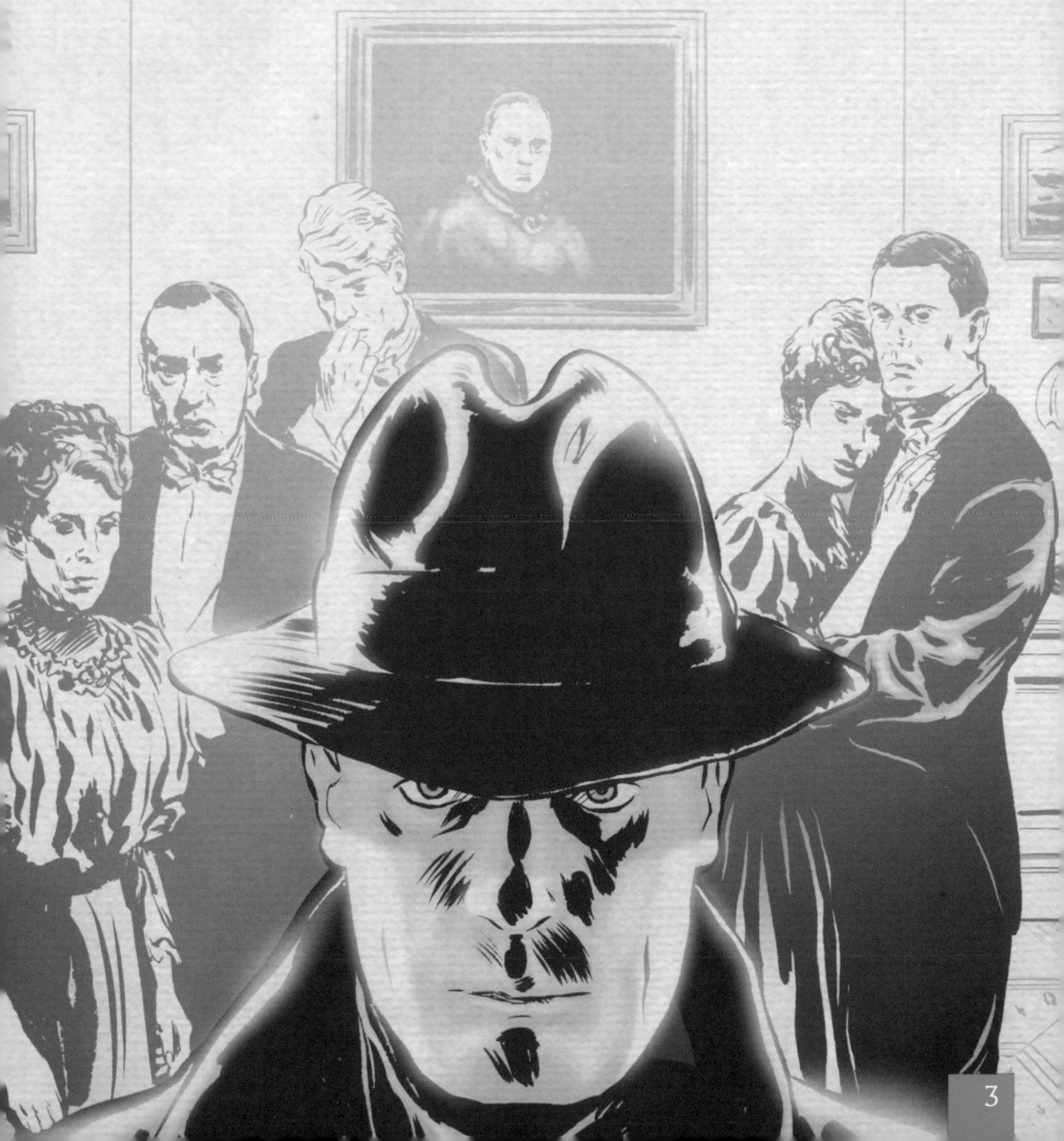

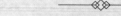

Dramatis Personæ

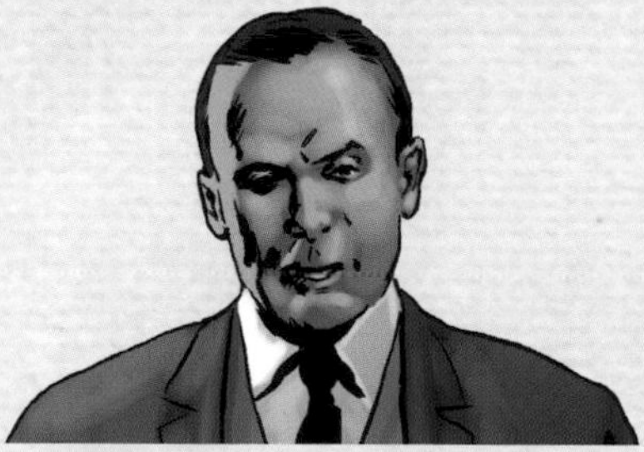

Inspector Goole

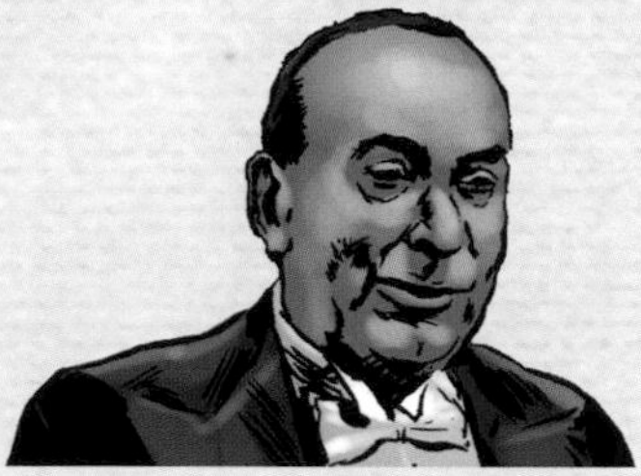

Arthur Birling
A wealthy industrialist

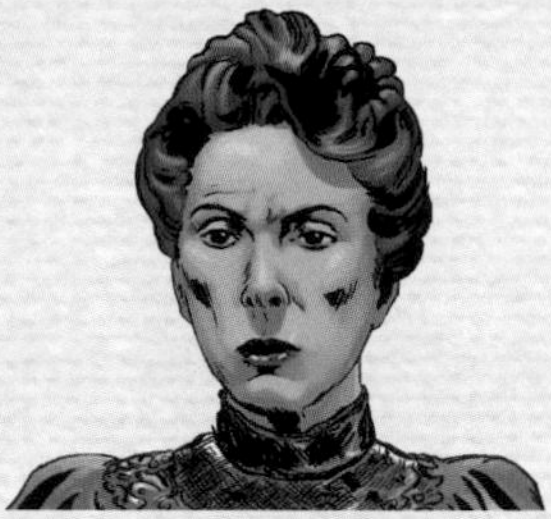

Sybil Birling
Arthur Birling's wife

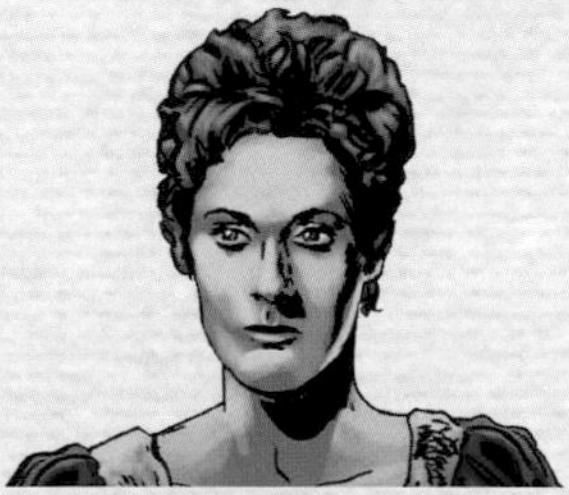

Sheila Birling
Arthur & Sybil's daughter

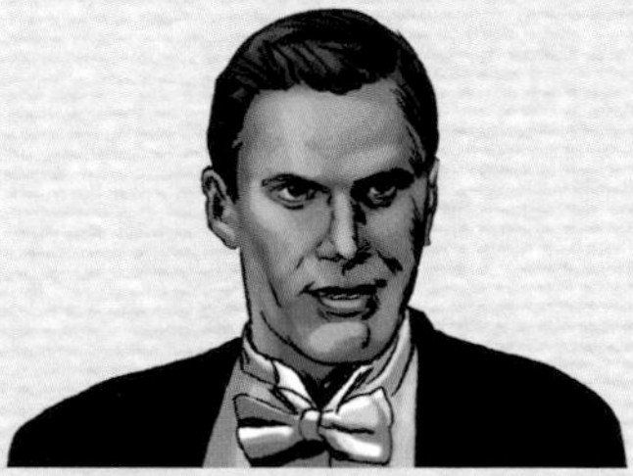

Gerald Croft
Sheila's fiancé

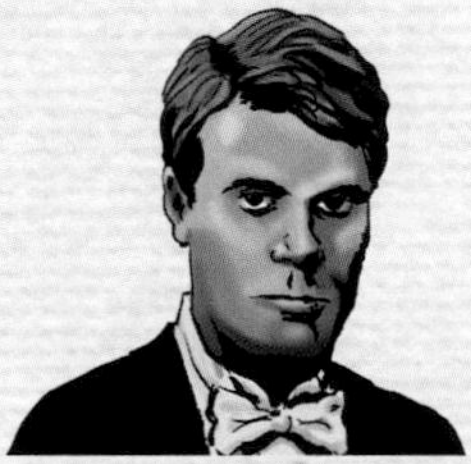

Eric Birling
Arthur & Sybil's son

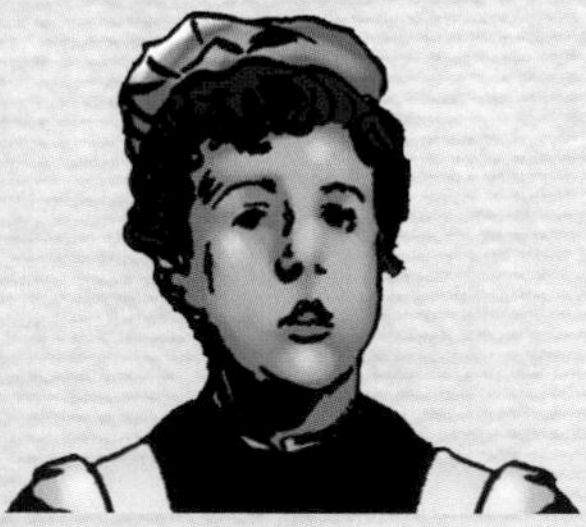

Edna
The Birlings' parlor-maid

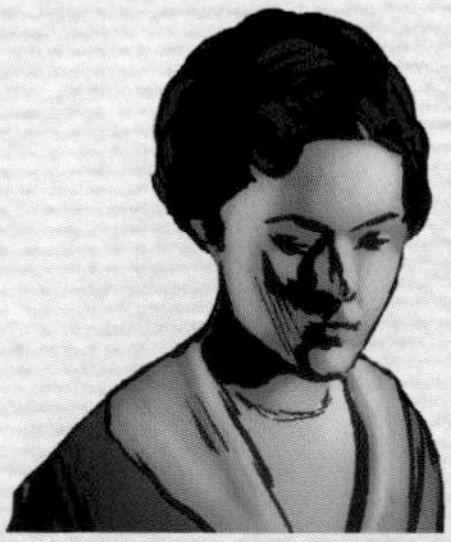

Eva Smith / Daisy Renton

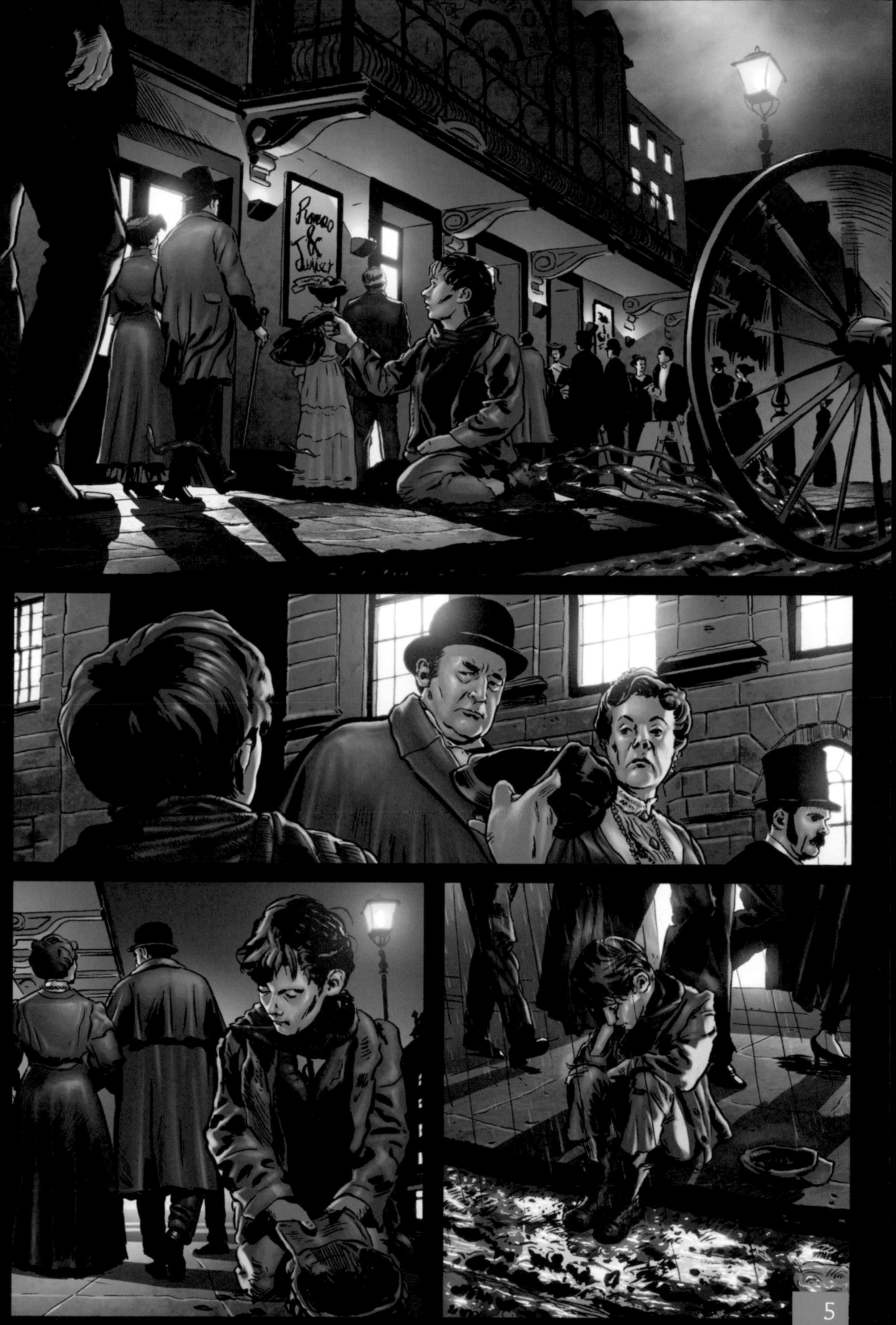
Romeo & Juliet

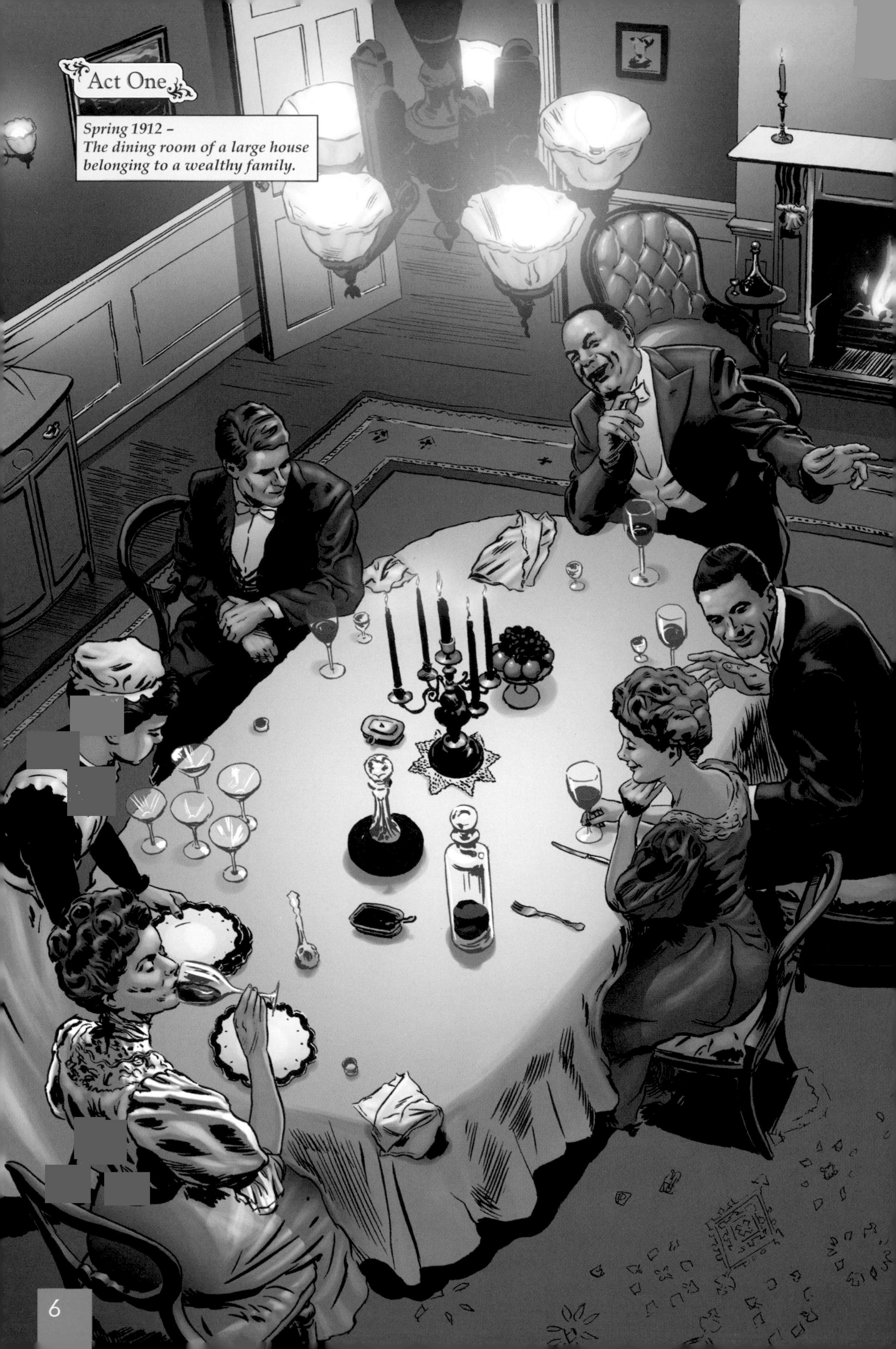
Act One
Spring 1912 –
The dining room of a large house
belonging to a wealthy family.

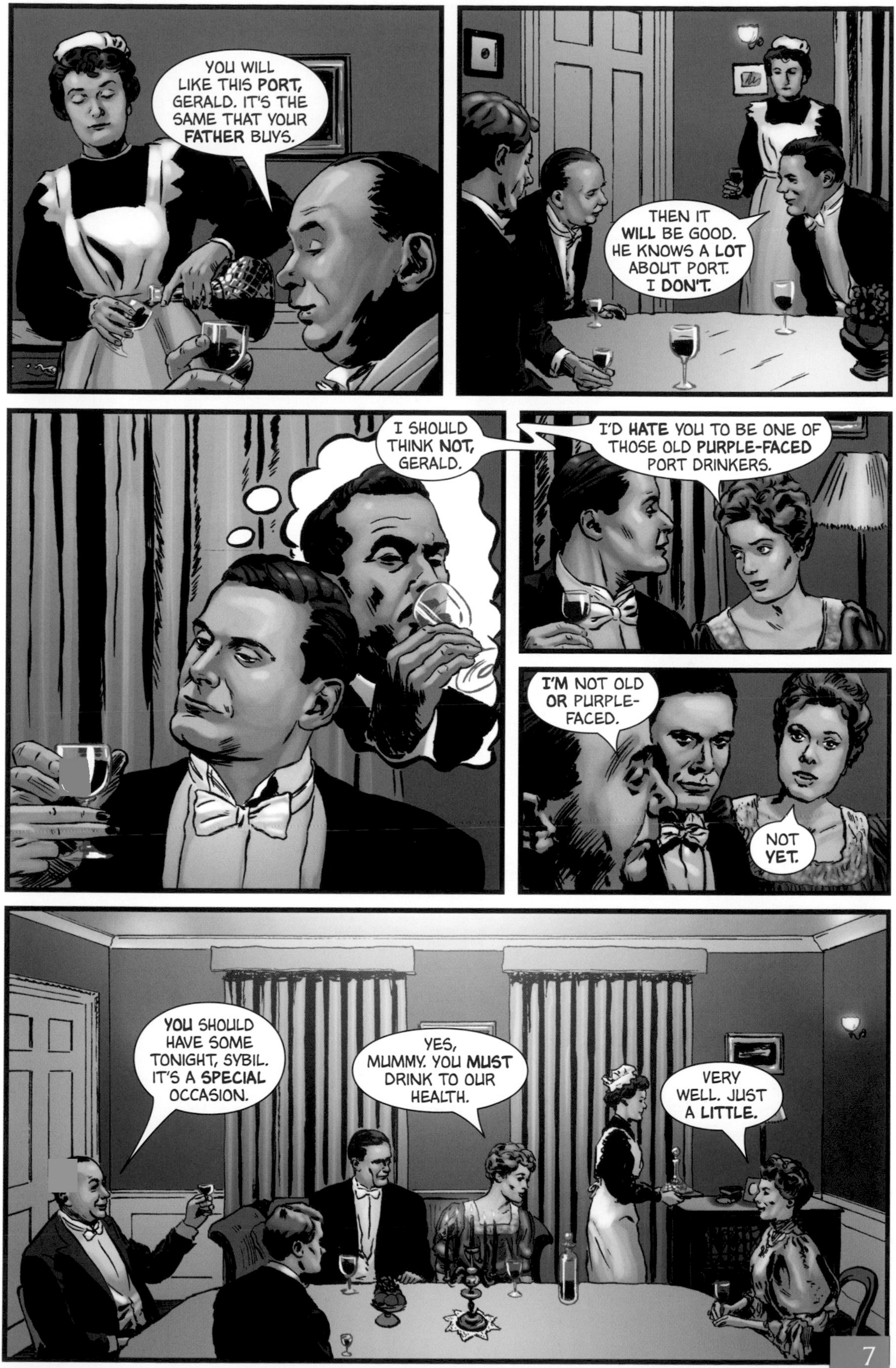
YOU WILL LIKE THIS PORT, GERALD. IT'S THE SAME THAT YOUR FATHER BUYS.
THEN IT WILL BE GOOD. HE KNOWS A LOT ABOUT PORT. I DON'T.
I SHOULD THINK NOT, GERALD.
I'D HATE YOU TO BE ONE OF THOSE OLD PURPLE-FACED PORT DRINKERS.
I'M NOT OLD OR PURPLE-FACED.
NOT YET.
YOU SHOULD HAVE SOME TONIGHT, SYBIL. IT'S A SPECIAL OCCASION.
YES, MUMMY. YOU MUST DRINK TO OUR HEALTH.
VERY WELL. JUST A LITTLE.

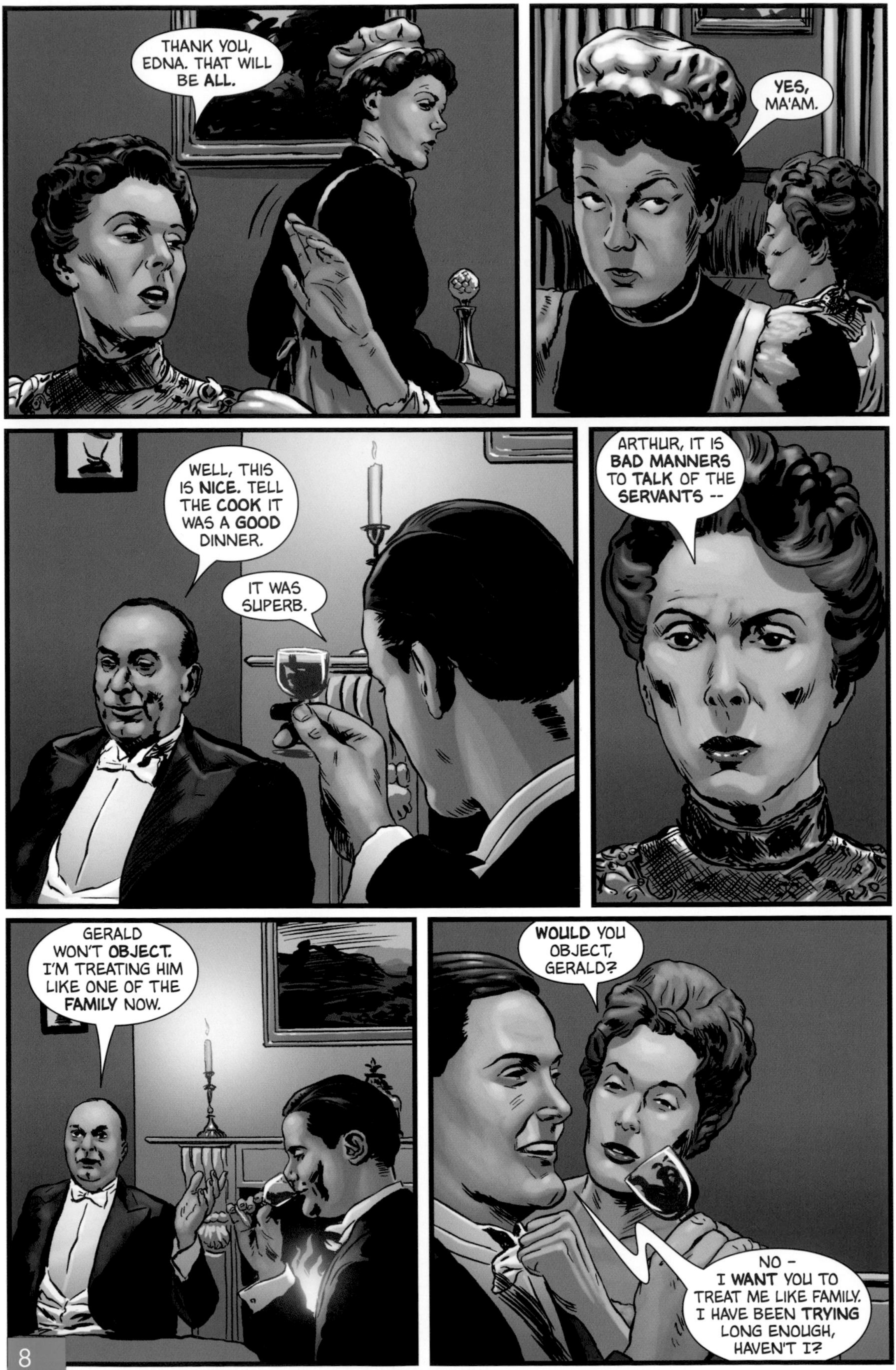
THANK YOU, EDNA. THAT WILL BE ALL.
YES, MA'AM.
WELL, THIS IS NICE. TELL THE COOK IT WAS A GOOD DINNER.
IT WAS SUPERB.
ARTHUR, IT IS BAD MANNERS TO TALK OF THE SERVANTS --
GERALD WON'T OBJECT. I'M TREATING HIM LIKE ONE OF THE FAMILY NOW.
WOULD YOU OBJECT, GERALD?
NO – I WANT YOU TO TREAT ME LIKE FAMILY. I HAVE BEEN TRYING LONG ENOUGH, HAVEN'T I?

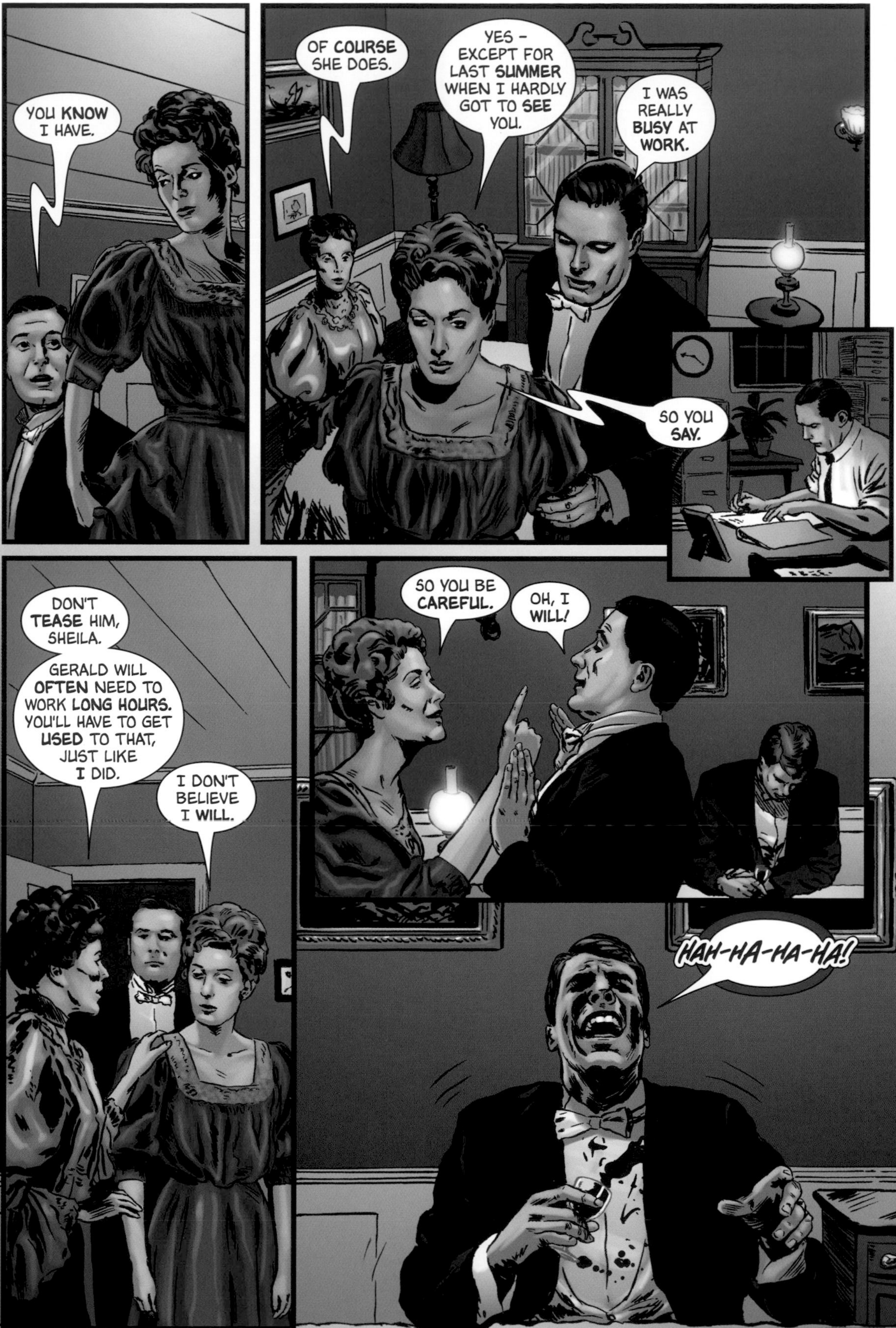

YOU KNOW I HAVE.
OF COURSE SHE DOES.
YES – EXCEPT FOR LAST SUMMER WHEN I HARDLY GOT TO SEE YOU.
I WAS REALLY BUSY AT WORK.
SO YOU SAY.
DON'T TEASE HIM, SHEILA.
GERALD WILL OFTEN NEED TO WORK LONG HOURS. YOU'LL HAVE TO GET USED TO THAT, JUST LIKE I DID.
I DON'T BELIEVE I WILL.
SO YOU BE CAREFUL.
OH, I WILL!
HAH-HA-HA-HA!

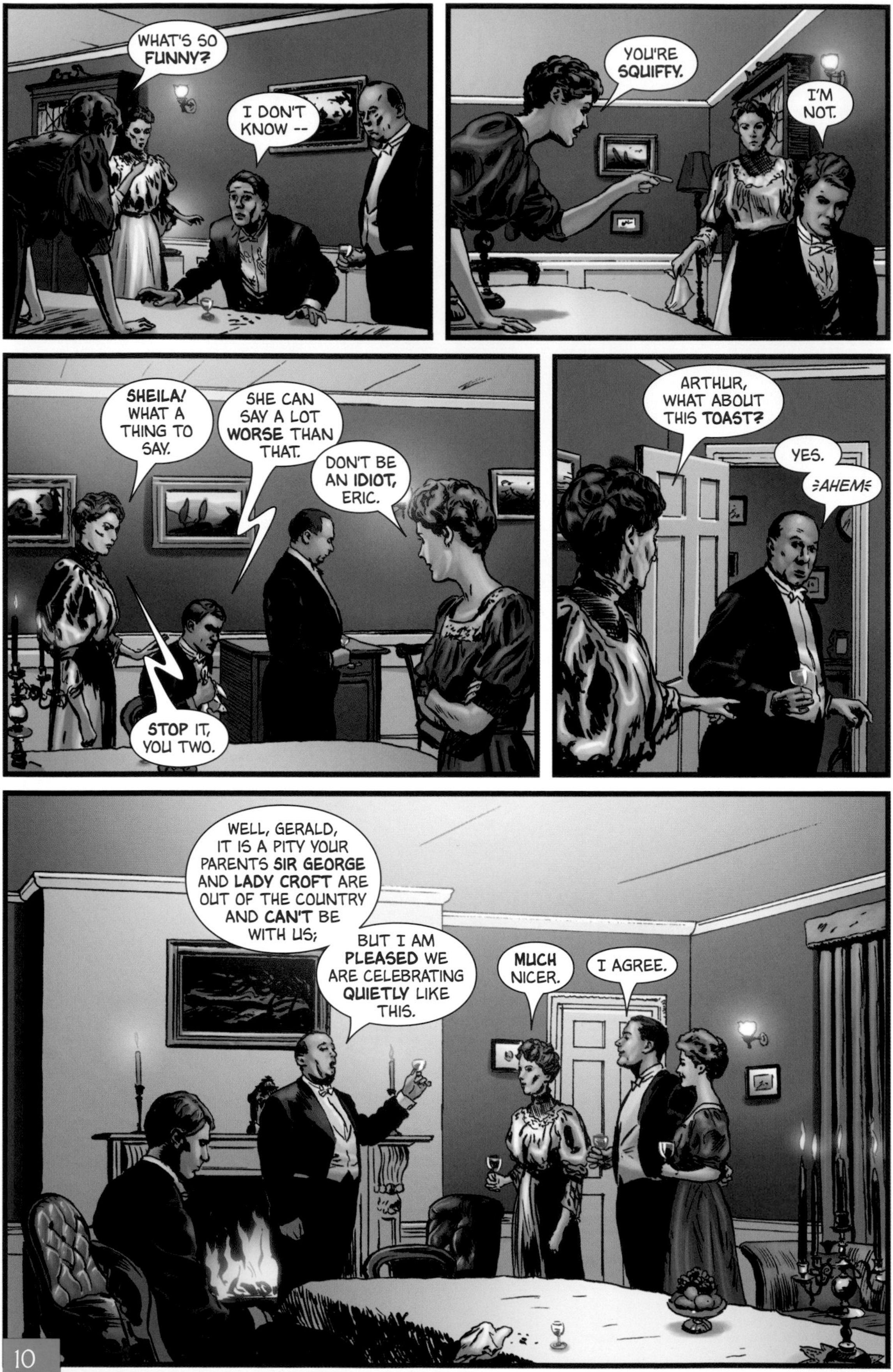

WHAT'S SO FUNNY?
I DON'T KNOW --
YOU'RE SQUIFFY.
I'M NOT.
SHEILA! WHAT A THING TO SAY.
SHE CAN SAY A LOT WORSE THAN THAT.
DON'T BE AN IDIOT, ERIC.
STOP IT, YOU TWO.
ARTHUR, WHAT ABOUT THIS TOAST?
YES.
AHEM
WELL, GERALD, IT IS A PITY YOUR PARENTS SIR GEORGE AND LADY CROFT ARE OUT OF THE COUNTRY AND CAN'T BE WITH US;
BUT I AM PLEASED WE ARE CELEBRATING QUIETLY LIKE THIS.
MUCH NICER.
I AGREE.

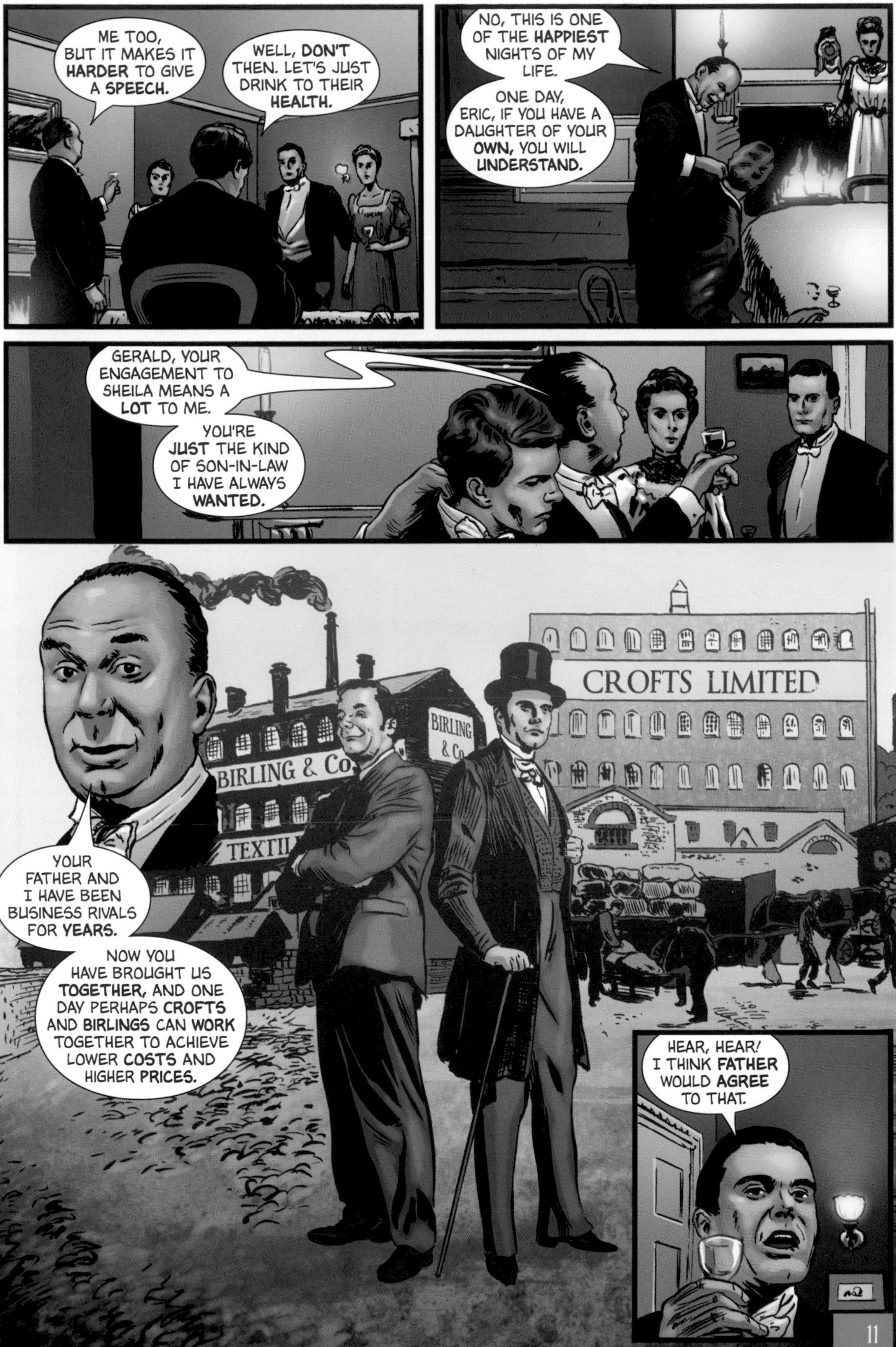
ME TOO, BUT IT MAKES IT HARDER TO GIVE A SPEECH.
WELL, DON'T THEN. LET'S JUST DRINK TO THEIR HEALTH.
NO, THIS IS ONE OF THE HAPPIEST NIGHTS OF MY LIFE.
ONE DAY, ERIC, IF YOU HAVE A DAUGHTER OF YOUR OWN, YOU WILL UNDERSTAND.
GERALD, YOUR ENGAGEMENT TO SHEILA MEANS A LOT TO ME.
YOU'RE JUST THE KIND OF SON-IN-LAW I HAVE ALWAYS WANTED.
CROFTS LIMITED
BIRLING & Co
BIRLING & Co
YOUR FATHER AND I HAVE BEEN BUSINESS RIVALS FOR YEARS.
NOW YOU HAVE BROUGHT US TOGETHER, AND ONE DAY PERHAPS CROFTS AND BIRLINGS CAN WORK TOGETHER TO ACHIEVE LOWER COSTS AND HIGHER PRICES.
HEAR, HEAR! I THINK FATHER WOULD AGREE TO THAT.

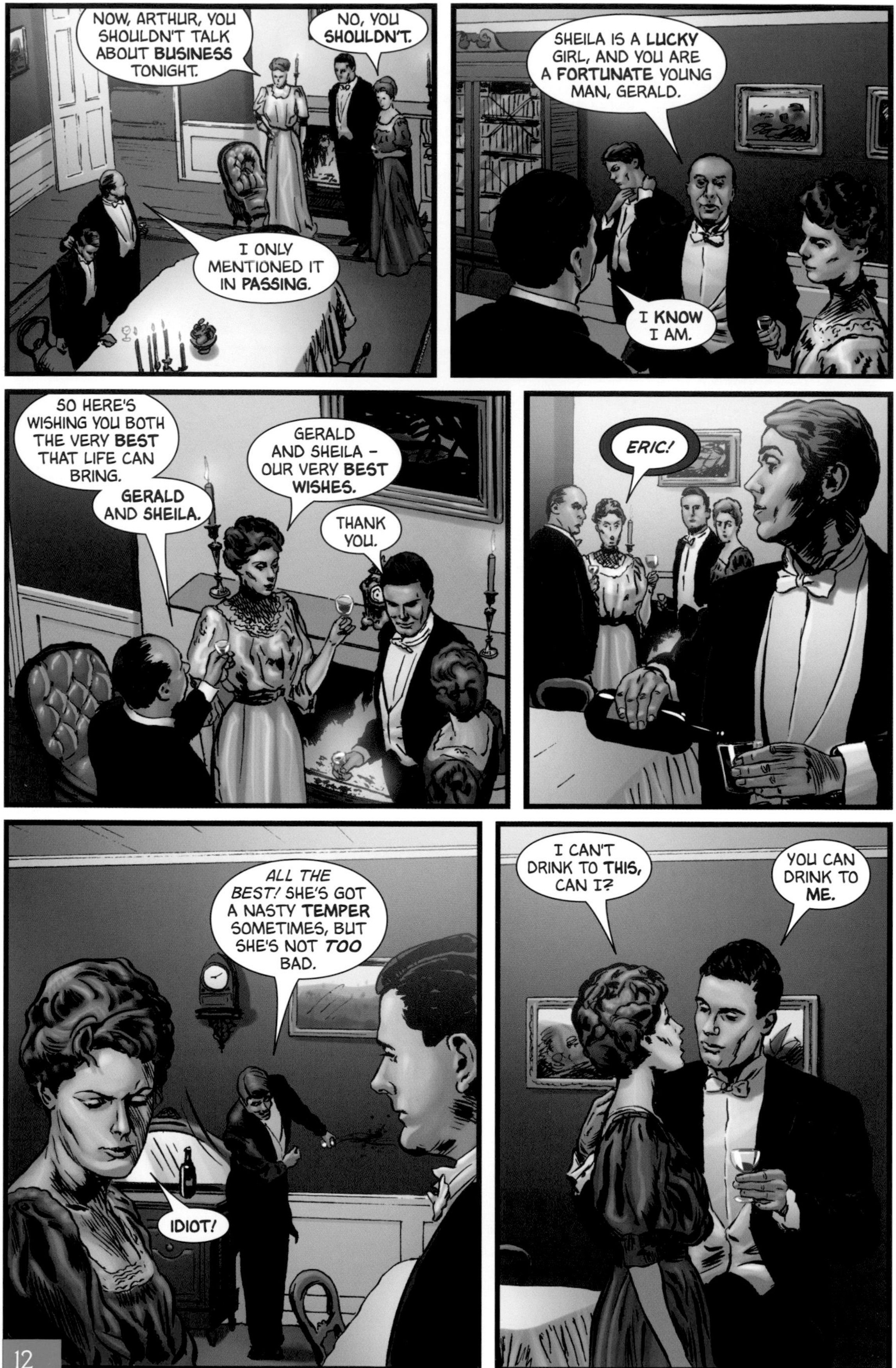
NOW, ARTHUR, YOU SHOULDN'T TALK ABOUT **BUSINESS** TONIGHT.
NO, YOU **SHOULDN'T.**
I ONLY MENTIONED IT IN **PASSING.**
SHEILA IS A **LUCKY** GIRL, AND YOU ARE A **FORTUNATE** YOUNG MAN, GERALD.
I **KNOW** I AM.
SO HERE'S WISHING YOU BOTH THE VERY **BEST** THAT LIFE CAN BRING.
GERALD AND SHEILA.
GERALD AND SHEILA – OUR VERY **BEST WISHES.**
THANK YOU.
ERIC!
ALL THE BEST! SHE'S GOT A NASTY **TEMPER** SOMETIMES, BUT SHE'S NOT ***TOO*** BAD.
IDIOT!
I CAN'T DRINK TO **THIS,** CAN I?
YOU CAN DRINK TO **ME.**

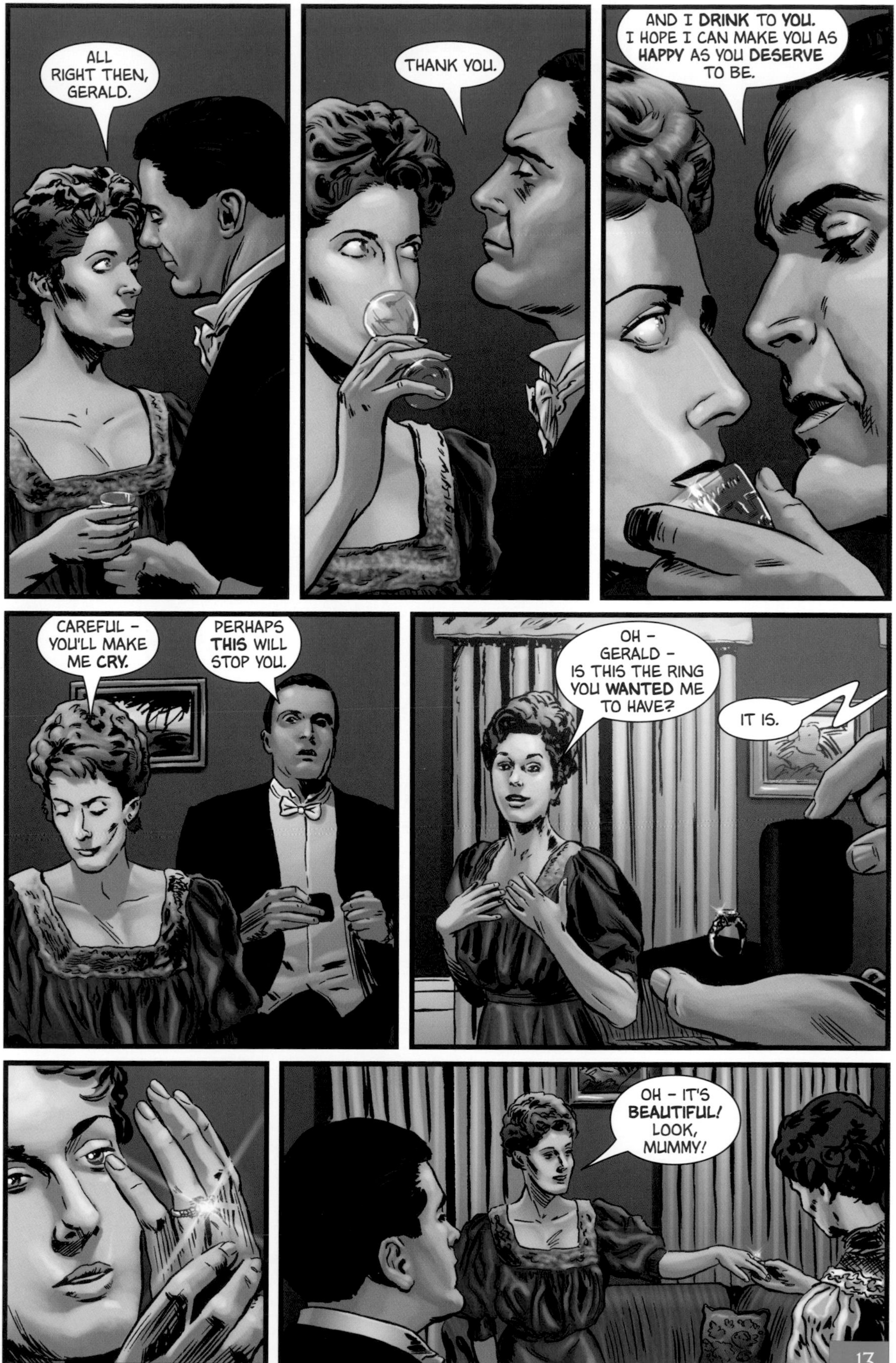
ALL RIGHT THEN, GERALD.
THANK YOU.
AND I DRINK TO YOU. I HOPE I CAN MAKE YOU AS HAPPY AS YOU DESERVE TO BE.
CAREFUL – YOU'LL MAKE ME CRY.
PERHAPS THIS WILL STOP YOU.
OH – GERALD – IS THIS THE RING YOU WANTED ME TO HAVE?
IT IS.
OH – IT'S BEAUTIFUL! LOOK, MUMMY!

OH – DARLING –

STEADY!

IT'S **PERFECT.** NOW I **REALLY** FEEL ENGAGED.

SO YOU **SHOULD,** DARLING. BE **CAREFUL** WITH IT.

I'LL **NEVER** LET IT OUT OF MY SIGHT.

THAT WAS GOOD **TIMING,** GERALD.

IF YOU'VE **FINISHED,** ARTHUR, SHEILA AND I WILL GO INTO THE **DRAWING-ROOM** AND LEAVE YOU **MEN** TO **TALK.**

I JUST WANTED TO **SAY** THIS.

ARE YOU **LISTENING,** SHEILA?

YES, DADDY.

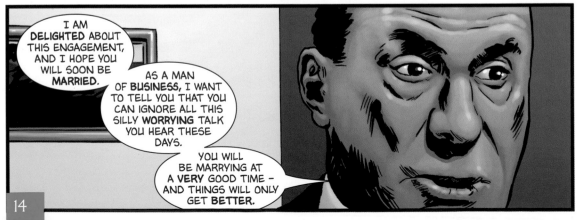

I AM **DELIGHTED** ABOUT THIS ENGAGEMENT, AND I HOPE YOU WILL SOON BE **MARRIED.**

AS A MAN OF **BUSINESS,** I WANT TO TELL YOU THAT YOU CAN IGNORE ALL THIS SILLY **WORRYING** TALK YOU HEAR THESE DAYS.

YOU WILL BE MARRYING AT A **VERY** GOOD TIME – AND THINGS WILL ONLY GET **BETTER.**

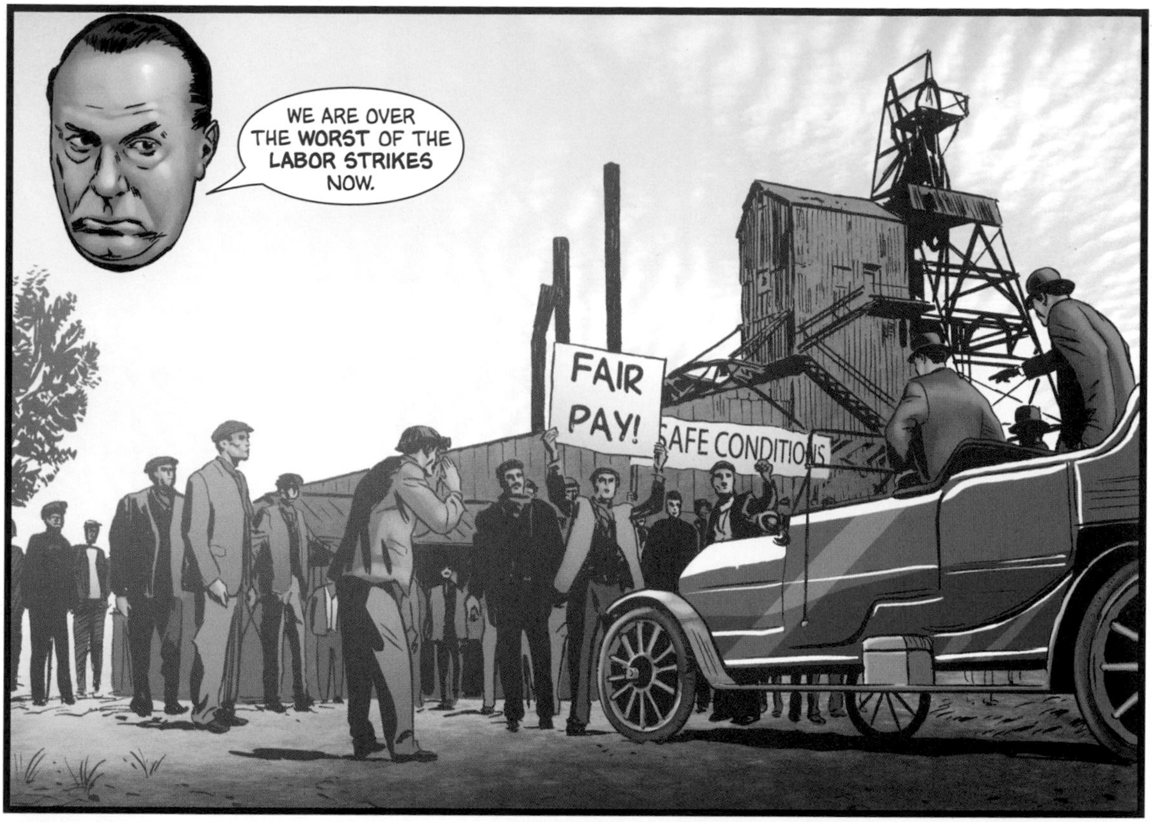
WE ARE OVER THE WORST OF THE LABOR STRIKES NOW.
FAIR PAY!
SAFE CONDITIONS

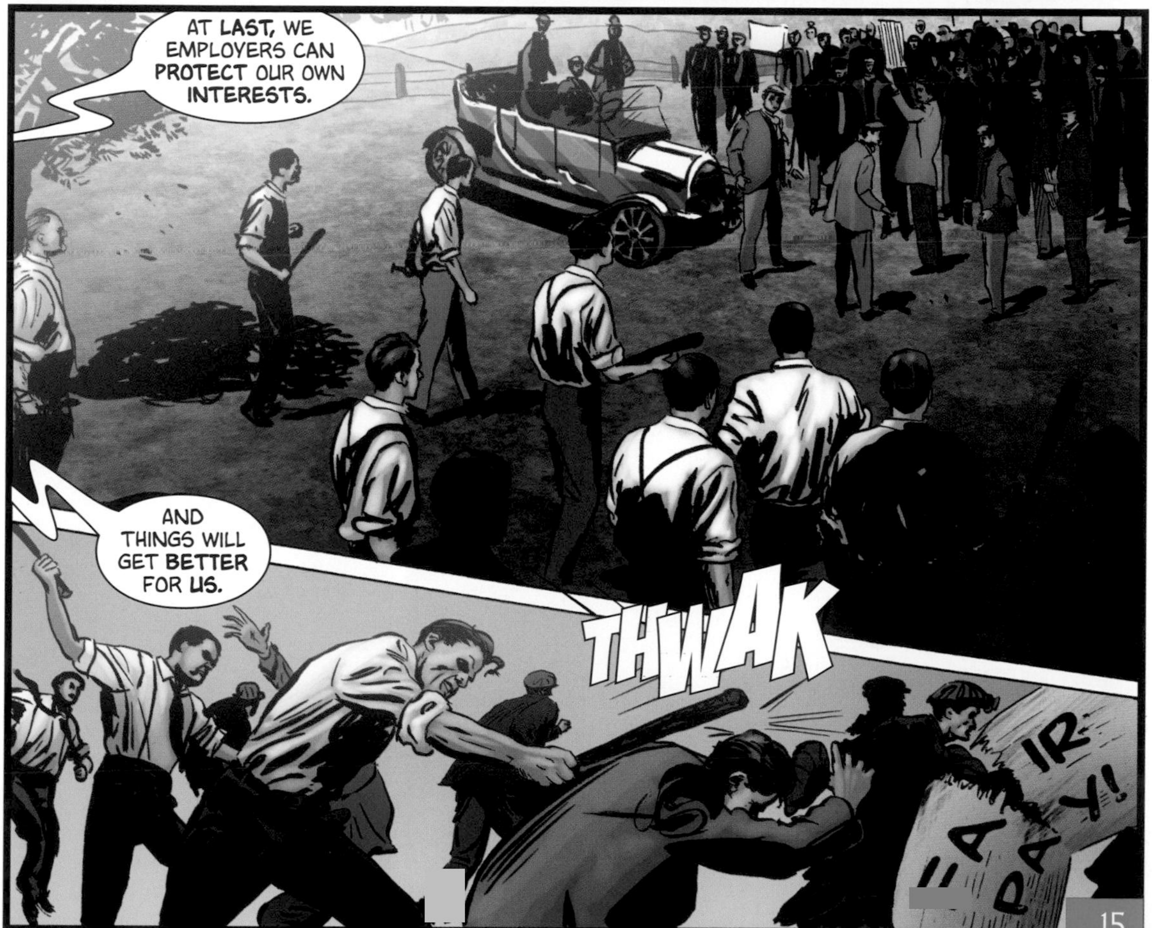
AT LAST, WE EMPLOYERS CAN PROTECT OUR OWN INTERESTS.
AND THINGS WILL GET BETTER FOR US.
THWAK

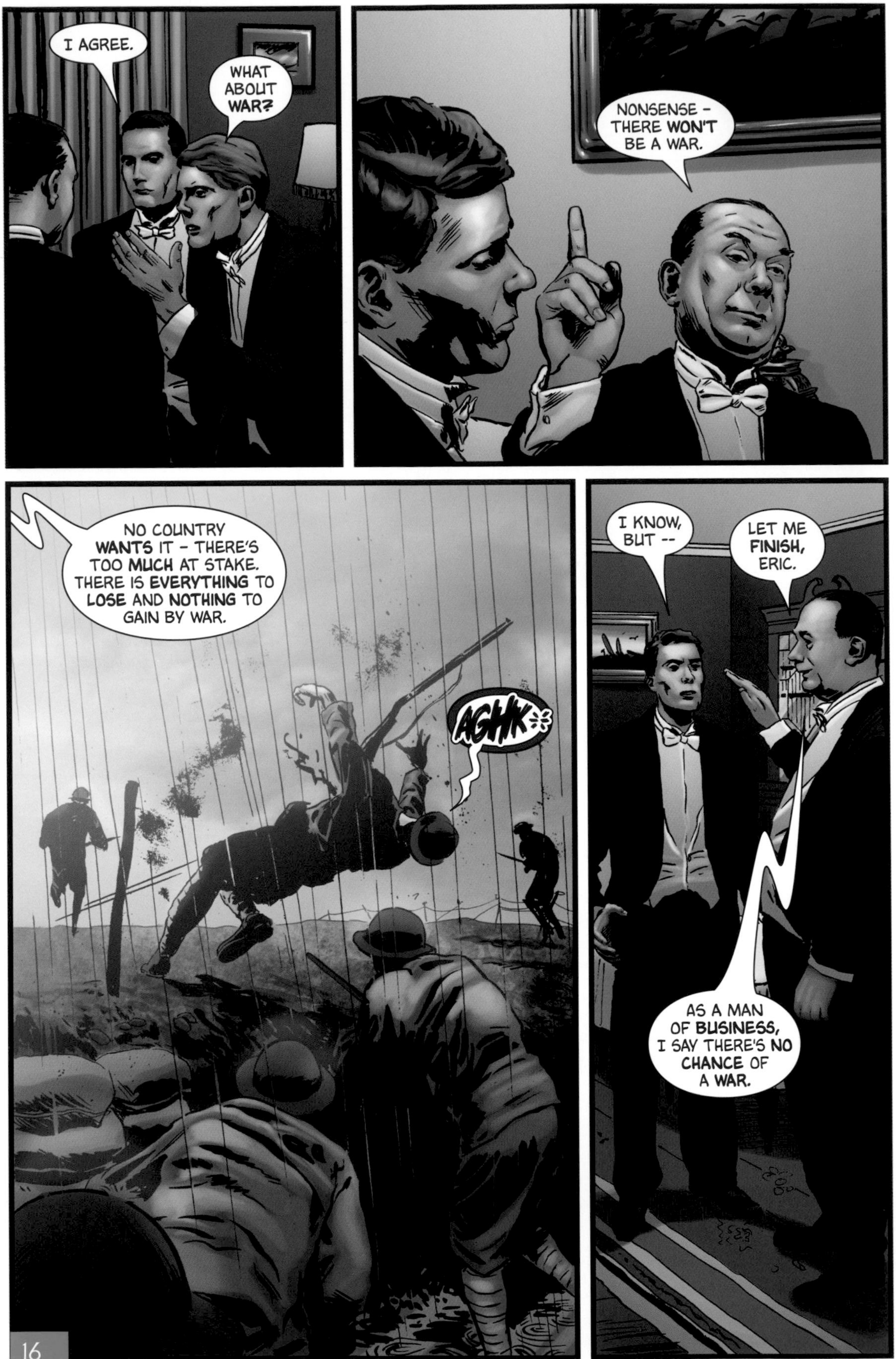
I AGREE.
WHAT ABOUT WAR?
NONSENSE – THERE WON'T BE A WAR.
NO COUNTRY WANTS IT – THERE'S TOO MUCH AT STAKE. THERE IS EVERYTHING TO LOSE AND NOTHING TO GAIN BY WAR.
AGHK
I KNOW, BUT --
LET ME FINISH, ERIC.
AS A MAN OF BUSINESS, I SAY THERE'S NO CHANCE OF A WAR.

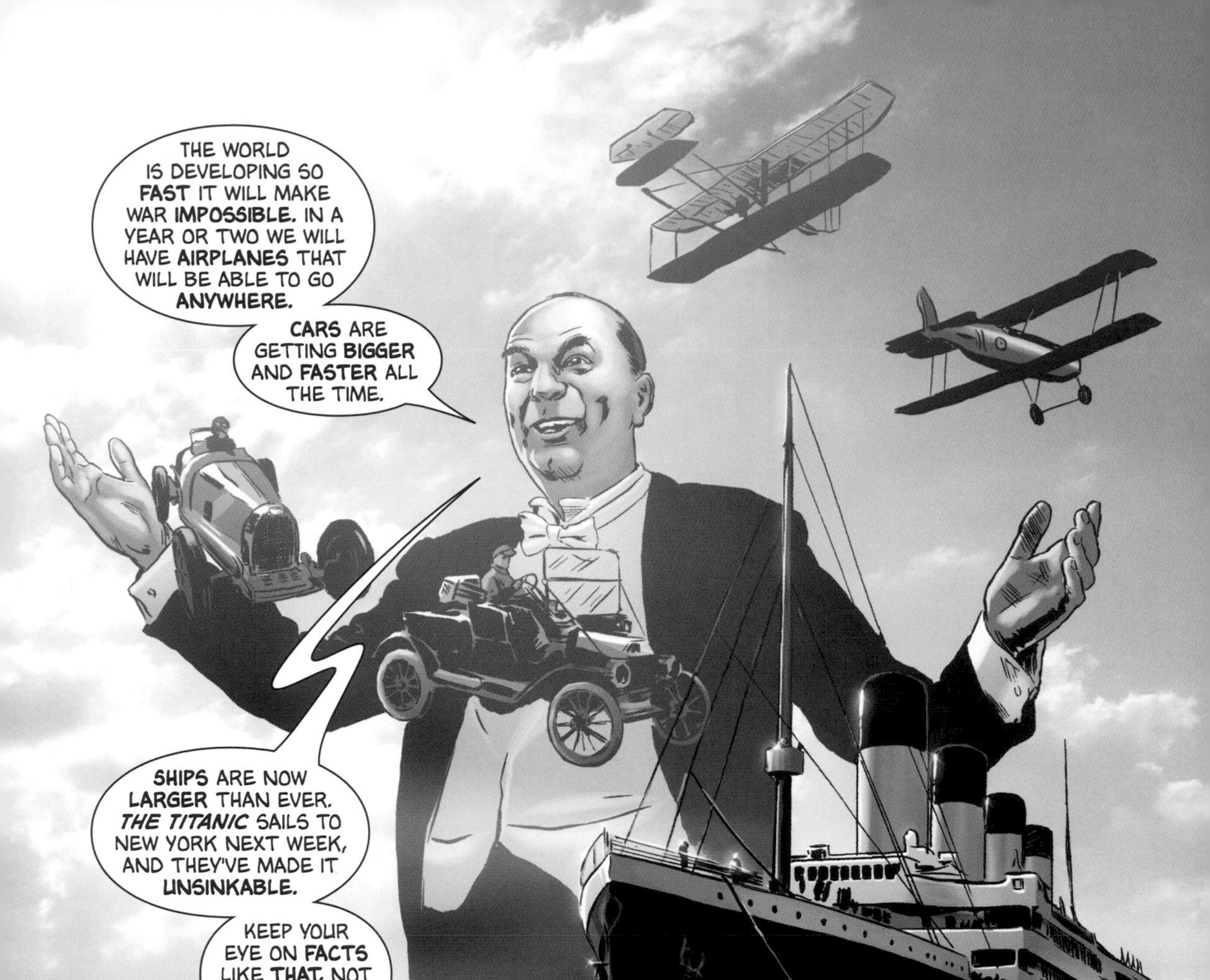
THE WORLD IS DEVELOPING SO FAST IT WILL MAKE WAR IMPOSSIBLE. IN A YEAR OR TWO WE WILL HAVE AIRPLANES THAT WILL BE ABLE TO GO ANYWHERE.
CARS ARE GETTING BIGGER AND FASTER ALL THE TIME.
SHIPS ARE NOW LARGER THAN EVER. THE TITANIC SAILS TO NEW YORK NEXT WEEK, AND THEY'VE MADE IT UNSINKABLE.
KEEP YOUR EYE ON FACTS LIKE THAT, NOT ON SILLY TALK ABOUT WAR.

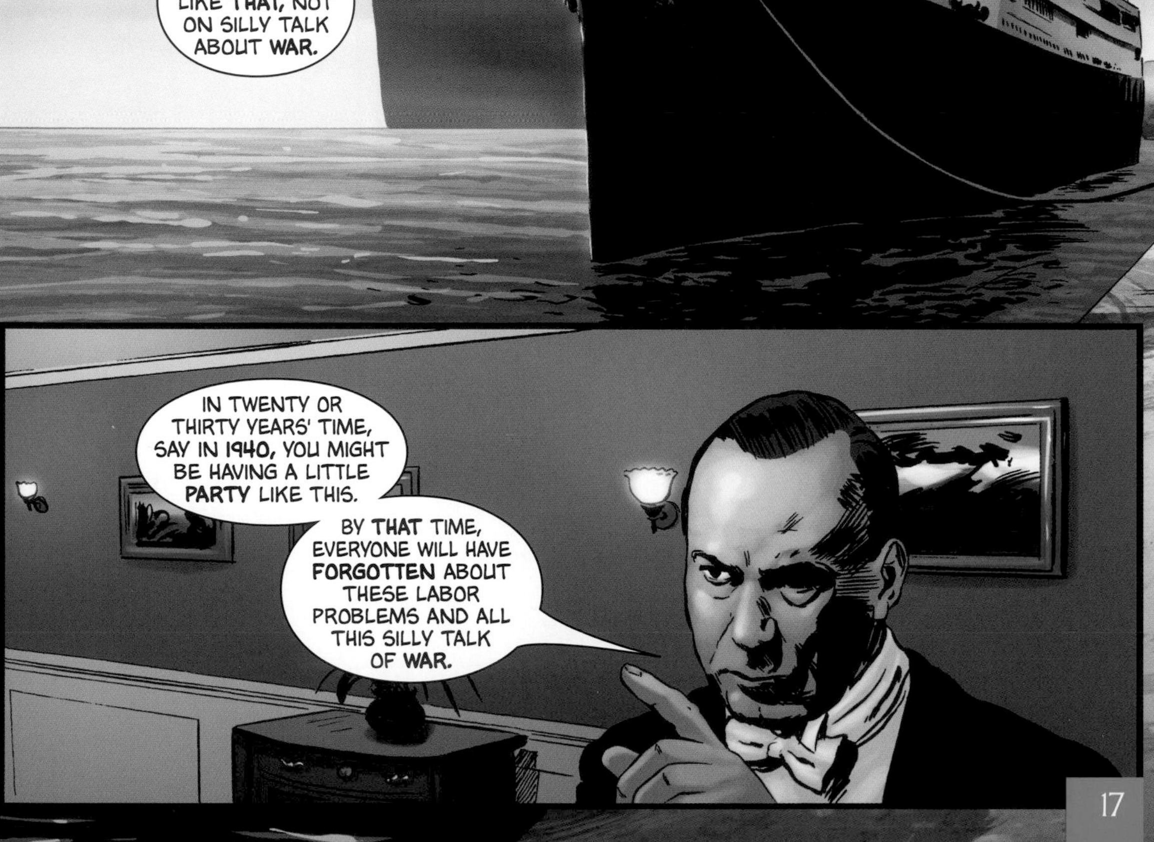
IN TWENTY OR THIRTY YEARS' TIME, SAY IN 1940, YOU MIGHT BE HAVING A LITTLE PARTY LIKE THIS.
BY THAT TIME, EVERYONE WILL HAVE FORGOTTEN ABOUT THESE LABOR PROBLEMS AND ALL THIS SILLY TALK OF WAR.

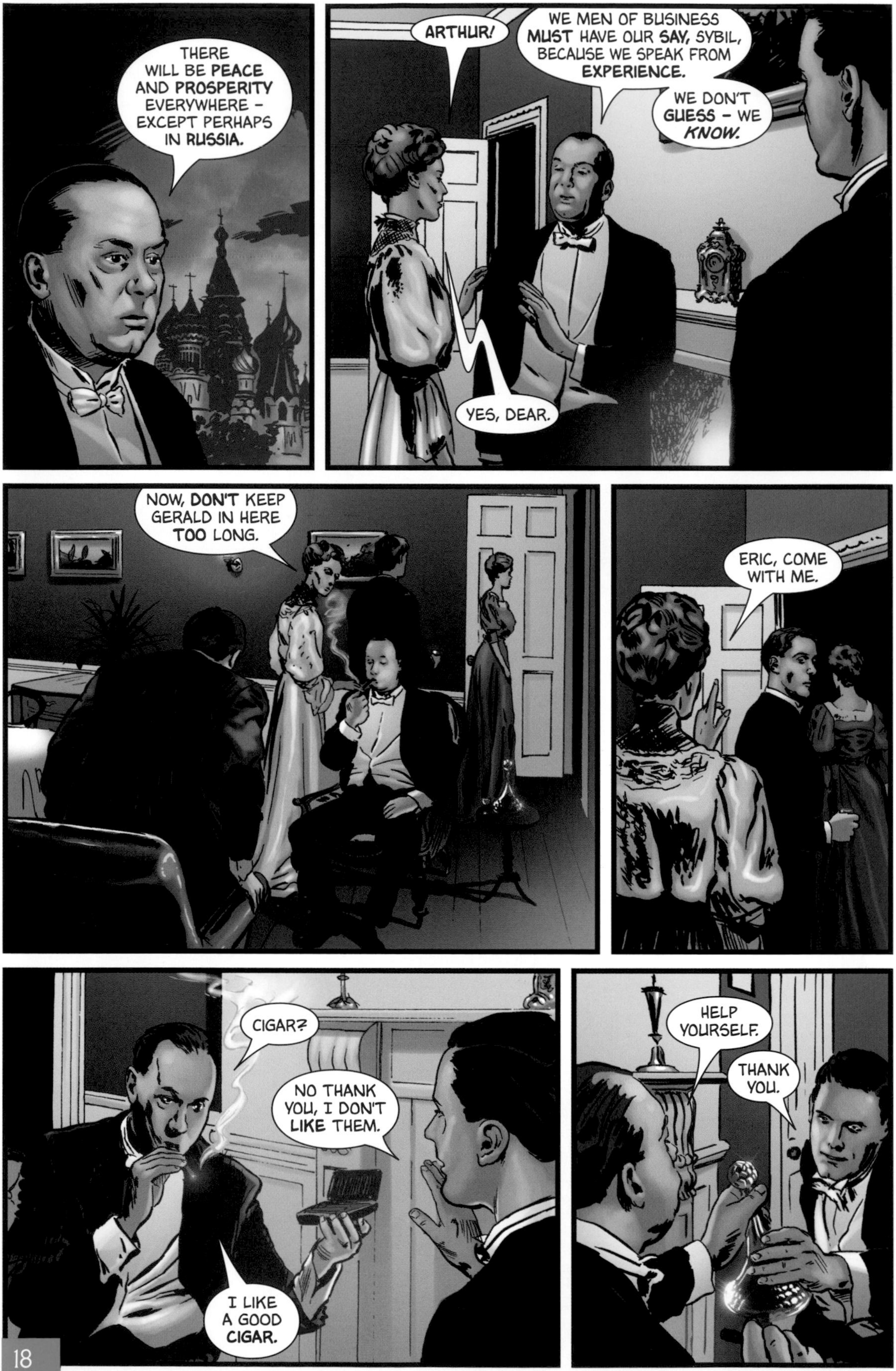
THERE WILL BE PEACE AND PROSPERITY EVERYWHERE – EXCEPT PERHAPS IN RUSSIA.
ARTHUR!
WE MEN OF BUSINESS MUST HAVE OUR SAY, SYBIL, BECAUSE WE SPEAK FROM EXPERIENCE.
WE DON'T GUESS – WE KNOW.
YES, DEAR.
NOW, DON'T KEEP GERALD IN HERE TOO LONG.
ERIC, COME WITH ME.
CIGAR?
NO THANK YOU, I DON'T LIKE THEM.
I LIKE A GOOD CIGAR.
HELP YOURSELF.
THANK YOU.

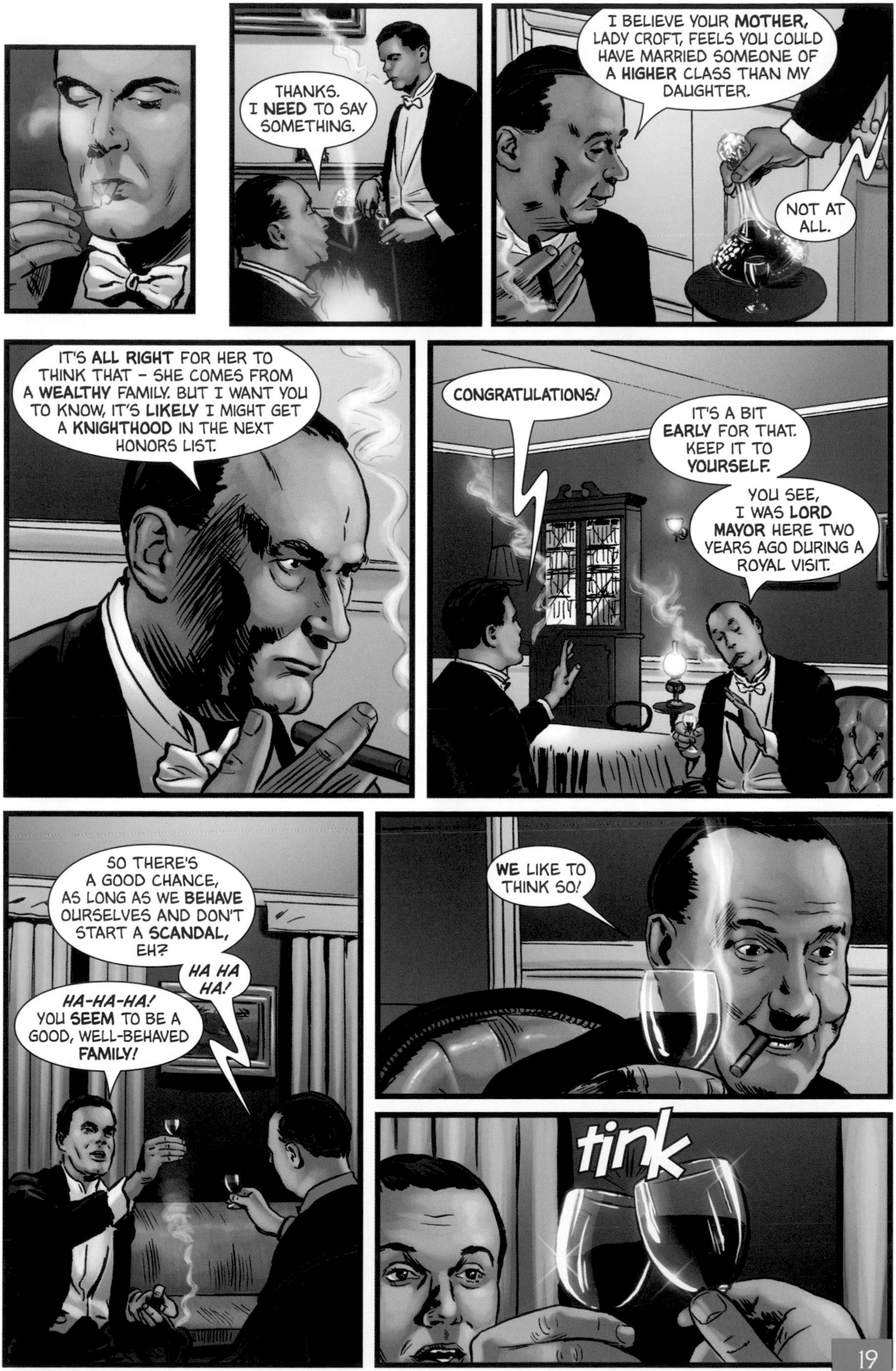
THANKS. I **NEED** TO SAY SOMETHING.
I BELIEVE YOUR **MOTHER,** LADY CROFT, FEELS YOU COULD HAVE MARRIED SOMEONE OF A **HIGHER** CLASS THAN MY DAUGHTER.
NOT AT ALL.
IT'S **ALL RIGHT** FOR HER TO THINK THAT – SHE COMES FROM A **WEALTHY** FAMILY. BUT I WANT YOU TO KNOW, IT'S **LIKELY** I MIGHT GET A **KNIGHTHOOD** IN THE NEXT HONORS LIST.
CONGRATULATIONS!
IT'S A BIT **EARLY** FOR THAT. KEEP IT TO **YOURSELF.**
YOU SEE, I WAS **LORD MAYOR** HERE TWO YEARS AGO DURING A ROYAL VISIT.
SO THERE'S A GOOD CHANCE, AS LONG AS WE **BEHAVE** OURSELVES AND DON'T START A **SCANDAL,** EH?
HA HA HA!
HA-HA-HA! YOU **SEEM** TO BE A GOOD, WELL-BEHAVED **FAMILY!**
WE LIKE TO THINK SO!
tink

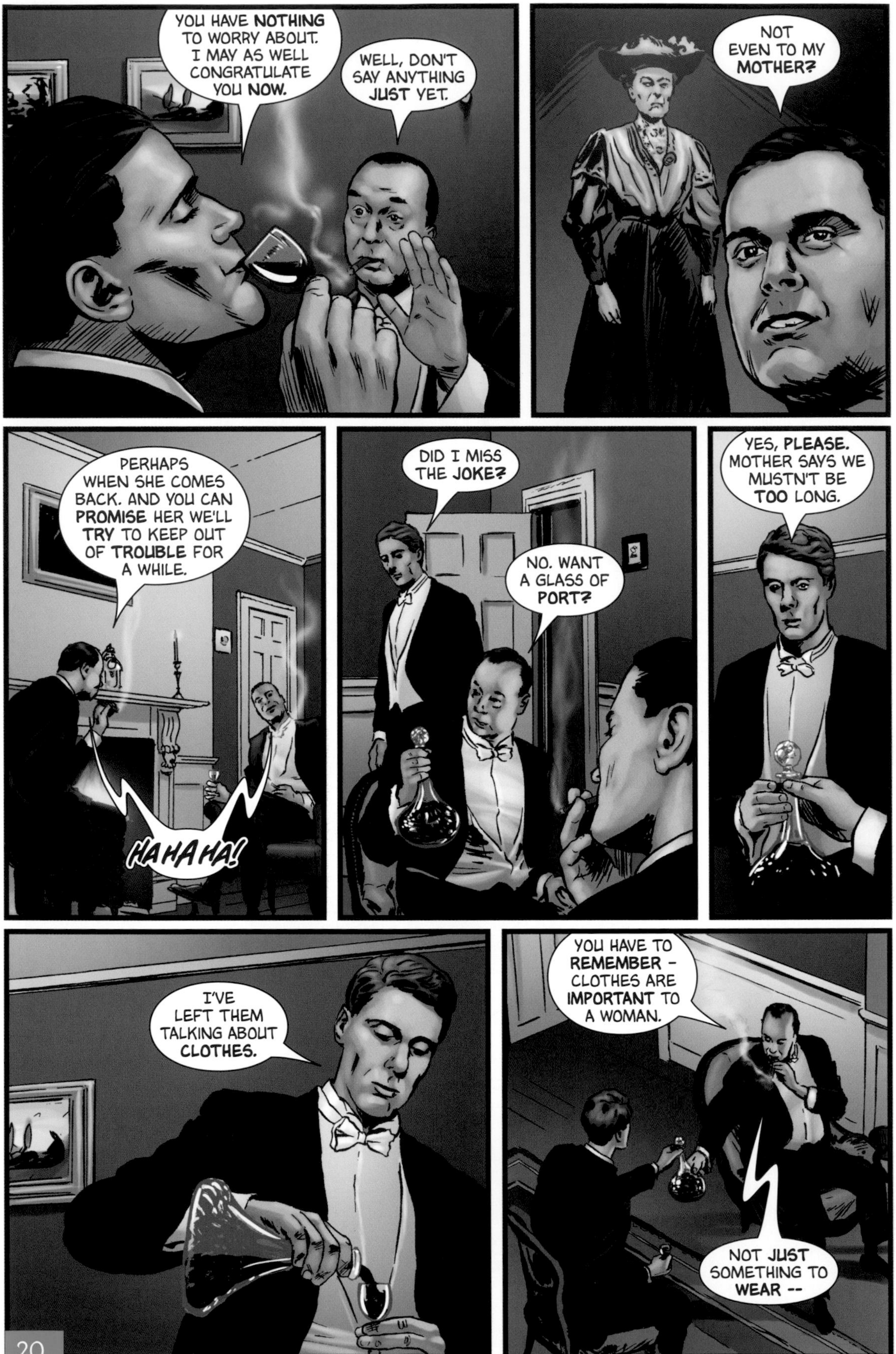
YOU HAVE NOTHING TO WORRY ABOUT. I MAY AS WELL CONGRATULATE YOU NOW.
WELL, DON'T SAY ANYTHING JUST YET.
NOT EVEN TO MY MOTHER?
PERHAPS WHEN SHE COMES BACK. AND YOU CAN PROMISE HER WE'LL TRY TO KEEP OUT OF TROUBLE FOR A WHILE.
HAHAHA!
DID I MISS THE JOKE?
NO. WANT A GLASS OF PORT?
YES, PLEASE. MOTHER SAYS WE MUSTN'T BE TOO LONG.
I'VE LEFT THEM TALKING ABOUT CLOTHES.
YOU HAVE TO REMEMBER - CLOTHES ARE IMPORTANT TO A WOMAN.
NOT JUST SOMETHING TO WEAR --

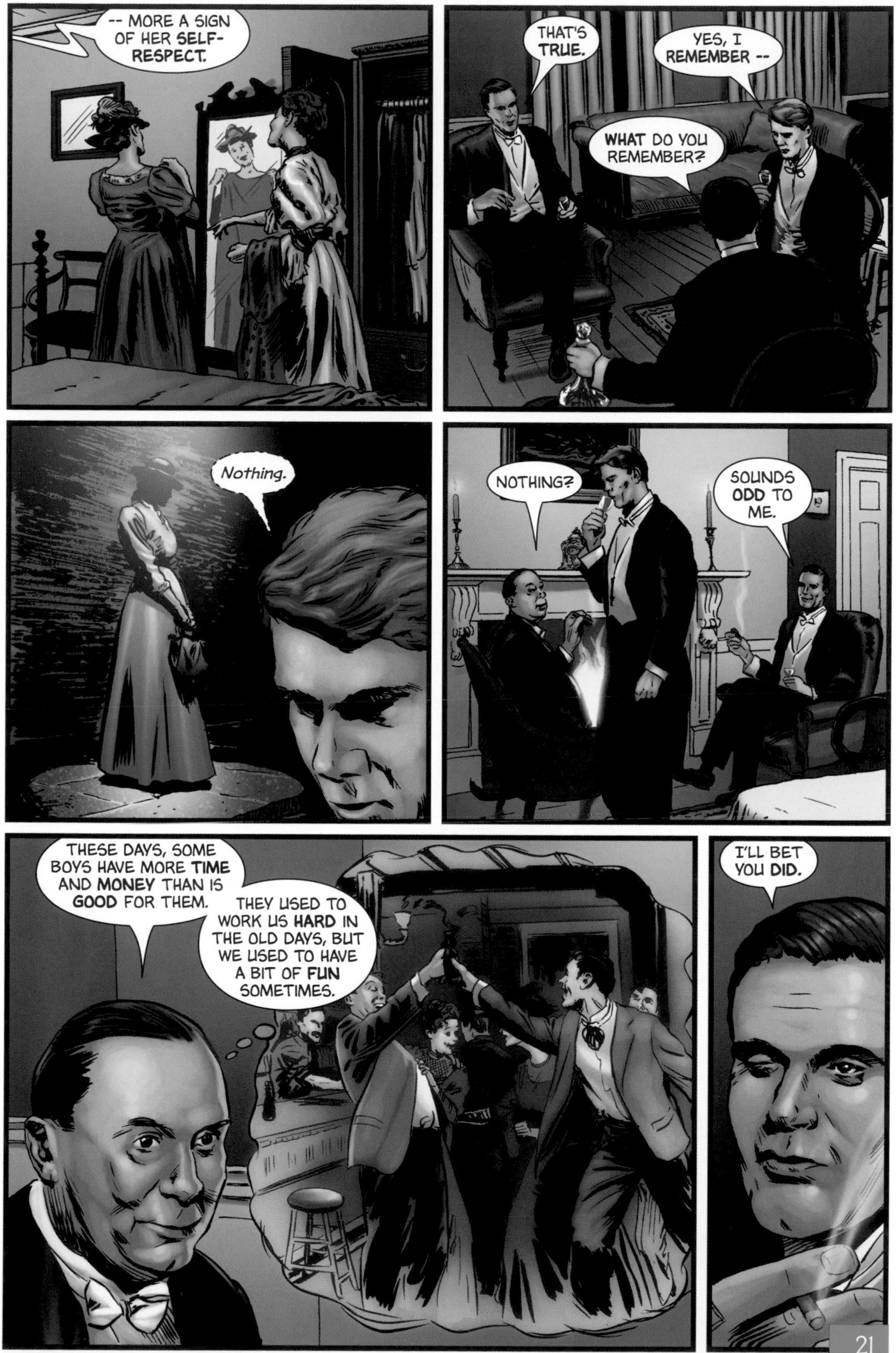

-- MORE A SIGN OF HER SELF-RESPECT.
THAT'S TRUE.
YES, I REMEMBER --
WHAT DO YOU REMEMBER?
Nothing.
NOTHING?
SOUNDS ODD TO ME.
THESE DAYS, SOME BOYS HAVE MORE TIME AND MONEY THAN IS GOOD FOR THEM.
THEY USED TO WORK US HARD IN THE OLD DAYS, BUT WE USED TO HAVE A BIT OF FUN SOMETIMES.
I'LL BET YOU DID.

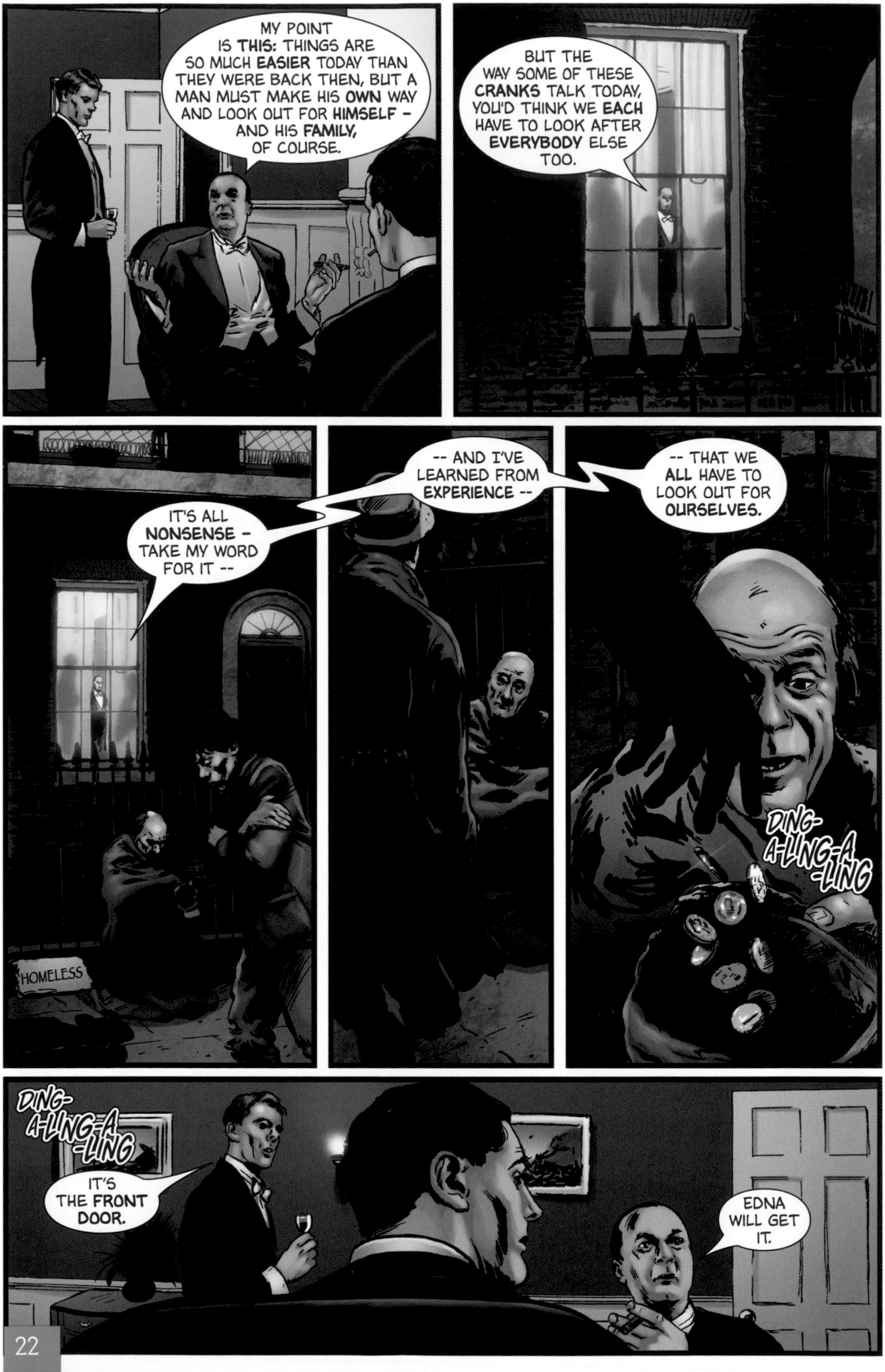
MY POINT IS THIS: THINGS ARE SO MUCH EASIER TODAY THAN THEY WERE BACK THEN, BUT A MAN MUST MAKE HIS OWN WAY AND LOOK OUT FOR HIMSELF – AND HIS FAMILY, OF COURSE.
BUT THE WAY SOME OF THESE CRANKS TALK TODAY, YOU'D THINK WE EACH HAVE TO LOOK AFTER EVERYBODY ELSE TOO.
IT'S ALL NONSENSE – TAKE MY WORD FOR IT --
HOMELESS
-- AND I'VE LEARNED FROM EXPERIENCE --
-- THAT WE ALL HAVE TO LOOK OUT FOR OURSELVES.
DING-A-LING-A-LING
DING-A-LING-A-LING
IT'S THE FRONT DOOR.
EDNA WILL GET IT.

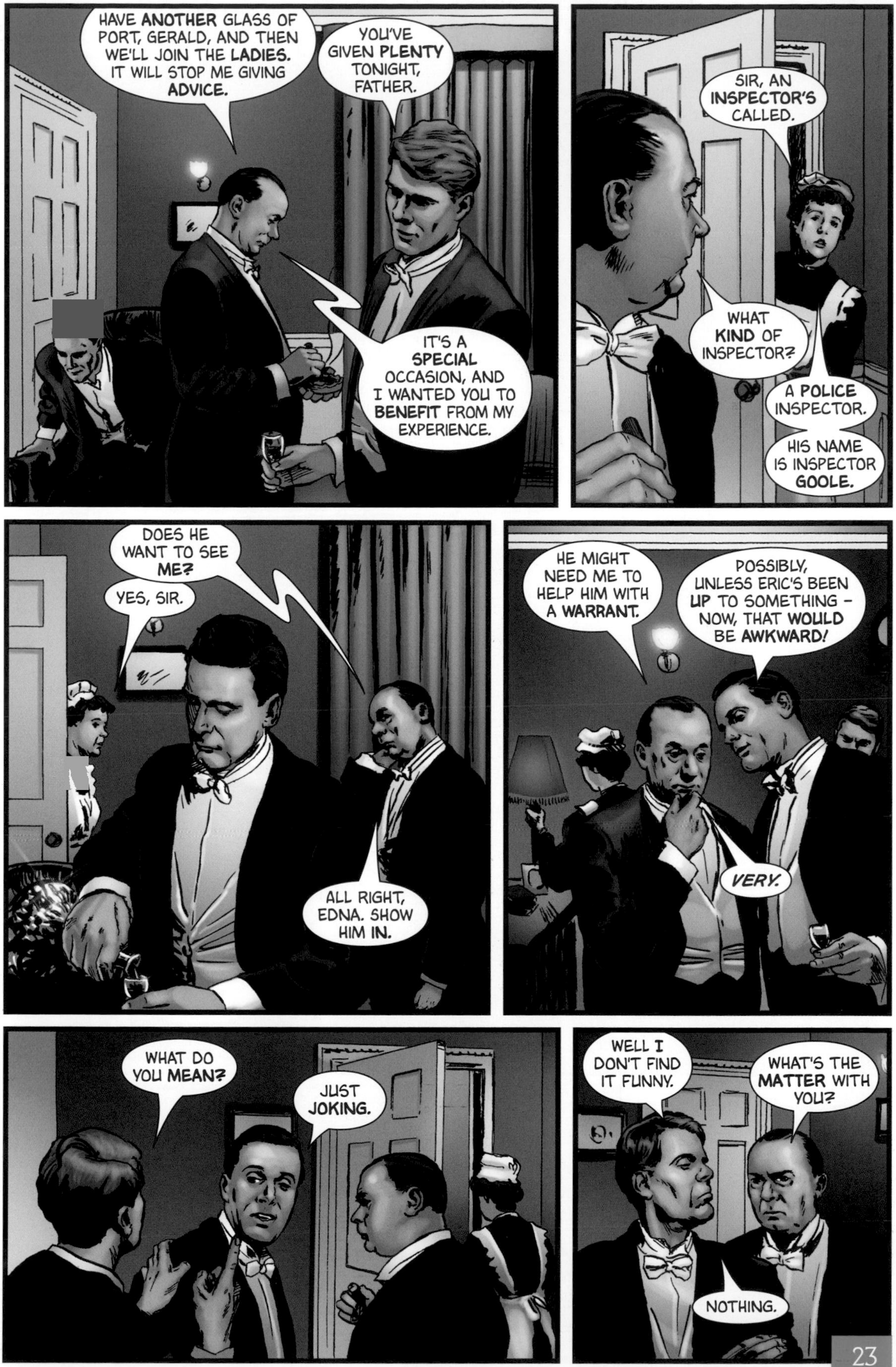
HAVE ANOTHER GLASS OF PORT, GERALD, AND THEN WE'LL JOIN THE LADIES. IT WILL STOP ME GIVING ADVICE.
YOU'VE GIVEN PLENTY TONIGHT, FATHER.
IT'S A SPECIAL OCCASION, AND I WANTED YOU TO BENEFIT FROM MY EXPERIENCE.
SIR, AN INSPECTOR'S CALLED.
WHAT KIND OF INSPECTOR?
A POLICE INSPECTOR.
HIS NAME IS INSPECTOR GOOLE.
DOES HE WANT TO SEE ME?
YES, SIR.
ALL RIGHT, EDNA. SHOW HIM IN.
HE MIGHT NEED ME TO HELP HIM WITH A WARRANT.
POSSIBLY, UNLESS ERIC'S BEEN UP TO SOMETHING – NOW, THAT WOULD BE AWKWARD!
VERY.
WHAT DO YOU MEAN?
JUST JOKING.
WELL I DON'T FIND IT FUNNY.
WHAT'S THE MATTER WITH YOU?
NOTHING.

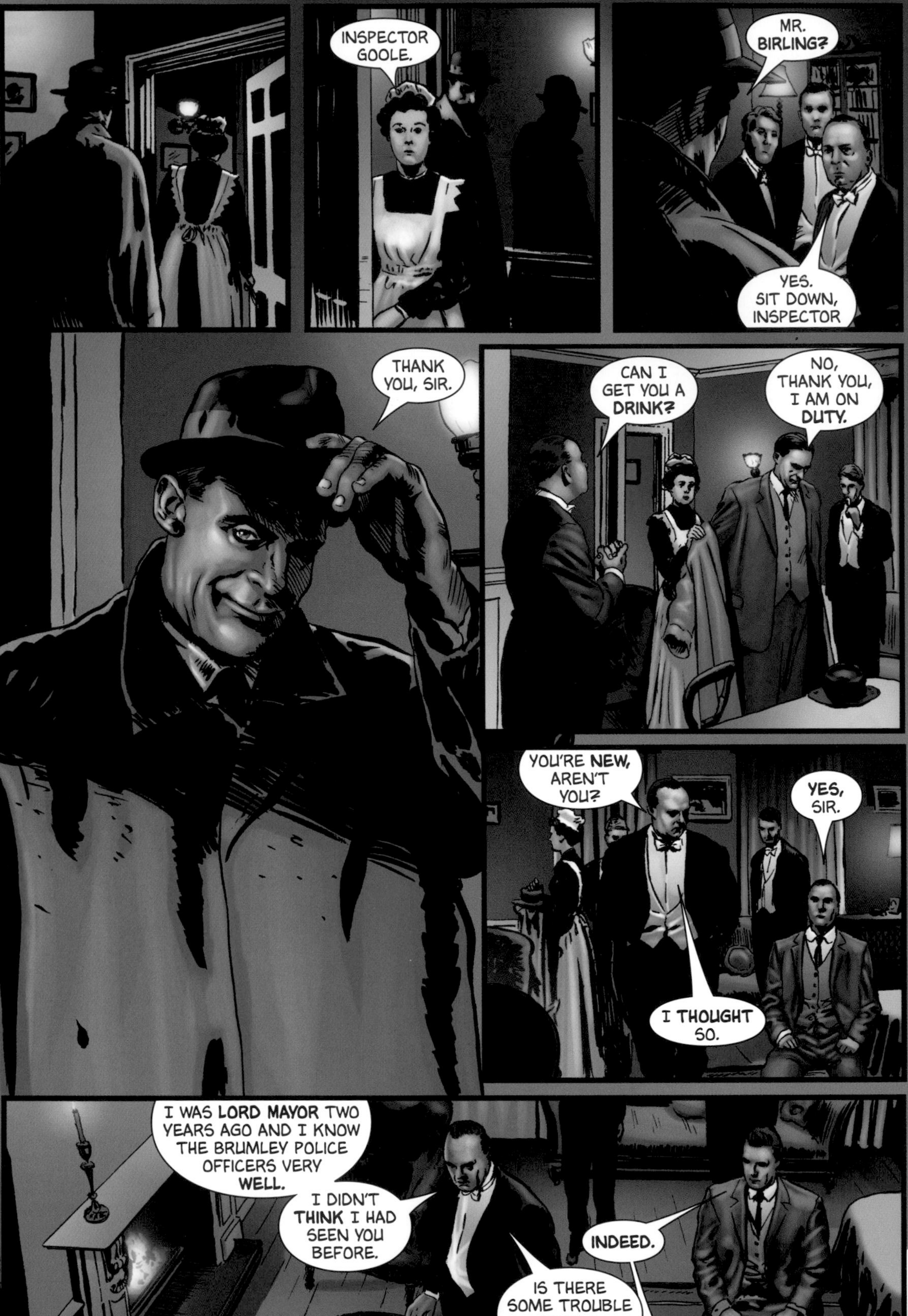
INSPECTOR GOOLE.
MR. BIRLING?
YES. SIT DOWN, INSPECTOR
THANK YOU, SIR.
CAN I GET YOU A DRINK?
NO, THANK YOU, I AM ON DUTY.
YOU'RE NEW, AREN'T YOU?
YES, SIR.
I THOUGHT SO.
I WAS LORD MAYOR TWO YEARS AGO AND I KNOW THE BRUMLEY POLICE OFFICERS VERY WELL.
I DIDN'T THINK I HAD SEEN YOU BEFORE.
INDEED.
IS THERE SOME TROUBLE WITH A WARRANT?
NO, MR. BIRLING.

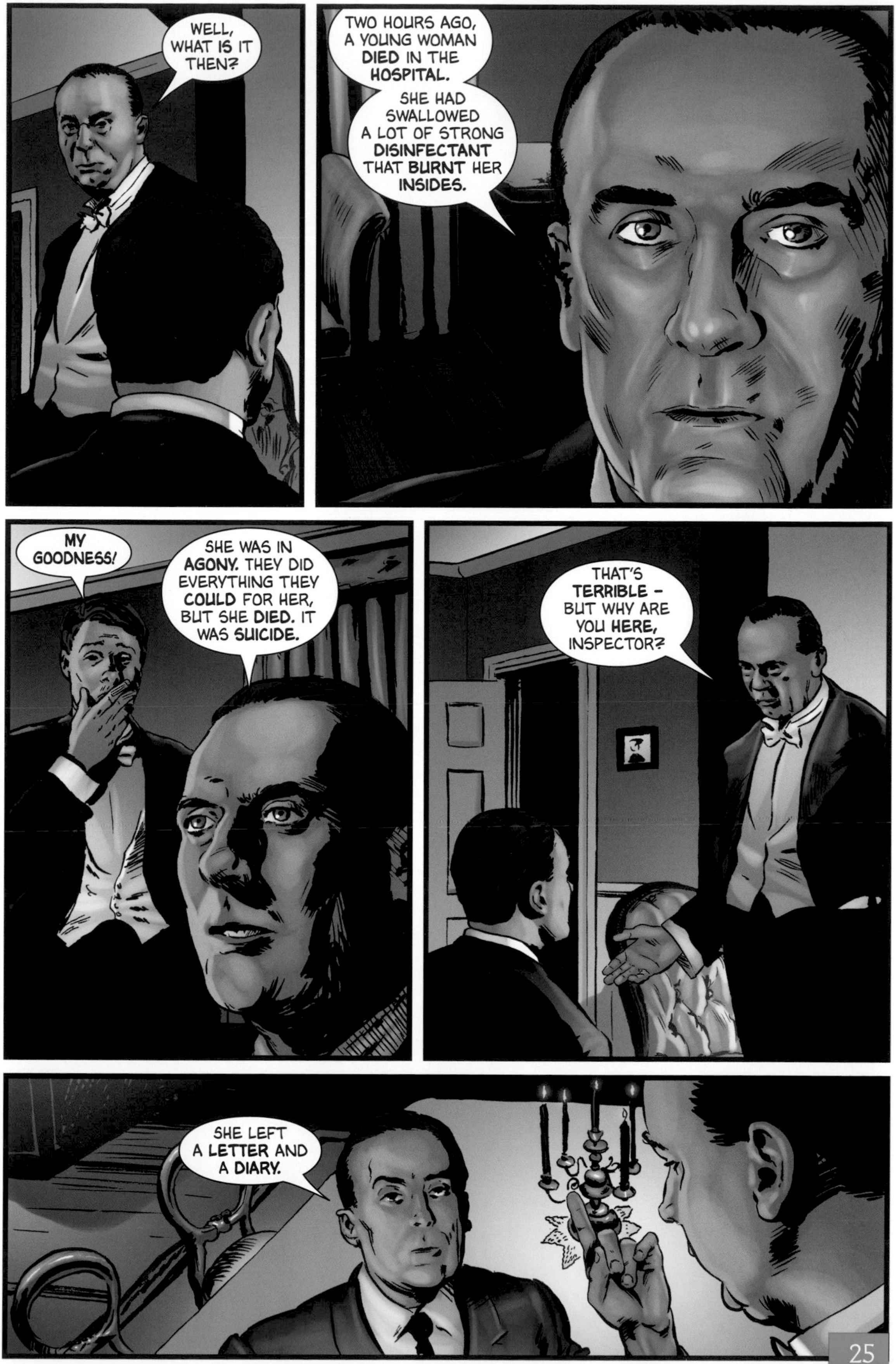
WELL, WHAT IS IT THEN?
TWO HOURS AGO, A YOUNG WOMAN DIED IN THE HOSPITAL.
SHE HAD SWALLOWED A LOT OF STRONG DISINFECTANT THAT BURNT HER INSIDES.
MY GOODNESS!
SHE WAS IN AGONY. THEY DID EVERYTHING THEY COULD FOR HER, BUT SHE DIED. IT WAS SUICIDE.
THAT'S TERRIBLE – BUT WHY ARE YOU HERE, INSPECTOR?
SHE LEFT A LETTER AND A DIARY.

LIKE MANY WOMEN WHO GET INTO TROUBLE, SHE USED **MORE** THAN ONE **NAME**.

BUT HER **REAL** NAME WAS EVA SMITH.

EVA SMITH?

DO YOU **REMEMBER** HER, MR. BIRLING?

NO, BUT HER NAME IS **FAMILIAR**. I DON'T **SEE** WHAT IT HAS TO DO WITH **ME**.

SHE USED TO **WORK** FOR **YOUR** COMPANY.

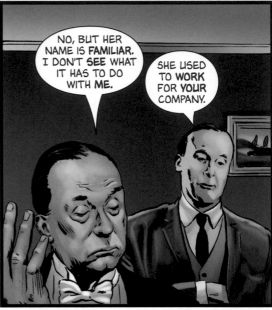

HUNDREDS OF WOMEN HAVE WORKED THERE.

EVA WAS **DIFFERENT**.

PERHAPS A **PHOTOGRAPH** WOULD REMIND YOU.

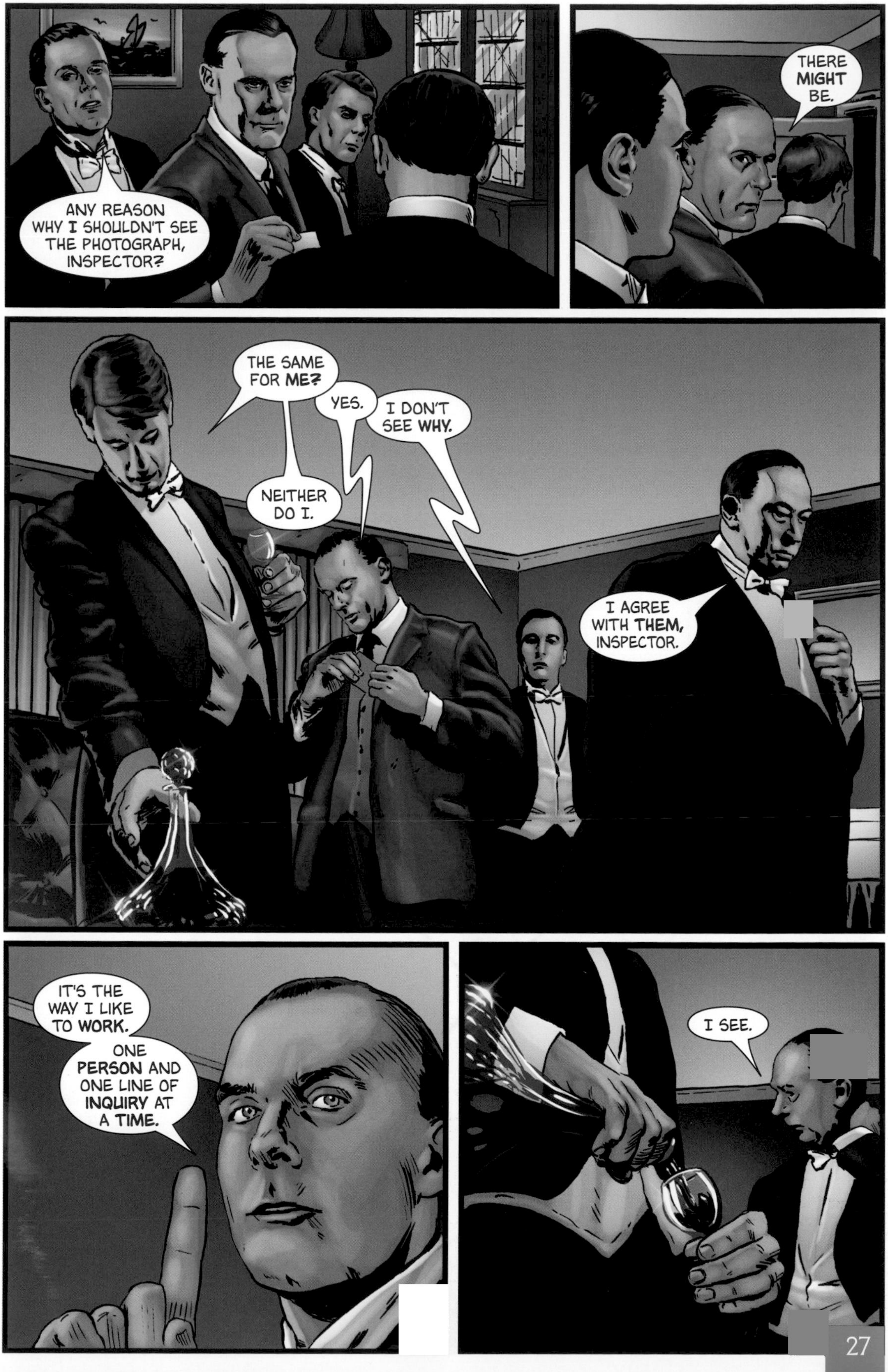
ANY REASON WHY I SHOULDN'T SEE THE PHOTOGRAPH, INSPECTOR?
THERE MIGHT BE.
THE SAME FOR ME?
YES.
I DON'T SEE WHY.
NEITHER DO I.
I AGREE WITH THEM, INSPECTOR.
IT'S THE WAY I LIKE TO WORK.
ONE PERSON AND ONE LINE OF INQUIRY AT A TIME.
I SEE.

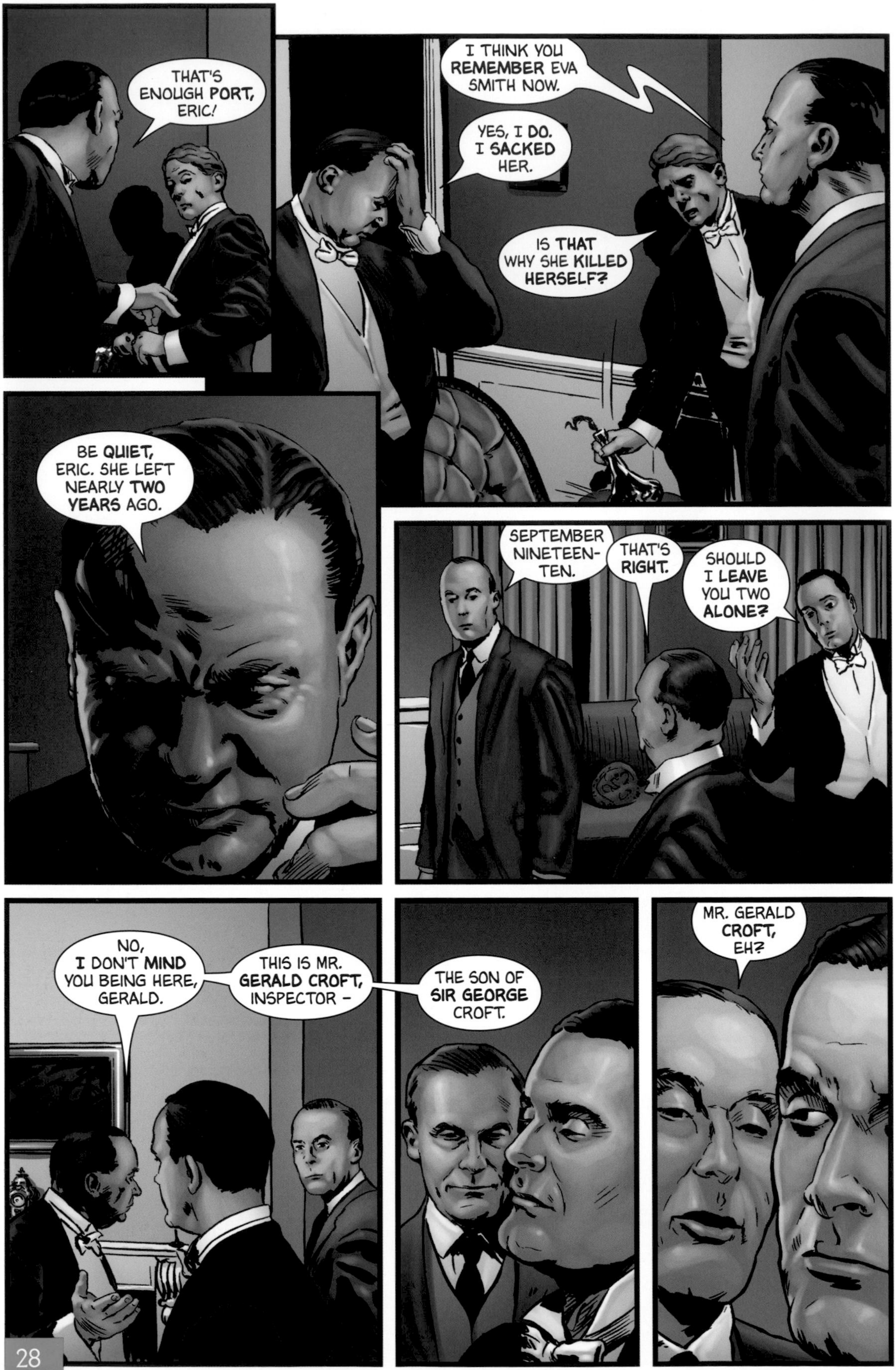
THAT'S ENOUGH PORT, ERIC!
I THINK YOU REMEMBER EVA SMITH NOW.
YES, I DO. I SACKED HER.
IS THAT WHY SHE KILLED HERSELF?
BE QUIET, ERIC. SHE LEFT NEARLY TWO YEARS AGO.
SEPTEMBER NINETEEN-TEN.
THAT'S RIGHT.
SHOULD I LEAVE YOU TWO ALONE?
NO, I DON'T MIND YOU BEING HERE, GERALD.
THIS IS MR. GERALD CROFT, INSPECTOR –
THE SON OF SIR GEORGE CROFT.
MR. GERALD CROFT, EH?

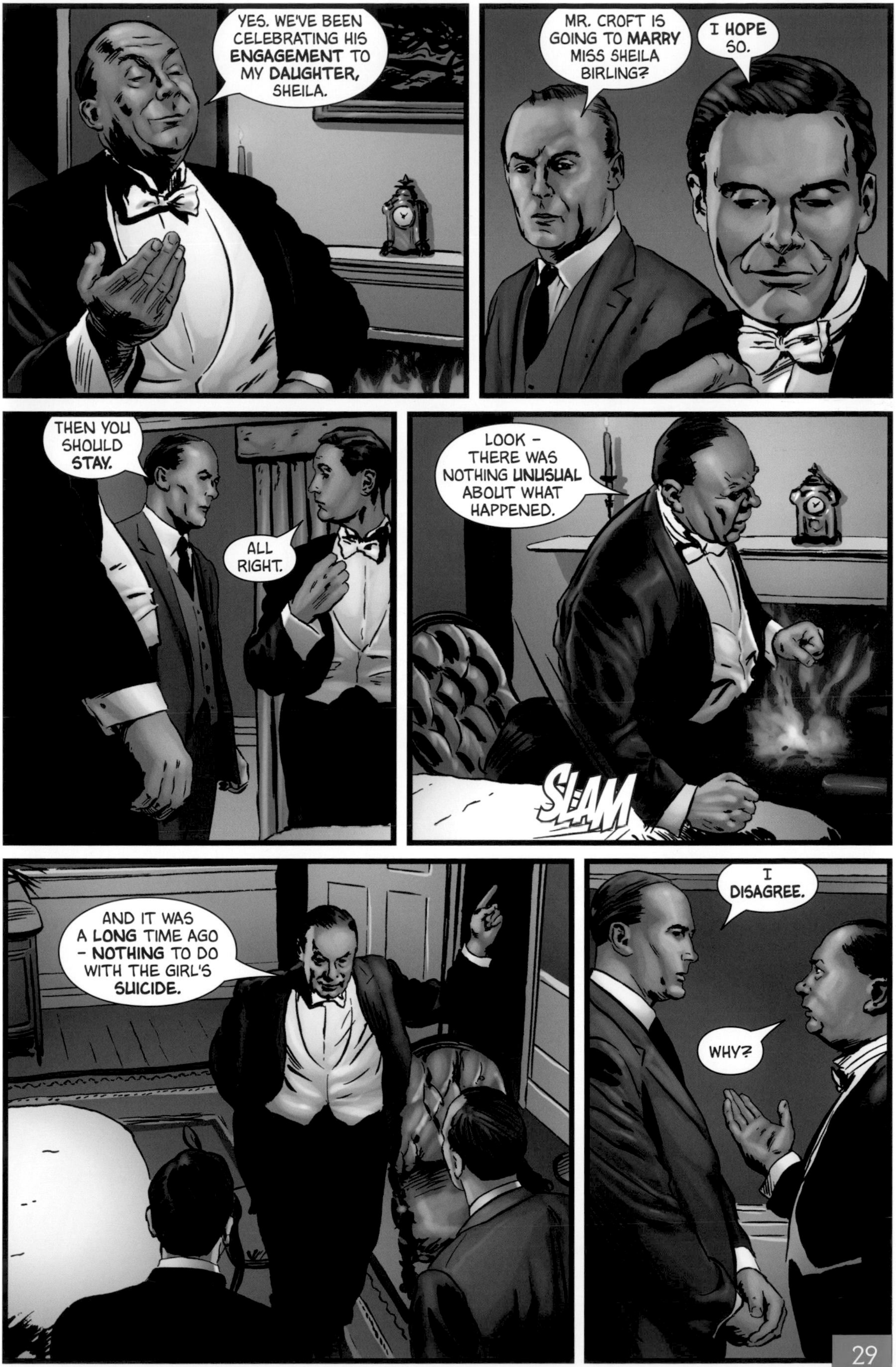
YES. WE'VE BEEN CELEBRATING HIS ENGAGEMENT TO MY DAUGHTER, SHEILA.
MR. CROFT IS GOING TO MARRY MISS SHEILA BIRLING?
I HOPE SO.
THEN YOU SHOULD STAY.
ALL RIGHT.
LOOK - THERE WAS NOTHING UNUSUAL ABOUT WHAT HAPPENED.
SLAM
AND IT WAS A LONG TIME AGO - NOTHING TO DO WITH THE GIRL'S SUICIDE.
I DISAGREE.
WHY?

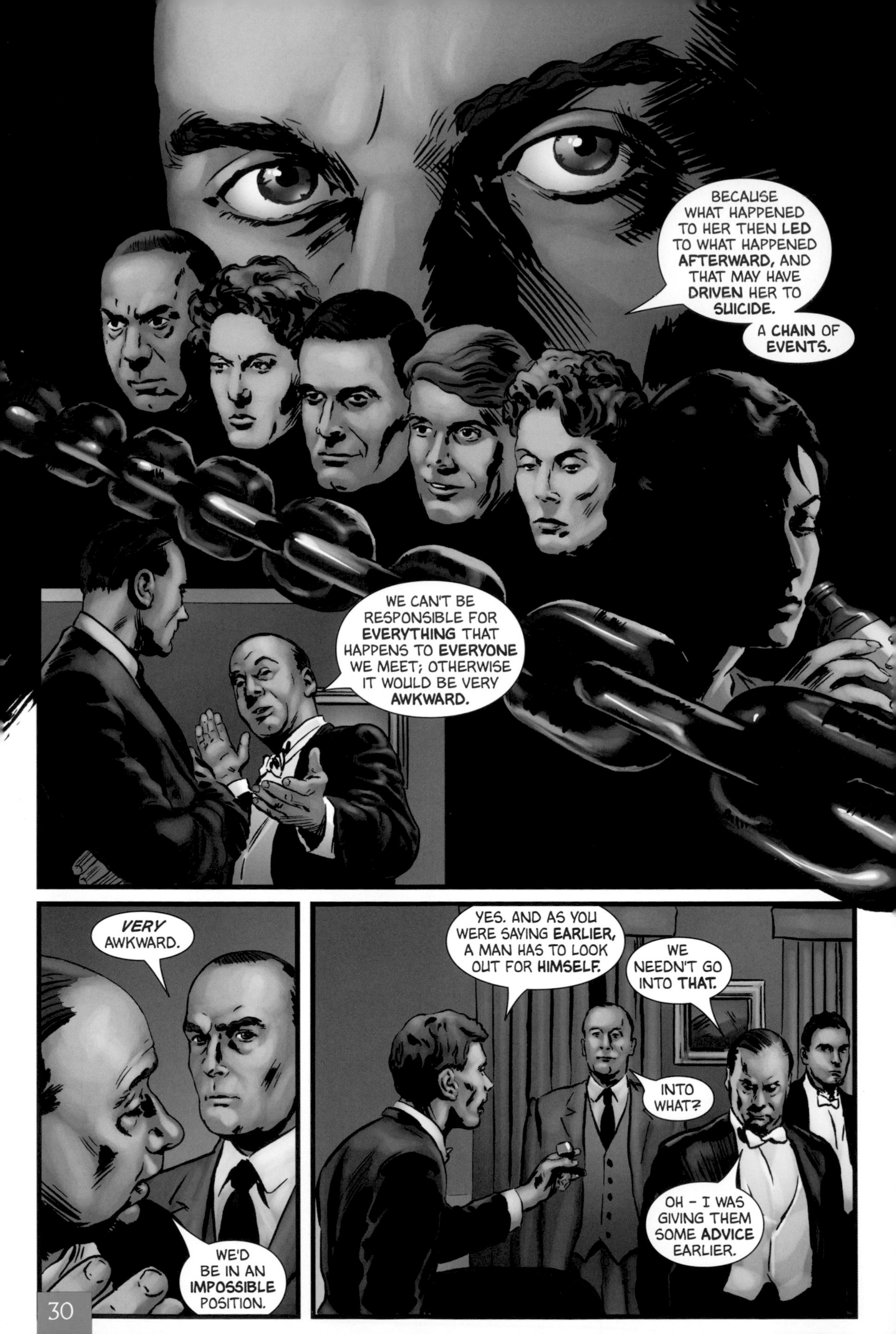

BECAUSE WHAT HAPPENED TO HER THEN LED TO WHAT HAPPENED AFTERWARD, AND THAT MAY HAVE DRIVEN HER TO SUICIDE.
A CHAIN OF EVENTS.
WE CAN'T BE RESPONSIBLE FOR EVERYTHING THAT HAPPENS TO EVERYONE WE MEET; OTHERWISE IT WOULD BE VERY AWKWARD.
VERY AWKWARD.
WE'D BE IN AN IMPOSSIBLE POSITION.
YES. AND AS YOU WERE SAYING EARLIER, A MAN HAS TO LOOK OUT FOR HIMSELF.
WE NEEDN'T GO INTO THAT.
INTO WHAT?
OH – I WAS GIVING THEM SOME ADVICE EARLIER.

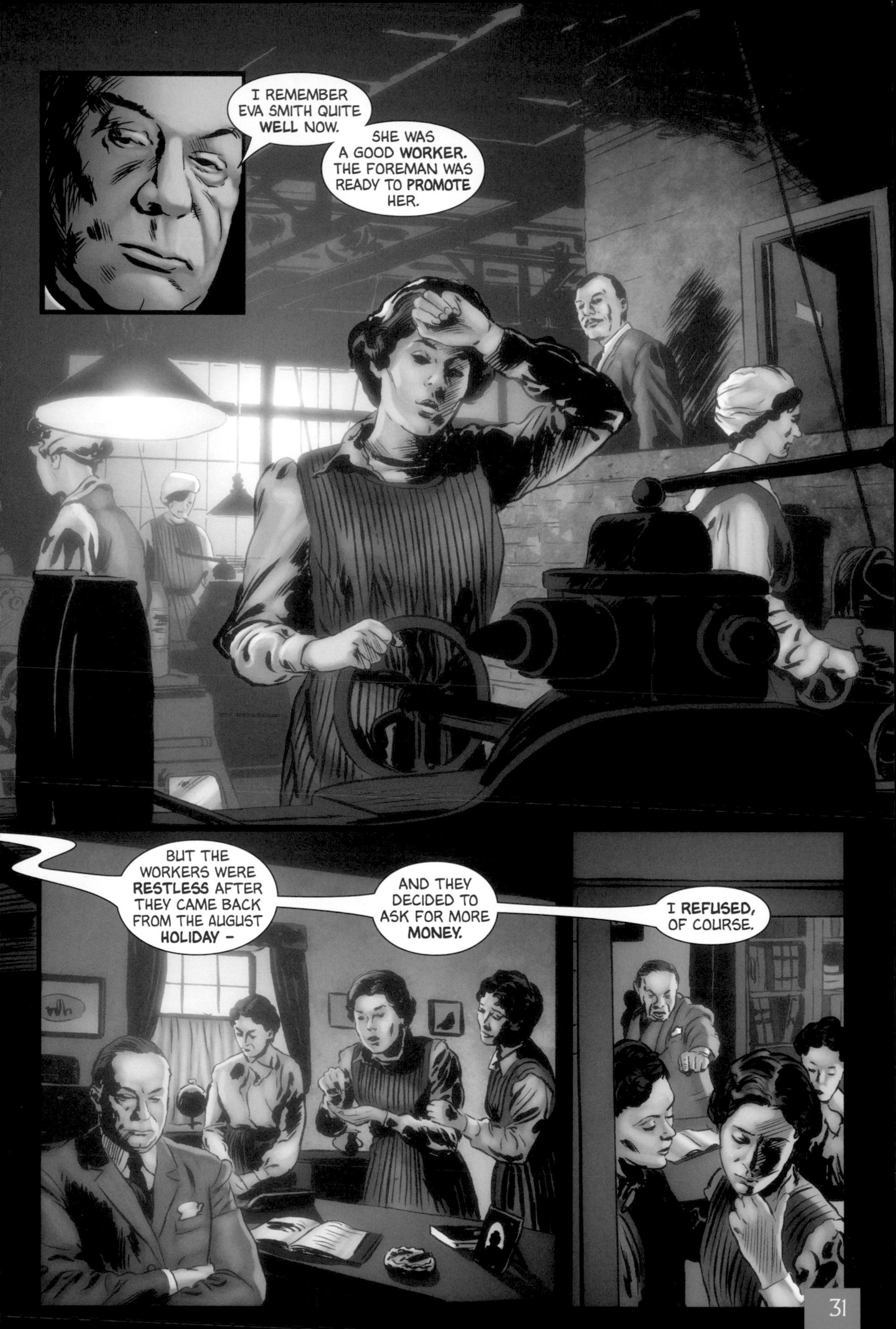

I REMEMBER EVA SMITH QUITE WELL NOW.
SHE WAS A GOOD WORKER. THE FOREMAN WAS READY TO PROMOTE HER.
BUT THE WORKERS WERE RESTLESS AFTER THEY CAME BACK FROM THE AUGUST HOLIDAY –
AND THEY DECIDED TO ASK FOR MORE MONEY.
I REFUSED, OF COURSE.

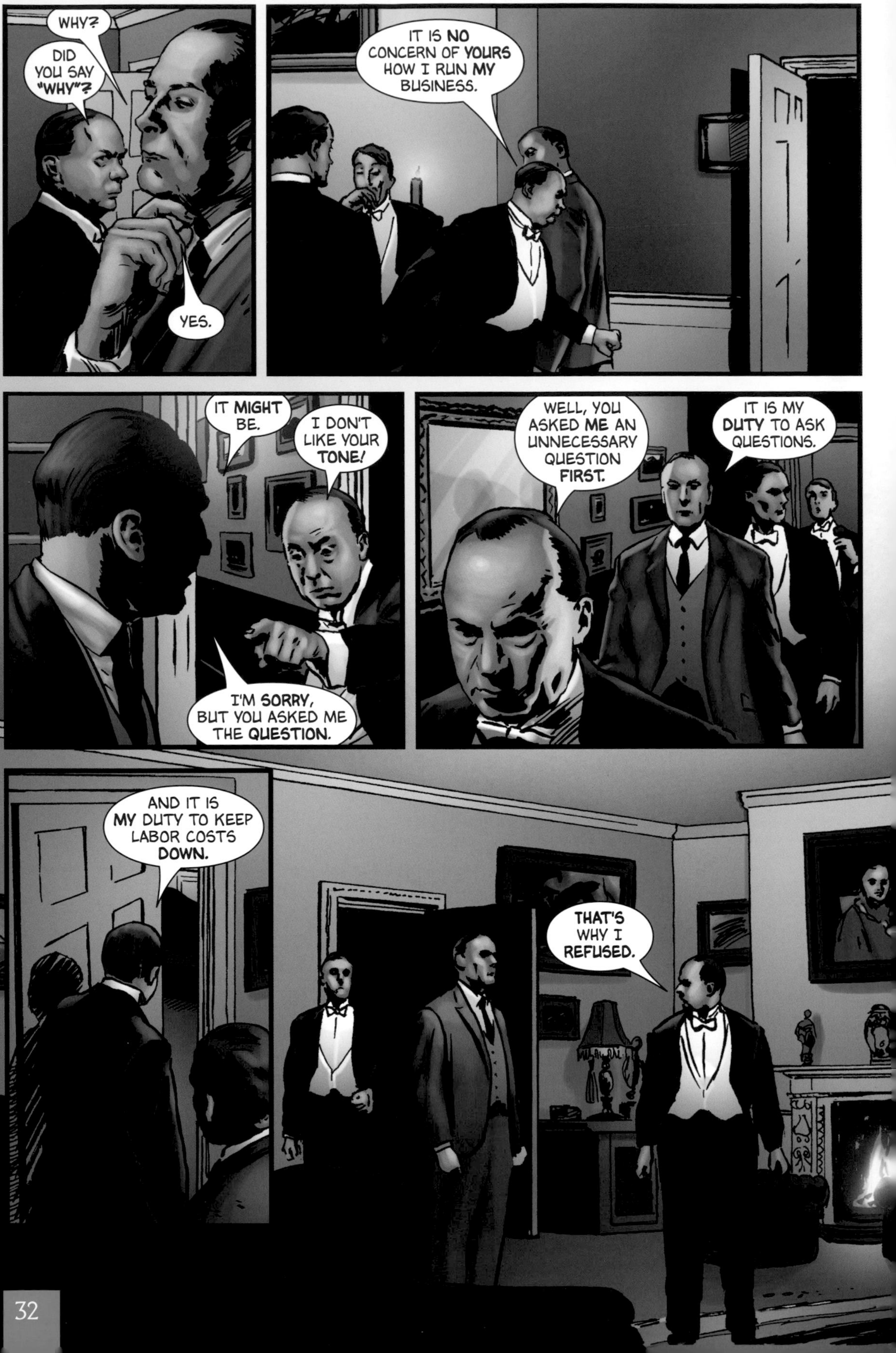
WHY?
DID YOU SAY "WHY"?
YES.
IT IS NO CONCERN OF YOURS HOW I RUN MY BUSINESS.
IT MIGHT BE.
I DON'T LIKE YOUR TONE!
I'M SORRY, BUT YOU ASKED ME THE QUESTION.
WELL, YOU ASKED ME AN UNNECESSARY QUESTION FIRST.
IT IS MY DUTY TO ASK QUESTIONS.
AND IT IS MY DUTY TO KEEP LABOR COSTS DOWN.
THAT'S WHY I REFUSED.

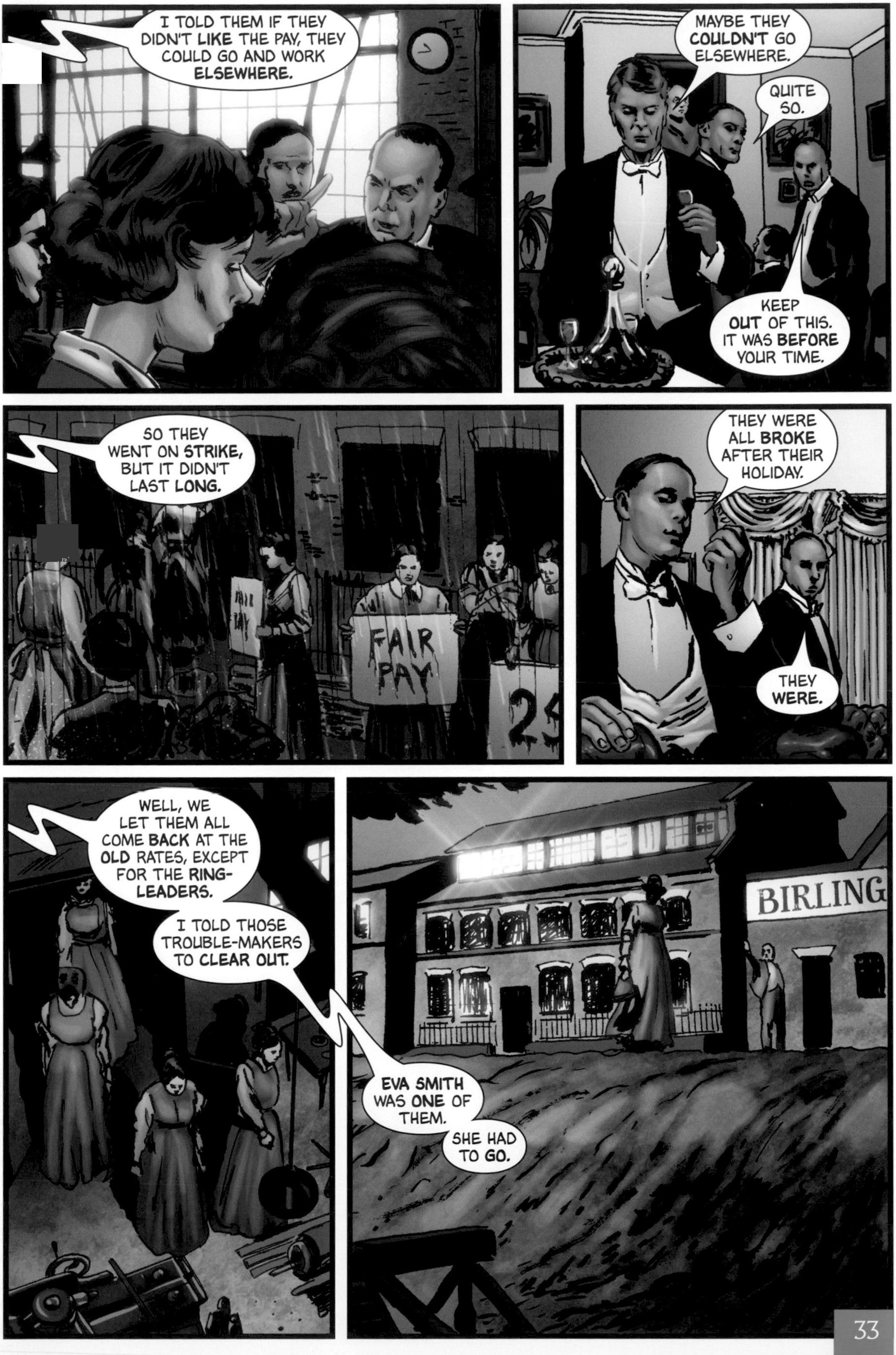
I TOLD THEM IF THEY DIDN'T LIKE THE PAY, THEY COULD GO AND WORK ELSEWHERE.
MAYBE THEY COULDN'T GO ELSEWHERE.
QUITE SO.
KEEP OUT OF THIS. IT WAS BEFORE YOUR TIME.
SO THEY WENT ON STRIKE, BUT IT DIDN'T LAST LONG.
FAIR PAY
25
THEY WERE ALL BROKE AFTER THEIR HOLIDAY.
THEY WERE.
WELL, WE LET THEM ALL COME BACK AT THE OLD RATES, EXCEPT FOR THE RING-LEADERS.
I TOLD THOSE TROUBLE-MAKERS TO CLEAR OUT.
BIRLING
EVA SMITH WAS ONE OF THEM.
SHE HAD TO GO.

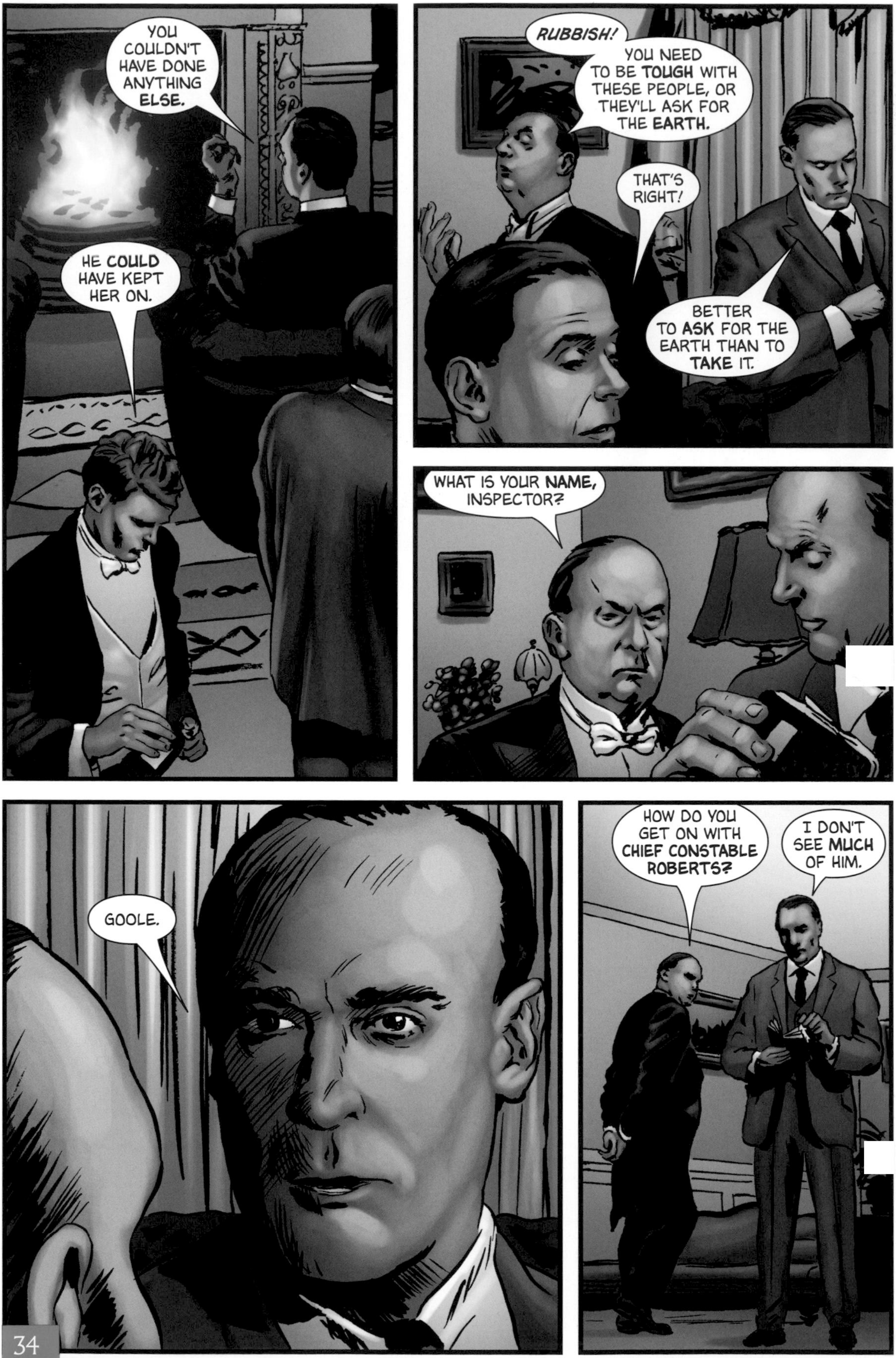
YOU COULDN'T HAVE DONE ANYTHING ELSE.
HE COULD HAVE KEPT HER ON.
RUBBISH!
YOU NEED TO BE TOUGH WITH THESE PEOPLE, OR THEY'LL ASK FOR THE EARTH.
THAT'S RIGHT!
BETTER TO ASK FOR THE EARTH THAN TO TAKE IT.
WHAT IS YOUR NAME, INSPECTOR?
GOOLE.
HOW DO YOU GET ON WITH CHIEF CONSTABLE ROBERTS?
I DON'T SEE MUCH OF HIM.

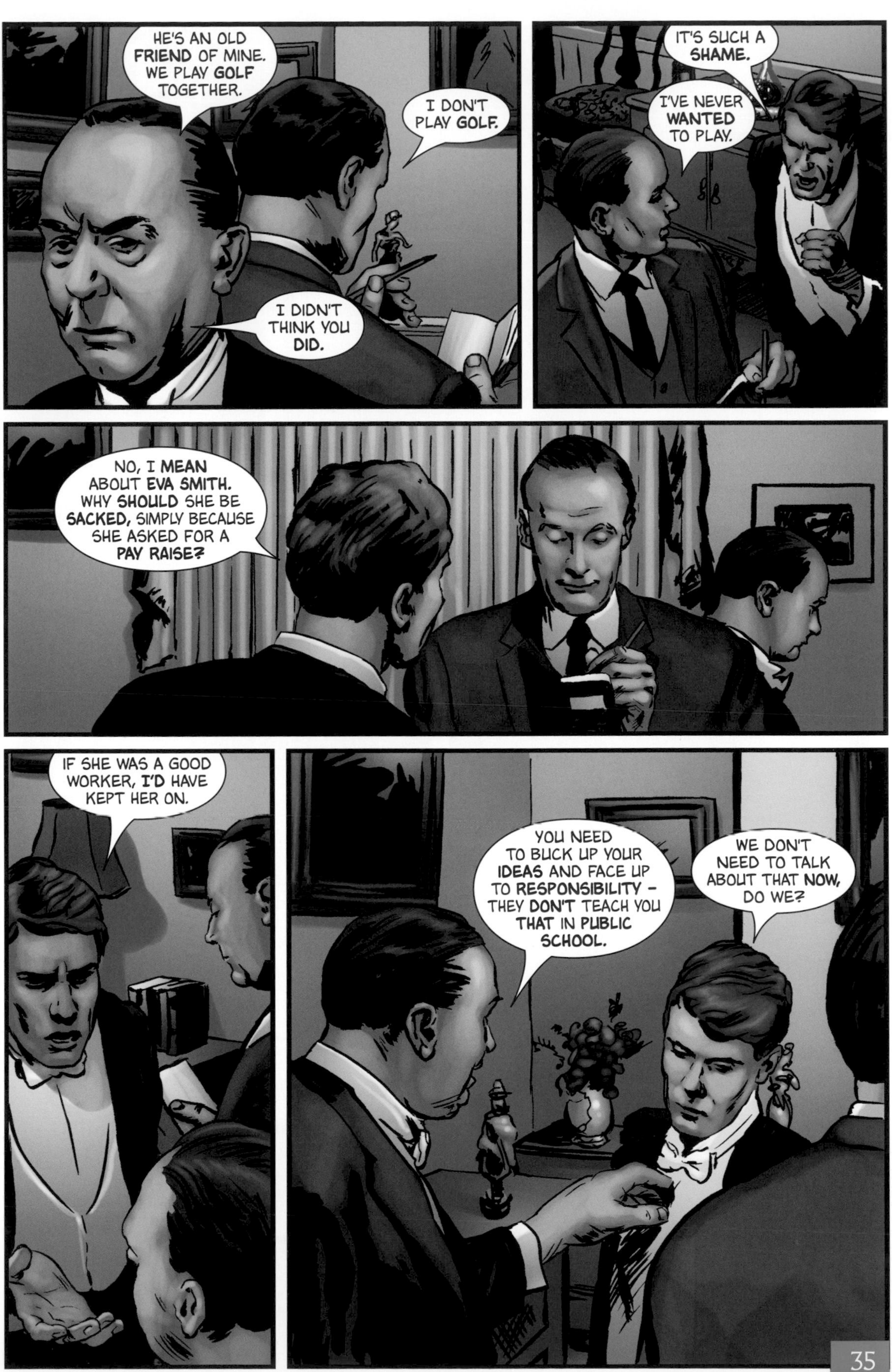
HE'S AN OLD FRIEND OF MINE. WE PLAY GOLF TOGETHER.
I DON'T PLAY GOLF.
I DIDN'T THINK YOU DID.
IT'S SUCH A SHAME.
I'VE NEVER WANTED TO PLAY.
NO, I MEAN ABOUT EVA SMITH. WHY SHOULD SHE BE SACKED, SIMPLY BECAUSE SHE ASKED FOR A PAY RAISE?
IF SHE WAS A GOOD WORKER, I'D HAVE KEPT HER ON.
YOU NEED TO BUCK UP YOUR IDEAS AND FACE UP TO RESPONSIBILITY – THEY DON'T TEACH YOU THAT IN PUBLIC SCHOOL.
WE DON'T NEED TO TALK ABOUT THAT NOW, DO WE?

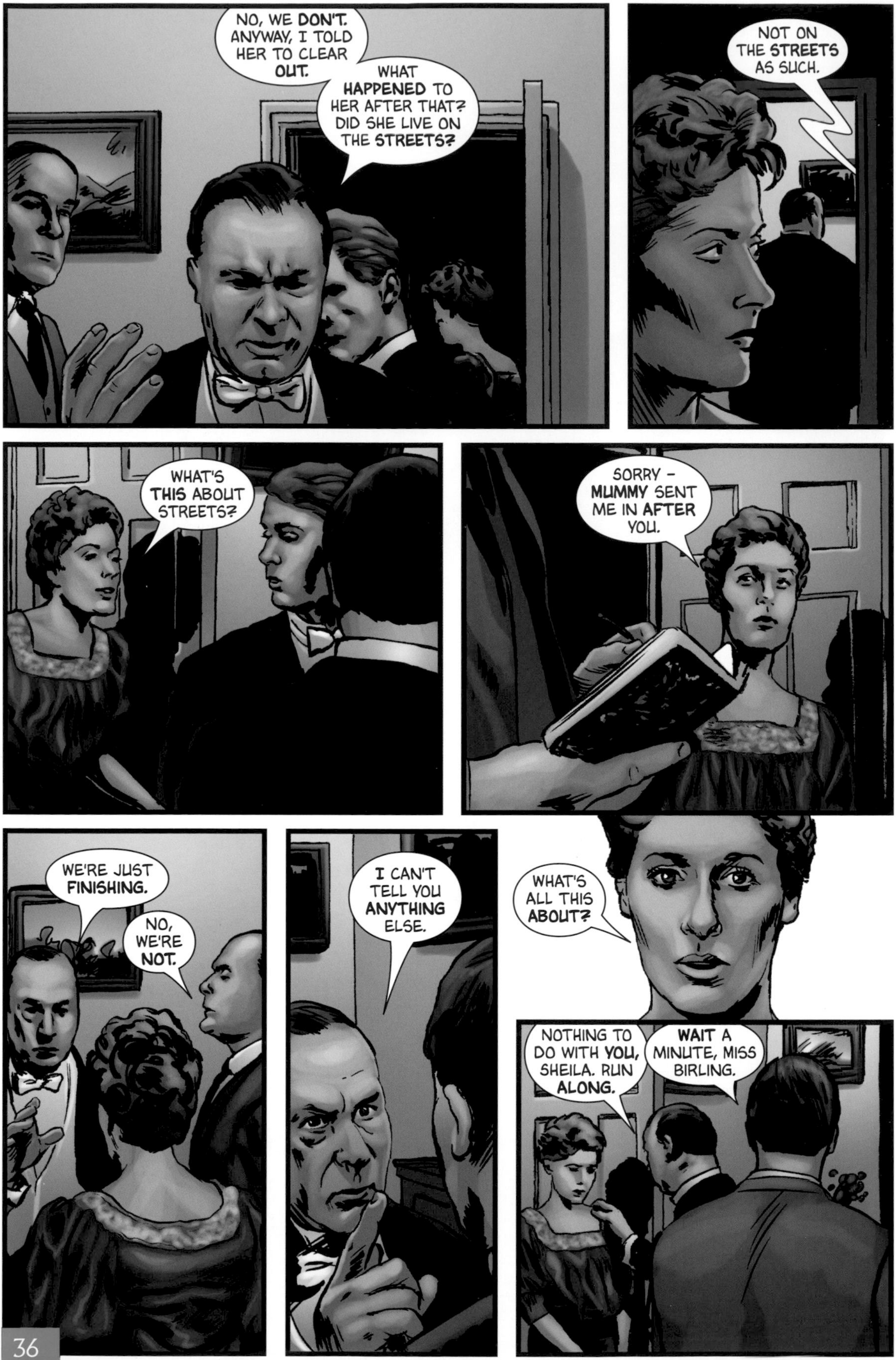
NO, WE DON'T. ANYWAY, I TOLD HER TO CLEAR OUT.
WHAT HAPPENED TO HER AFTER THAT? DID SHE LIVE ON THE STREETS?
NOT ON THE STREETS AS SUCH.
WHAT'S THIS ABOUT STREETS?
SORRY – MUMMY SENT ME IN AFTER YOU.
WE'RE JUST FINISHING.
NO, WE'RE NOT.
I CAN'T TELL YOU ANYTHING ELSE.
WHAT'S ALL THIS ABOUT?
NOTHING TO DO WITH YOU, SHEILA. RUN ALONG.
WAIT A MINUTE, MISS BIRLING.

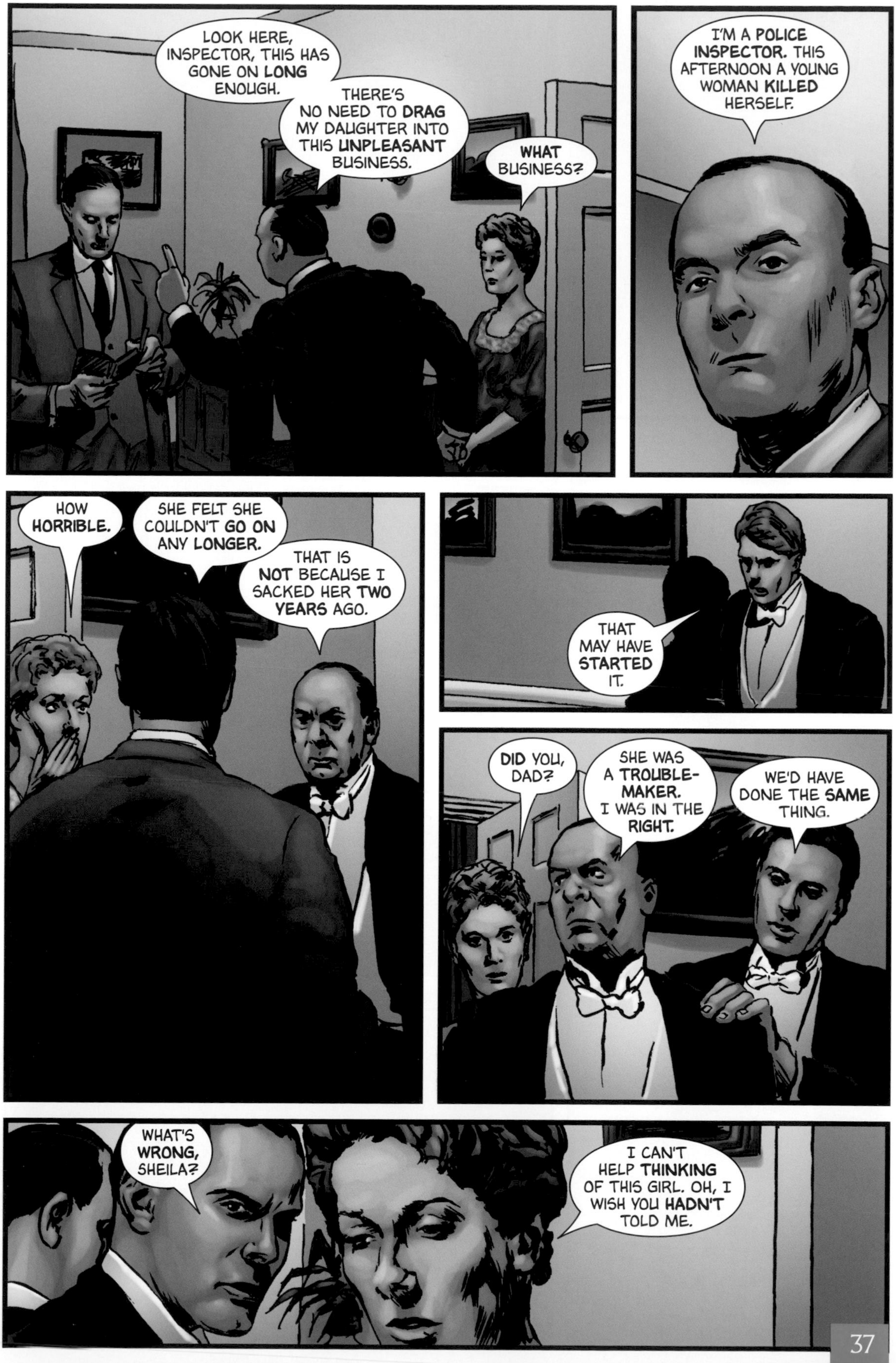
LOOK HERE, INSPECTOR, THIS HAS GONE ON LONG ENOUGH.
THERE'S NO NEED TO DRAG MY DAUGHTER INTO THIS UNPLEASANT BUSINESS.
WHAT BUSINESS?
I'M A POLICE INSPECTOR. THIS AFTERNOON A YOUNG WOMAN KILLED HERSELF.
HOW HORRIBLE.
SHE FELT SHE COULDN'T GO ON ANY LONGER.
THAT IS NOT BECAUSE I SACKED HER TWO YEARS AGO.
THAT MAY HAVE STARTED IT.
DID YOU, DAD?
SHE WAS A TROUBLE-MAKER. I WAS IN THE RIGHT.
WE'D HAVE DONE THE SAME THING.
WHAT'S WRONG, SHEILA?
I CAN'T HELP THINKING OF THIS GIRL. OH, I WISH YOU HADN'T TOLD ME.

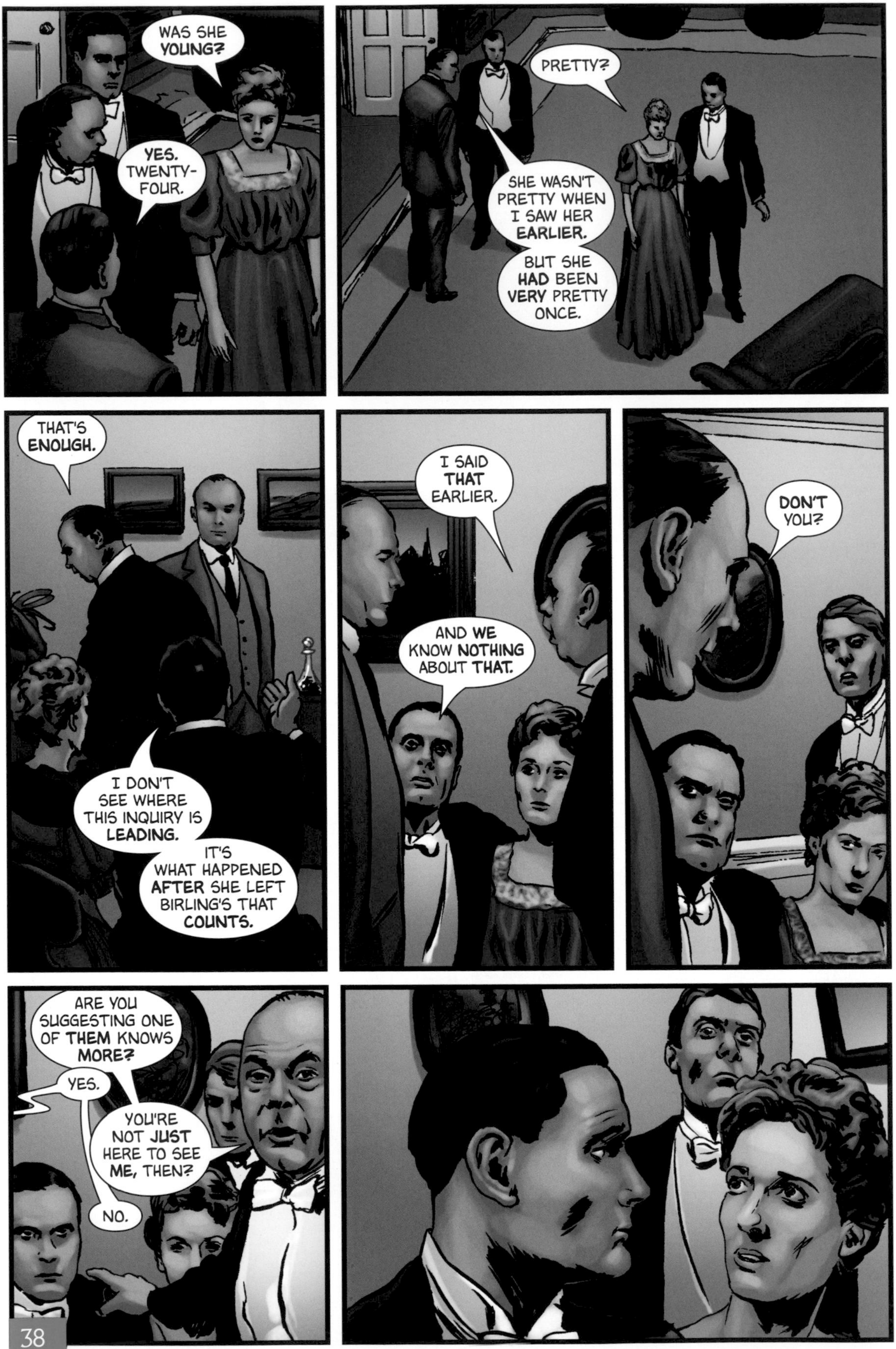
WAS SHE YOUNG?
YES. TWENTY-FOUR.
PRETTY?
SHE WASN'T PRETTY WHEN I SAW HER EARLIER.
BUT SHE HAD BEEN VERY PRETTY ONCE.
THAT'S ENOUGH.
I DON'T SEE WHERE THIS INQUIRY IS LEADING.
IT'S WHAT HAPPENED AFTER SHE LEFT BIRLING'S THAT COUNTS.
I SAID THAT EARLIER.
AND WE KNOW NOTHING ABOUT THAT.
DON'T YOU?
ARE YOU SUGGESTING ONE OF THEM KNOWS MORE?
YES.
YOU'RE NOT JUST HERE TO SEE ME, THEN?
NO.

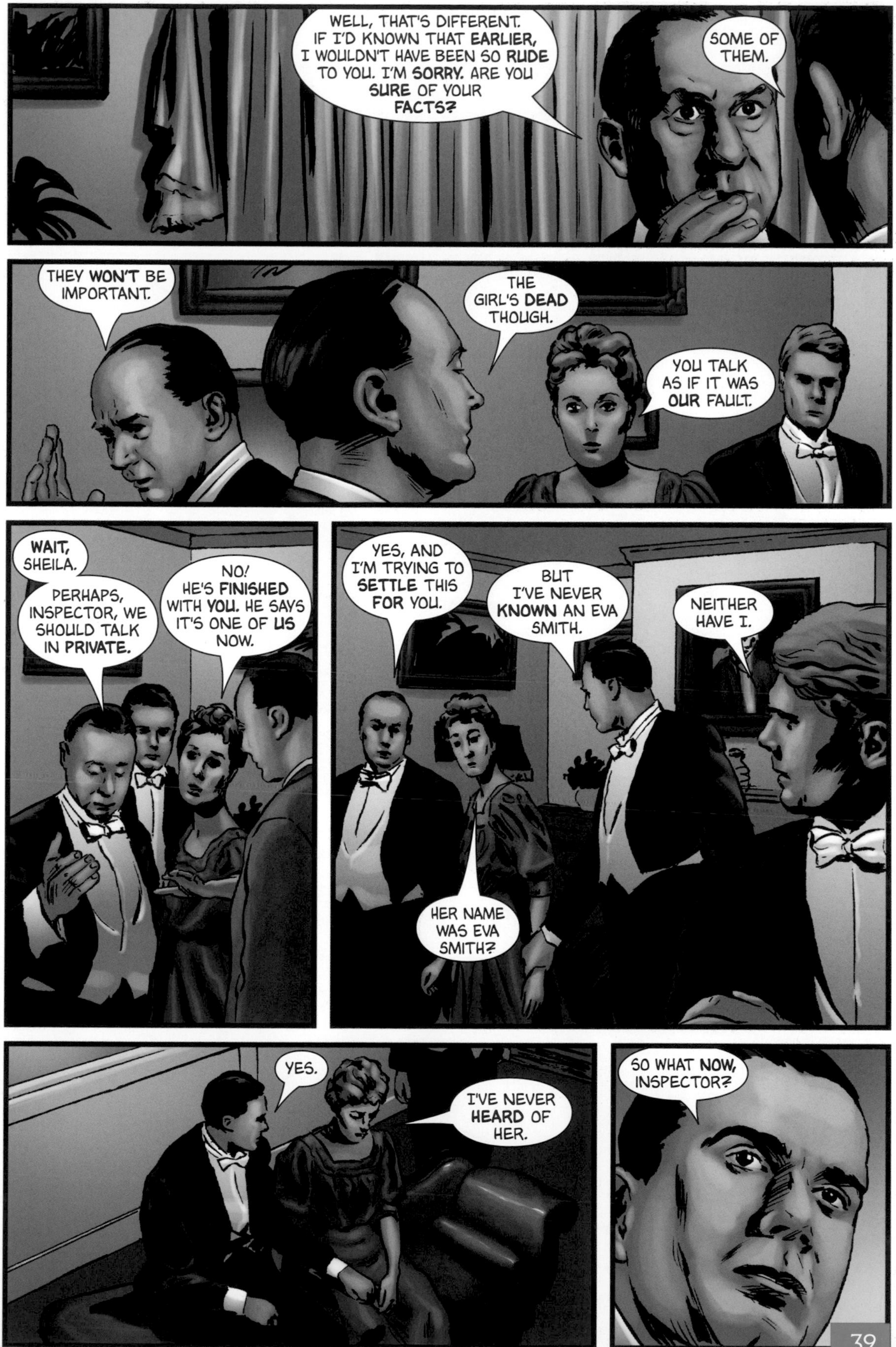
WELL, THAT'S DIFFERENT. IF I'D KNOWN THAT EARLIER, I WOULDN'T HAVE BEEN SO RUDE TO YOU. I'M SORRY. ARE YOU SURE OF YOUR FACTS?
SOME OF THEM.
THEY WON'T BE IMPORTANT.
THE GIRL'S DEAD THOUGH.
YOU TALK AS IF IT WAS OUR FAULT.
WAIT, SHEILA.
PERHAPS, INSPECTOR, WE SHOULD TALK IN PRIVATE.
NO! HE'S FINISHED WITH YOU. HE SAYS IT'S ONE OF US NOW.
YES, AND I'M TRYING TO SETTLE THIS FOR YOU.
BUT I'VE NEVER KNOWN AN EVA SMITH.
NEITHER HAVE I.
HER NAME WAS EVA SMITH?
YES.
I'VE NEVER HEARD OF HER.
SO WHAT NOW, INSPECTOR?

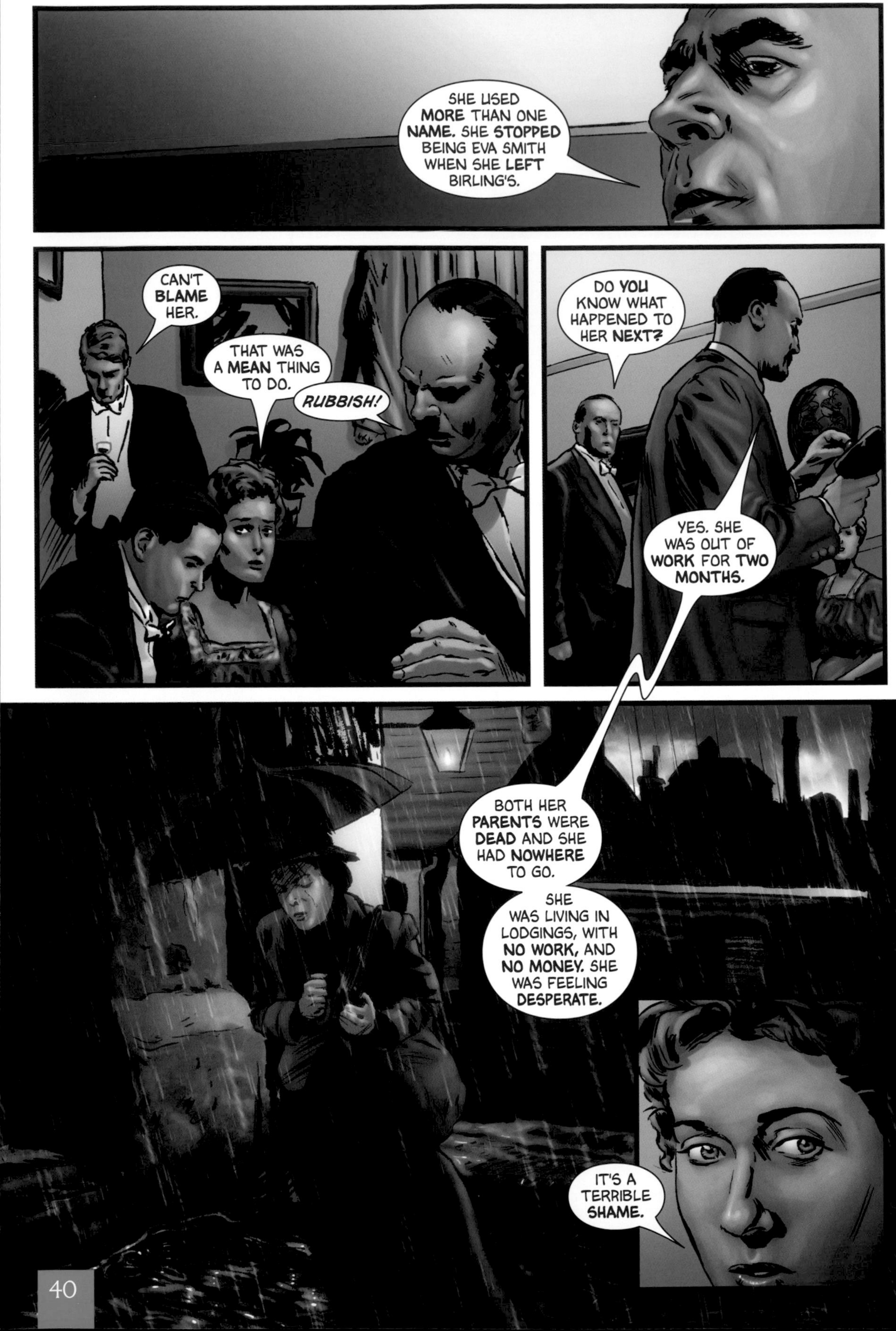
SHE USED MORE THAN ONE NAME. SHE STOPPED BEING EVA SMITH WHEN SHE LEFT BIRLING'S.
CAN'T BLAME HER.
THAT WAS A MEAN THING TO DO.
RUBBISH!
DO YOU KNOW WHAT HAPPENED TO HER NEXT?
YES. SHE WAS OUT OF WORK FOR TWO MONTHS.
BOTH HER PARENTS WERE DEAD AND SHE HAD NOWHERE TO GO.
SHE WAS LIVING IN LODGINGS, WITH NO WORK, AND NO MONEY. SHE WAS FEELING DESPERATE.
IT'S A TERRIBLE SHAME.

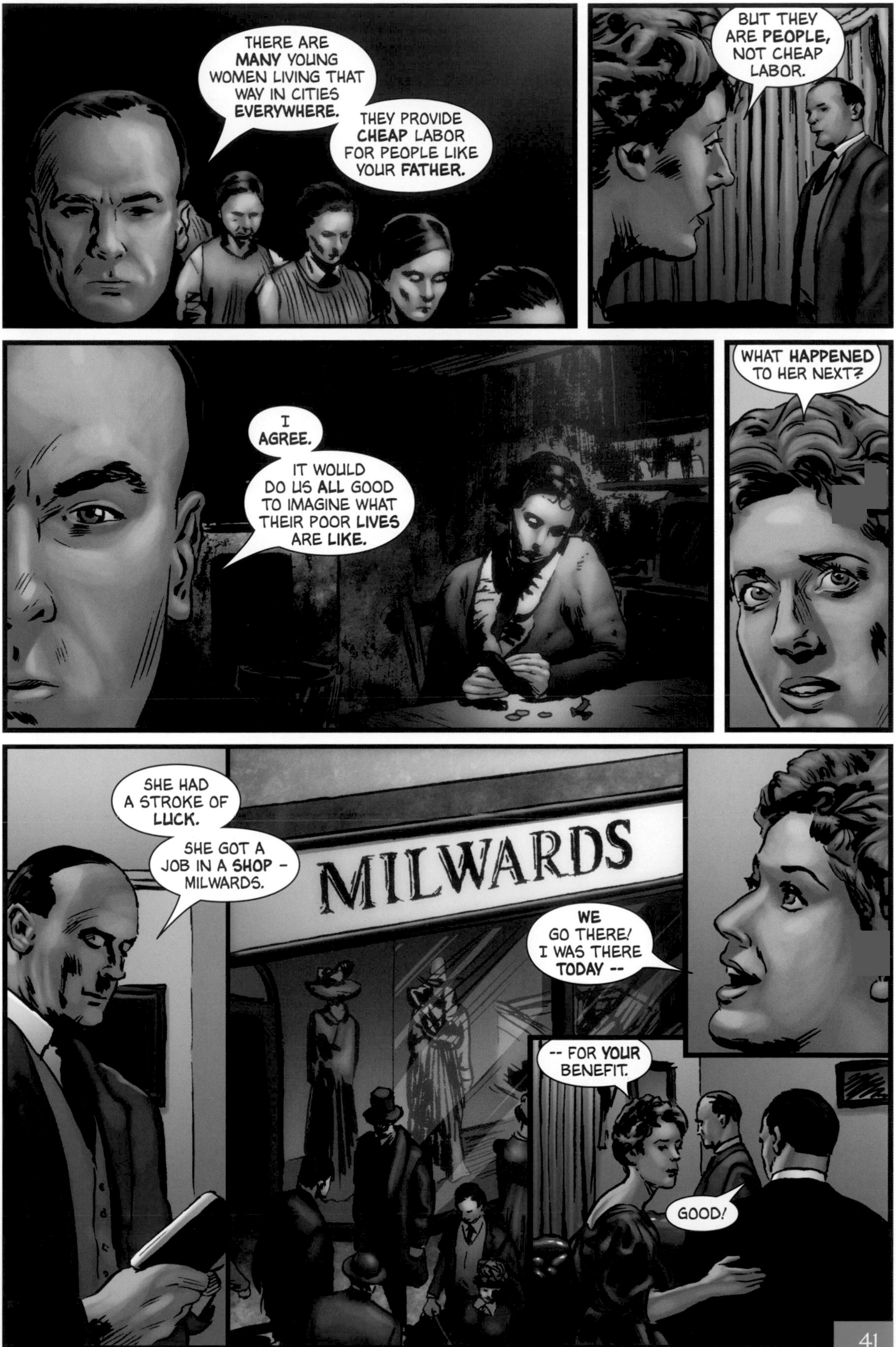
THERE ARE MANY YOUNG WOMEN LIVING THAT WAY IN CITIES EVERYWHERE.
THEY PROVIDE CHEAP LABOR FOR PEOPLE LIKE YOUR FATHER.
BUT THEY ARE PEOPLE, NOT CHEAP LABOR.
I AGREE.
IT WOULD DO US ALL GOOD TO IMAGINE WHAT THEIR POOR LIVES ARE LIKE.
WHAT HAPPENED TO HER NEXT?
SHE HAD A STROKE OF LUCK.
SHE GOT A JOB IN A SHOP – MILWARDS.
MILWARDS
WE GO THERE! I WAS THERE TODAY --
-- FOR YOUR BENEFIT.
GOOD!

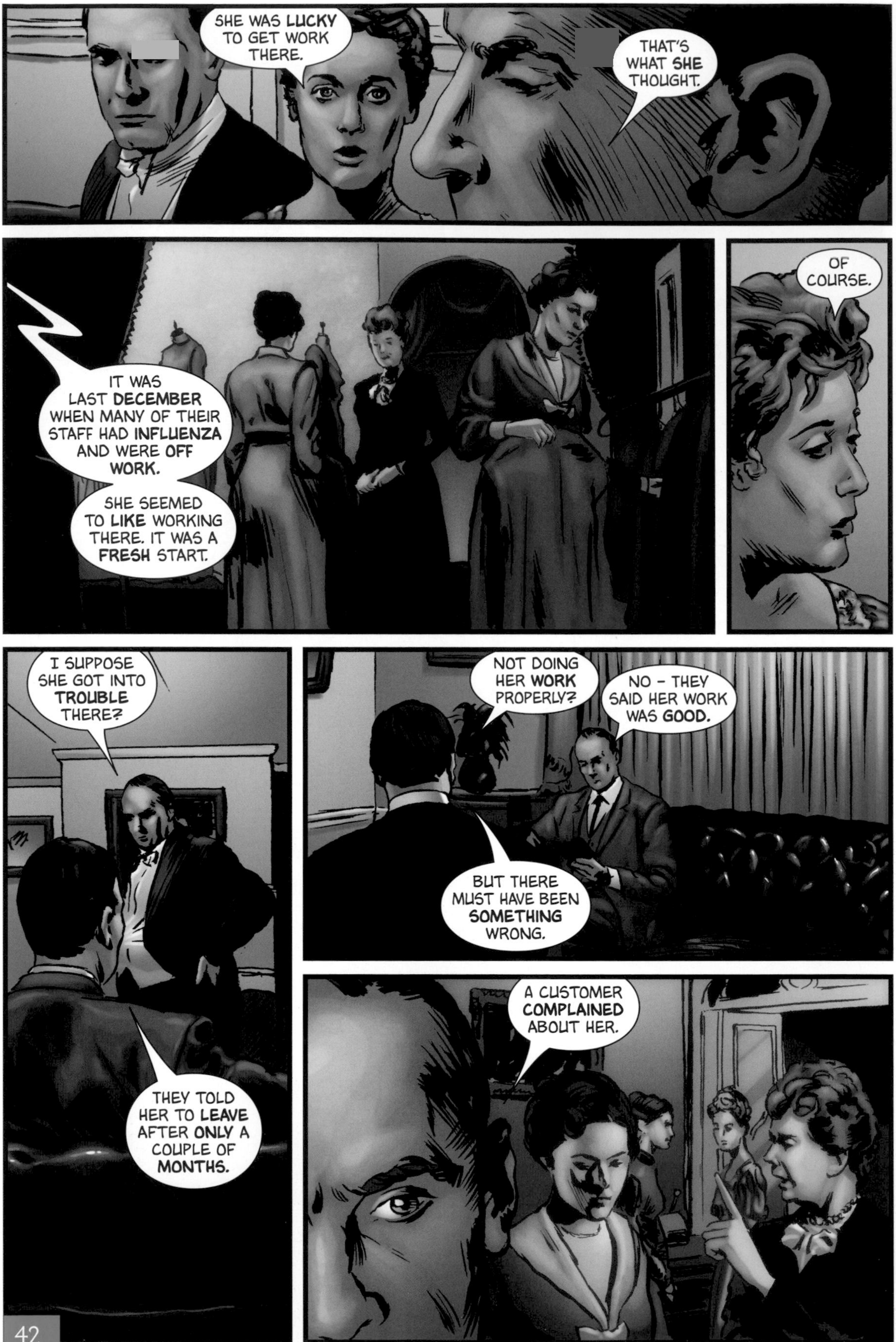
SHE WAS LUCKY TO GET WORK THERE.
THAT'S WHAT SHE THOUGHT.
IT WAS LAST DECEMBER WHEN MANY OF THEIR STAFF HAD INFLUENZA AND WERE OFF WORK.
SHE SEEMED TO LIKE WORKING THERE. IT WAS A FRESH START.
OF COURSE.
I SUPPOSE SHE GOT INTO TROUBLE THERE?
THEY TOLD HER TO LEAVE AFTER ONLY A COUPLE OF MONTHS.
NOT DOING HER WORK PROPERLY?
NO – THEY SAID HER WORK WAS GOOD.
BUT THERE MUST HAVE BEEN SOMETHING WRONG.
A CUSTOMER COMPLAINED ABOUT HER.

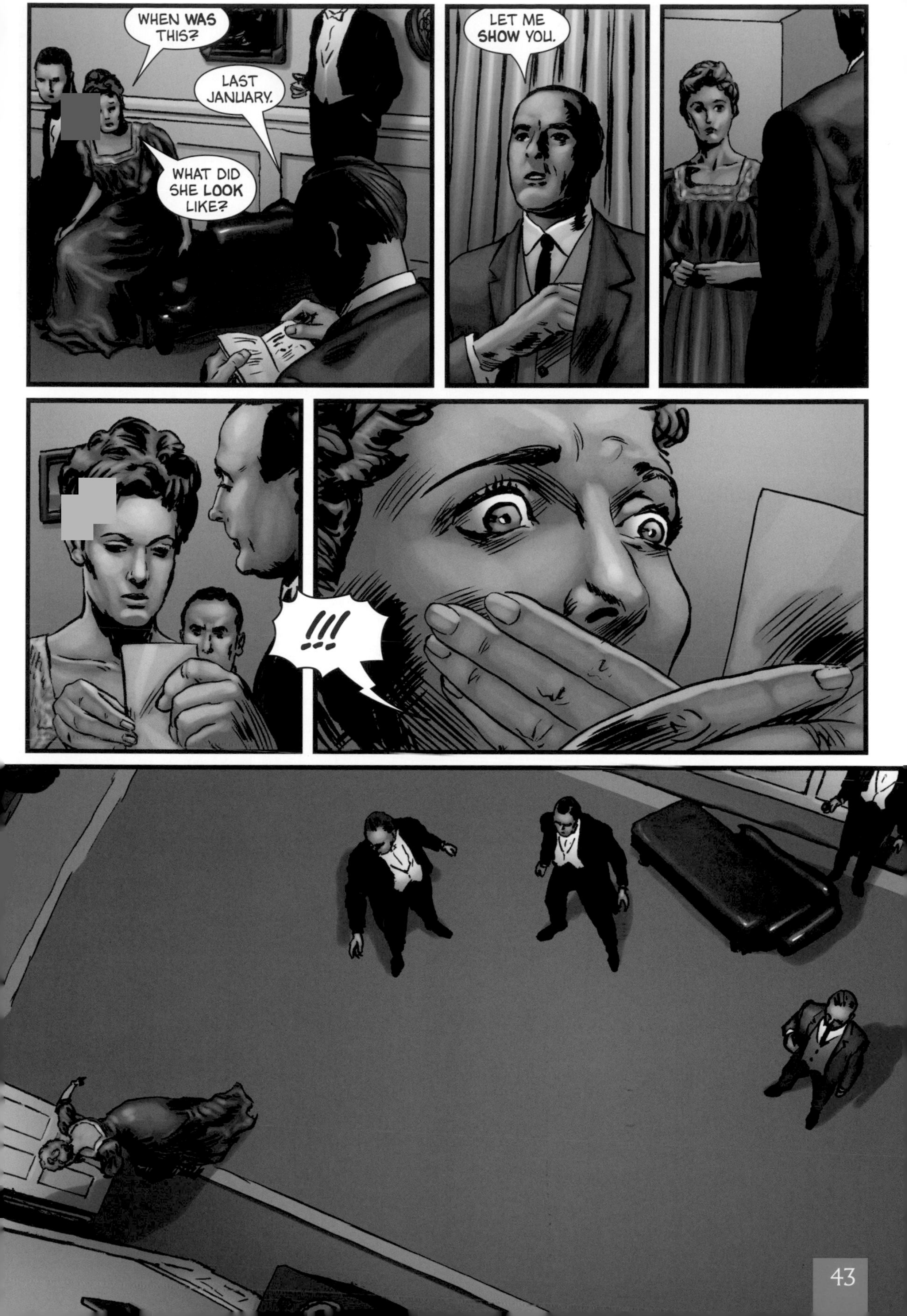
WHEN WAS THIS?
LAST JANUARY.
WHAT DID SHE LOOK LIKE?
LET ME SHOW YOU.
!!!

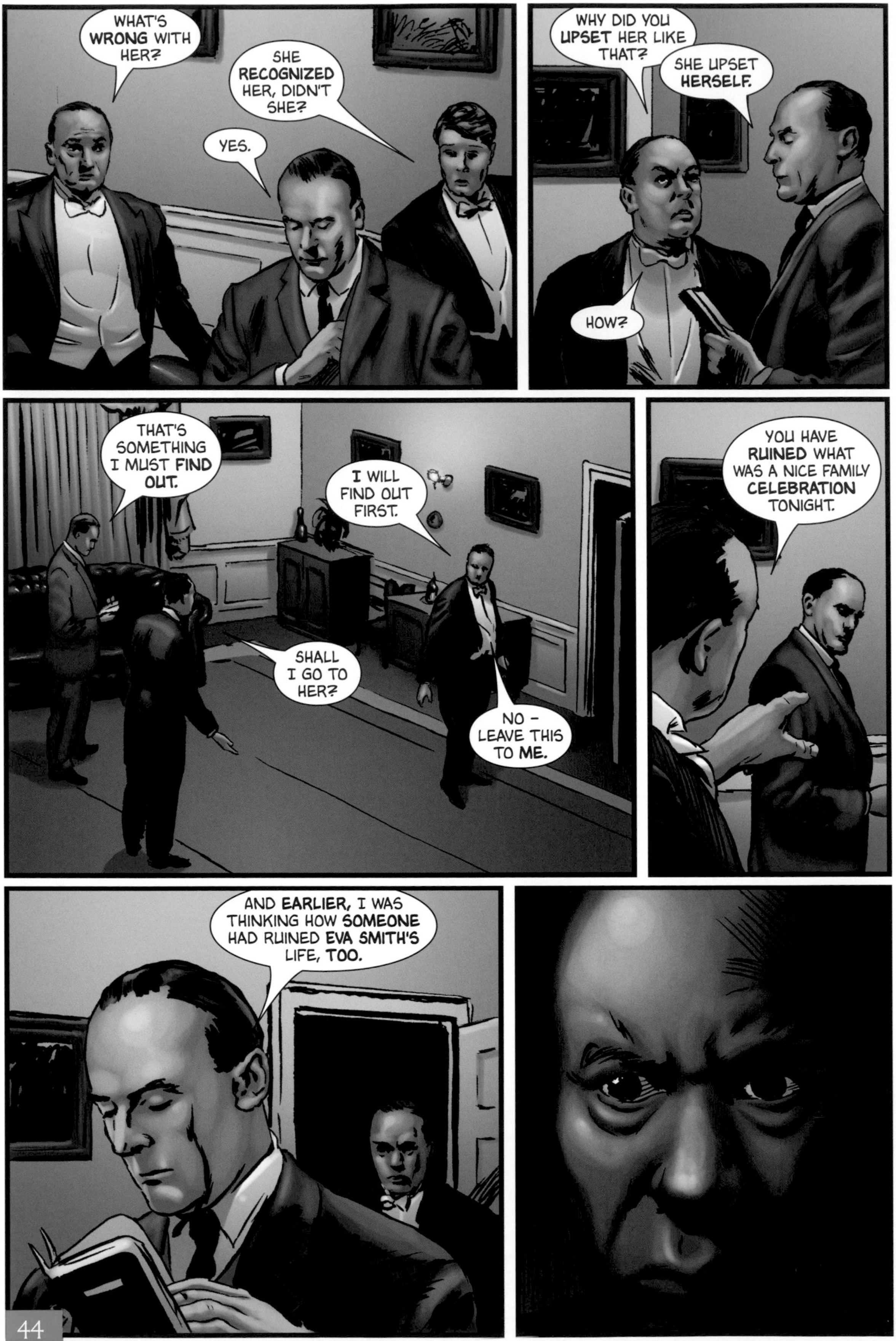
WHAT'S WRONG WITH HER?
SHE RECOGNIZED HER, DIDN'T SHE?
YES.
WHY DID YOU UPSET HER LIKE THAT?
SHE UPSET HERSELF.
HOW?
THAT'S SOMETHING I MUST FIND OUT.
I WILL FIND OUT FIRST.
SHALL I GO TO HER?
NO - LEAVE THIS TO ME.
YOU HAVE RUINED WHAT WAS A NICE FAMILY CELEBRATION TONIGHT.
AND EARLIER, I WAS THINKING HOW SOMEONE HAD RUINED EVA SMITH'S LIFE, TOO.

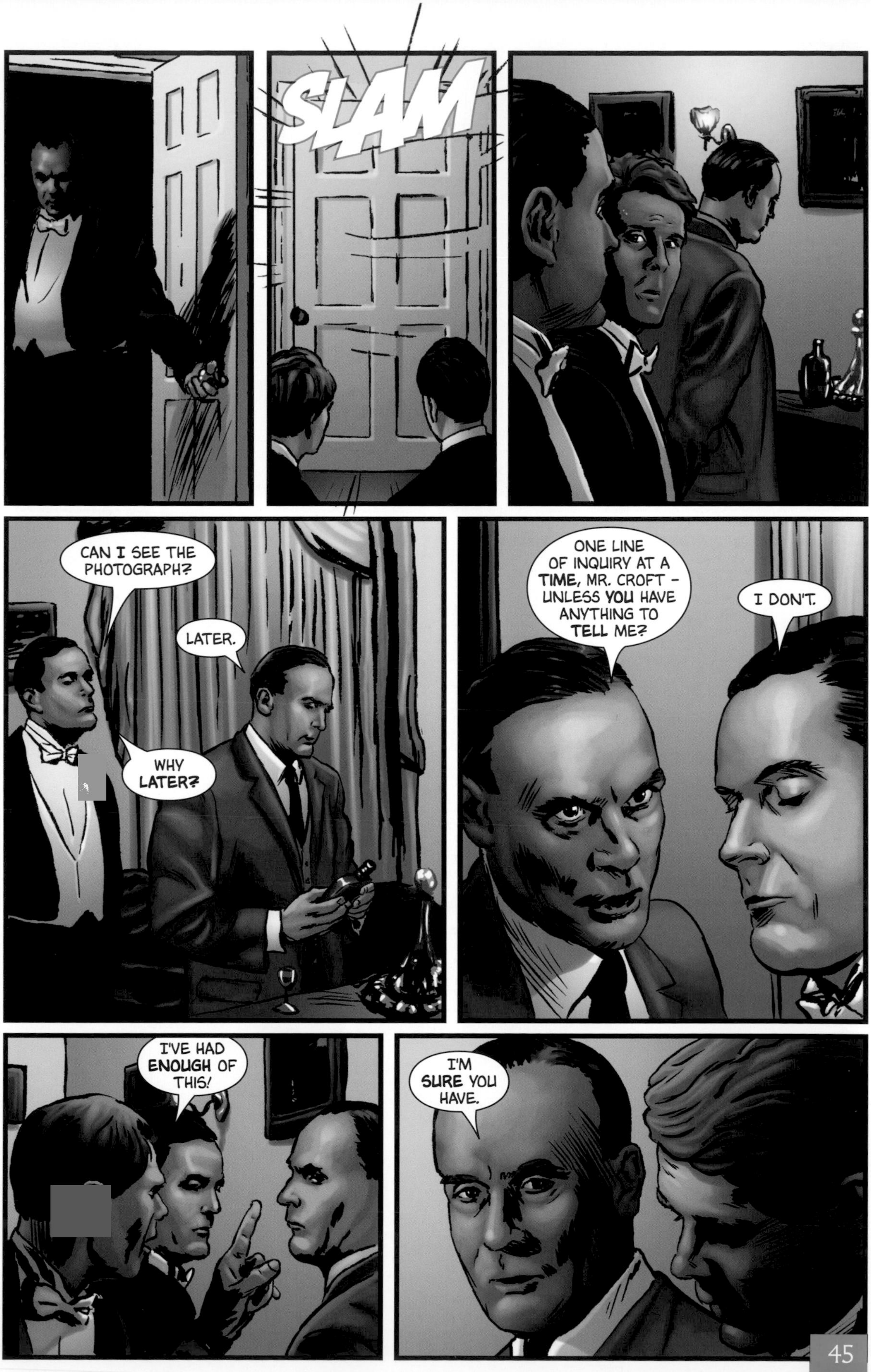
SLAM
CAN I SEE THE PHOTOGRAPH?
LATER.
WHY LATER?
ONE LINE OF INQUIRY AT A TIME, MR. CROFT – UNLESS YOU HAVE ANYTHING TO TELL ME?
I DON'T.
I'VE HAD ENOUGH OF THIS!
I'M SURE YOU HAVE.

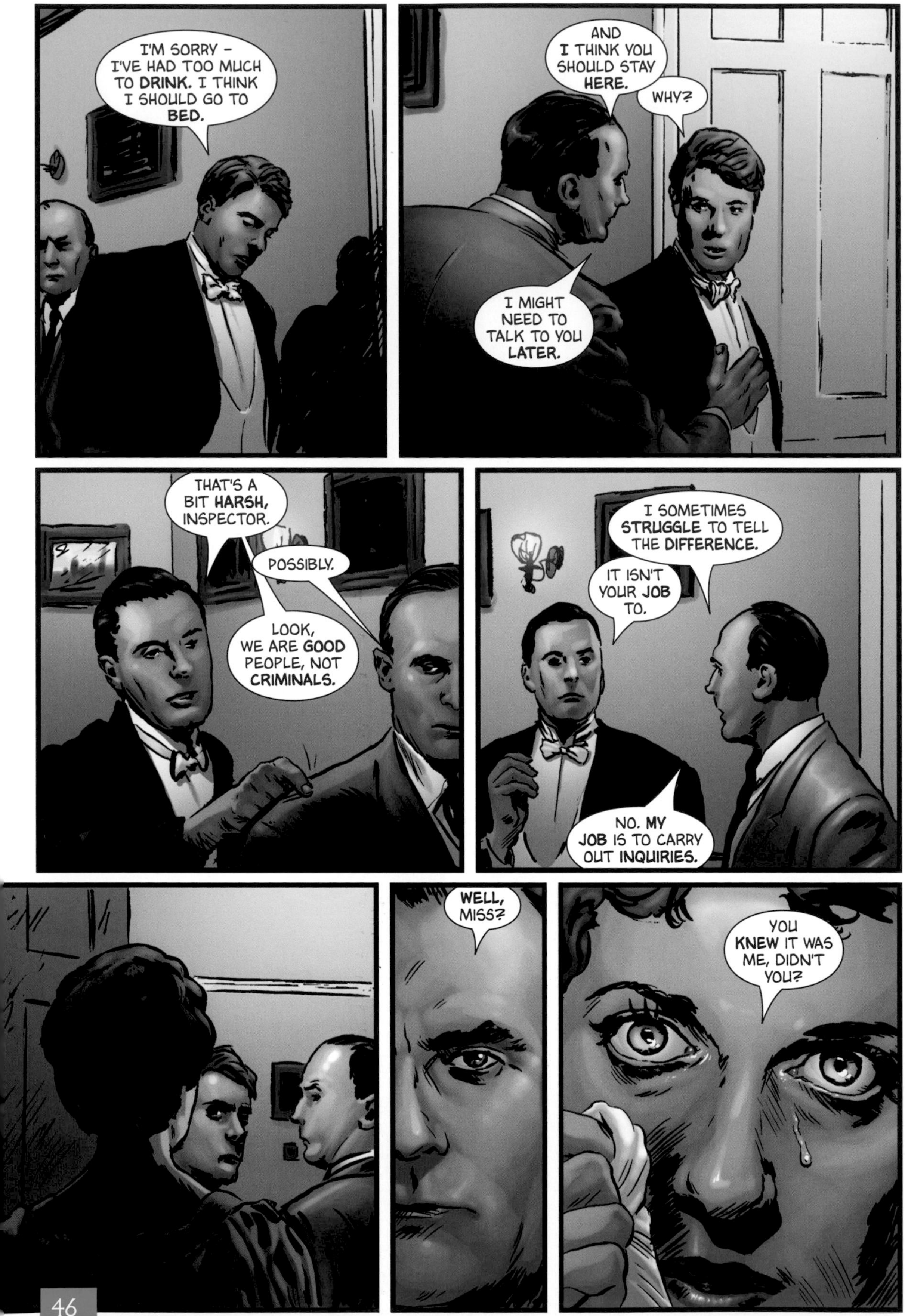
I'M SORRY – I'VE HAD TOO MUCH TO DRINK. I THINK I SHOULD GO TO BED.
AND I THINK YOU SHOULD STAY HERE.
WHY?
I MIGHT NEED TO TALK TO YOU LATER.
THAT'S A BIT HARSH, INSPECTOR.
POSSIBLY.
LOOK, WE ARE GOOD PEOPLE, NOT CRIMINALS.
I SOMETIMES STRUGGLE TO TELL THE DIFFERENCE.
IT ISN'T YOUR JOB TO.
NO. MY JOB IS TO CARRY OUT INQUIRIES.
WELL, MISS?
YOU KNEW IT WAS ME, DIDN'T YOU?

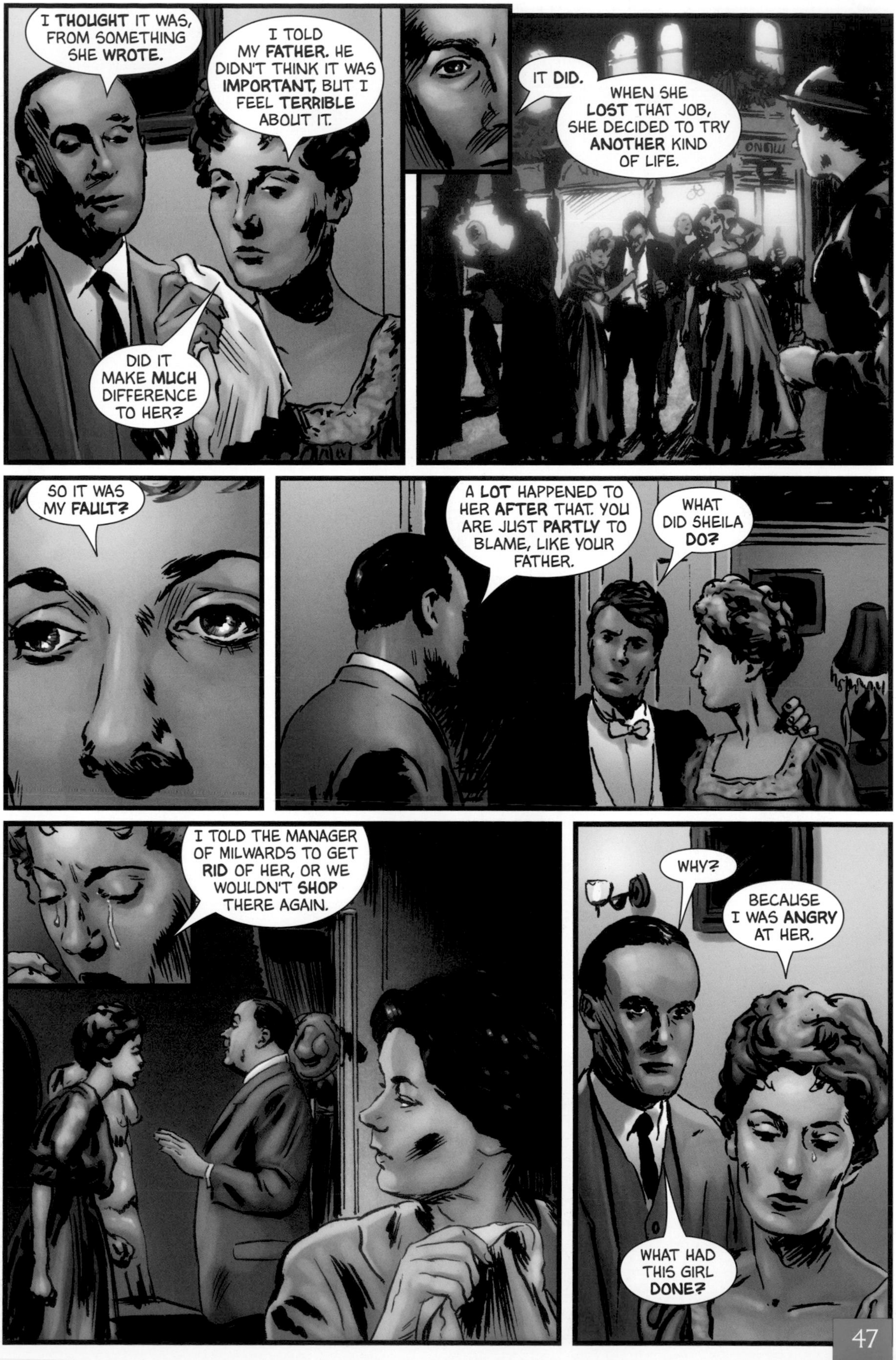

I THOUGHT IT WAS, FROM SOMETHING SHE WROTE.
I TOLD MY FATHER. HE DIDN'T THINK IT WAS IMPORTANT, BUT I FEEL TERRIBLE ABOUT IT.
DID IT MAKE MUCH DIFFERENCE TO HER?
IT DID.
WHEN SHE LOST THAT JOB, SHE DECIDED TO TRY ANOTHER KIND OF LIFE.
SO IT WAS MY FAULT?
A LOT HAPPENED TO HER AFTER THAT. YOU ARE JUST PARTLY TO BLAME, LIKE YOUR FATHER.
WHAT DID SHEILA DO?
I TOLD THE MANAGER OF MILWARDS TO GET RID OF HER, OR WE WOULDN'T SHOP THERE AGAIN.
WHY?
BECAUSE I WAS ANGRY AT HER.
WHAT HAD THIS GIRL DONE?

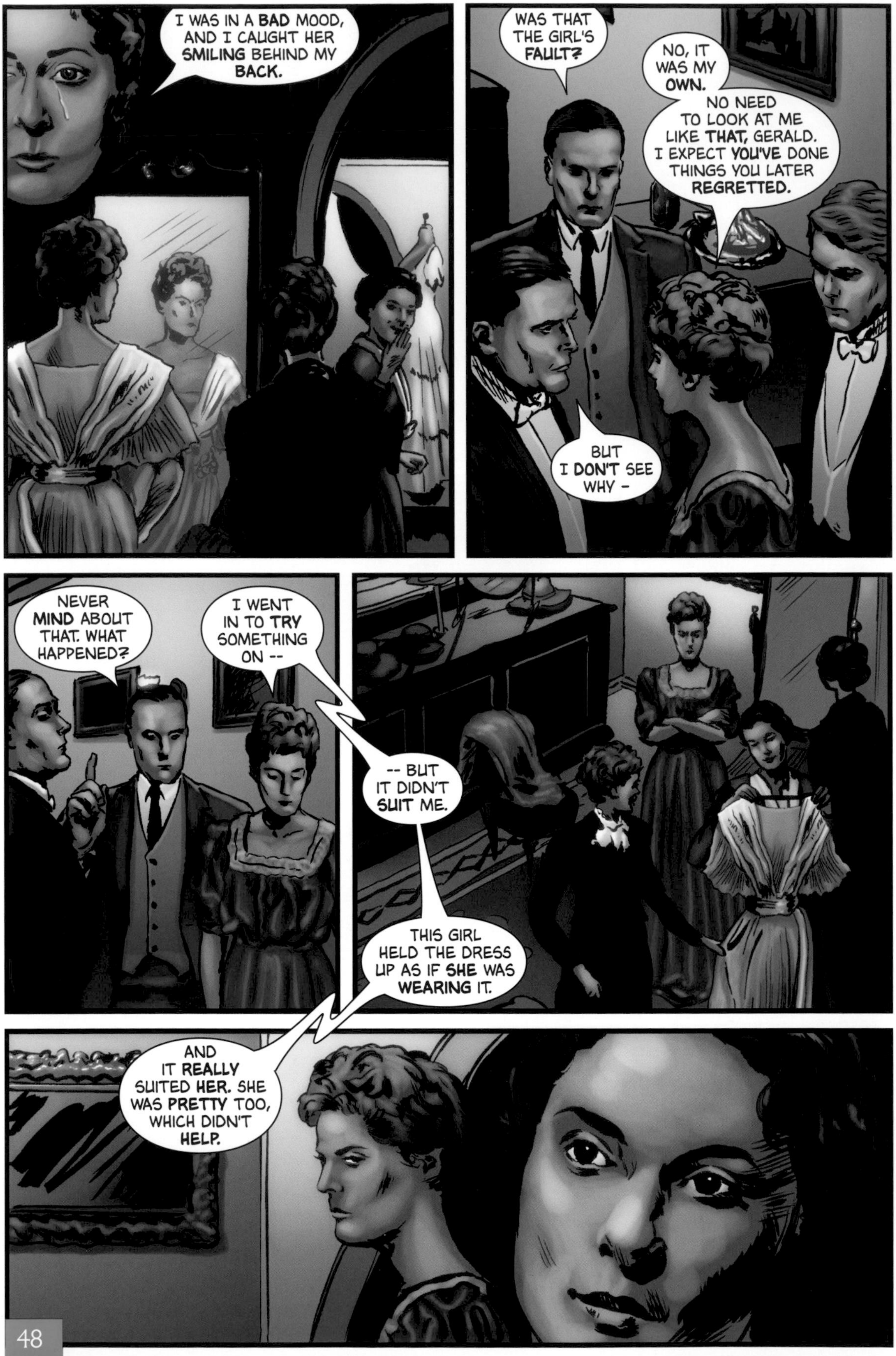
I WAS IN A BAD MOOD, AND I CAUGHT HER SMILING BEHIND MY BACK.
WAS THAT THE GIRL'S FAULT?
NO, IT WAS MY OWN.
NO NEED TO LOOK AT ME LIKE THAT, GERALD. I EXPECT YOU'VE DONE THINGS YOU LATER REGRETTED.
BUT I DON'T SEE WHY -
NEVER MIND ABOUT THAT. WHAT HAPPENED?
I WENT IN TO TRY SOMETHING ON --
-- BUT IT DIDN'T SUIT ME.
THIS GIRL HELD THE DRESS UP AS IF SHE WAS WEARING IT.
AND IT REALLY SUITED HER. SHE WAS PRETTY TOO, WHICH DIDN'T HELP.

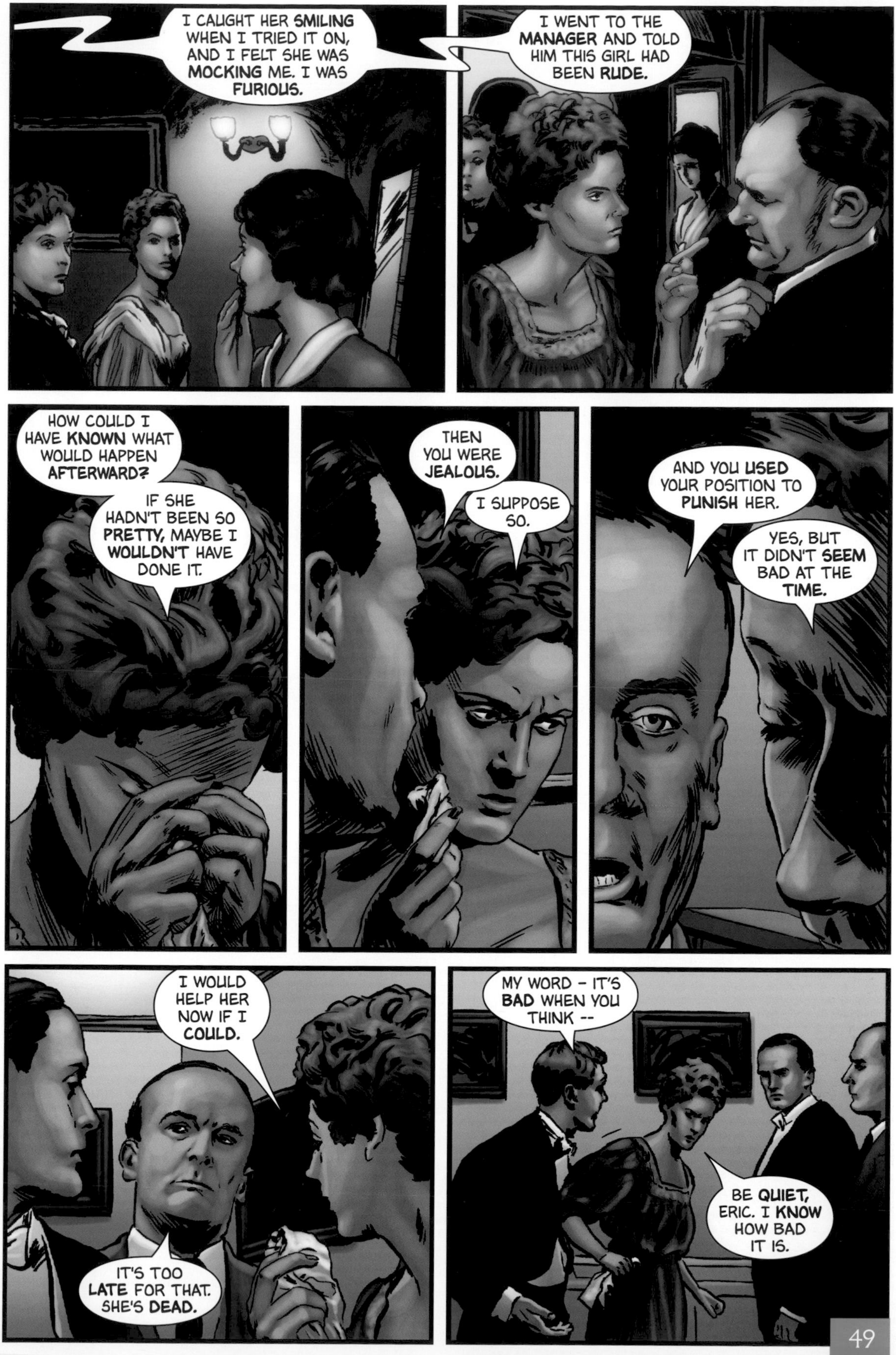

I CAUGHT HER SMILING WHEN I TRIED IT ON, AND I FELT SHE WAS MOCKING ME. I WAS FURIOUS.
I WENT TO THE MANAGER AND TOLD HIM THIS GIRL HAD BEEN RUDE.
HOW COULD I HAVE KNOWN WHAT WOULD HAPPEN AFTERWARD?
IF SHE HADN'T BEEN SO PRETTY, MAYBE I WOULDN'T HAVE DONE IT.
THEN YOU WERE JEALOUS.
I SUPPOSE SO.
AND YOU USED YOUR POSITION TO PUNISH HER.
YES, BUT IT DIDN'T SEEM BAD AT THE TIME.
I WOULD HELP HER NOW IF I COULD.
IT'S TOO LATE FOR THAT. SHE'S DEAD.
MY WORD – IT'S BAD WHEN YOU THINK --
BE QUIET, ERIC. I KNOW HOW BAD IT IS.

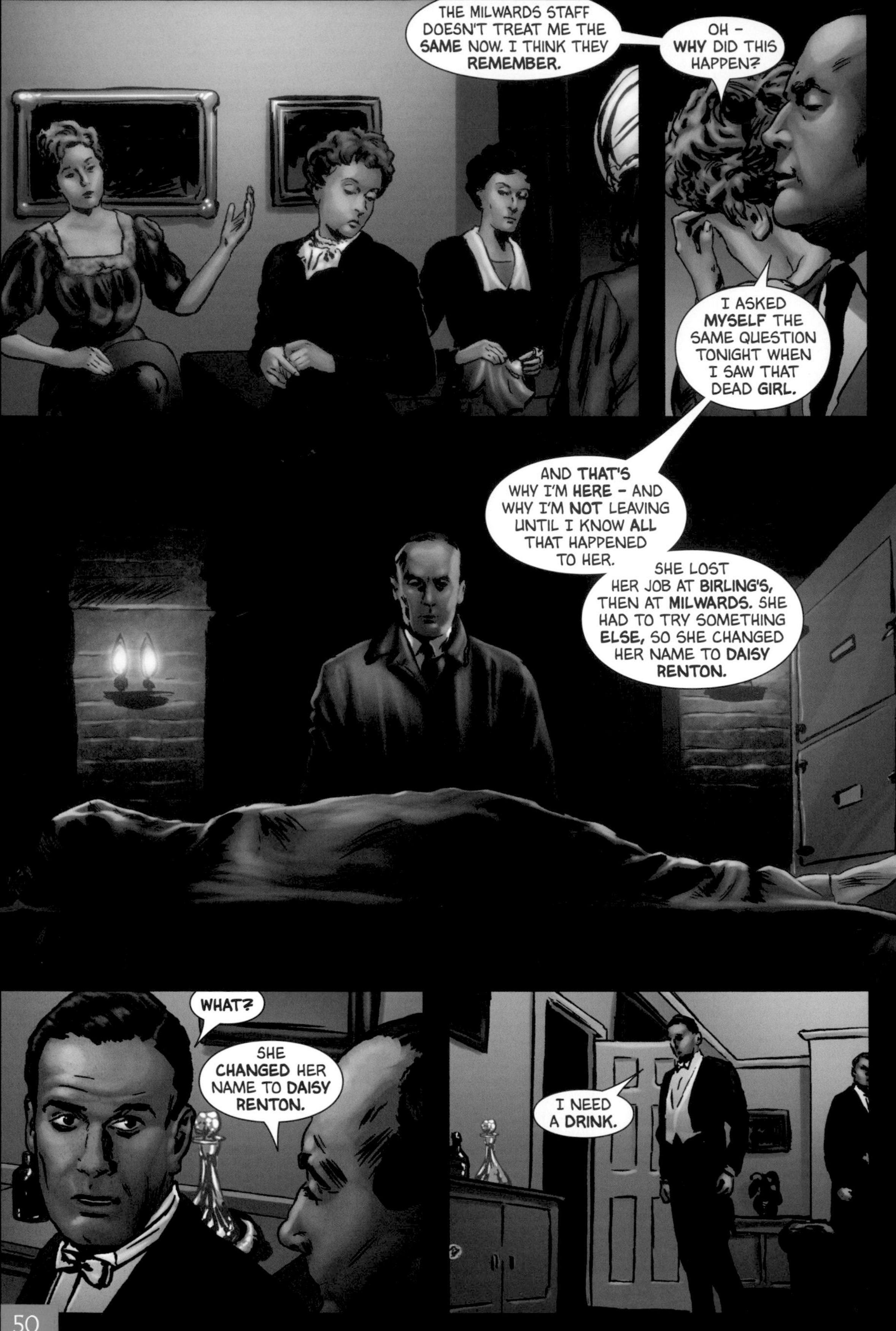
THE MILWARDS STAFF DOESN'T TREAT ME THE SAME NOW. I THINK THEY REMEMBER.
OH – WHY DID THIS HAPPEN?
I ASKED MYSELF THE SAME QUESTION TONIGHT WHEN I SAW THAT DEAD GIRL.
AND THAT'S WHY I'M HERE – AND WHY I'M NOT LEAVING UNTIL I KNOW ALL THAT HAPPENED TO HER.
SHE LOST HER JOB AT BIRLING'S, THEN AT MILWARDS. SHE HAD TO TRY SOMETHING ELSE, SO SHE CHANGED HER NAME TO DAISY RENTON.
WHAT?
SHE CHANGED HER NAME TO DAISY RENTON.
I NEED A DRINK.

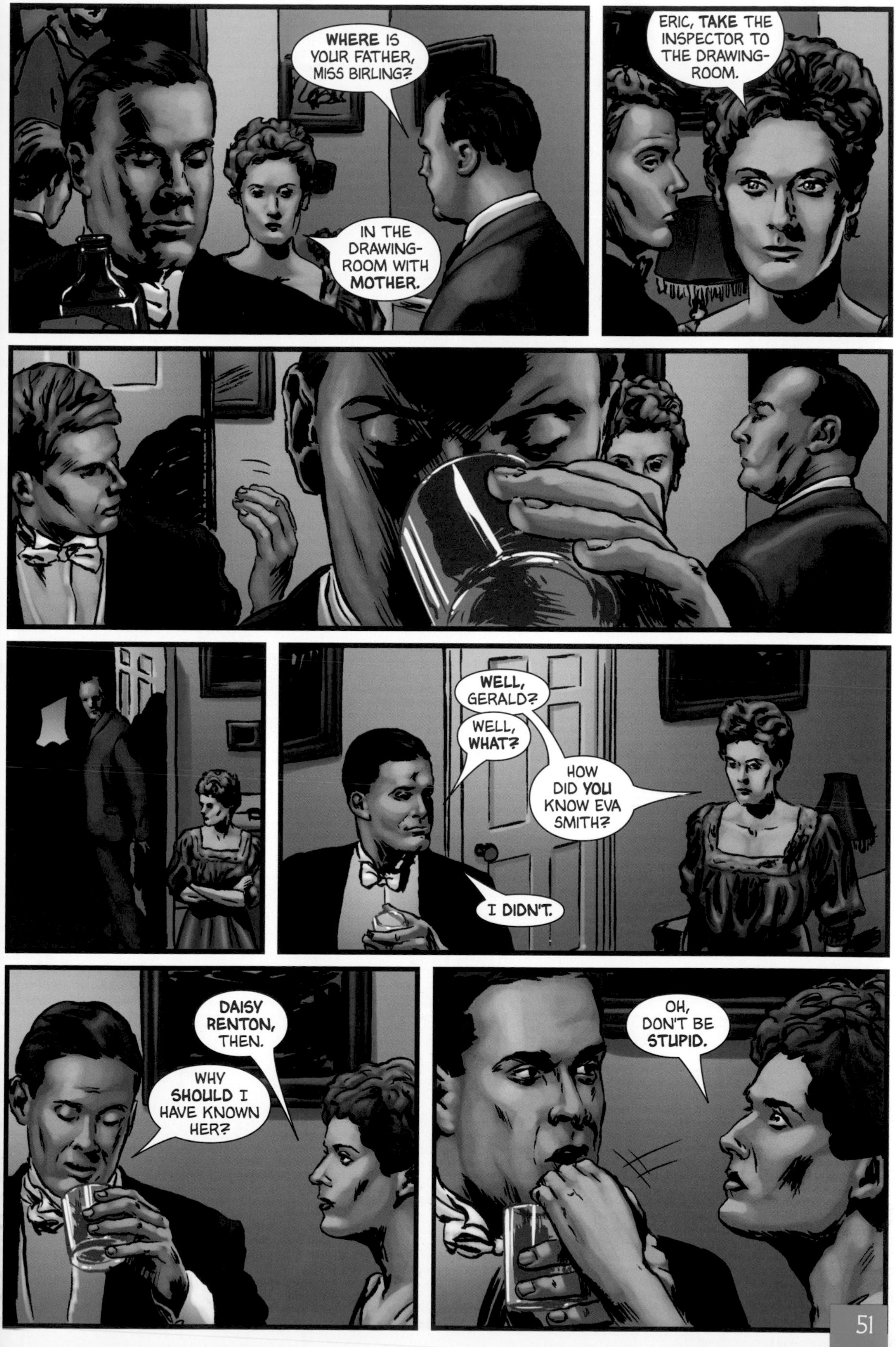
WHERE IS YOUR FATHER, MISS BIRLING?
IN THE DRAWING-ROOM WITH MOTHER.
ERIC, TAKE THE INSPECTOR TO THE DRAWING-ROOM.
WELL, GERALD?
WELL, WHAT?
HOW DID YOU KNOW EVA SMITH?
I DIDN'T.
DAISY RENTON, THEN.
WHY SHOULD I HAVE KNOWN HER?
OH, DON'T BE STUPID.

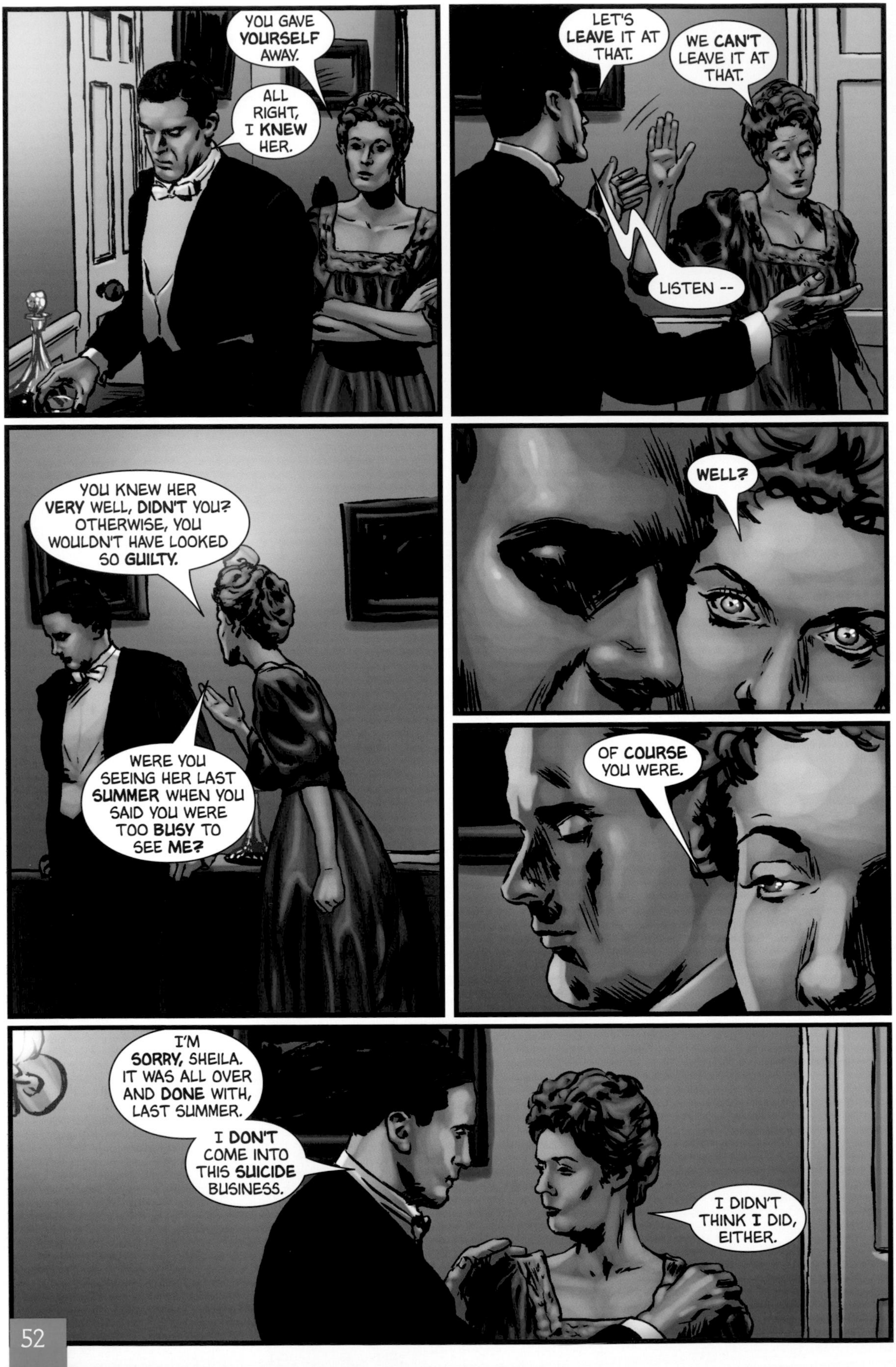
YOU GAVE YOURSELF AWAY.
ALL RIGHT, I KNEW HER.
LET'S LEAVE IT AT THAT.
WE CAN'T LEAVE IT AT THAT.
LISTEN --
YOU KNEW HER VERY WELL, DIDN'T YOU? OTHERWISE, YOU WOULDN'T HAVE LOOKED SO GUILTY.
WERE YOU SEEING HER LAST SUMMER WHEN YOU SAID YOU WERE TOO BUSY TO SEE ME?
WELL?
OF COURSE YOU WERE.
I'M SORRY, SHEILA. IT WAS ALL OVER AND DONE WITH, LAST SUMMER.
I DON'T COME INTO THIS SUICIDE BUSINESS.
I DIDN'T THINK I DID, EITHER.

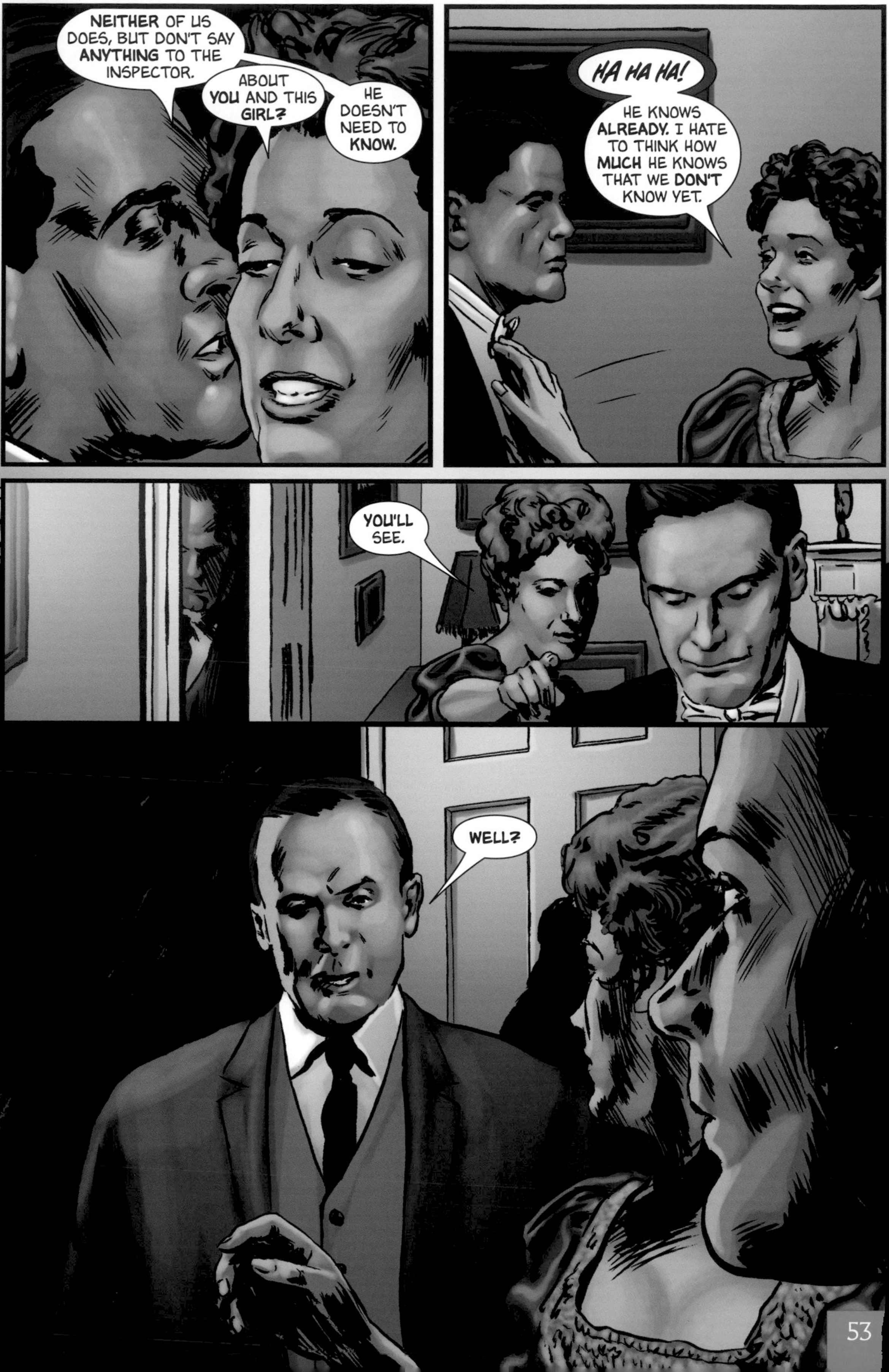
NEITHER OF US DOES, BUT DON'T SAY ANYTHING TO THE INSPECTOR.
ABOUT YOU AND THIS GIRL?
HE DOESN'T NEED TO KNOW.
HA HA HA!
HE KNOWS ALREADY. I HATE TO THINK HOW MUCH HE KNOWS THAT WE DON'T KNOW YET.
YOU'LL SEE.
WELL?

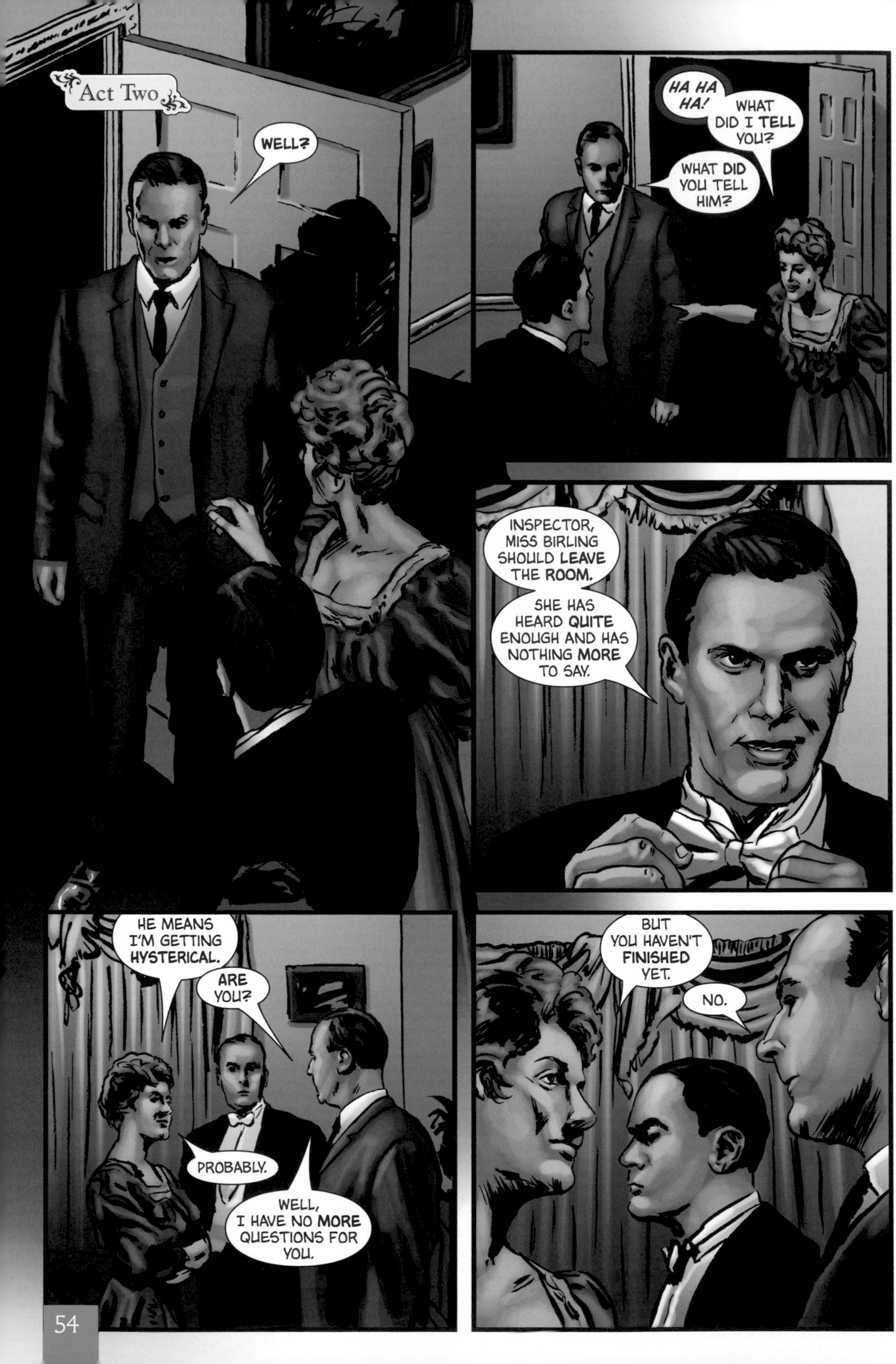
WELL?
HA HA HA!
WHAT DID I TELL YOU?
WHAT DID YOU TELL HIM?
INSPECTOR, MISS BIRLING SHOULD LEAVE THE ROOM.
SHE HAS HEARD QUITE ENOUGH AND HAS NOTHING MORE TO SAY.
HE MEANS I'M GETTING HYSTERICAL.
ARE YOU?
PROBABLY.
WELL, I HAVE NO MORE QUESTIONS FOR YOU.
BUT YOU HAVEN'T FINISHED YET.
NO.

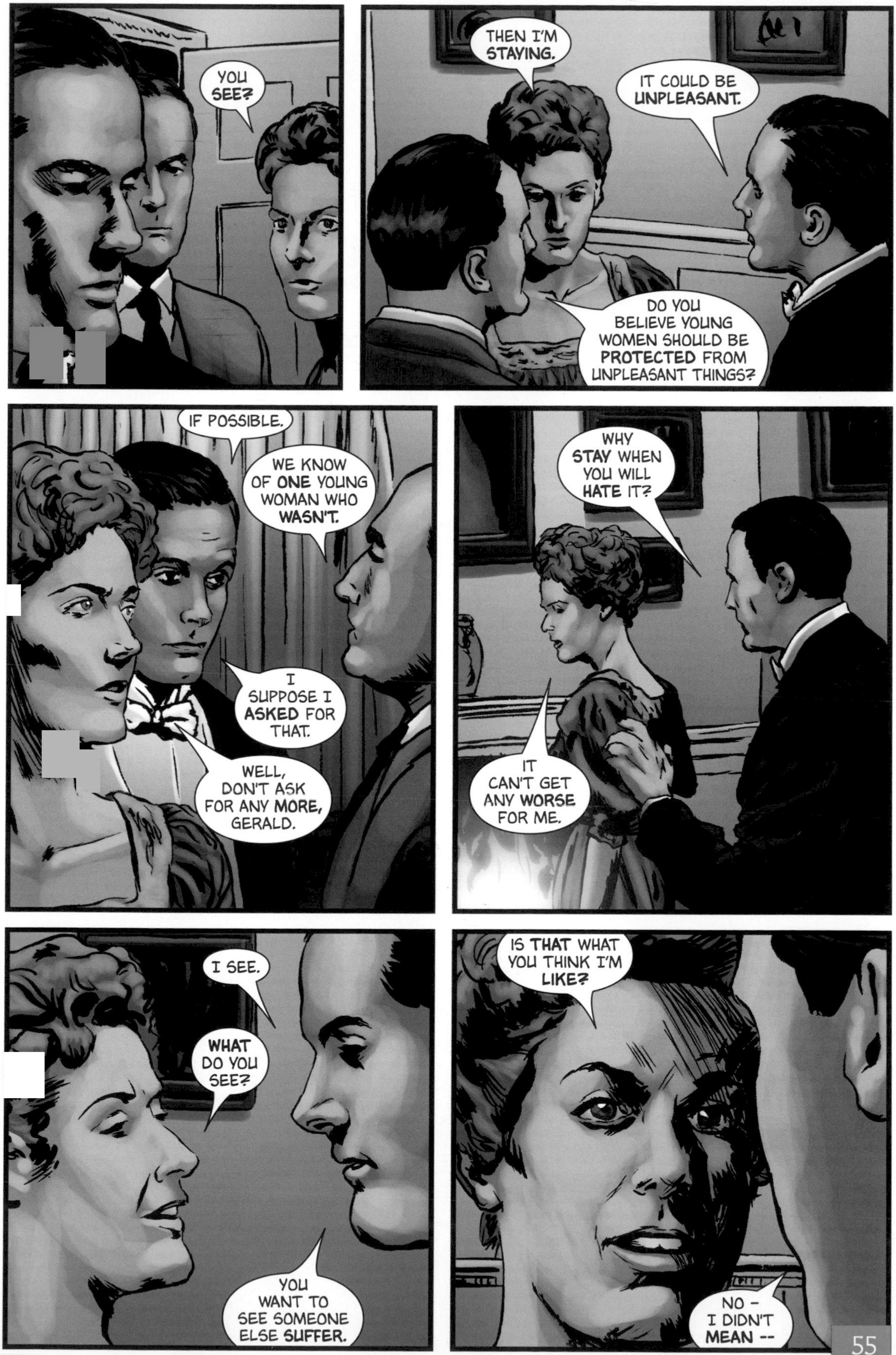
YOU SEE?
THEN I'M STAYING.
IT COULD BE UNPLEASANT.
DO YOU BELIEVE YOUNG WOMEN SHOULD BE PROTECTED FROM UNPLEASANT THINGS?
IF POSSIBLE.
WE KNOW OF ONE YOUNG WOMAN WHO WASN'T.
I SUPPOSE I ASKED FOR THAT.
WELL, DON'T ASK FOR ANY MORE, GERALD.
WHY STAY WHEN YOU WILL HATE IT?
IT CAN'T GET ANY WORSE FOR ME.
I SEE.
WHAT DO YOU SEE?
YOU WANT TO SEE SOMEONE ELSE SUFFER.
IS THAT WHAT YOU THINK I'M LIKE?
NO – I DIDN'T MEAN --

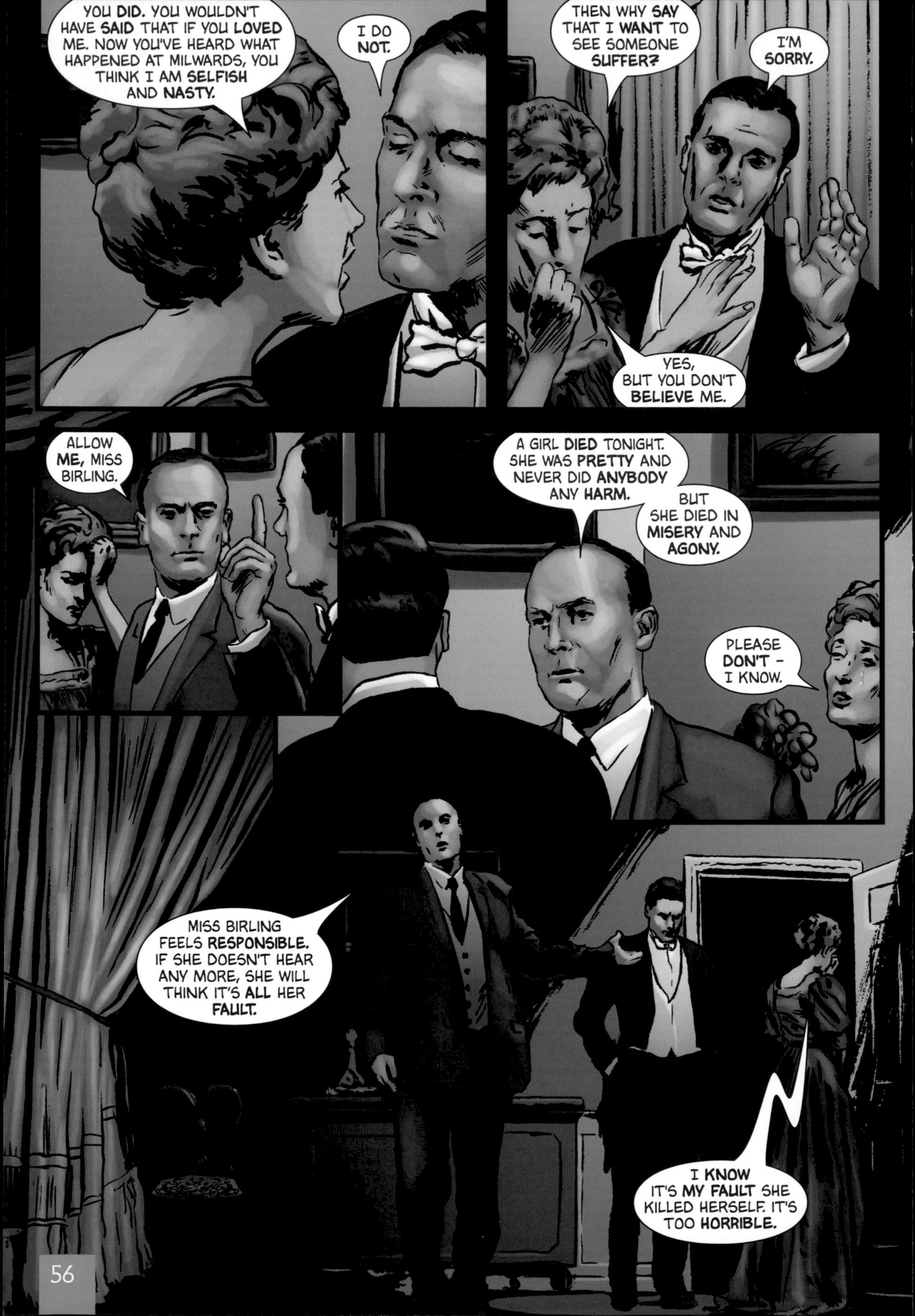
YOU DID. YOU WOULDN'T HAVE SAID THAT IF YOU LOVED ME. NOW YOU'VE HEARD WHAT HAPPENED AT MILWARDS, YOU THINK I AM SELFISH AND NASTY.
I DO NOT.
THEN WHY SAY THAT I WANT TO SEE SOMEONE SUFFER?
I'M SORRY.
YES, BUT YOU DON'T BELIEVE ME.
ALLOW ME, MISS BIRLING.
A GIRL DIED TONIGHT. SHE WAS PRETTY AND NEVER DID ANYBODY ANY HARM.
BUT SHE DIED IN MISERY AND AGONY.
PLEASE DON'T - I KNOW.
MISS BIRLING FEELS RESPONSIBLE. IF SHE DOESN'T HEAR ANY MORE, SHE WILL THINK IT'S ALL HER FAULT.
I KNOW IT'S MY FAULT SHE KILLED HERSELF. IT'S TOO HORRIBLE.

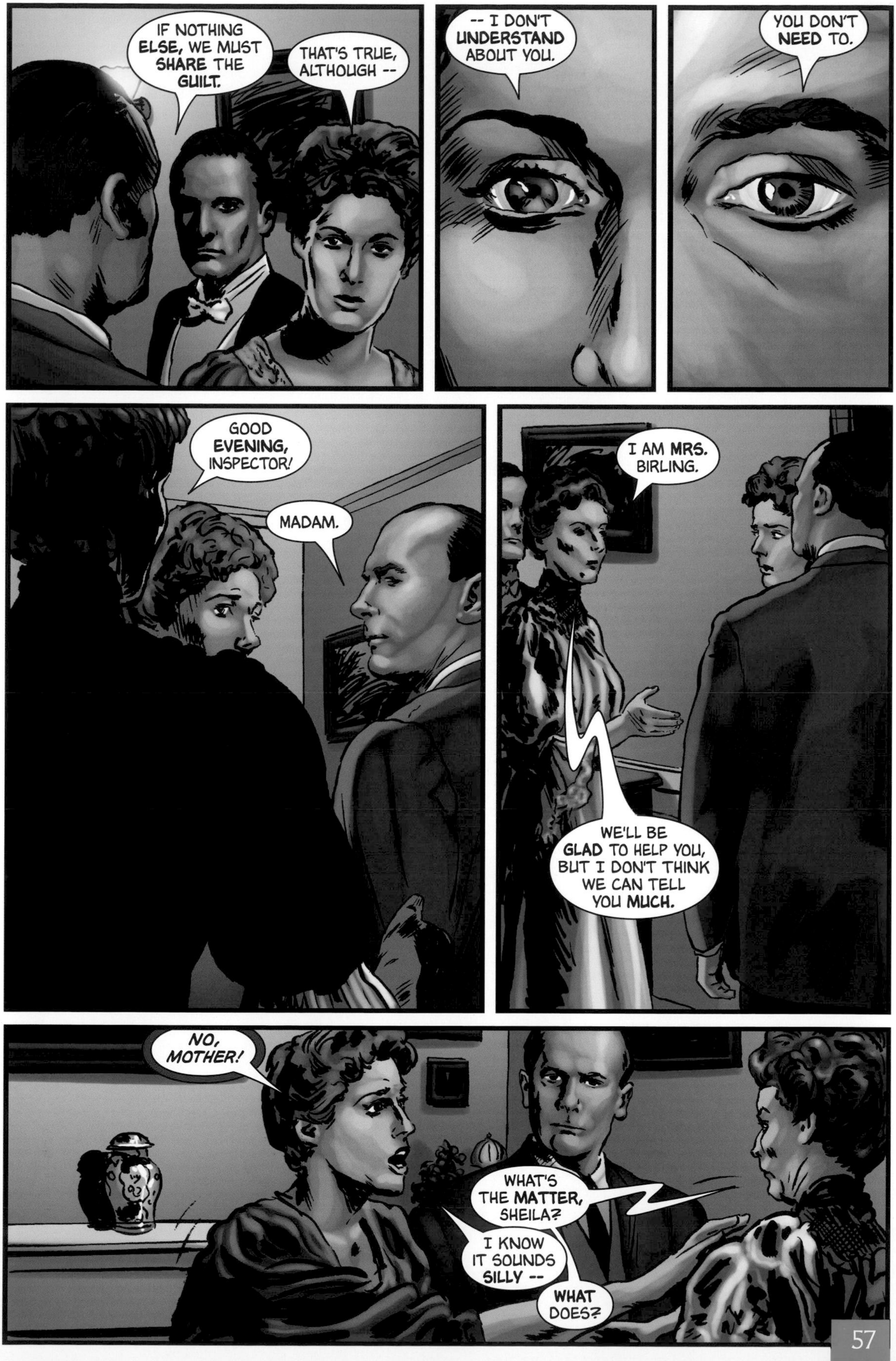
IF NOTHING ELSE, WE MUST SHARE THE GUILT.
THAT'S TRUE, ALTHOUGH --
-- I DON'T UNDERSTAND ABOUT YOU.
YOU DON'T NEED TO.
GOOD EVENING, INSPECTOR!
MADAM.
I AM MRS. BIRLING.
WE'LL BE GLAD TO HELP YOU, BUT I DON'T THINK WE CAN TELL YOU MUCH.
NO, MOTHER!
WHAT'S THE MATTER, SHEILA?
I KNOW IT SOUNDS SILLY --
WHAT DOES?

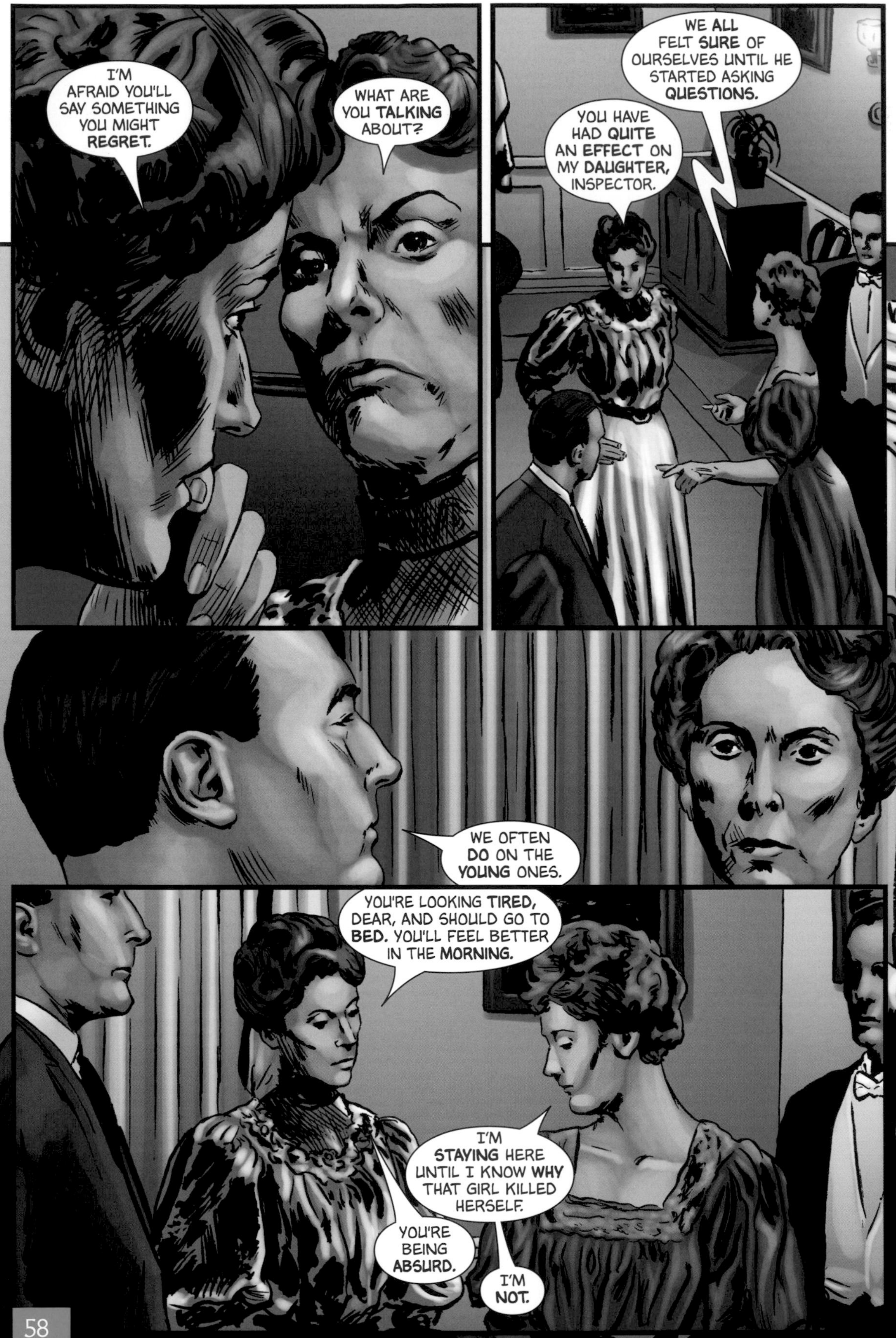

I'M AFRAID YOU'LL SAY SOMETHING YOU MIGHT REGRET.
WHAT ARE YOU TALKING ABOUT?
YOU HAVE HAD QUITE AN EFFECT ON MY DAUGHTER, INSPECTOR.
WE ALL FELT SURE OF OURSELVES UNTIL HE STARTED ASKING QUESTIONS.
WE OFTEN DO ON THE YOUNG ONES.
YOU'RE LOOKING TIRED, DEAR, AND SHOULD GO TO BED. YOU'LL FEEL BETTER IN THE MORNING.
I'M STAYING HERE UNTIL I KNOW WHY THAT GIRL KILLED HERSELF.
YOU'RE BEING ABSURD.
I'M NOT.

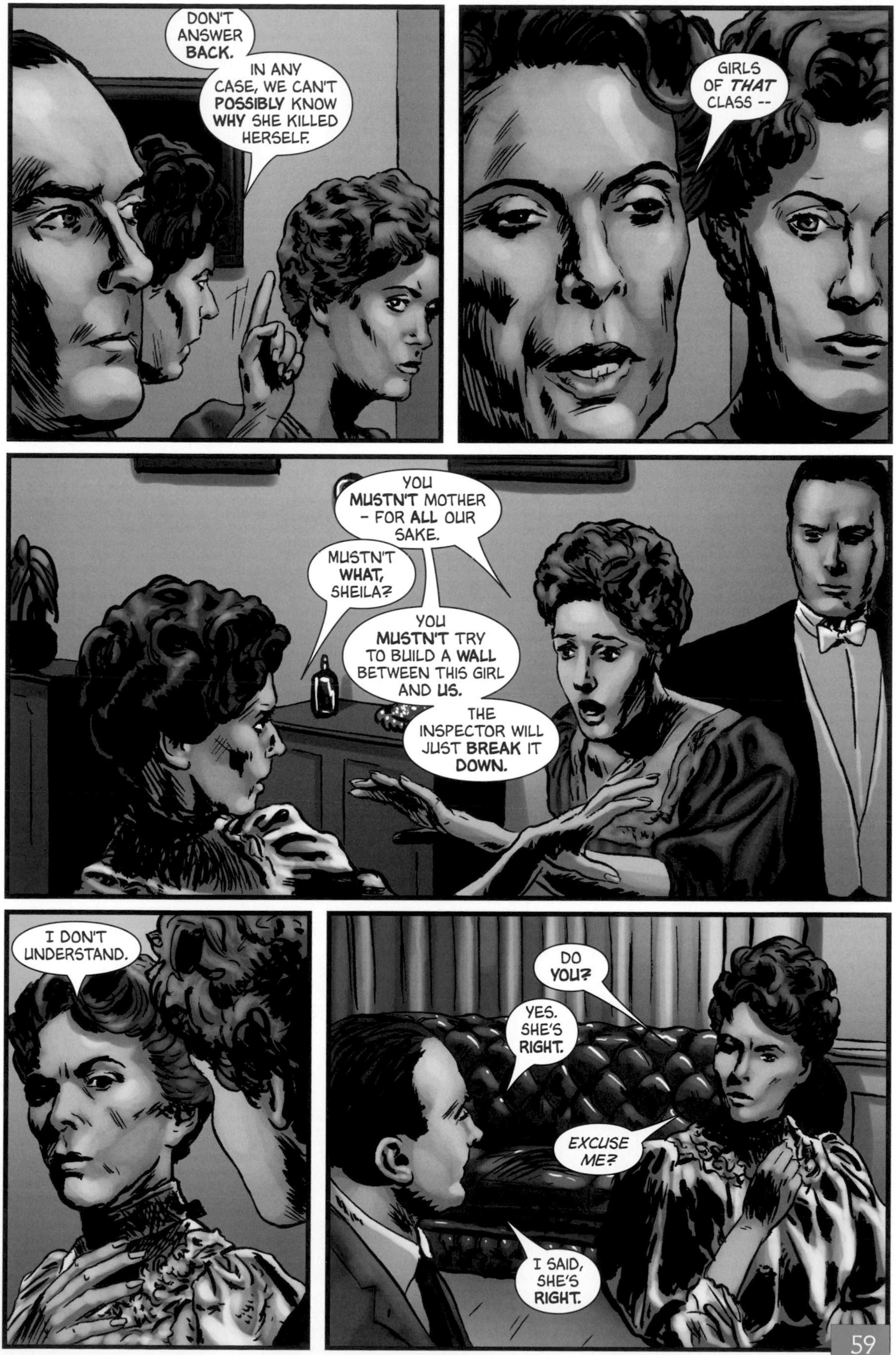
DON'T ANSWER BACK.
IN ANY CASE, WE CAN'T POSSIBLY KNOW WHY SHE KILLED HERSELF.
GIRLS OF THAT CLASS --
YOU MUSTN'T MOTHER - FOR ALL OUR SAKE.
MUSTN'T WHAT, SHEILA?
YOU MUSTN'T TRY TO BUILD A WALL BETWEEN THIS GIRL AND US.
THE INSPECTOR WILL JUST BREAK IT DOWN.
I DON'T UNDERSTAND.
DO YOU?
YES. SHE'S RIGHT.
EXCUSE ME?
I SAID, SHE'S RIGHT.

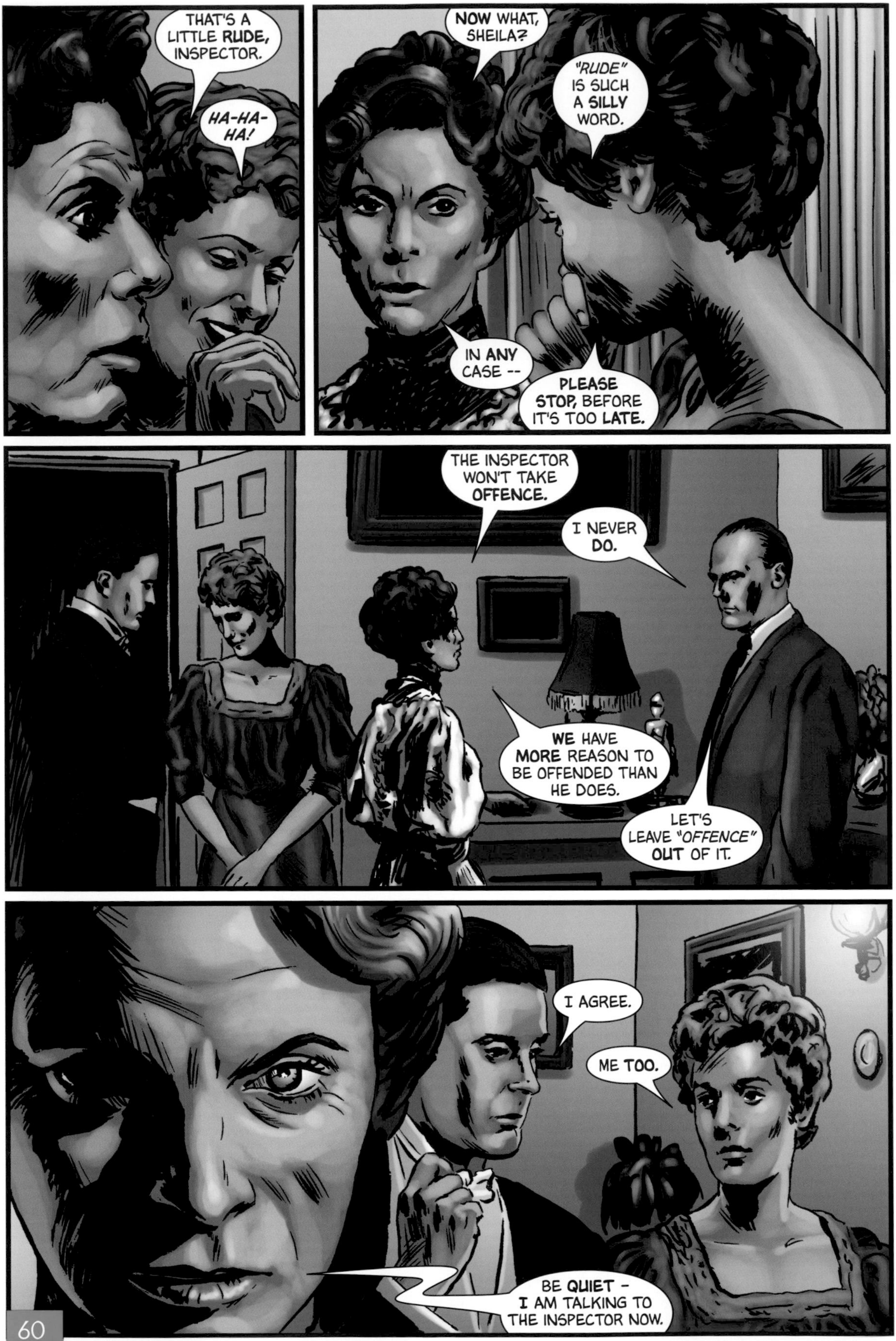
THAT'S A LITTLE RUDE, INSPECTOR.
HA-HA-HA!
NOW WHAT, SHEILA?
"RUDE" IS SUCH A SILLY WORD.
IN ANY CASE --
PLEASE STOP, BEFORE IT'S TOO LATE.
THE INSPECTOR WON'T TAKE OFFENCE.
I NEVER DO.
WE HAVE MORE REASON TO BE OFFENDED THAN HE DOES.
LET'S LEAVE "OFFENCE" OUT OF IT.
I AGREE.
ME TOO.
BE QUIET – I AM TALKING TO THE INSPECTOR NOW.

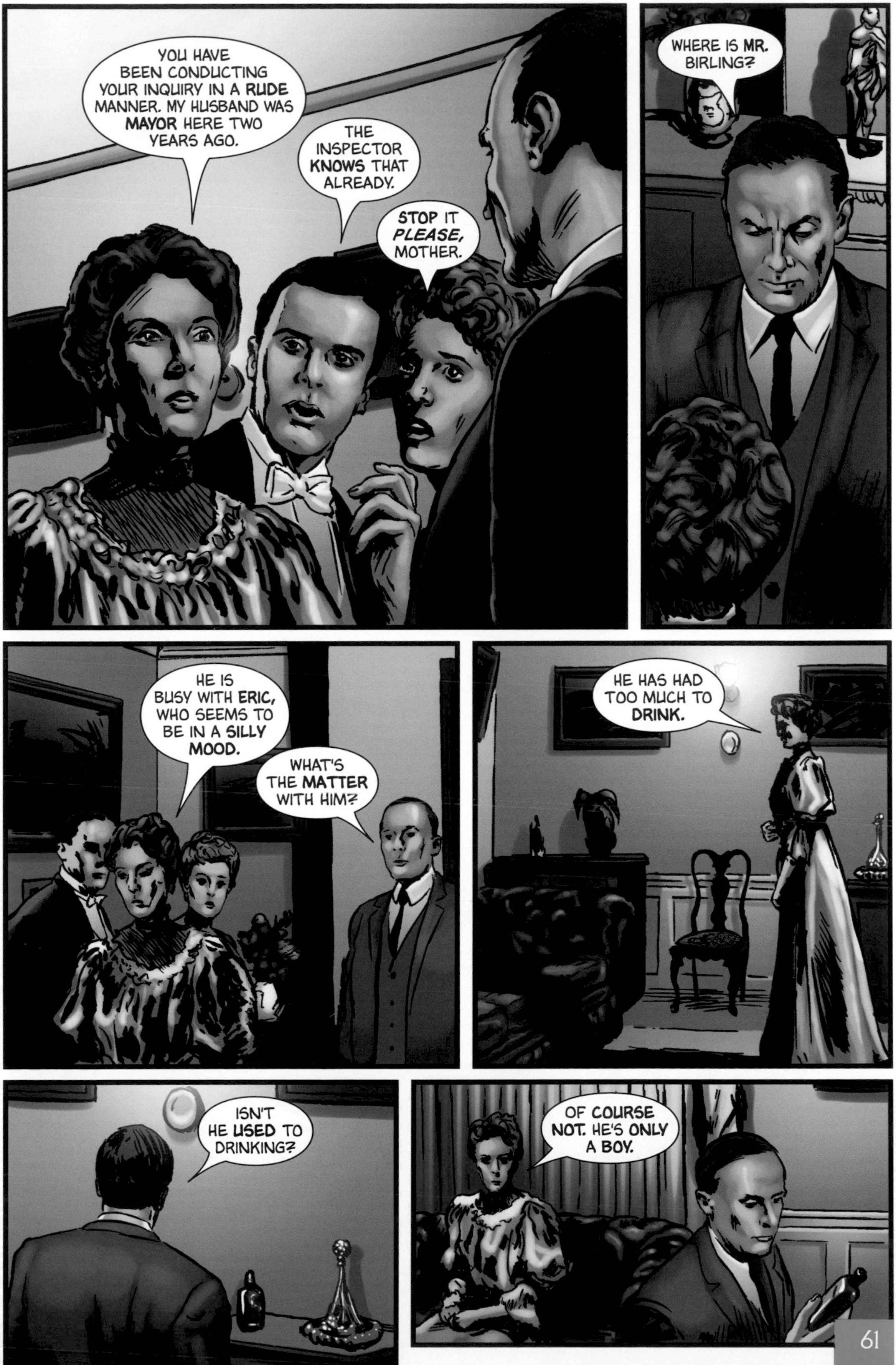
YOU HAVE BEEN CONDUCTING YOUR INQUIRY IN A RUDE MANNER. MY HUSBAND WAS MAYOR HERE TWO YEARS AGO.
THE INSPECTOR KNOWS THAT ALREADY.
STOP IT PLEASE, MOTHER.
WHERE IS MR. BIRLING?
HE IS BUSY WITH ERIC, WHO SEEMS TO BE IN A SILLY MOOD.
WHAT'S THE MATTER WITH HIM?
HE HAS HAD TOO MUCH TO DRINK.
ISN'T HE USED TO DRINKING?
OF COURSE NOT. HE'S ONLY A BOY.

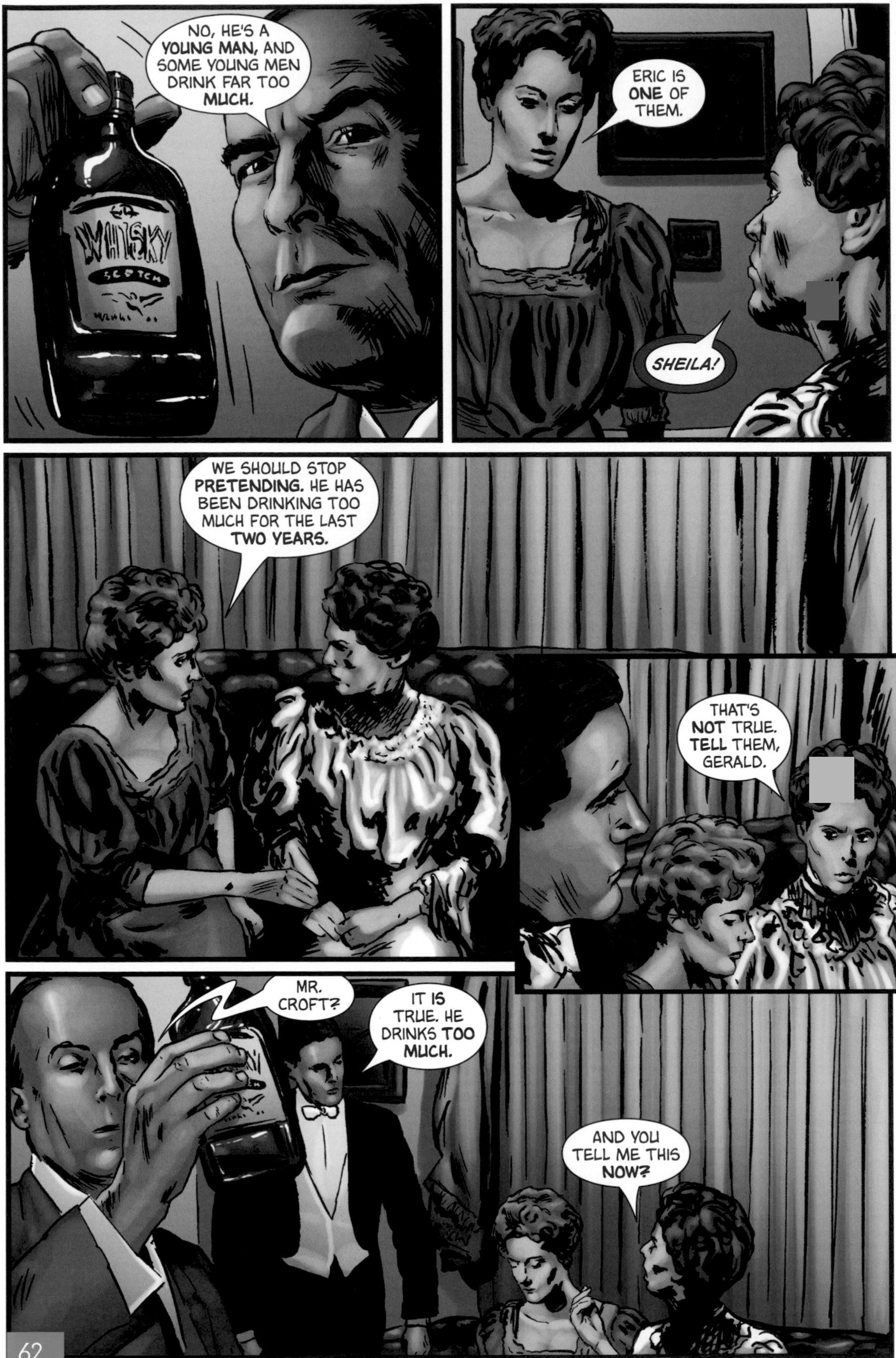
NO, HE'S A YOUNG MAN, AND SOME YOUNG MEN DRINK FAR TOO MUCH.
WHISKY SCOTCH
ERIC IS ONE OF THEM.
SHEILA!
WE SHOULD STOP PRETENDING. HE HAS BEEN DRINKING TOO MUCH FOR THE LAST TWO YEARS.
THAT'S NOT TRUE. TELL THEM, GERALD.
MR. CROFT?
IT IS TRUE. HE DRINKS TOO MUCH.
AND YOU TELL ME THIS NOW?

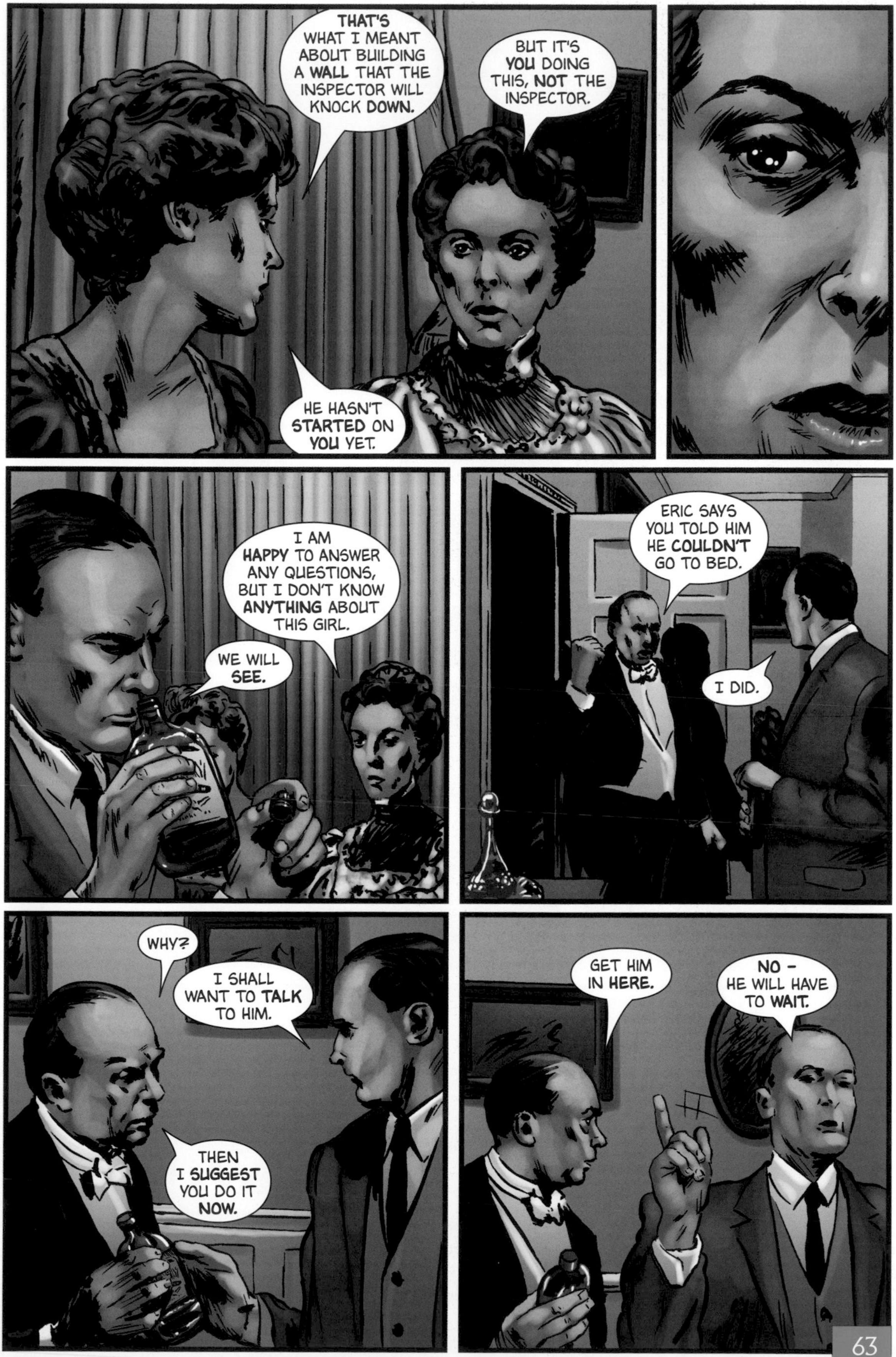
THAT'S WHAT I MEANT ABOUT BUILDING A WALL THAT THE INSPECTOR WILL KNOCK DOWN.
BUT IT'S YOU DOING THIS, NOT THE INSPECTOR.
HE HASN'T STARTED ON YOU YET.
I AM HAPPY TO ANSWER ANY QUESTIONS, BUT I DON'T KNOW ANYTHING ABOUT THIS GIRL.
WE WILL SEE.
ERIC SAYS YOU TOLD HIM HE COULDN'T GO TO BED.
I DID.
WHY?
I SHALL WANT TO TALK TO HIM.
THEN I SUGGEST YOU DO IT NOW.
GET HIM IN HERE.
NO - HE WILL HAVE TO WAIT.

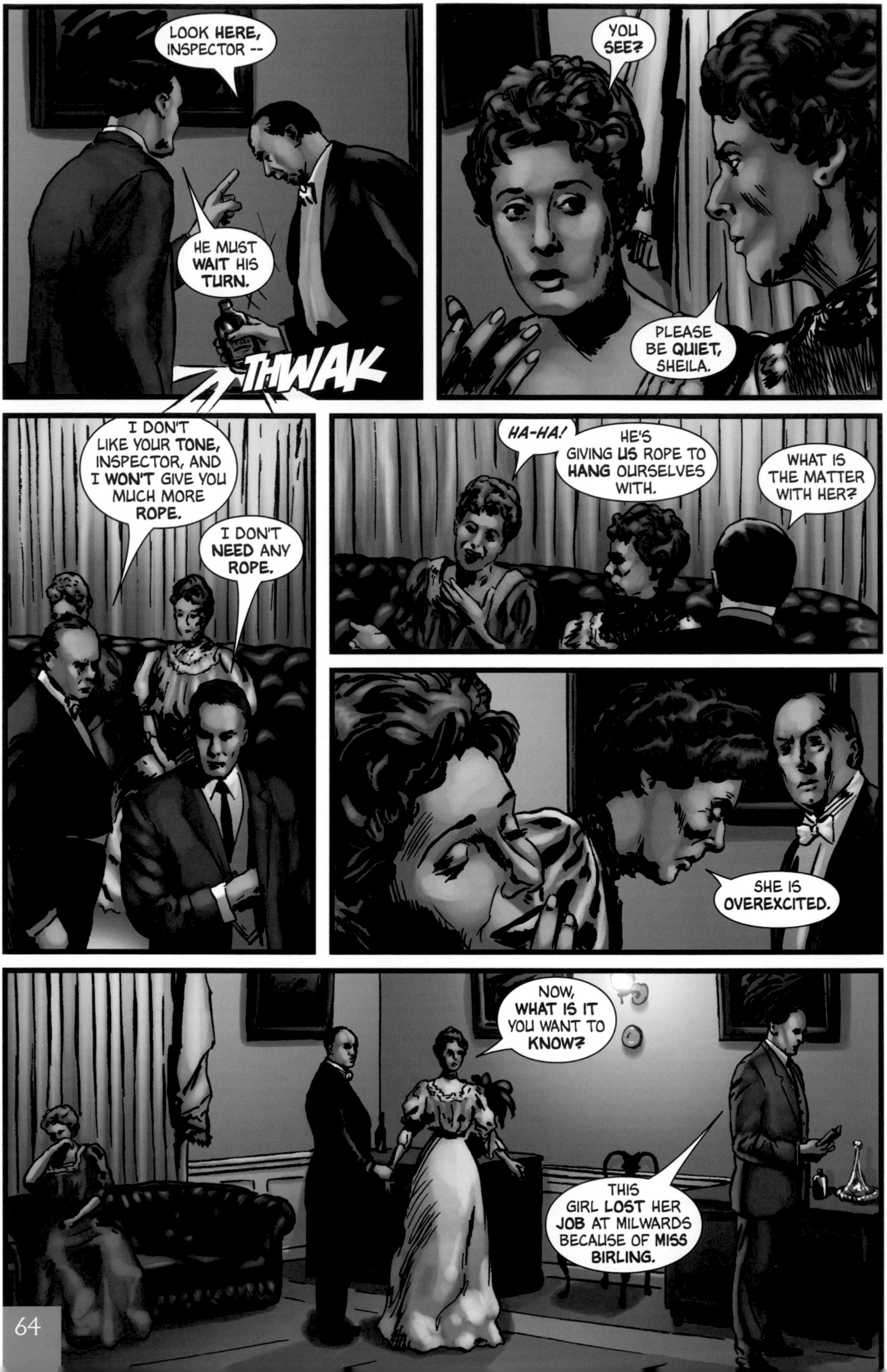

LOOK HERE, INSPECTOR --
HE MUST WAIT HIS TURN.
THWAK
YOU SEE?
PLEASE BE QUIET, SHEILA.
I DON'T LIKE YOUR TONE, INSPECTOR, AND I WON'T GIVE YOU MUCH MORE ROPE.
I DON'T NEED ANY ROPE.
HA-HA!
HE'S GIVING US ROPE TO HANG OURSELVES WITH.
WHAT IS THE MATTER WITH HER?
SHE IS OVEREXCITED.
NOW, WHAT IS IT YOU WANT TO KNOW?
THIS GIRL LOST HER JOB AT MILWARDS BECAUSE OF MISS BIRLING.

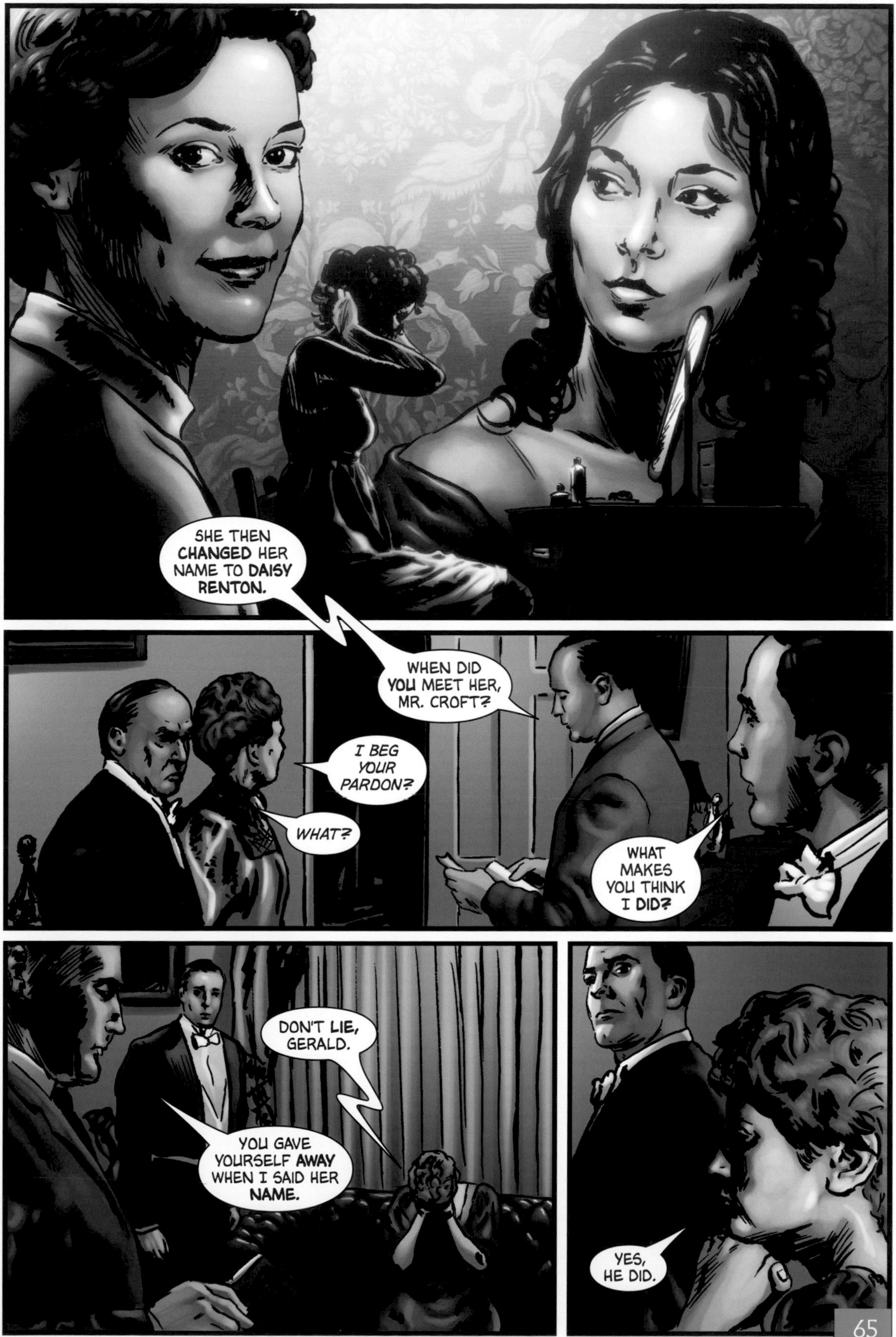
SHE THEN CHANGED HER NAME TO DAISY RENTON.
WHEN DID YOU MEET HER, MR. CROFT?
I BEG YOUR PARDON?
WHAT?
WHAT MAKES YOU THINK I DID?
DON'T LIE, GERALD.
YOU GAVE YOURSELF AWAY WHEN I SAID HER NAME.
YES, HE DID.

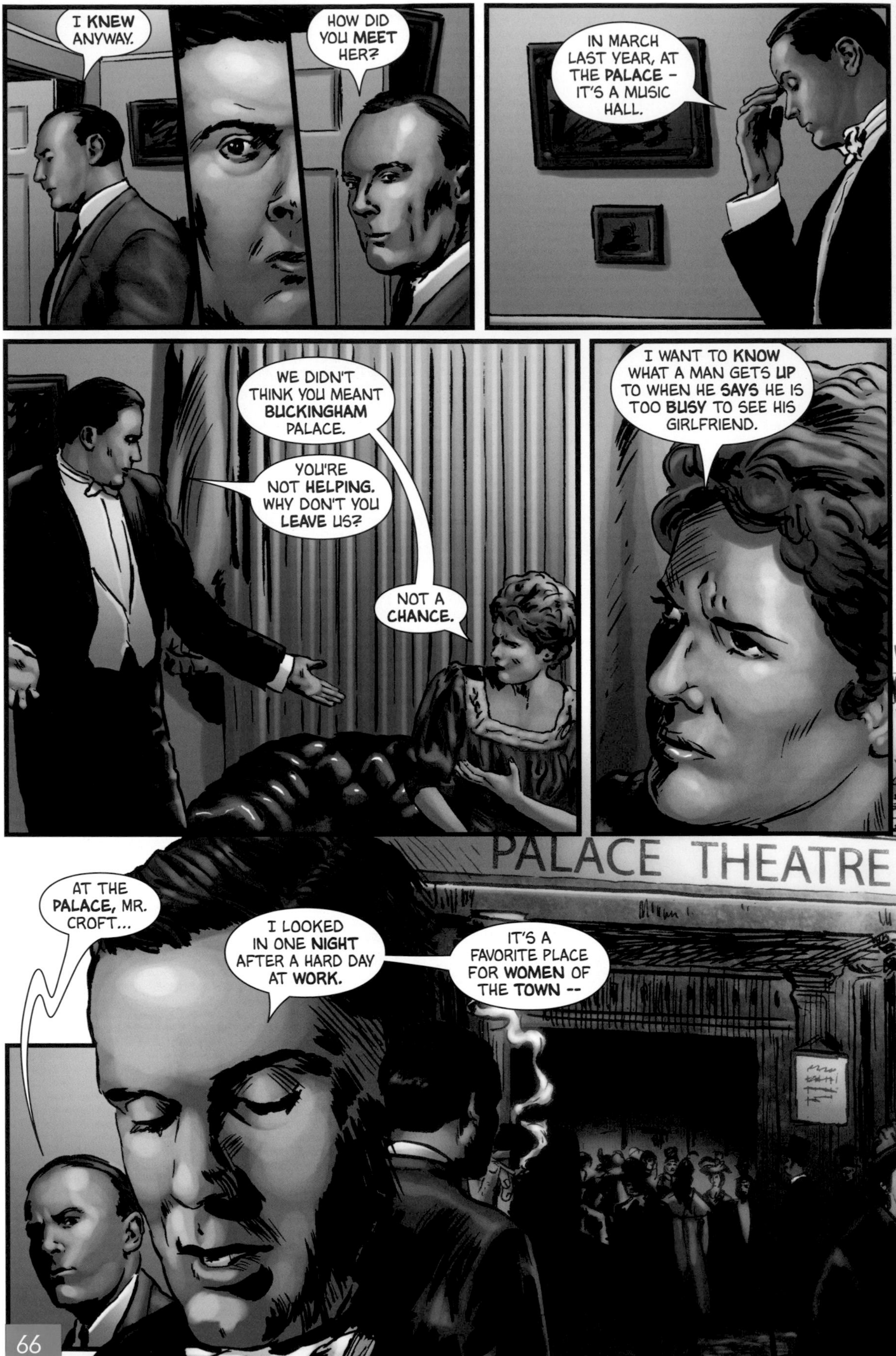
I KNEW ANYWAY.
HOW DID YOU MEET HER?
IN MARCH LAST YEAR, AT THE PALACE – IT'S A MUSIC HALL.
WE DIDN'T THINK YOU MEANT BUCKINGHAM PALACE.
YOU'RE NOT HELPING. WHY DON'T YOU LEAVE US?
NOT A CHANCE.
I WANT TO KNOW WHAT A MAN GETS UP TO WHEN HE SAYS HE IS TOO BUSY TO SEE HIS GIRLFRIEND.
PALACE THEATRE
AT THE PALACE, MR. CROFT...
I LOOKED IN ONE NIGHT AFTER A HARD DAY AT WORK.
IT'S A FAVORITE PLACE FOR WOMEN OF THE TOWN --

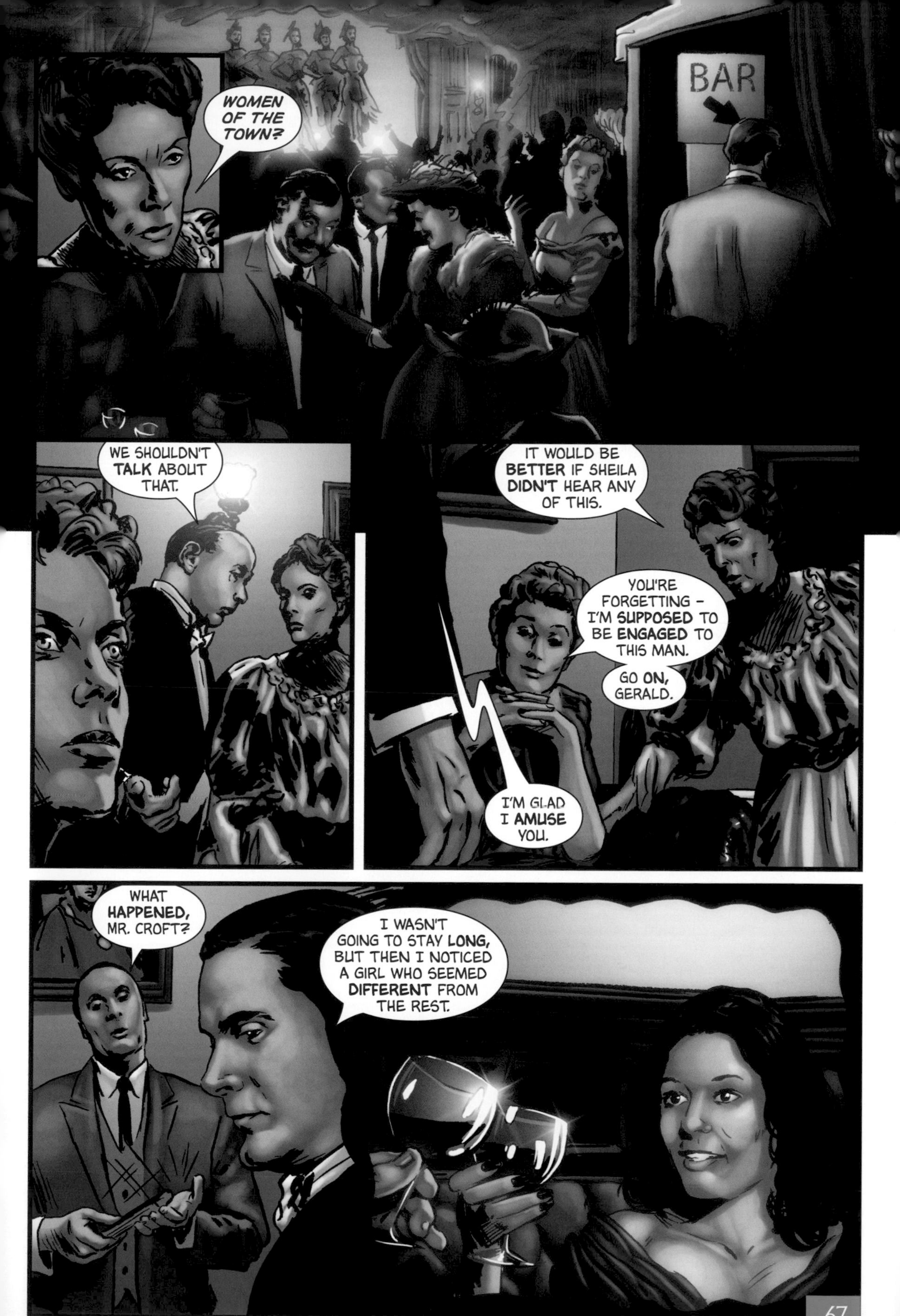

WOMEN OF THE TOWN?
WE SHOULDN'T TALK ABOUT THAT.
IT WOULD BE BETTER IF SHEILA DIDN'T HEAR ANY OF THIS.
YOU'RE FORGETTING – I'M SUPPOSED TO BE ENGAGED TO THIS MAN.
GO ON, GERALD.
I'M GLAD I AMUSE YOU.
WHAT HAPPENED, MR. CROFT?
I WASN'T GOING TO STAY LONG, BUT THEN I NOTICED A GIRL WHO SEEMED DIFFERENT FROM THE REST.
BAR

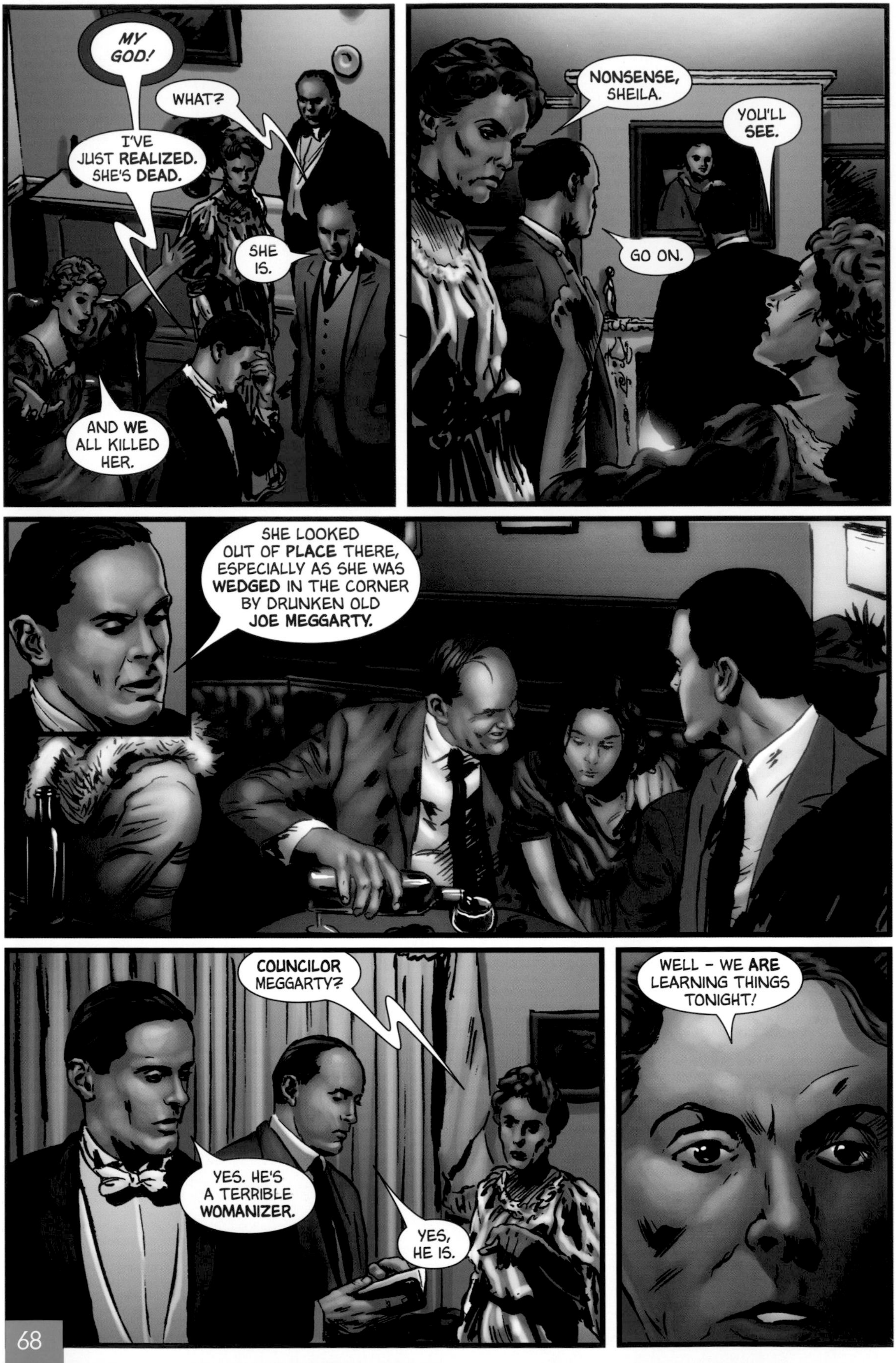
MY GOD!
WHAT?
I'VE JUST REALIZED. SHE'S DEAD.
SHE IS.
AND WE ALL KILLED HER.
NONSENSE, SHEILA.
YOU'LL SEE.
GO ON.
SHE LOOKED OUT OF PLACE THERE, ESPECIALLY AS SHE WAS WEDGED IN THE CORNER BY DRUNKEN OLD JOE MEGGARTY.
COUNCILOR MEGGARTY?
YES. HE'S A TERRIBLE WOMANIZER.
YES, HE IS.
WELL - WE ARE LEARNING THINGS TONIGHT!

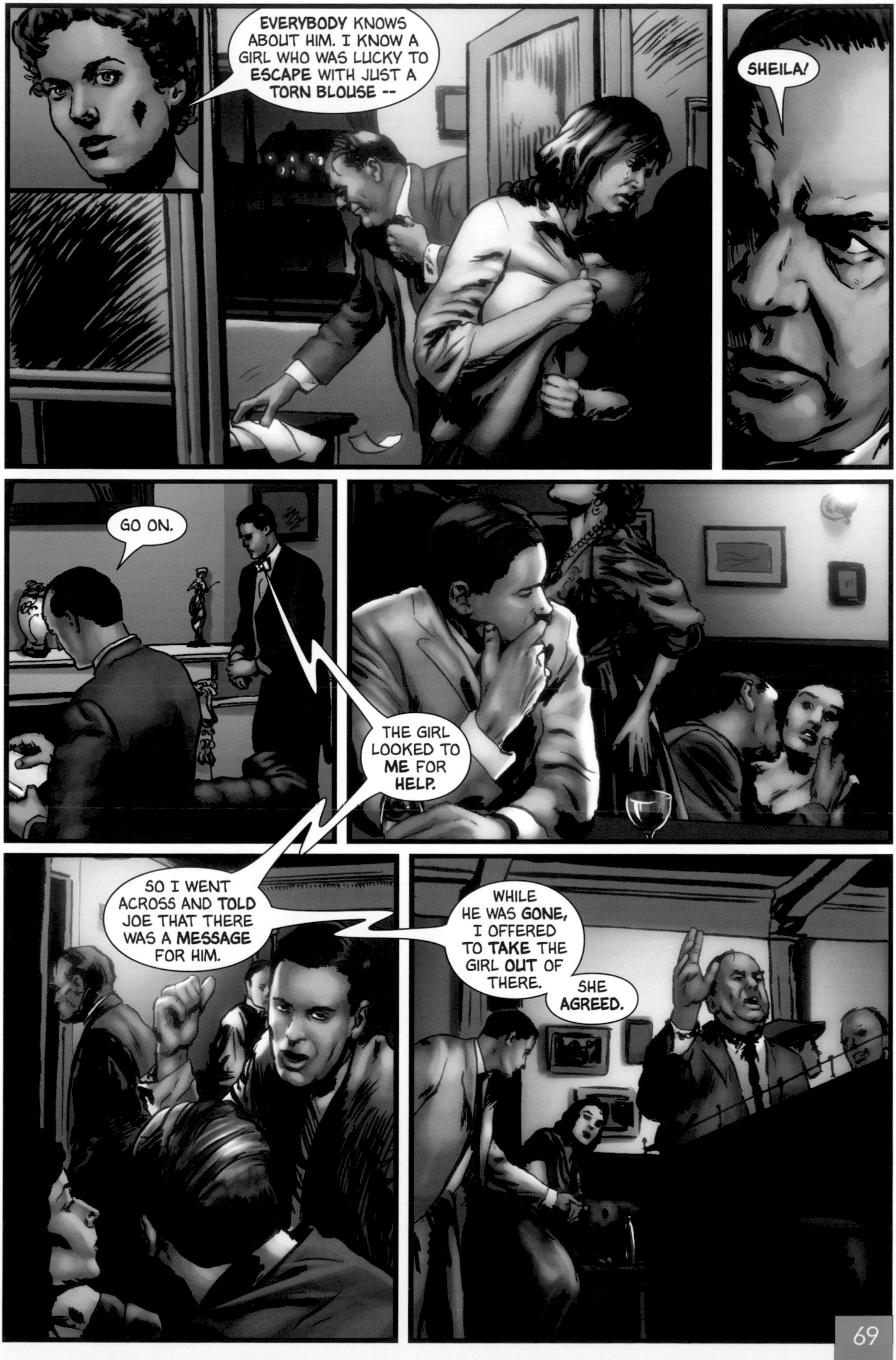
EVERYBODY KNOWS ABOUT HIM. I KNOW A GIRL WHO WAS LUCKY TO ESCAPE WITH JUST A TORN BLOUSE --
SHEILA!
GO ON.
THE GIRL LOOKED TO ME FOR HELP.
SO I WENT ACROSS AND TOLD JOE THAT THERE WAS A MESSAGE FOR HIM.
WHILE HE WAS GONE, I OFFERED TO TAKE THE GIRL OUT OF THERE.
SHE AGREED.

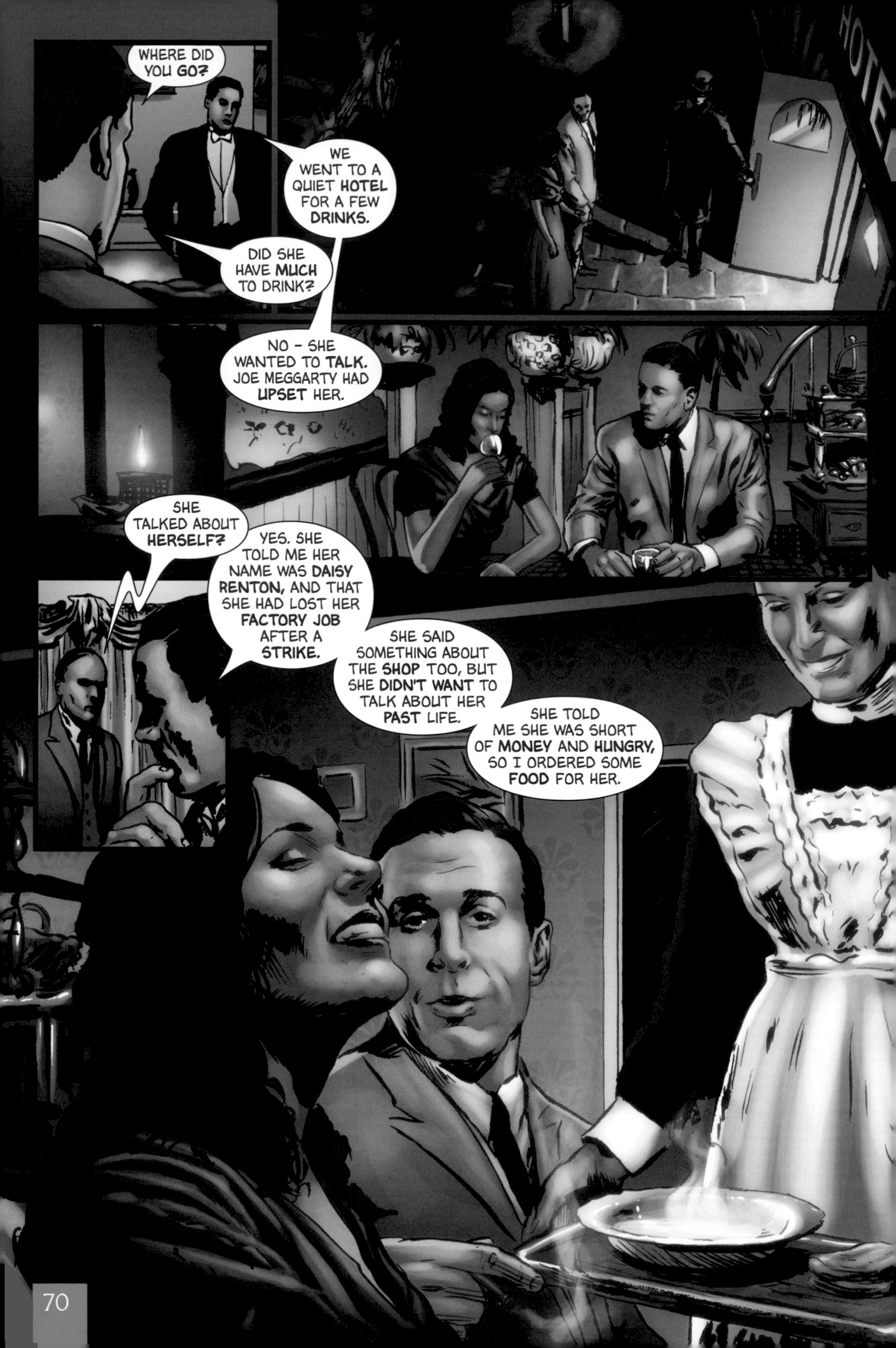

WHERE DID YOU GO?
WE WENT TO A QUIET HOTEL FOR A FEW DRINKS.
DID SHE HAVE MUCH TO DRINK?
NO - SHE WANTED TO TALK. JOE MEGGARTY HAD UPSET HER.
SHE TALKED ABOUT HERSELF?
YES. SHE TOLD ME HER NAME WAS DAISY RENTON, AND THAT SHE HAD LOST HER FACTORY JOB AFTER A STRIKE.
SHE SAID SOMETHING ABOUT THE SHOP TOO, BUT SHE DIDN'T WANT TO TALK ABOUT HER PAST LIFE.
SHE TOLD ME SHE WAS SHORT OF MONEY AND HUNGRY, SO I ORDERED SOME FOOD FOR HER.
HOTEL

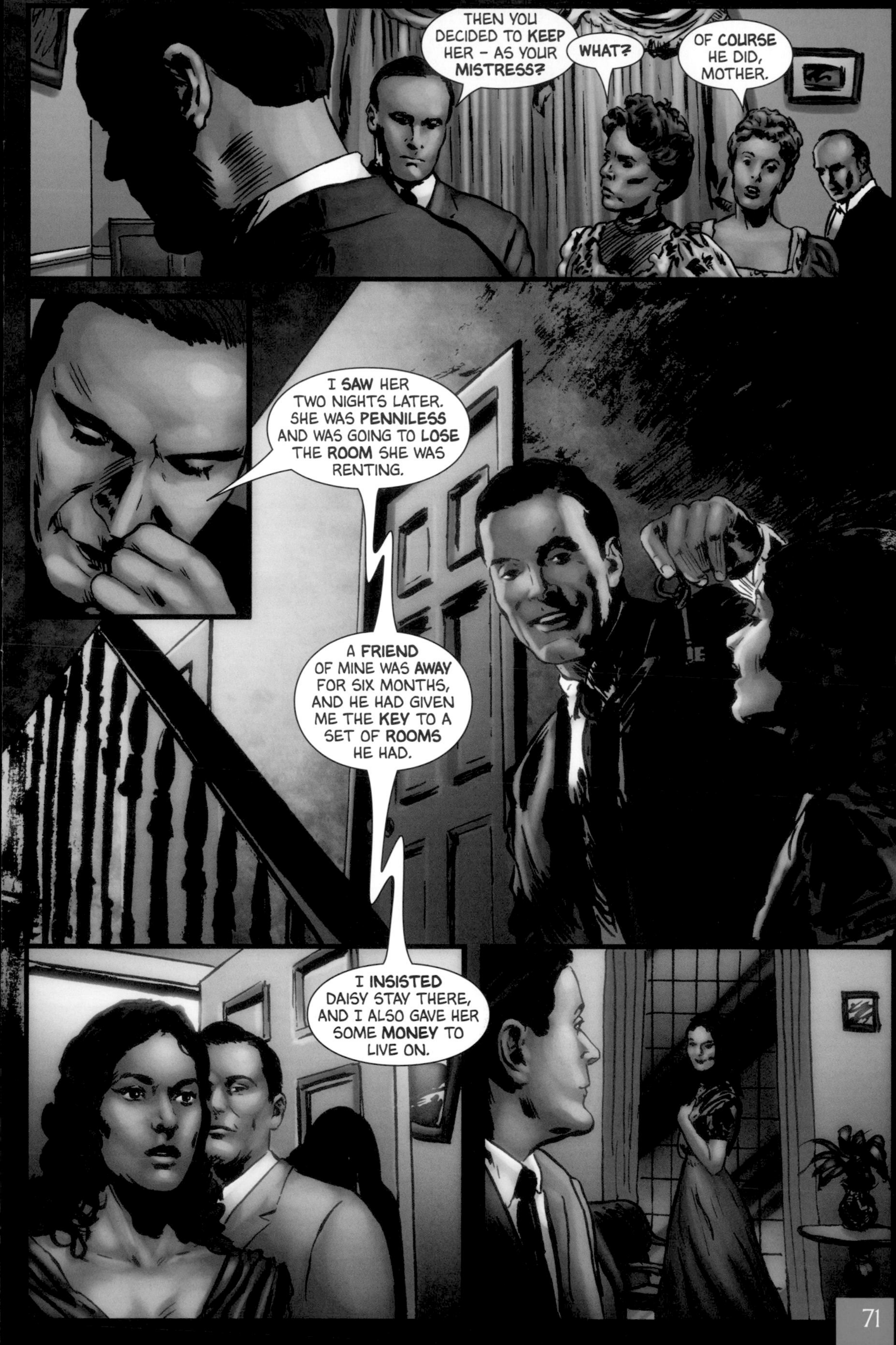
THEN YOU DECIDED TO KEEP HER – AS YOUR MISTRESS?
WHAT?
OF COURSE HE DID, MOTHER.
I SAW HER TWO NIGHTS LATER. SHE WAS PENNILESS AND WAS GOING TO LOSE THE ROOM SHE WAS RENTING.
A FRIEND OF MINE WAS AWAY FOR SIX MONTHS, AND HE HAD GIVEN ME THE KEY TO A SET OF ROOMS HE HAD.
I INSISTED DAISY STAY THERE, AND I ALSO GAVE HER SOME MONEY TO LIVE ON.

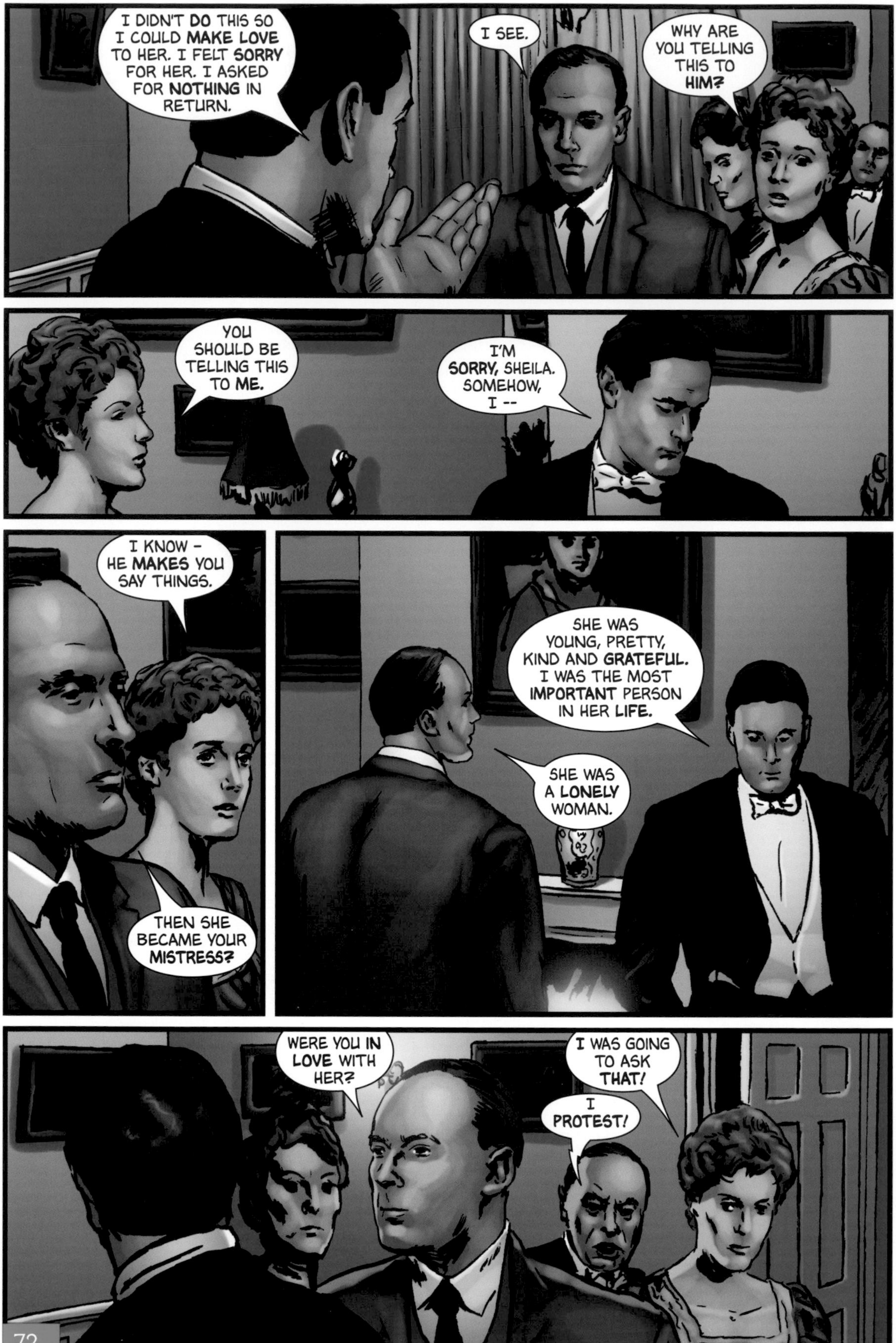

I DIDN'T DO THIS SO I COULD MAKE LOVE TO HER. I FELT SORRY FOR HER. I ASKED FOR NOTHING IN RETURN.
I SEE.
WHY ARE YOU TELLING THIS TO HIM?
YOU SHOULD BE TELLING THIS TO ME.
I'M SORRY, SHEILA. SOMEHOW, I --
I KNOW - HE MAKES YOU SAY THINGS.
THEN SHE BECAME YOUR MISTRESS?
SHE WAS YOUNG, PRETTY, KIND AND GRATEFUL. I WAS THE MOST IMPORTANT PERSON IN HER LIFE.
SHE WAS A LONELY WOMAN.
WERE YOU IN LOVE WITH HER?
I WAS GOING TO ASK THAT!
I PROTEST!

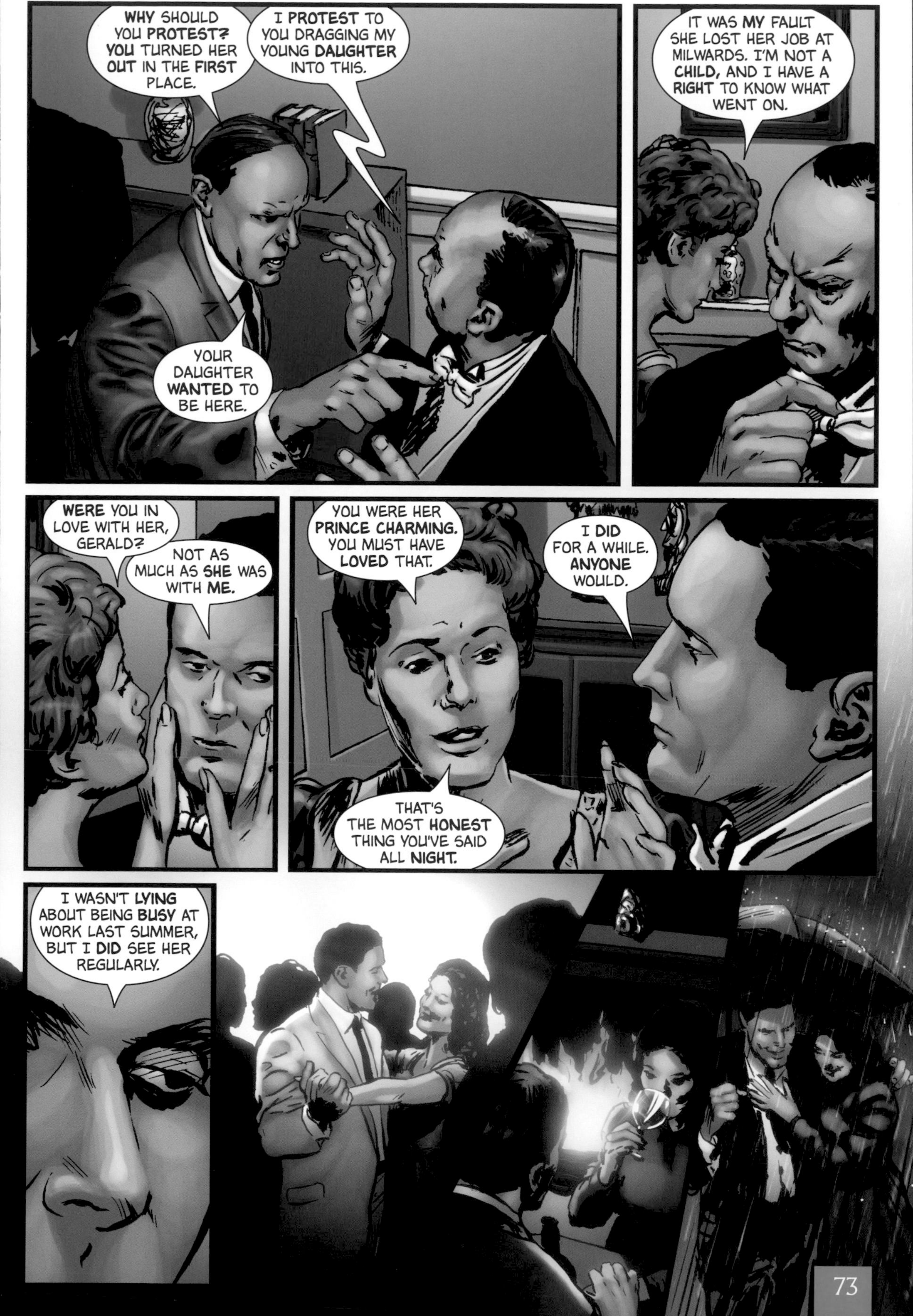
WHY SHOULD YOU PROTEST? YOU TURNED HER OUT IN THE FIRST PLACE.
I PROTEST TO YOU DRAGGING MY YOUNG DAUGHTER INTO THIS.
YOUR DAUGHTER WANTED TO BE HERE.
IT WAS MY FAULT SHE LOST HER JOB AT MILWARDS. I'M NOT A CHILD, AND I HAVE A RIGHT TO KNOW WHAT WENT ON.
WERE YOU IN LOVE WITH HER, GERALD?
NOT AS MUCH AS SHE WAS WITH ME.
YOU WERE HER PRINCE CHARMING. YOU MUST HAVE LOVED THAT.
I DID FOR A WHILE. ANYONE WOULD.
THAT'S THE MOST HONEST THING YOU'VE SAID ALL NIGHT.
I WASN'T LYING ABOUT BEING BUSY AT WORK LAST SUMMER, BUT I DID SEE HER REGULARLY.

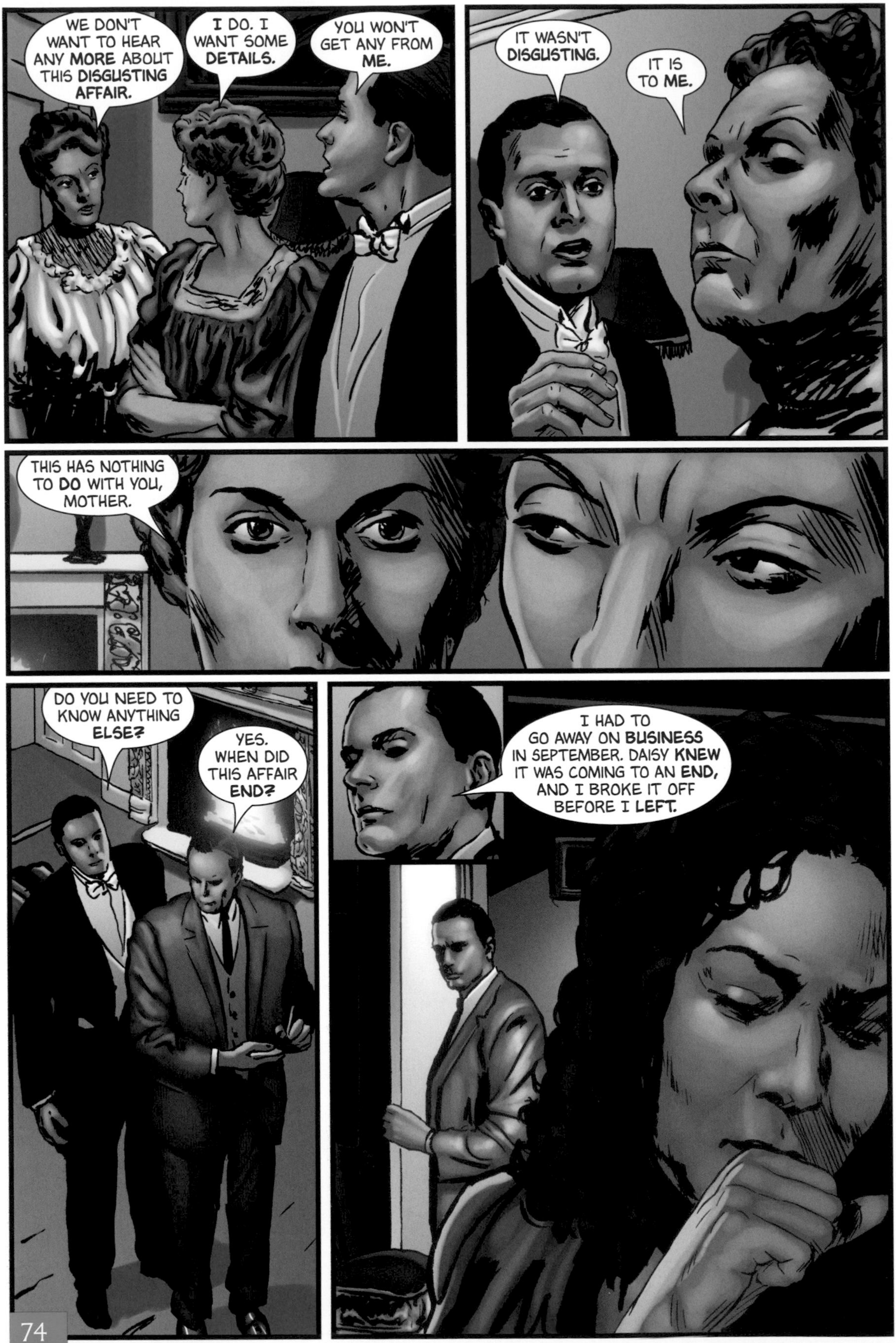
WE DON'T WANT TO HEAR ANY MORE ABOUT THIS DISGUSTING AFFAIR.
I DO. I WANT SOME DETAILS.
YOU WON'T GET ANY FROM ME.
IT WASN'T DISGUSTING.
IT IS TO ME.
THIS HAS NOTHING TO DO WITH YOU, MOTHER.
DO YOU NEED TO KNOW ANYTHING ELSE?
YES. WHEN DID THIS AFFAIR END?
I HAD TO GO AWAY ON BUSINESS IN SEPTEMBER. DAISY KNEW IT WAS COMING TO AN END, AND I BROKE IT OFF BEFORE I LEFT.

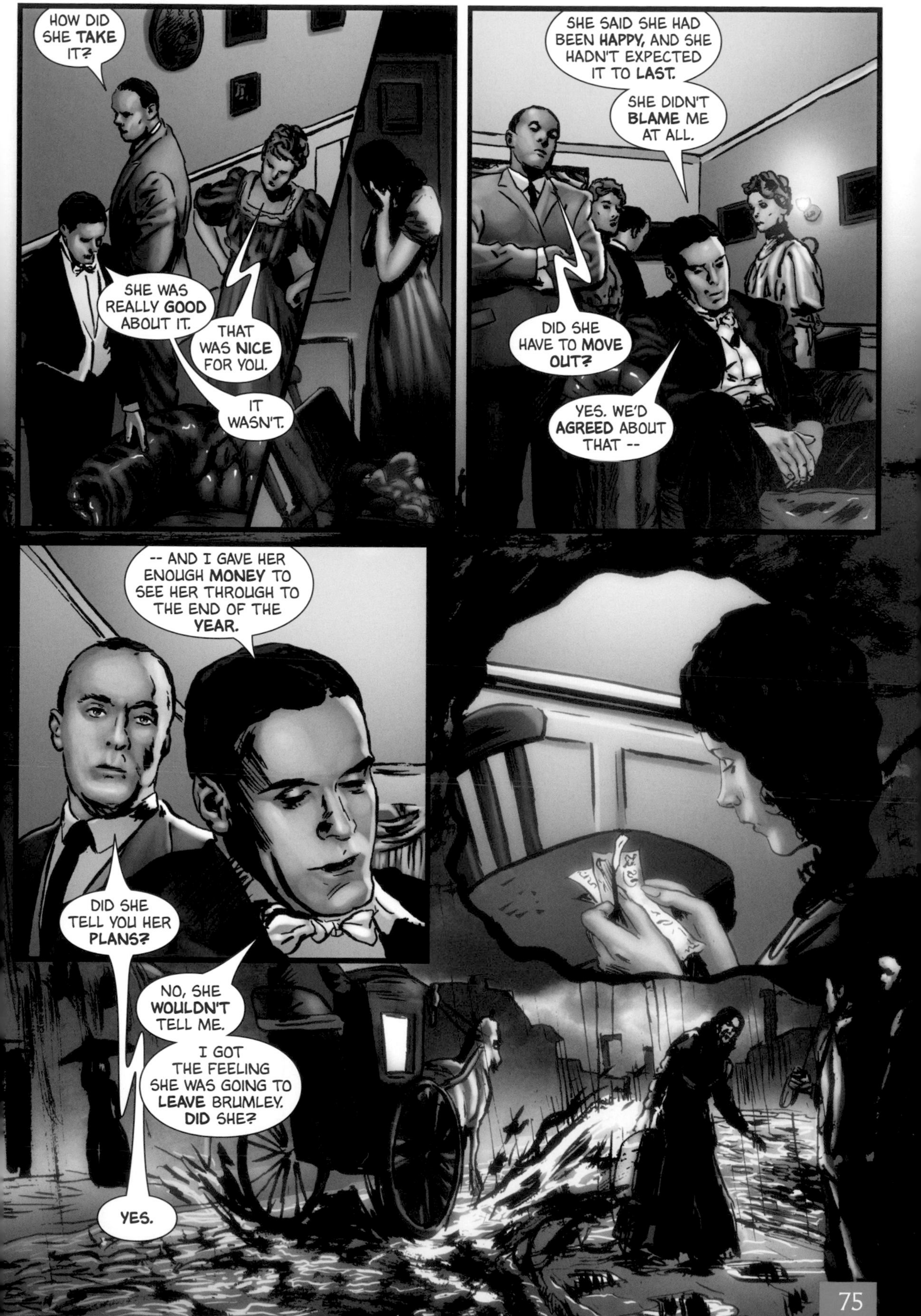
HOW DID SHE TAKE IT?
SHE WAS REALLY GOOD ABOUT IT.
THAT WAS NICE FOR YOU.
IT WASN'T.
SHE SAID SHE HAD BEEN HAPPY, AND SHE HADN'T EXPECTED IT TO LAST.
SHE DIDN'T BLAME ME AT ALL.
DID SHE HAVE TO MOVE OUT?
YES. WE'D AGREED ABOUT THAT --
-- AND I GAVE HER ENOUGH MONEY TO SEE HER THROUGH TO THE END OF THE YEAR.
DID SHE TELL YOU HER PLANS?
NO, SHE WOULDN'T TELL ME.
I GOT THE FEELING SHE WAS GOING TO LEAVE BRUMLEY. DID SHE?
YES.

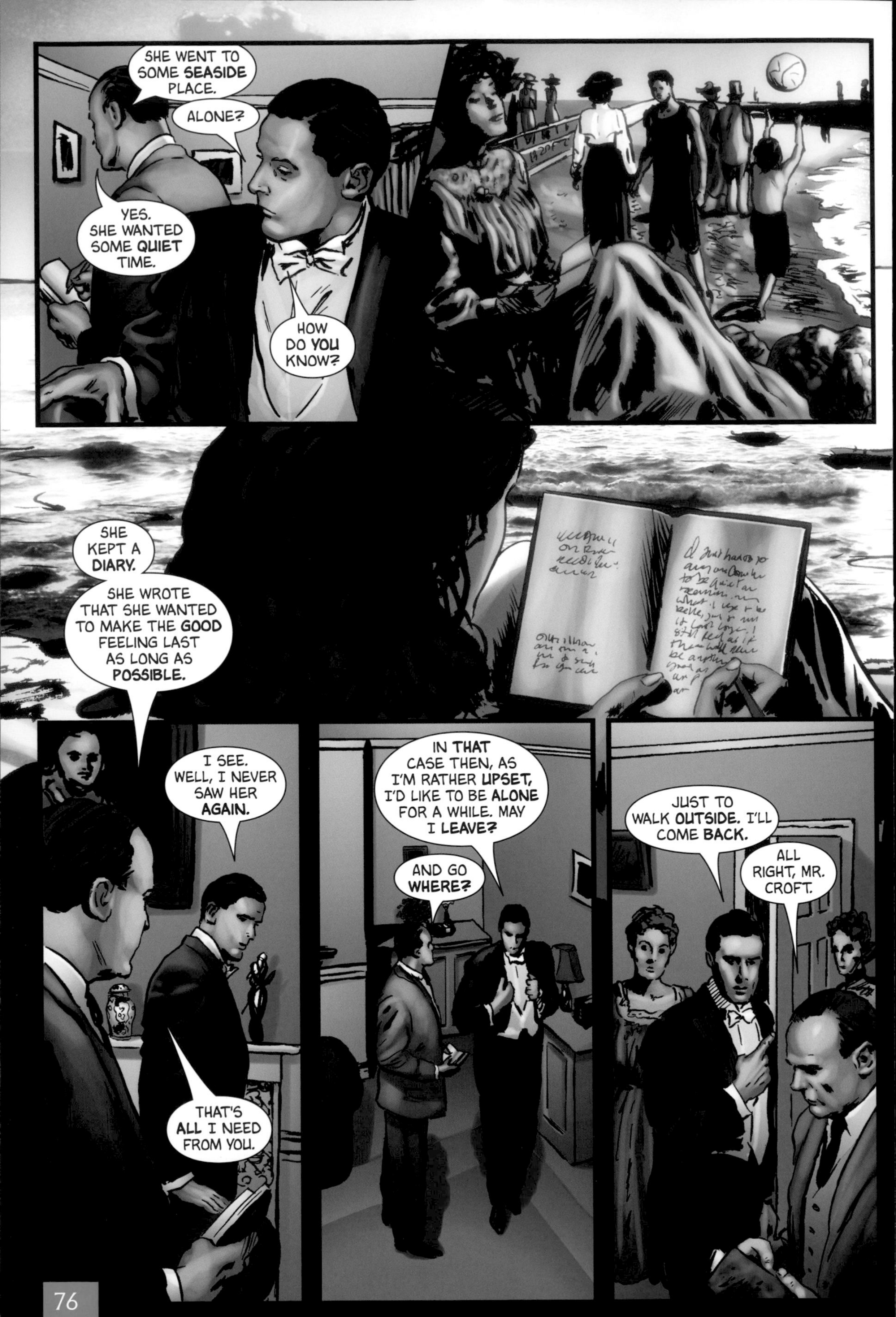

SHE WENT TO SOME SEASIDE PLACE.
ALONE?
YES. SHE WANTED SOME QUIET TIME.
HOW DO YOU KNOW?
SHE KEPT A DIARY.
SHE WROTE THAT SHE WANTED TO MAKE THE GOOD FEELING LAST AS LONG AS POSSIBLE.
I SEE. WELL, I NEVER SAW HER AGAIN.
THAT'S ALL I NEED FROM YOU.
IN THAT CASE THEN, AS I'M RATHER UPSET, I'D LIKE TO BE ALONE FOR A WHILE. MAY I LEAVE?
AND GO WHERE?
JUST TO WALK OUTSIDE. I'LL COME BACK.
ALL RIGHT, MR. CROFT.

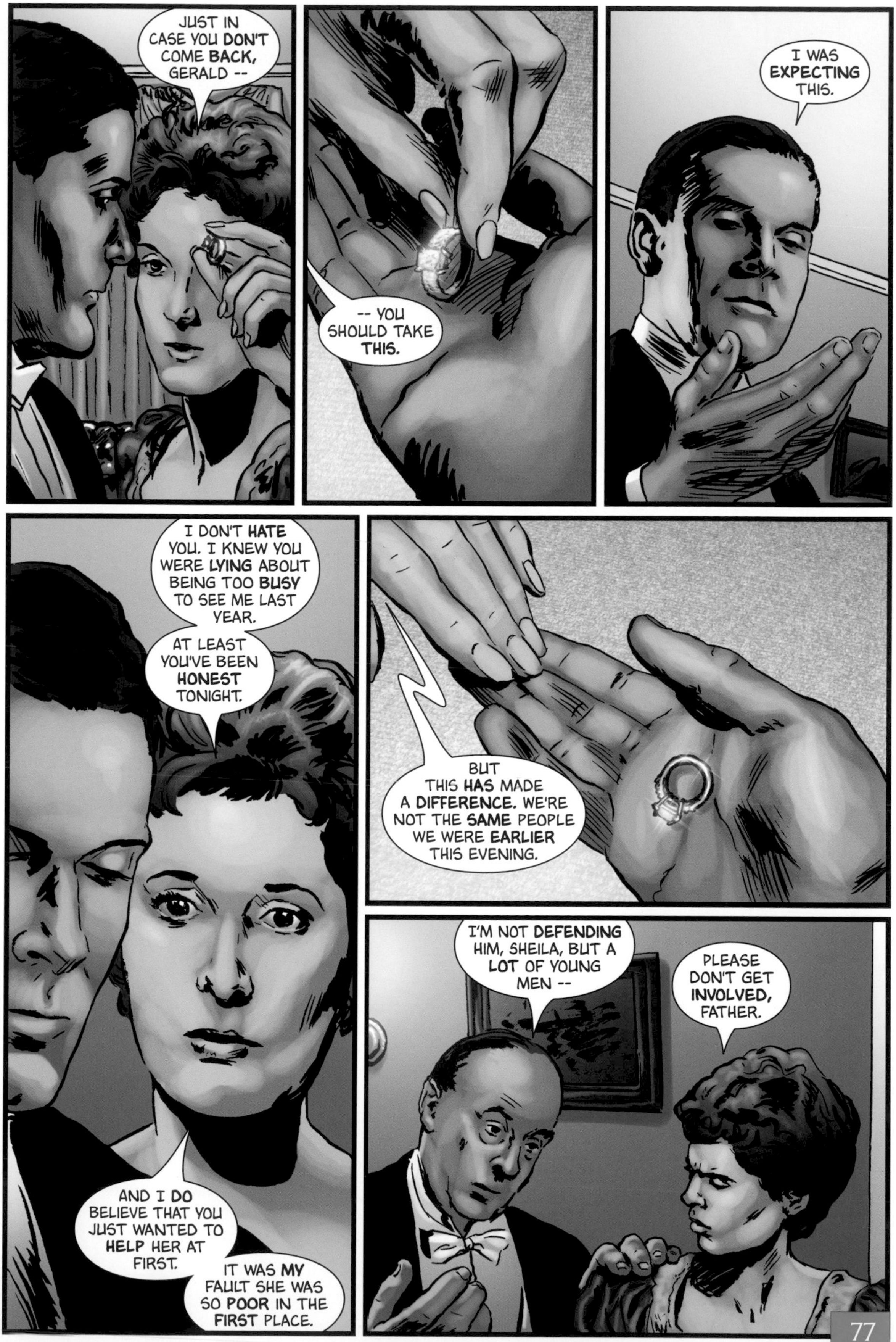

JUST IN CASE YOU DON'T COME BACK, GERALD --
-- YOU SHOULD TAKE THIS.
I WAS EXPECTING THIS.
I DON'T HATE YOU. I KNEW YOU WERE LYING ABOUT BEING TOO BUSY TO SEE ME LAST YEAR.
AT LEAST YOU'VE BEEN HONEST TONIGHT.
AND I DO BELIEVE THAT YOU JUST WANTED TO HELP HER AT FIRST.
IT WAS MY FAULT SHE WAS SO POOR IN THE FIRST PLACE.
BUT THIS HAS MADE A DIFFERENCE. WE'RE NOT THE SAME PEOPLE WE WERE EARLIER THIS EVENING.
I'M NOT DEFENDING HIM, SHEILA, BUT A LOT OF YOUNG MEN --
PLEASE DON'T GET INVOLVED, FATHER.

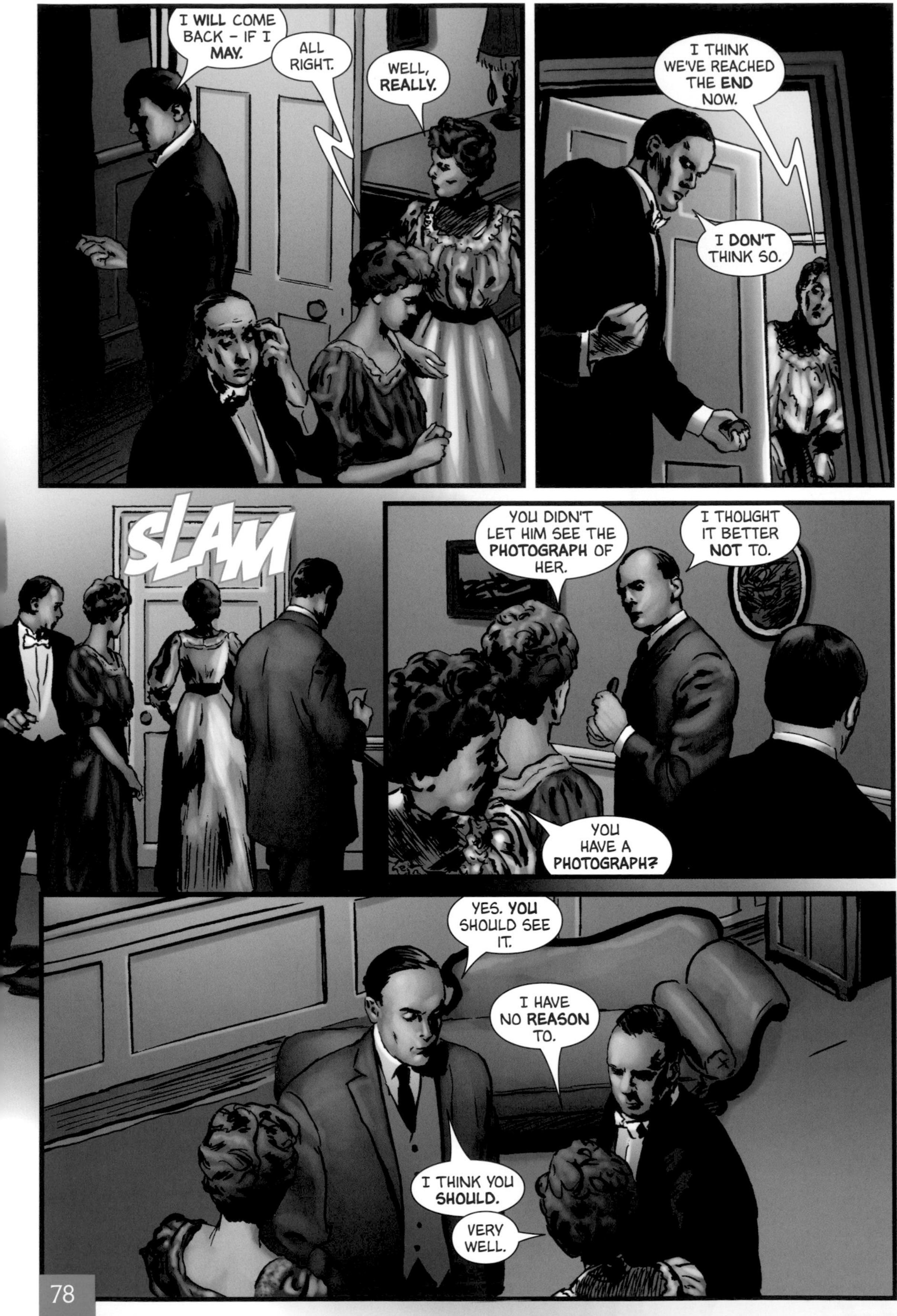

I WILL COME BACK – IF I MAY.
ALL RIGHT.
WELL, REALLY.
I THINK WE'VE REACHED THE END NOW.
I DON'T THINK SO.
SLAM
YOU DIDN'T LET HIM SEE THE PHOTOGRAPH OF HER.
I THOUGHT IT BETTER NOT TO.
YOU HAVE A PHOTOGRAPH?
YES. YOU SHOULD SEE IT.
I HAVE NO REASON TO.
I THINK YOU SHOULD.
VERY WELL.

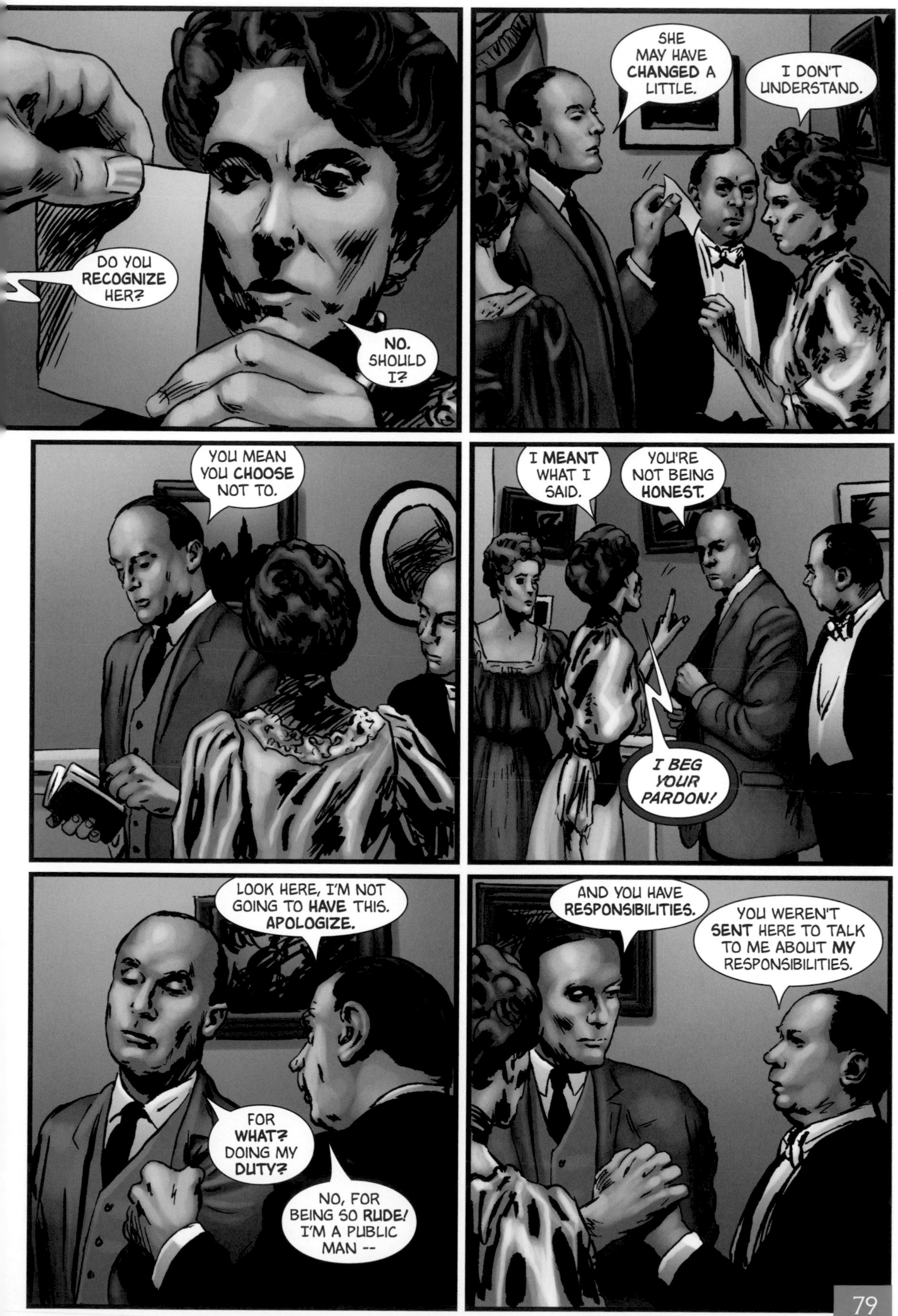
DO YOU RECOGNIZE HER?
NO. SHOULD I?
SHE MAY HAVE CHANGED A LITTLE.
I DON'T UNDERSTAND.
YOU MEAN YOU CHOOSE NOT TO.
I MEANT WHAT I SAID.
YOU'RE NOT BEING HONEST.
I BEG YOUR PARDON!
LOOK HERE, I'M NOT GOING TO HAVE THIS. APOLOGIZE.
FOR WHAT? DOING MY DUTY?
NO, FOR BEING SO RUDE! I'M A PUBLIC MAN --
AND YOU HAVE RESPONSIBILITIES.
YOU WEREN'T SENT HERE TO TALK TO ME ABOUT MY RESPONSIBILITIES.

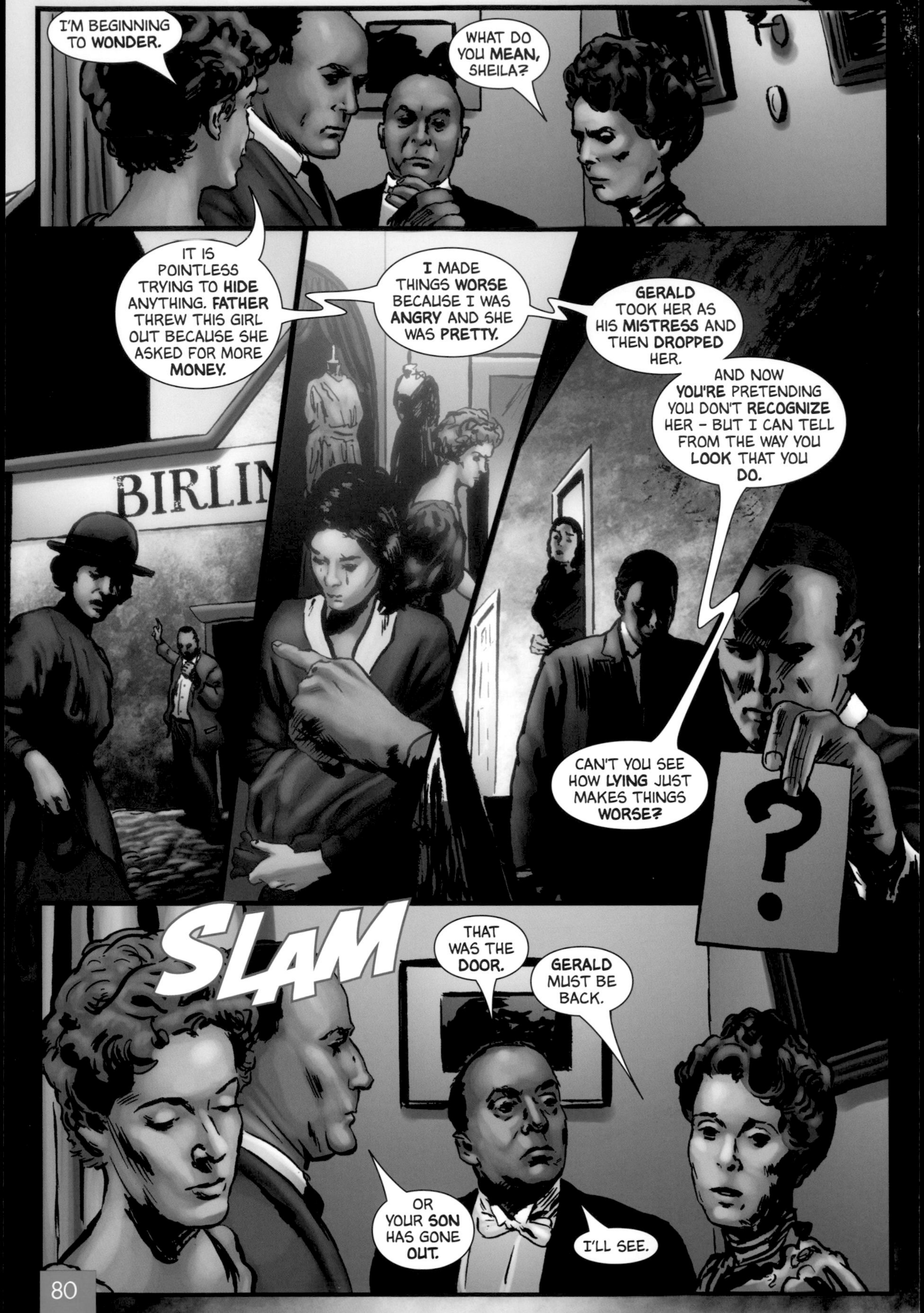
I'M BEGINNING TO WONDER.
WHAT DO YOU MEAN, SHEILA?
IT IS POINTLESS TRYING TO HIDE ANYTHING. FATHER THREW THIS GIRL OUT BECAUSE SHE ASKED FOR MORE MONEY.
BIRLIN
I MADE THINGS WORSE BECAUSE I WAS ANGRY AND SHE WAS PRETTY.
GERALD TOOK HER AS HIS MISTRESS AND THEN DROPPED HER.
AND NOW YOU'RE PRETENDING YOU DON'T RECOGNIZE HER – BUT I CAN TELL FROM THE WAY YOU LOOK THAT YOU DO.
CAN'T YOU SEE HOW LYING JUST MAKES THINGS WORSE?
?
SLAM
THAT WAS THE DOOR.
GERALD MUST BE BACK.
OR YOUR SON HAS GONE OUT.
I'LL SEE.

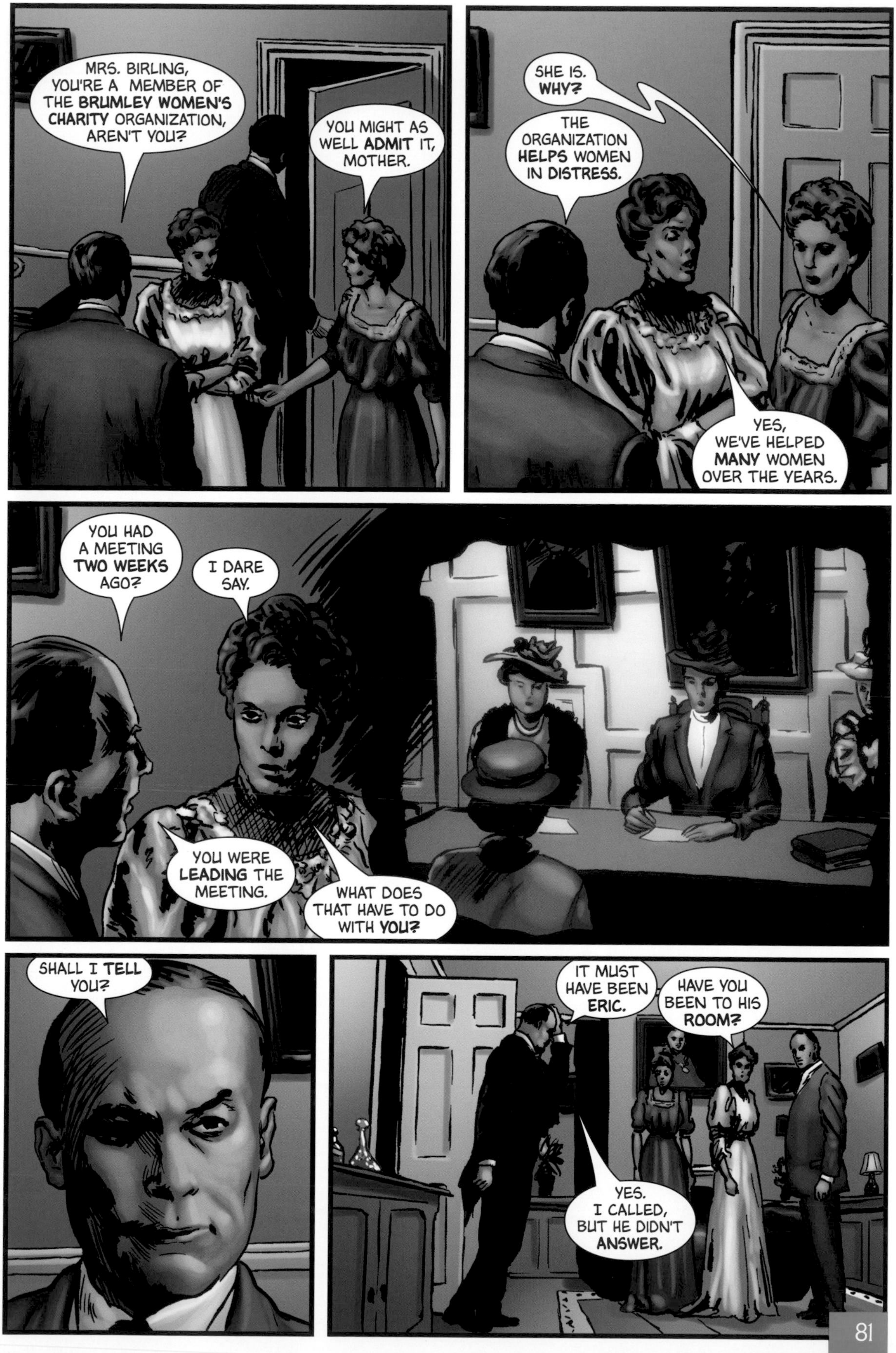

MRS. BIRLING, YOU'RE A MEMBER OF THE BRUMLEY WOMEN'S CHARITY ORGANIZATION, AREN'T YOU?
YOU MIGHT AS WELL ADMIT IT, MOTHER.
SHE IS. WHY?
THE ORGANIZATION HELPS WOMEN IN DISTRESS.
YES, WE'VE HELPED MANY WOMEN OVER THE YEARS.
YOU HAD A MEETING TWO WEEKS AGO?
I DARE SAY.
YOU WERE LEADING THE MEETING.
WHAT DOES THAT HAVE TO DO WITH YOU?
SHALL I TELL YOU?
IT MUST HAVE BEEN ERIC.
HAVE YOU BEEN TO HIS ROOM?
YES. I CALLED, BUT HE DIDN'T ANSWER.

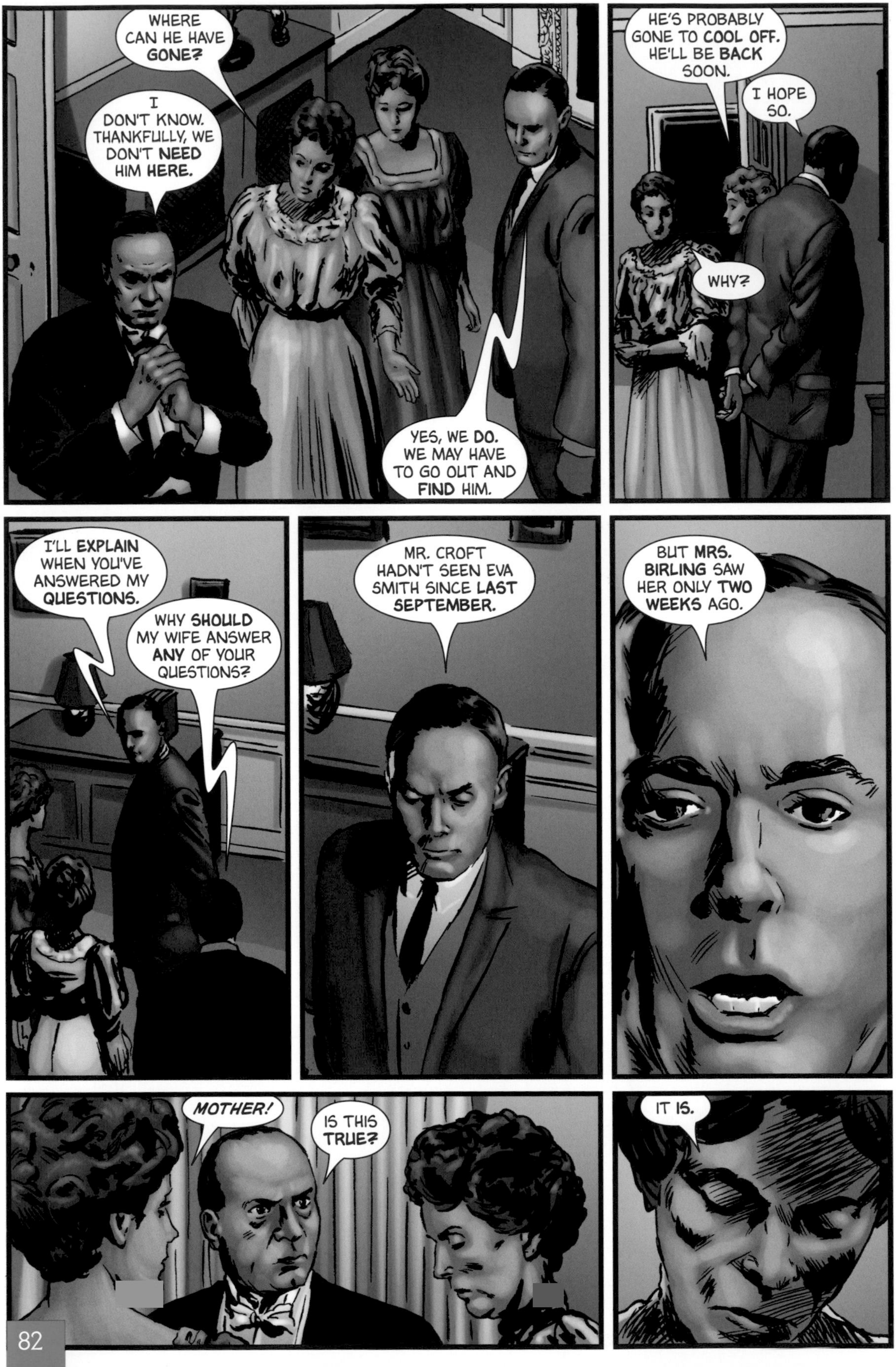

WHERE CAN HE HAVE GONE?
I DON'T KNOW. THANKFULLY, WE DON'T NEED HIM HERE.
YES, WE DO. WE MAY HAVE TO GO OUT AND FIND HIM.
HE'S PROBABLY GONE TO COOL OFF. HE'LL BE BACK SOON.
I HOPE SO.
WHY?
I'LL EXPLAIN WHEN YOU'VE ANSWERED MY QUESTIONS.
WHY SHOULD MY WIFE ANSWER ANY OF YOUR QUESTIONS?
MR. CROFT HADN'T SEEN EVA SMITH SINCE LAST SEPTEMBER.
BUT MRS. BIRLING SAW HER ONLY TWO WEEKS AGO.
MOTHER!
IS THIS TRUE?
IT IS.

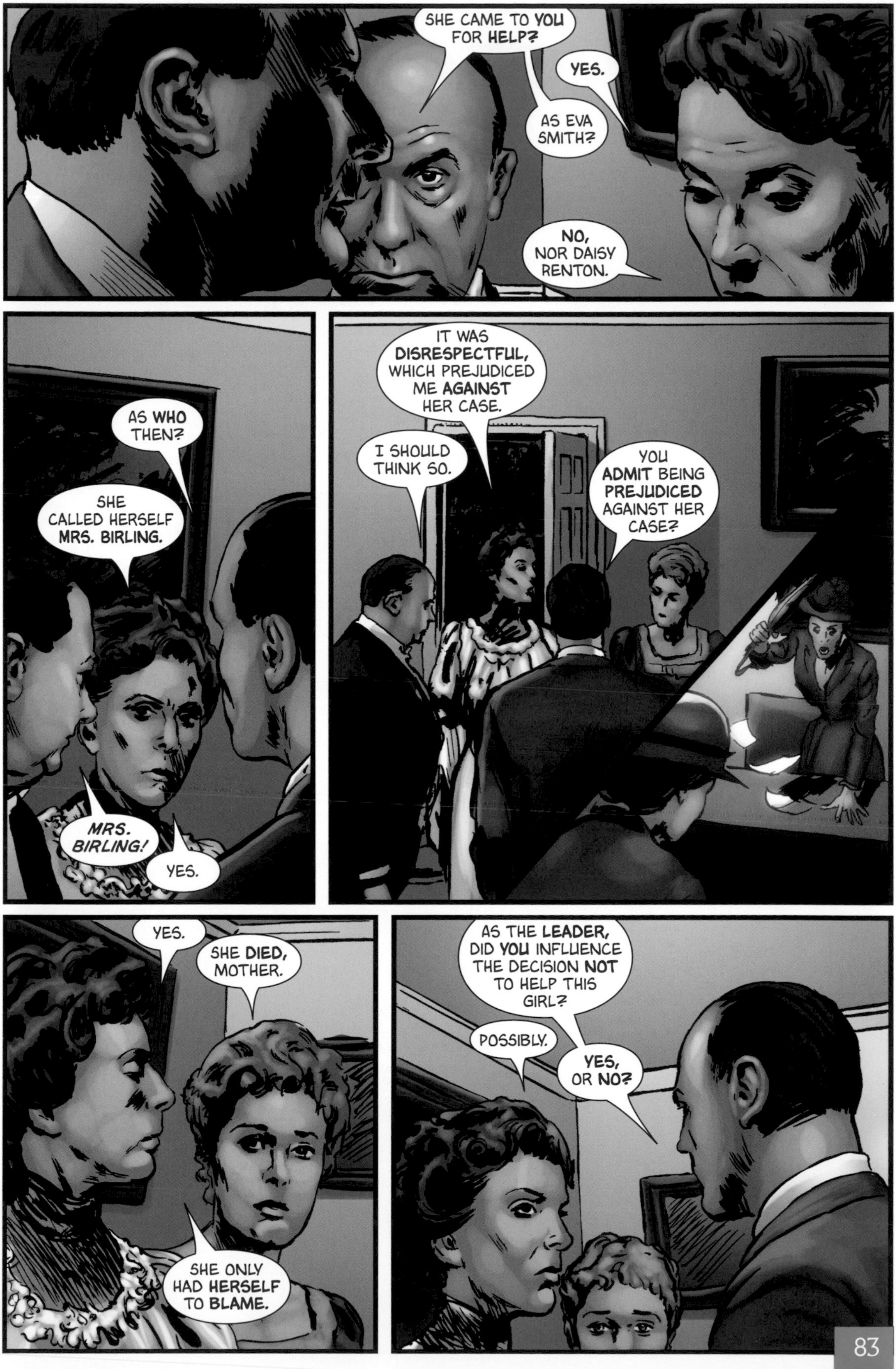
SHE CAME TO YOU FOR HELP?
YES.
AS EVA SMITH?
NO, NOR DAISY RENTON.
AS WHO THEN?
SHE CALLED HERSELF MRS. BIRLING.
MRS. BIRLING!
YES.
IT WAS DISRESPECTFUL, WHICH PREJUDICED ME AGAINST HER CASE.
I SHOULD THINK SO.
YOU ADMIT BEING PREJUDICED AGAINST HER CASE?
YES.
SHE DIED, MOTHER.
SHE ONLY HAD HERSELF TO BLAME.
AS THE LEADER, DID YOU INFLUENCE THE DECISION NOT TO HELP THIS GIRL?
POSSIBLY.
YES, OR NO?

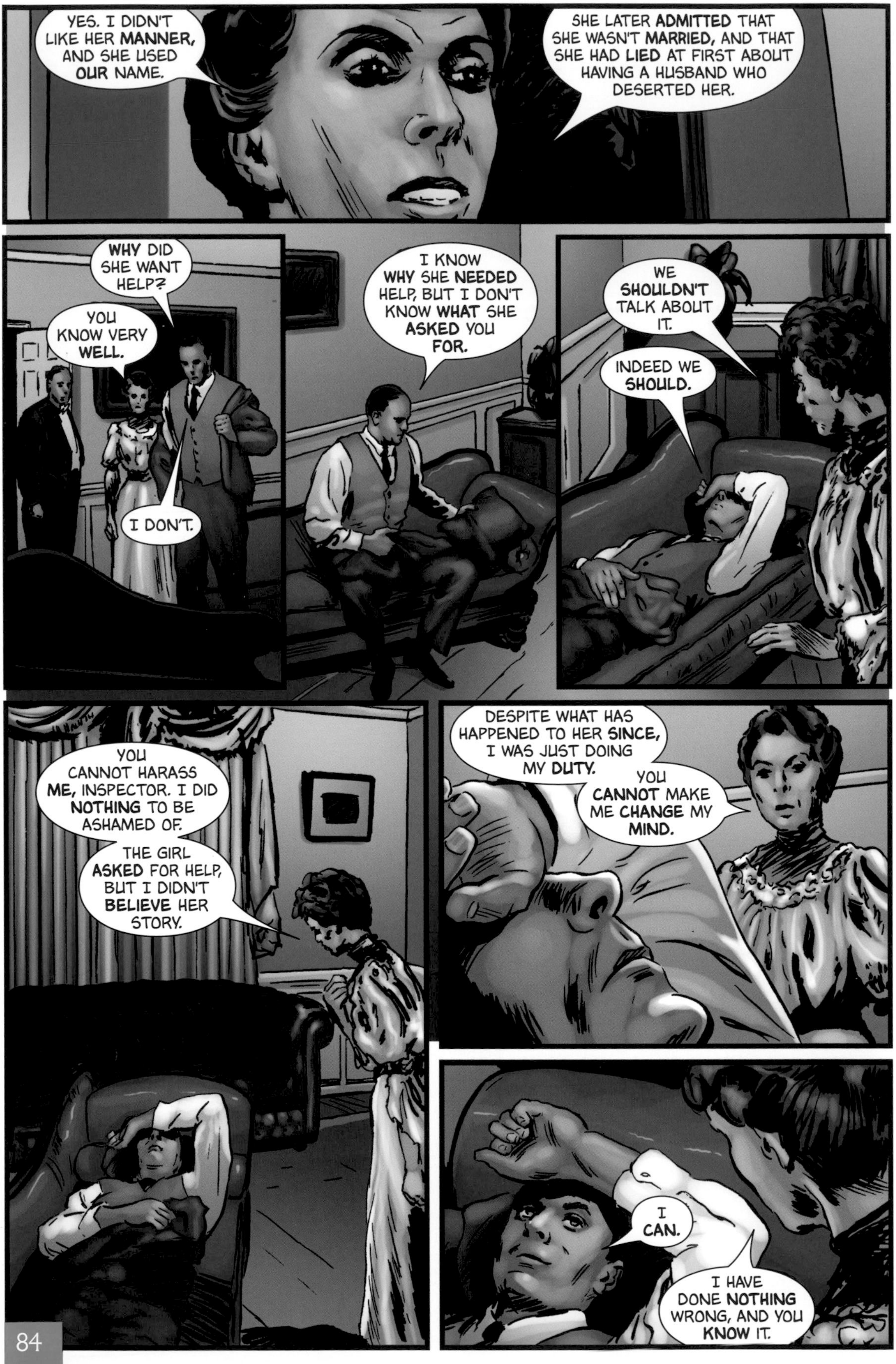
YES. I DIDN'T LIKE HER MANNER, AND SHE USED OUR NAME.
SHE LATER ADMITTED THAT SHE WASN'T MARRIED, AND THAT SHE HAD LIED AT FIRST ABOUT HAVING A HUSBAND WHO DESERTED HER.
WHY DID SHE WANT HELP?
YOU KNOW VERY WELL.
I DON'T.
I KNOW WHY SHE NEEDED HELP, BUT I DON'T KNOW WHAT SHE ASKED YOU FOR.
WE SHOULDN'T TALK ABOUT IT.
INDEED WE SHOULD.
YOU CANNOT HARASS ME, INSPECTOR. I DID NOTHING TO BE ASHAMED OF.
THE GIRL ASKED FOR HELP, BUT I DIDN'T BELIEVE HER STORY.
DESPITE WHAT HAS HAPPENED TO HER SINCE, I WAS JUST DOING MY DUTY.
YOU CANNOT MAKE ME CHANGE MY MIND.
I CAN.
I HAVE DONE NOTHING WRONG, AND YOU KNOW IT.

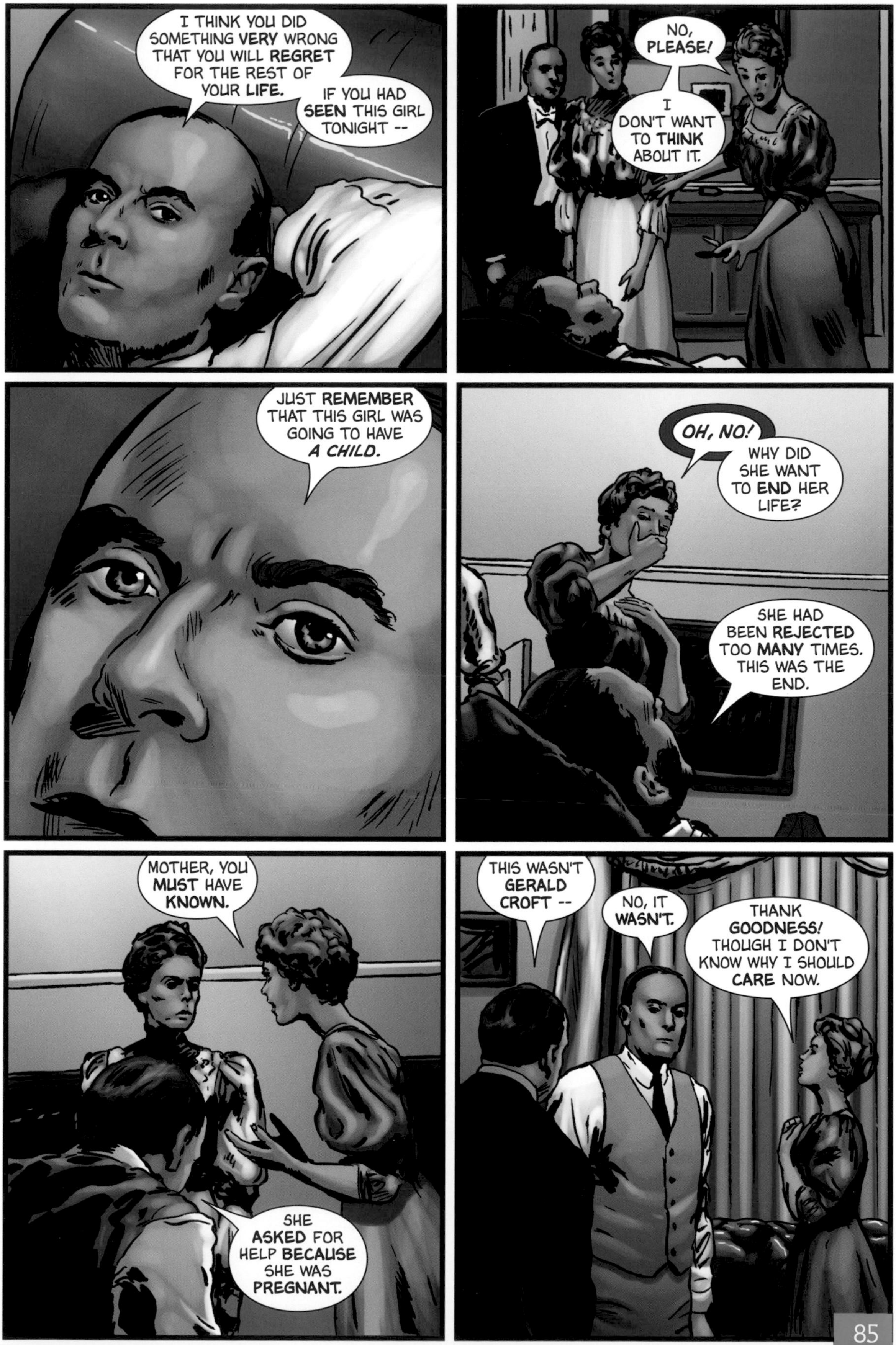
I THINK YOU DID SOMETHING VERY WRONG THAT YOU WILL REGRET FOR THE REST OF YOUR LIFE.
IF YOU HAD SEEN THIS GIRL TONIGHT --
NO, PLEASE!
I DON'T WANT TO THINK ABOUT IT.
JUST REMEMBER THAT THIS GIRL WAS GOING TO HAVE A CHILD.
OH, NO!
WHY DID SHE WANT TO END HER LIFE?
SHE HAD BEEN REJECTED TOO MANY TIMES. THIS WAS THE END.
MOTHER, YOU MUST HAVE KNOWN.
SHE ASKED FOR HELP BECAUSE SHE WAS PREGNANT.
THIS WASN'T GERALD CROFT --
NO, IT WASN'T.
THANK GOODNESS! THOUGH I DON'T KNOW WHY I SHOULD CARE NOW.

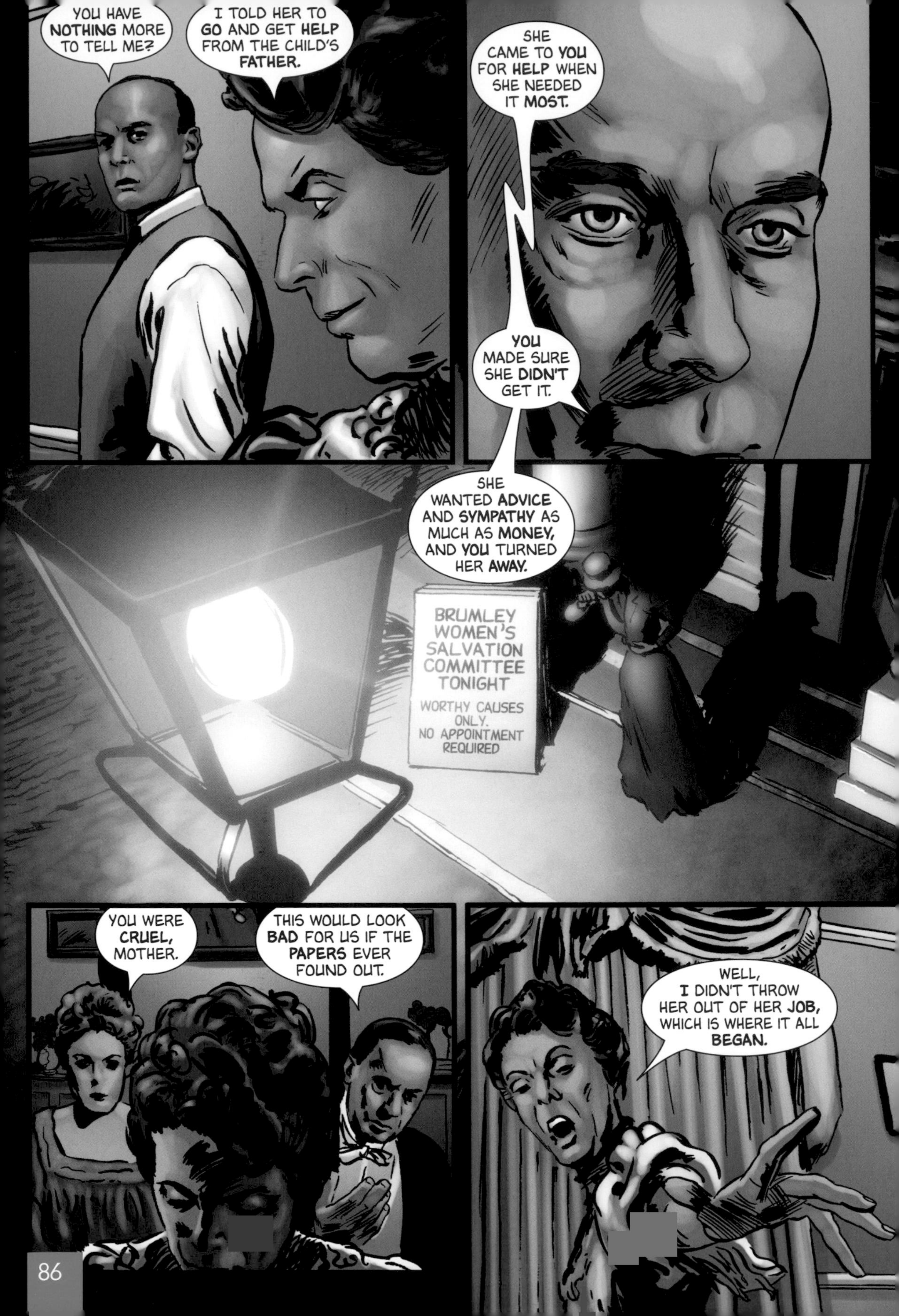
YOU HAVE NOTHING MORE TO TELL ME?
I TOLD HER TO GO AND GET HELP FROM THE CHILD'S FATHER.
SHE CAME TO YOU FOR HELP WHEN SHE NEEDED IT MOST.
YOU MADE SURE SHE DIDN'T GET IT.
SHE WANTED ADVICE AND SYMPATHY AS MUCH AS MONEY, AND YOU TURNED HER AWAY.
BRUMLEY WOMEN'S SALVATION COMMITTEE TONIGHT
WORTHY CAUSES ONLY. NO APPOINTMENT REQUIRED
YOU WERE CRUEL, MOTHER.
THIS WOULD LOOK BAD FOR US IF THE PAPERS EVER FOUND OUT.
WELL, I DIDN'T THROW HER OUT OF HER JOB, WHICH IS WHERE IT ALL BEGAN.

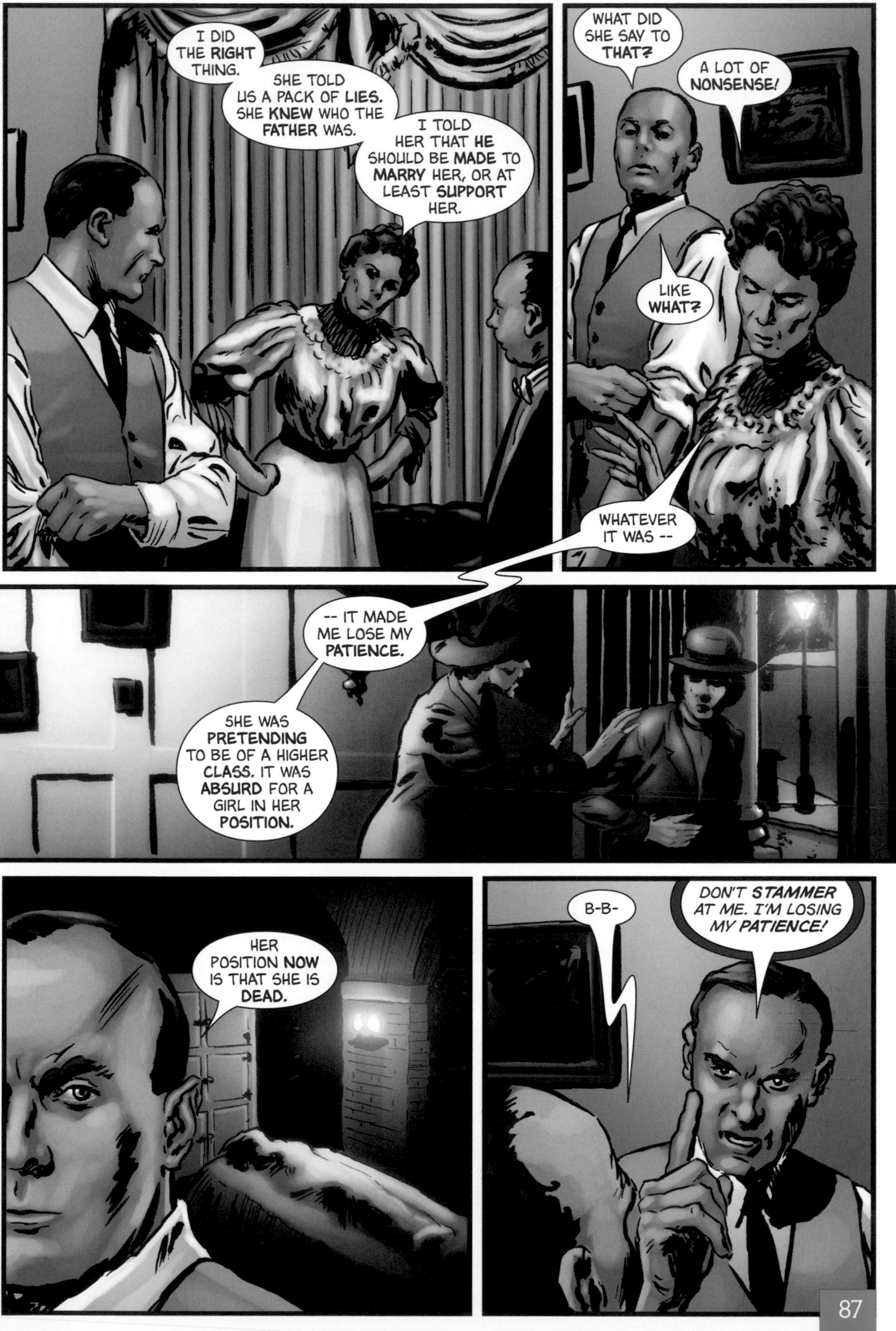
I DID THE RIGHT THING.
SHE TOLD US A PACK OF LIES. SHE KNEW WHO THE FATHER WAS.
I TOLD HER THAT HE SHOULD BE MADE TO MARRY HER, OR AT LEAST SUPPORT HER.
WHAT DID SHE SAY TO THAT?
A LOT OF NONSENSE!
LIKE WHAT?
WHATEVER IT WAS --
-- IT MADE ME LOSE MY PATIENCE.
SHE WAS PRETENDING TO BE OF A HIGHER CLASS. IT WAS ABSURD FOR A GIRL IN HER POSITION.
HER POSITION NOW IS THAT SHE IS DEAD.
B-B-
DON'T STAMMER AT ME. I'M LOSING MY PATIENCE!

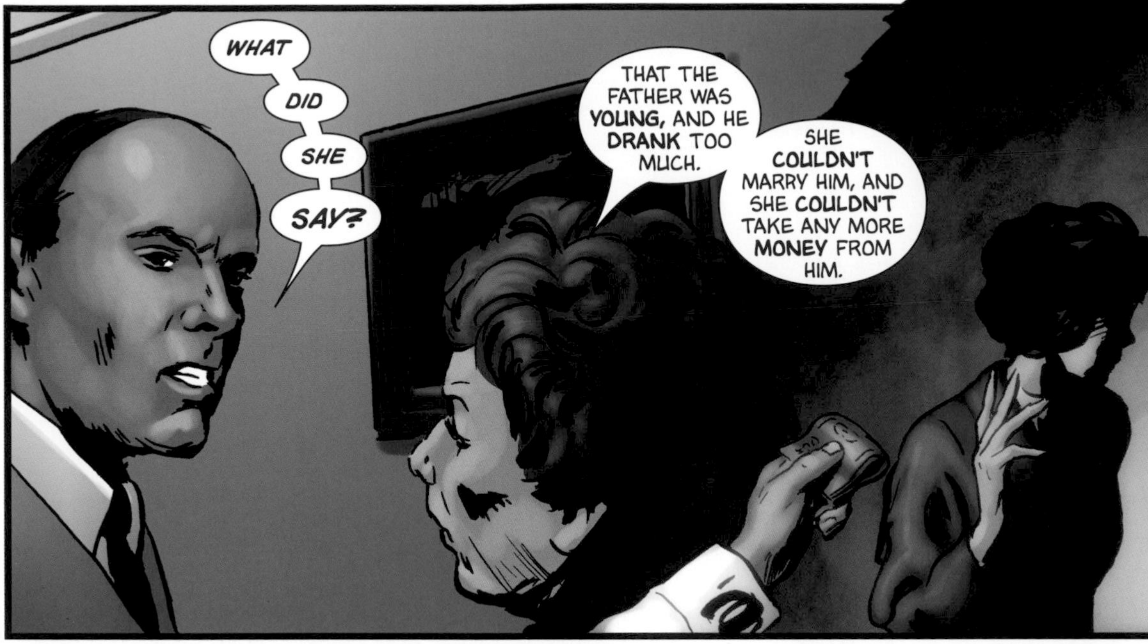
WHAT DID SHE SAY?
THAT THE FATHER WAS YOUNG, AND HE DRANK TOO MUCH.
SHE COULDN'T MARRY HIM, AND SHE COULDN'T TAKE ANY MORE MONEY FROM HIM.

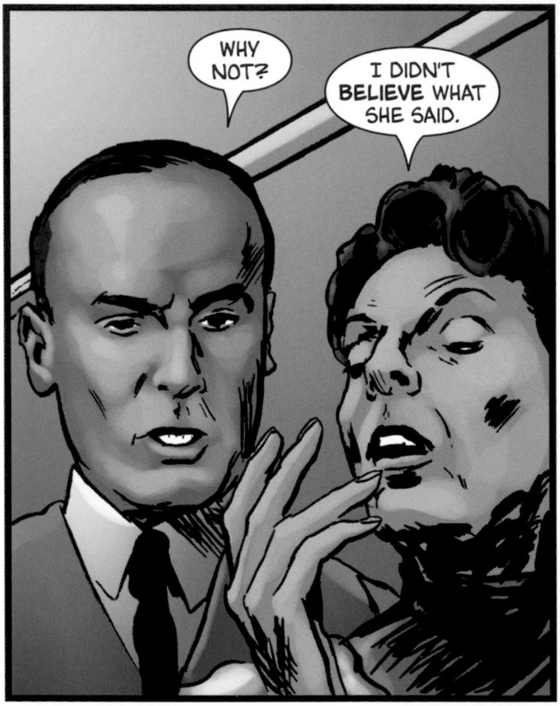
WHY NOT?
I DIDN'T BELIEVE WHAT SHE SAID.

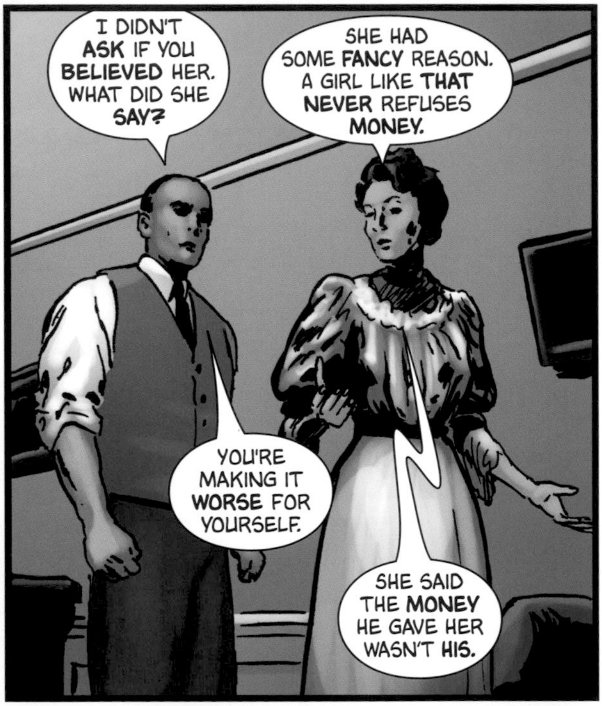
I DIDN'T ASK IF YOU BELIEVED HER. WHAT DID SHE SAY?
SHE HAD SOME FANCY REASON. A GIRL LIKE THAT NEVER REFUSES MONEY.
YOU'RE MAKING IT WORSE FOR YOURSELF.
SHE SAID THE MONEY HE GAVE HER WASN'T HIS.

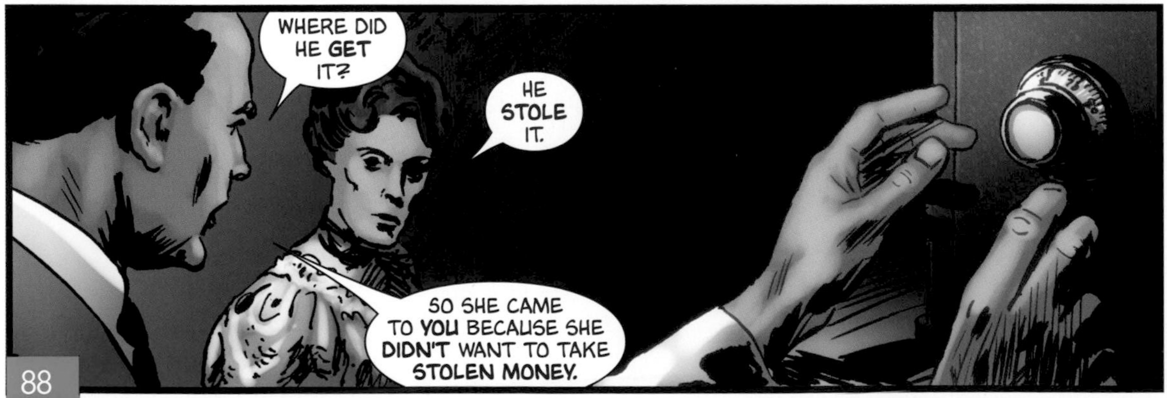
WHERE DID HE GET IT?
HE STOLE IT.
SO SHE CAME TO YOU BECAUSE SHE DIDN'T WANT TO TAKE STOLEN MONEY.

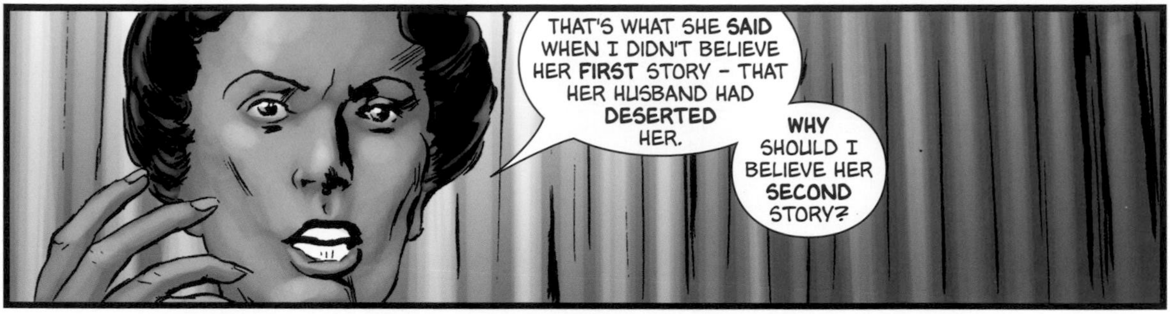
THAT'S WHAT SHE SAID WHEN I DIDN'T BELIEVE HER FIRST STORY – THAT HER HUSBAND HAD DESERTED HER.
WHY SHOULD I BELIEVE HER SECOND STORY?

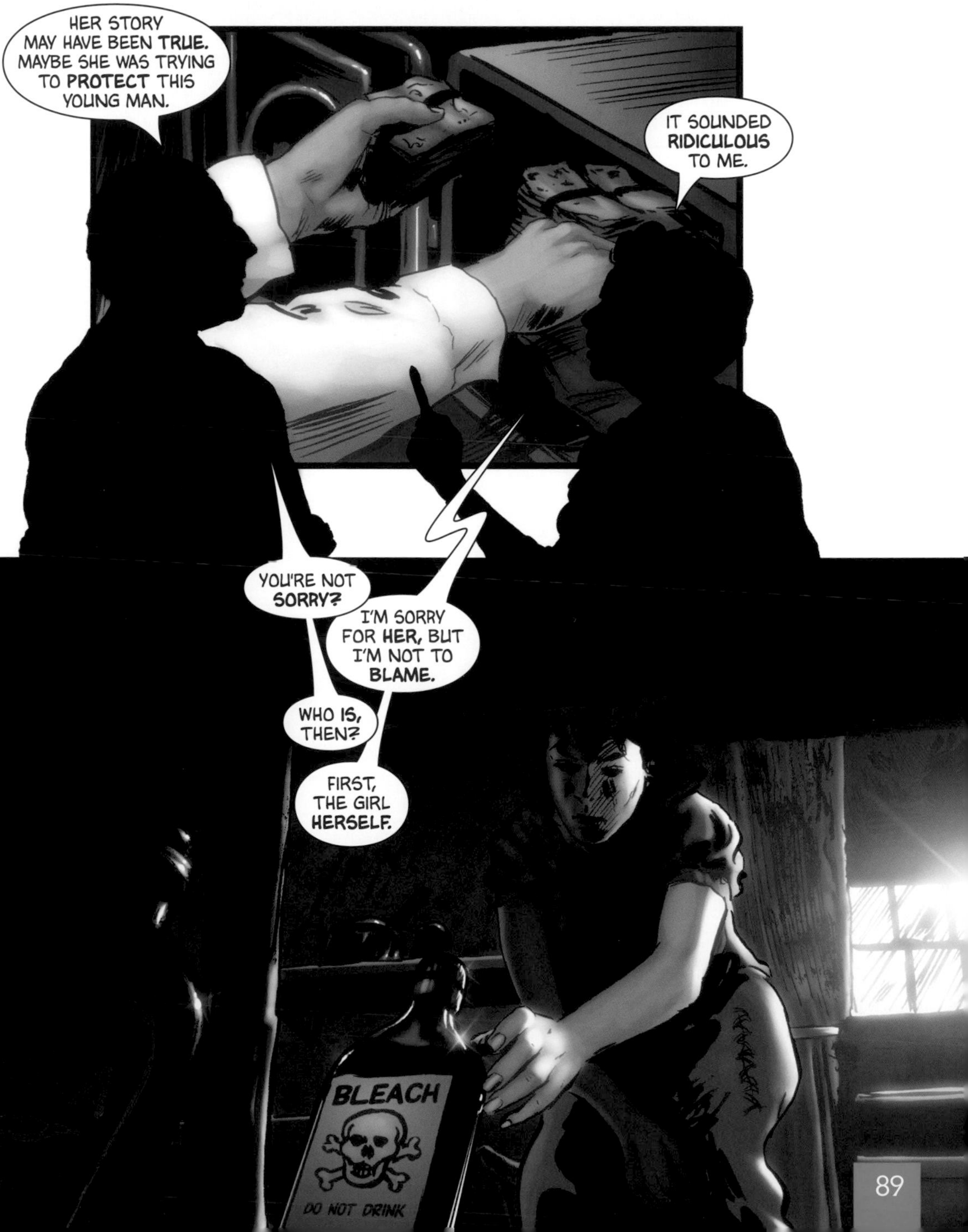
HER STORY MAY HAVE BEEN TRUE. MAYBE SHE WAS TRYING TO PROTECT THIS YOUNG MAN.
IT SOUNDED RIDICULOUS TO ME.
YOU'RE NOT SORRY?
I'M SORRY FOR HER, BUT I'M NOT TO BLAME.
WHO IS, THEN?
FIRST, THE GIRL HERSELF.
BLEACH
DO NOT DRINK

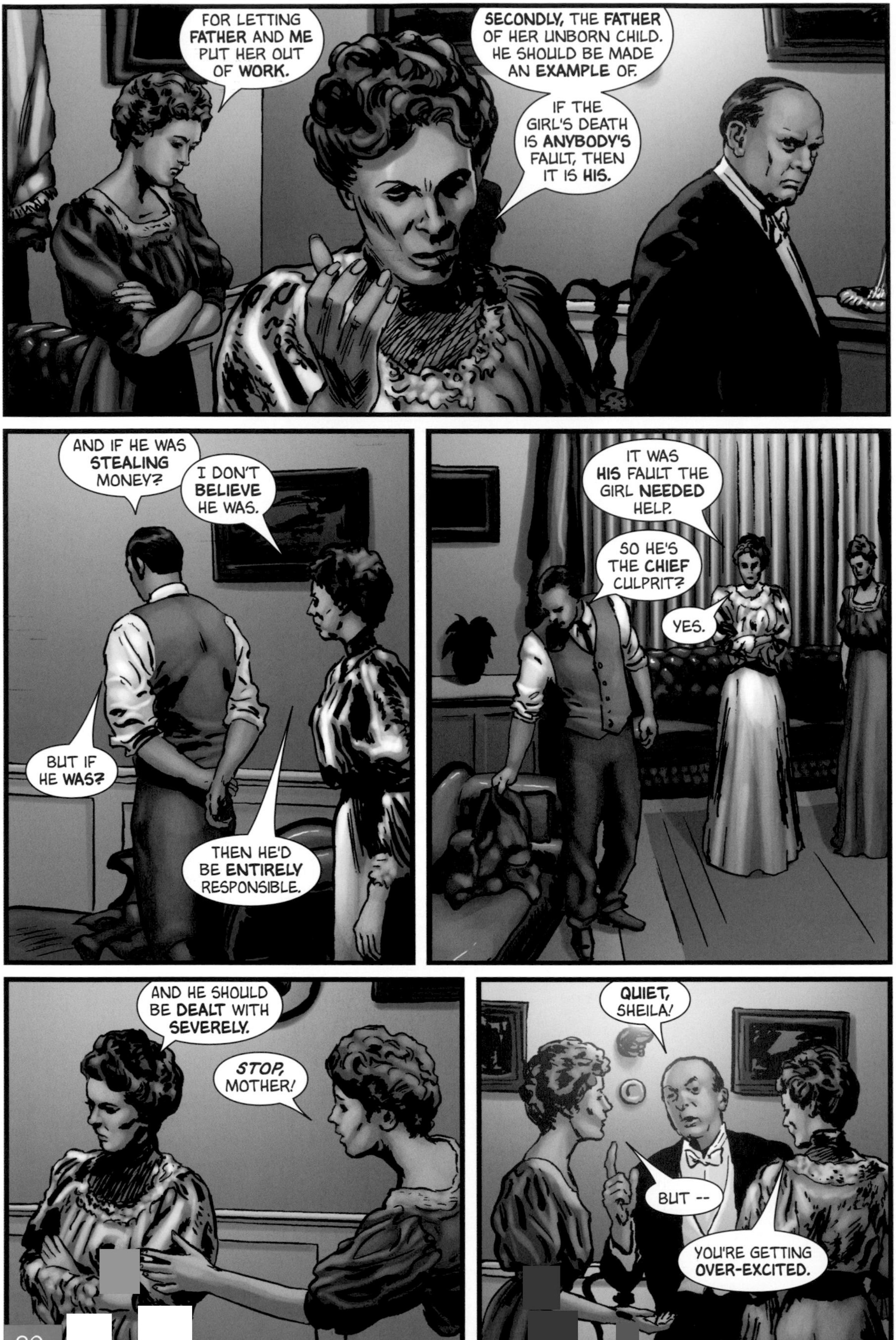
FOR LETTING FATHER AND ME PUT HER OUT OF WORK.
SECONDLY, THE FATHER OF HER UNBORN CHILD. HE SHOULD BE MADE AN EXAMPLE OF.
IF THE GIRL'S DEATH IS ANYBODY'S FAULT, THEN IT IS HIS.
AND IF HE WAS STEALING MONEY?
I DON'T BELIEVE HE WAS.
BUT IF HE WAS?
THEN HE'D BE ENTIRELY RESPONSIBLE.
IT WAS HIS FAULT THE GIRL NEEDED HELP.
SO HE'S THE CHIEF CULPRIT?
YES.
AND HE SHOULD BE DEALT WITH SEVERELY.
STOP, MOTHER!
QUIET, SHEILA!
BUT --
YOU'RE GETTING OVER-EXCITED.

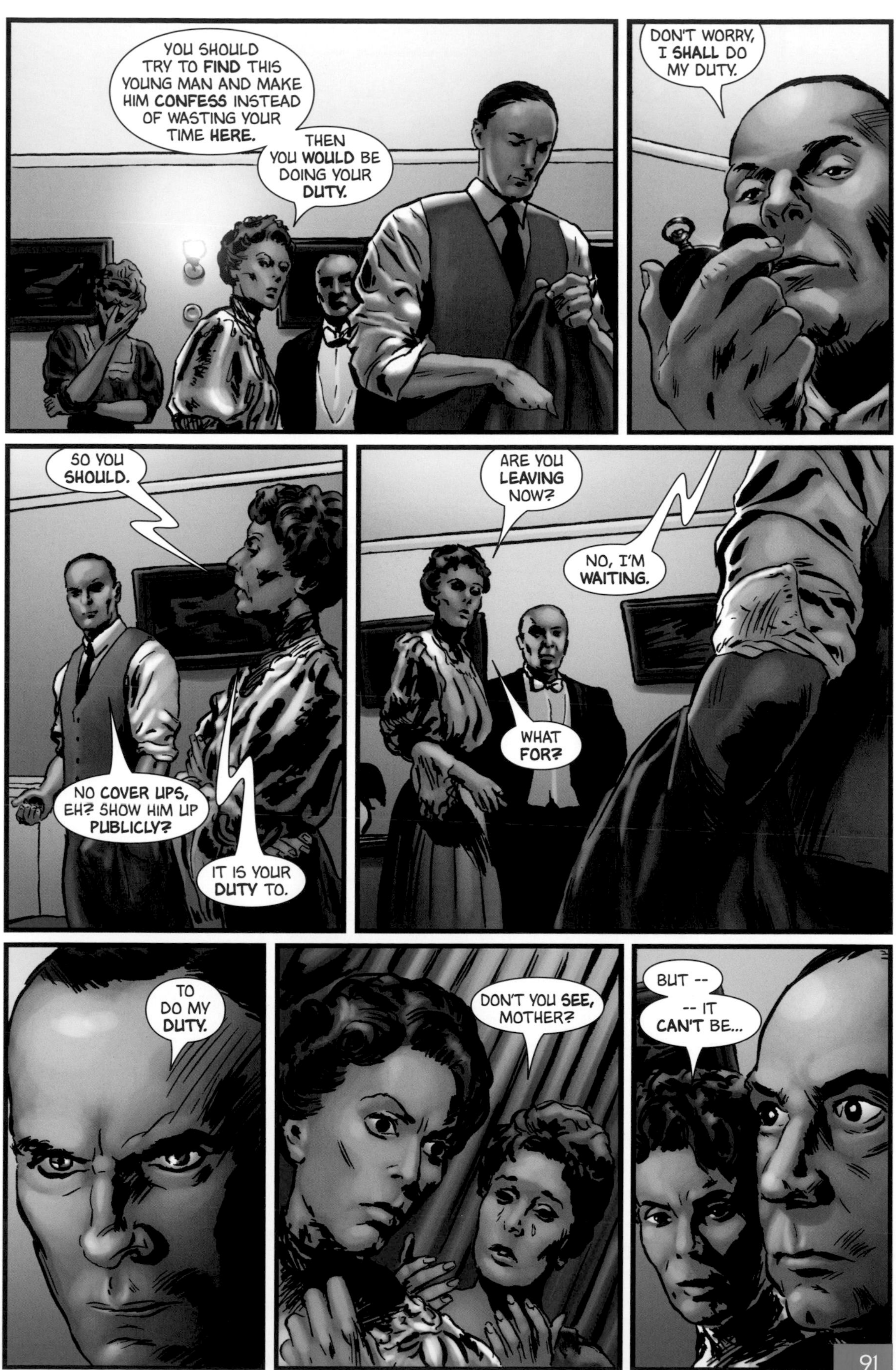
YOU SHOULD TRY TO FIND THIS YOUNG MAN AND MAKE HIM CONFESS INSTEAD OF WASTING YOUR TIME HERE.
THEN YOU WOULD BE DOING YOUR DUTY.
DON'T WORRY, I SHALL DO MY DUTY.
SO YOU SHOULD.
NO COVER UPS, EH? SHOW HIM UP PUBLICLY?
IT IS YOUR DUTY TO.
ARE YOU LEAVING NOW?
NO, I'M WAITING.
WHAT FOR?
TO DO MY DUTY.
DON'T YOU SEE, MOTHER?
BUT --
-- IT CAN'T BE...

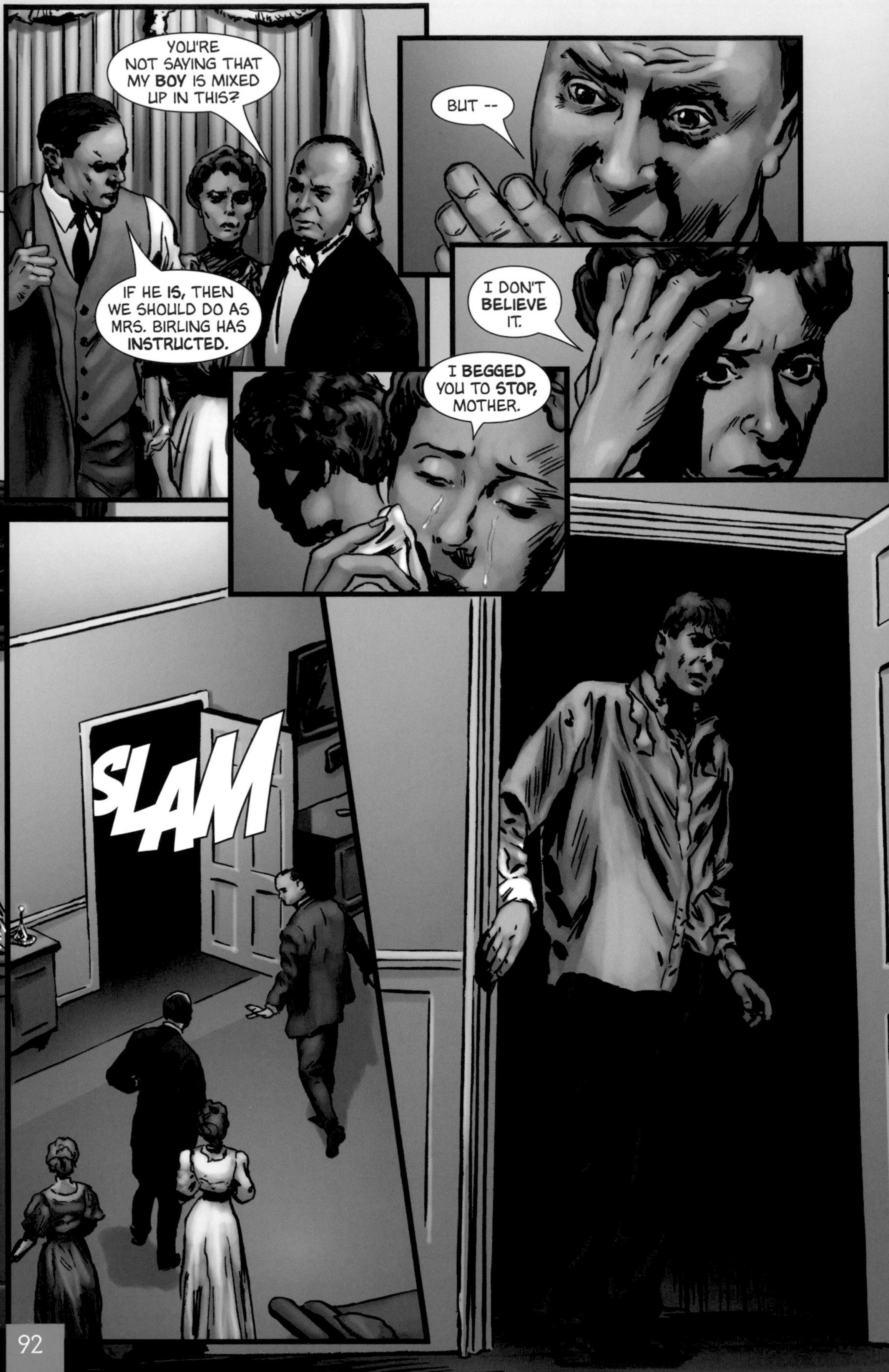
YOU'RE NOT SAYING THAT MY BOY IS MIXED UP IN THIS?
IF HE IS, THEN WE SHOULD DO AS MRS. BIRLING HAS INSTRUCTED.
BUT --
I DON'T BELIEVE IT.
I BEGGED YOU TO STOP, MOTHER.
SLAM

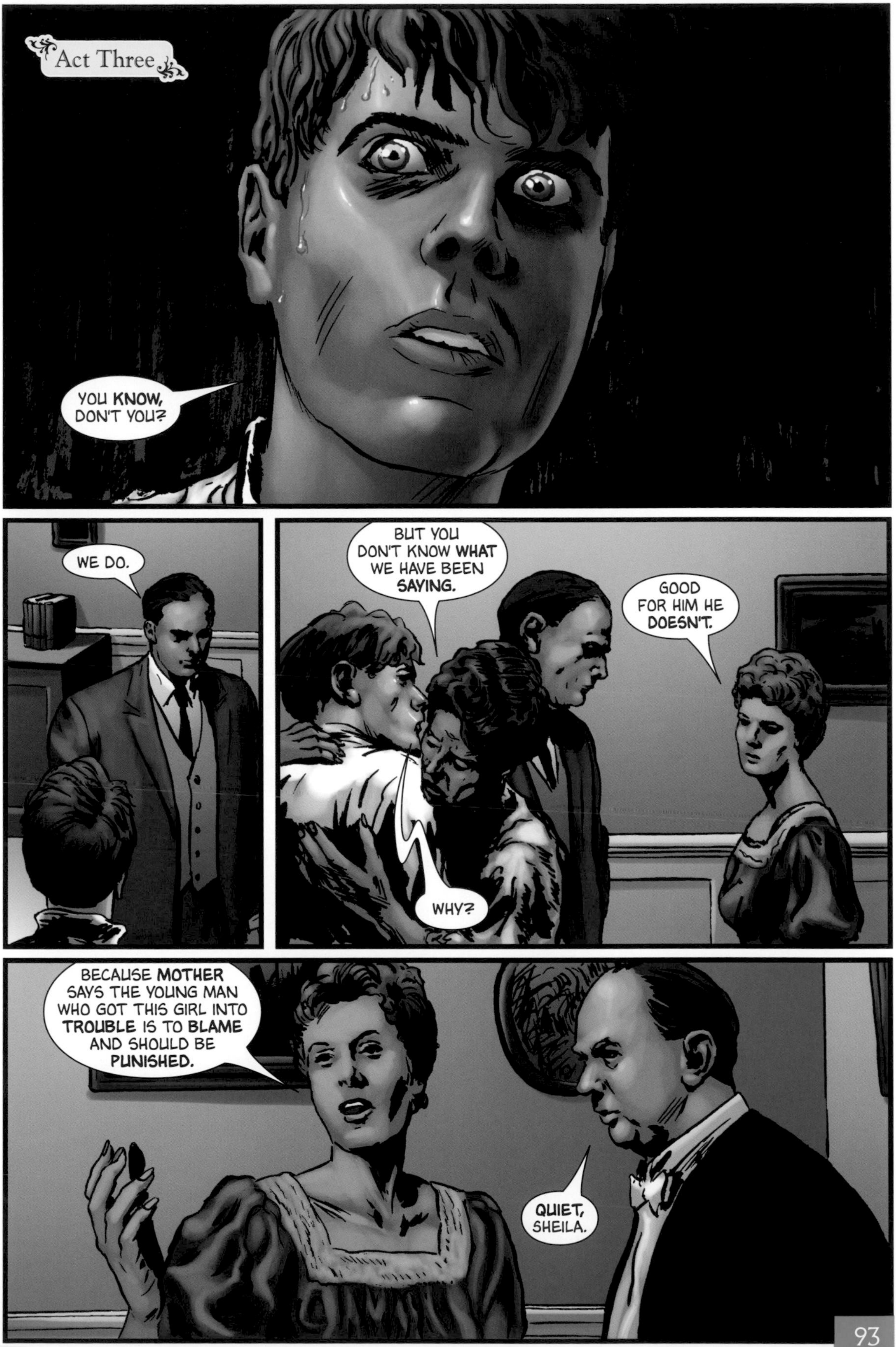
Act Three
YOU KNOW, DON'T YOU?
WE DO.
BUT YOU DON'T KNOW WHAT WE HAVE BEEN SAYING.
WHY?
GOOD FOR HIM HE DOESN'T.
BECAUSE MOTHER SAYS THE YOUNG MAN WHO GOT THIS GIRL INTO TROUBLE IS TO BLAME AND SHOULD BE PUNISHED.
QUIET, SHEILA.

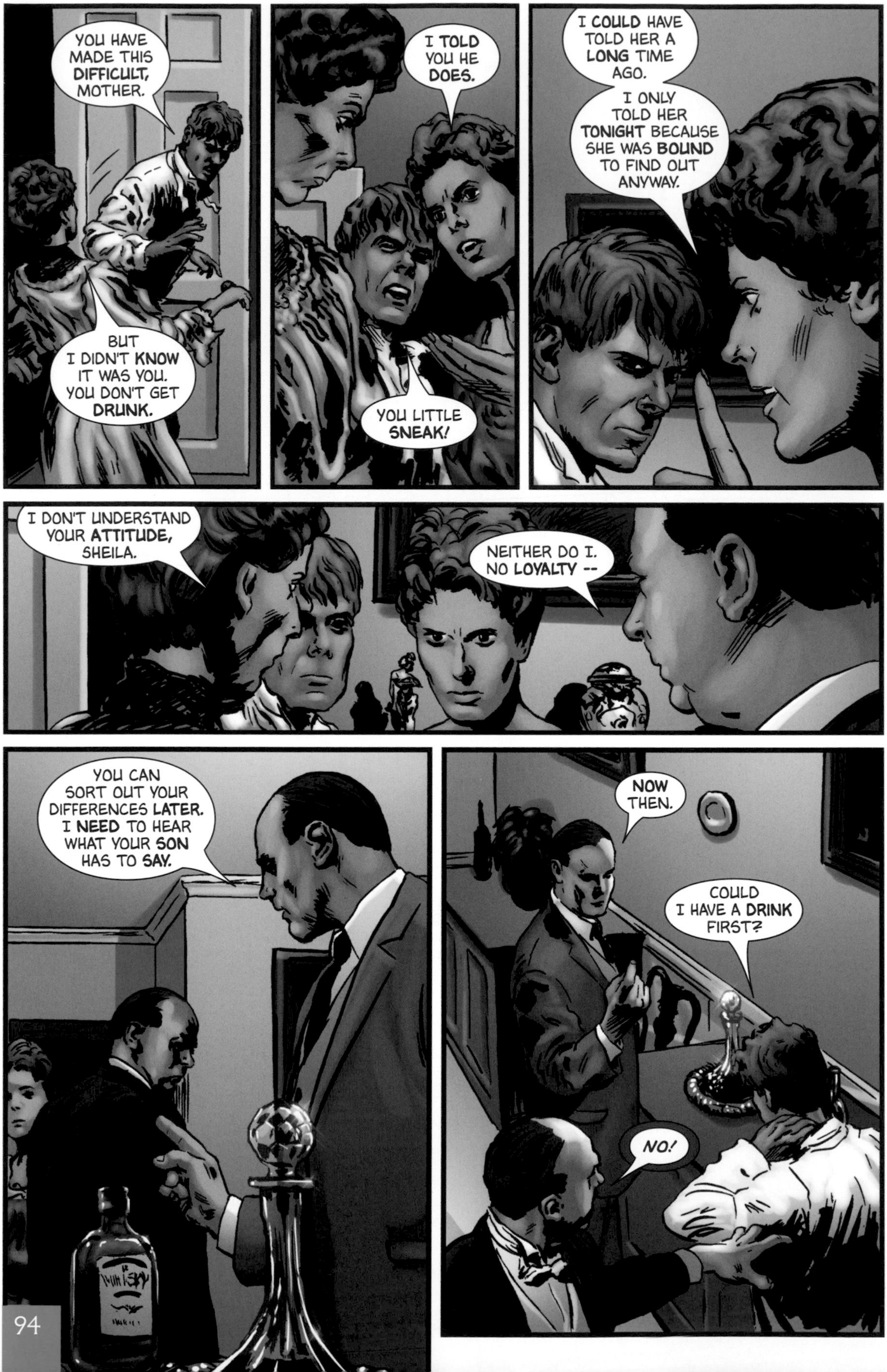
YOU HAVE MADE THIS DIFFICULT, MOTHER.
BUT I DIDN'T KNOW IT WAS YOU. YOU DON'T GET DRUNK.
I TOLD YOU HE DOES.
YOU LITTLE SNEAK!
I COULD HAVE TOLD HER A LONG TIME AGO.
I ONLY TOLD HER TONIGHT BECAUSE SHE WAS BOUND TO FIND OUT ANYWAY.
I DON'T UNDERSTAND YOUR ATTITUDE, SHEILA.
NEITHER DO I. NO LOYALTY --
YOU CAN SORT OUT YOUR DIFFERENCES LATER. I NEED TO HEAR WHAT YOUR SON HAS TO SAY.
NOW THEN.
COULD I HAVE A DRINK FIRST?
NO!

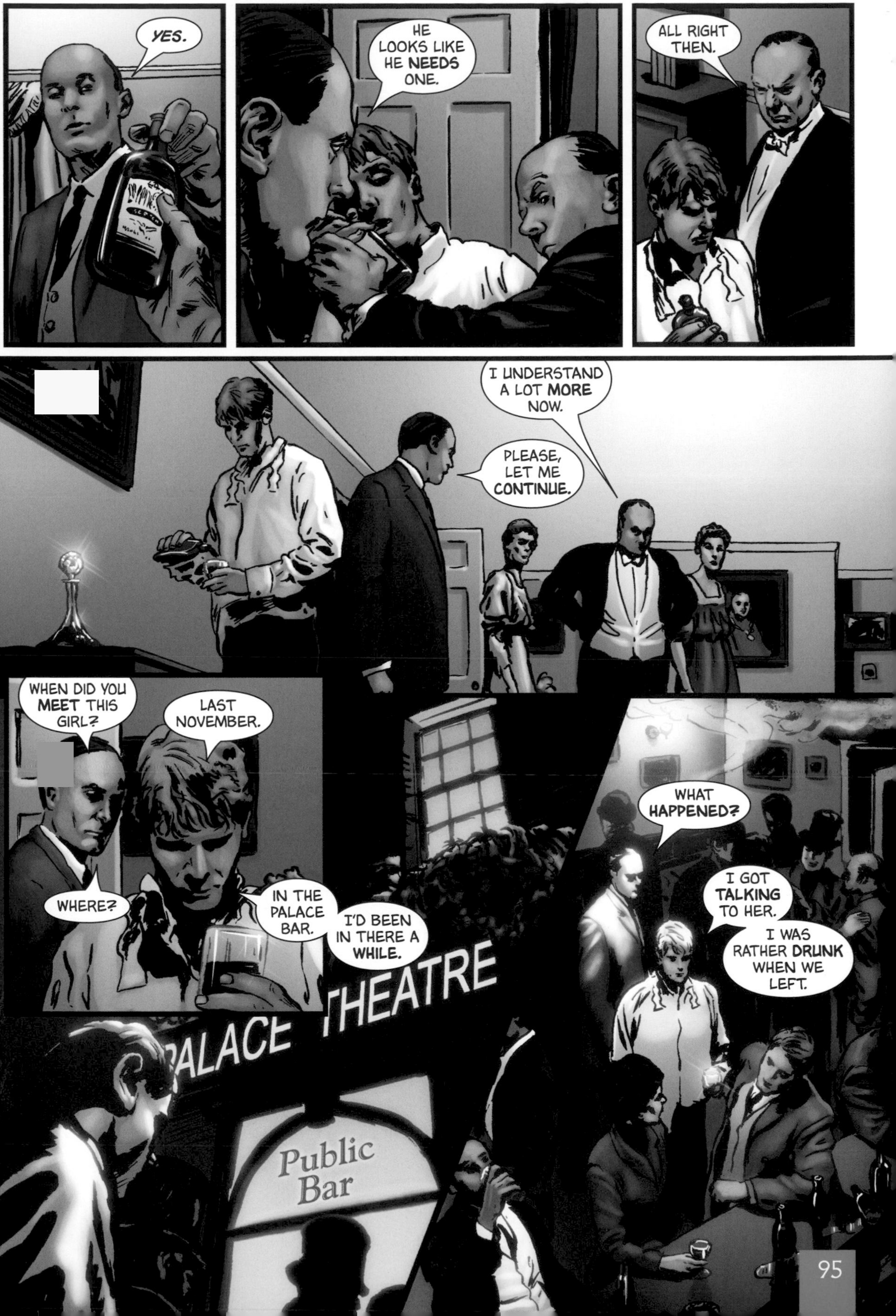
YES.
HE LOOKS LIKE HE NEEDS ONE.
ALL RIGHT THEN.
I UNDERSTAND A LOT MORE NOW.
PLEASE, LET ME CONTINUE.
WHEN DID YOU MEET THIS GIRL?
LAST NOVEMBER.
WHERE?
IN THE PALACE BAR.
I'D BEEN IN THERE A WHILE.
PALACE THEATRE
Public Bar
WHAT HAPPENED?
I GOT TALKING TO HER.
I WAS RATHER DRUNK WHEN WE LEFT.

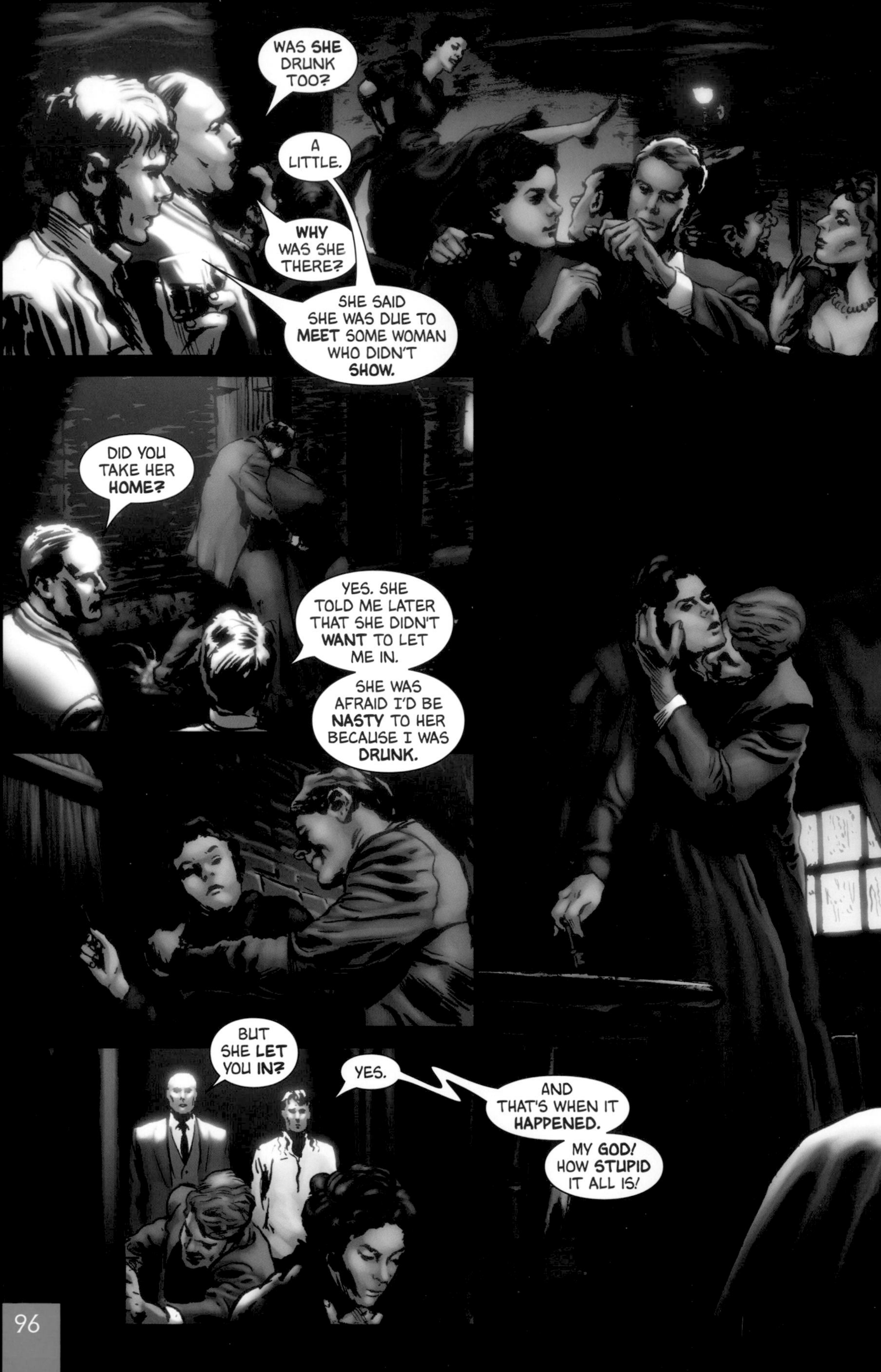
WAS SHE DRUNK TOO?
A LITTLE.
WHY WAS SHE THERE?
SHE SAID SHE WAS DUE TO MEET SOME WOMAN WHO DIDN'T SHOW.
DID YOU TAKE HER HOME?
YES. SHE TOLD ME LATER THAT SHE DIDN'T WANT TO LET ME IN.
SHE WAS AFRAID I'D BE NASTY TO HER BECAUSE I WAS DRUNK.
BUT SHE LET YOU IN?
YES.
AND THAT'S WHEN IT HAPPENED.
MY GOD! HOW STUPID IT ALL IS!

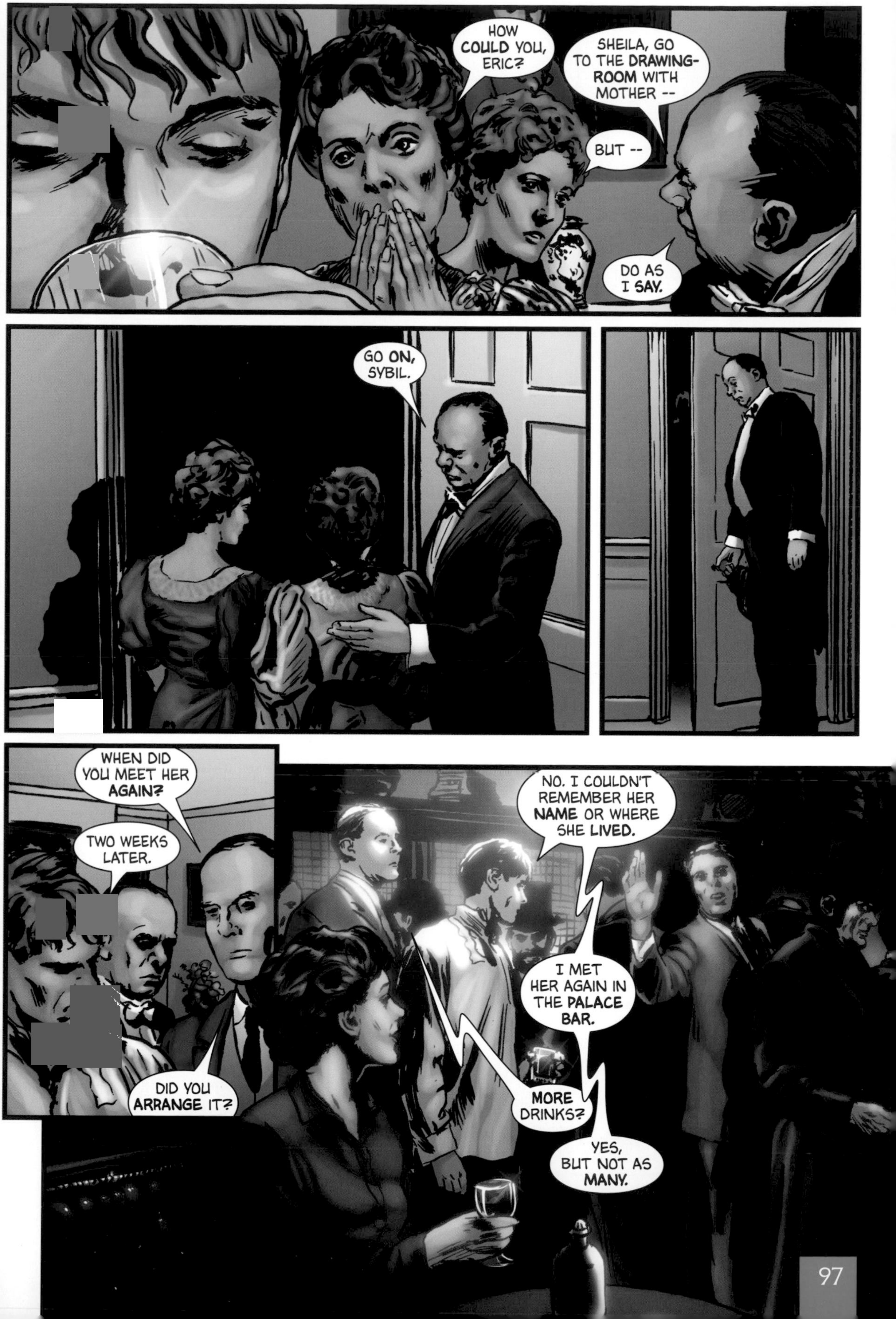
HOW COULD YOU, ERIC?
SHEILA, GO TO THE DRAWING-ROOM WITH MOTHER --
BUT --
DO AS I SAY.
GO ON, SYBIL.
WHEN DID YOU MEET HER AGAIN?
TWO WEEKS LATER.
DID YOU ARRANGE IT?
NO. I COULDN'T REMEMBER HER NAME OR WHERE SHE LIVED.
I MET HER AGAIN IN THE PALACE BAR.
MORE DRINKS?
YES, BUT NOT AS MANY.

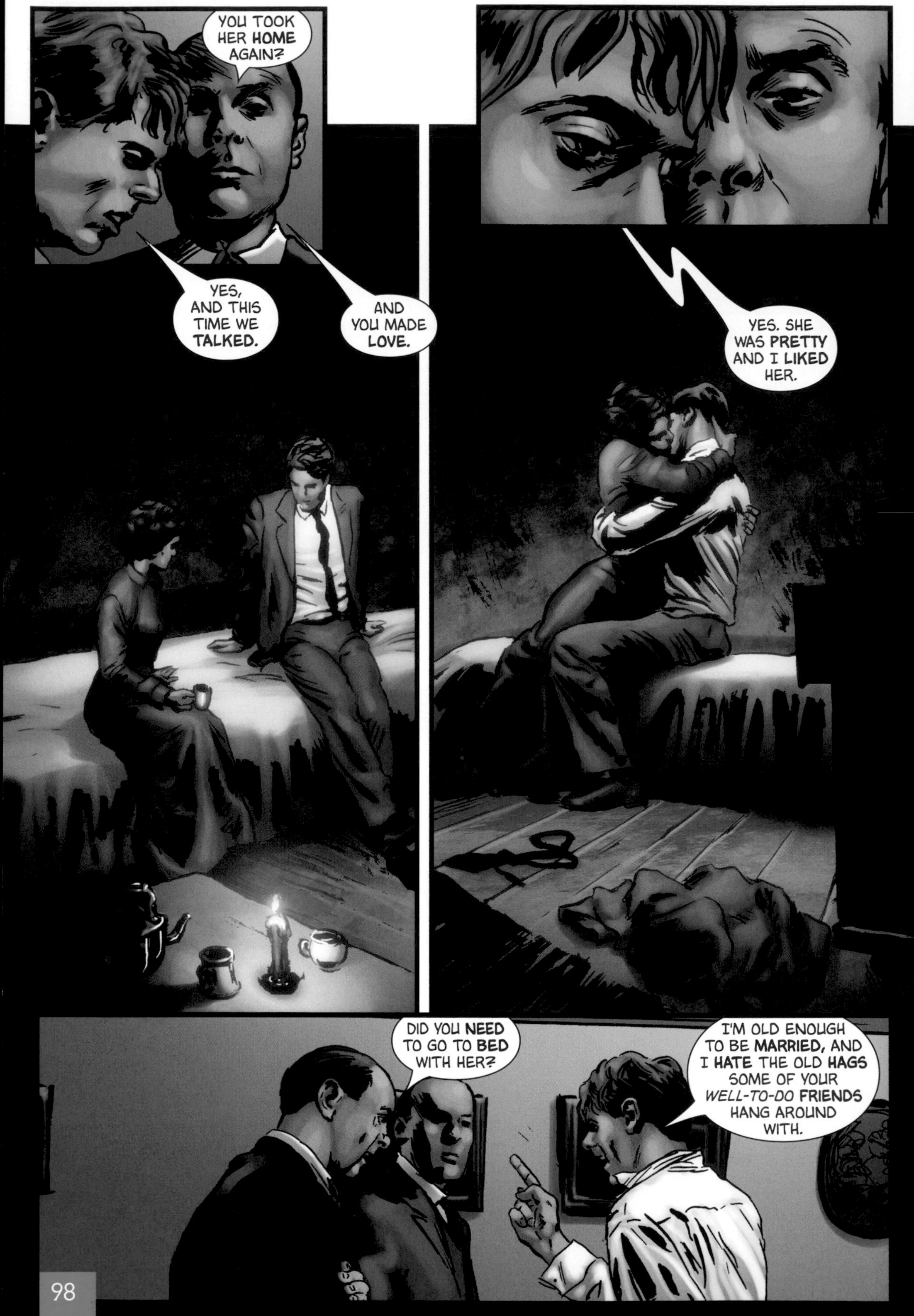
YOU TOOK HER HOME AGAIN?
YES, AND THIS TIME WE TALKED.
AND YOU MADE LOVE.
YES. SHE WAS PRETTY AND I LIKED HER.
DID YOU NEED TO GO TO BED WITH HER?
I'M OLD ENOUGH TO BE MARRIED, AND I HATE THE OLD HAGS SOME OF YOUR WELL-TO-DO FRIENDS HANG AROUND WITH.

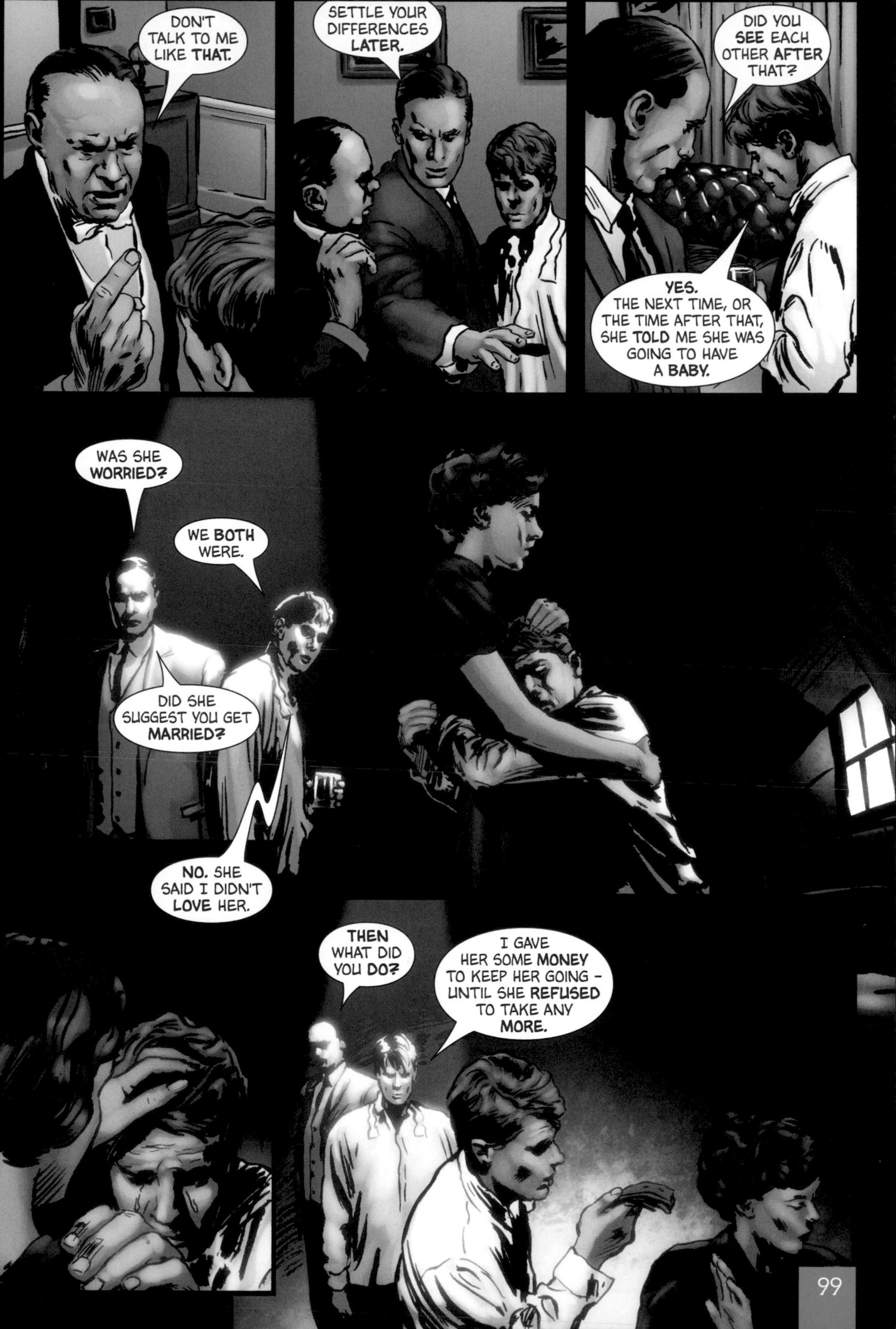

DON'T TALK TO ME LIKE THAT.
SETTLE YOUR DIFFERENCES LATER.
DID YOU SEE EACH OTHER AFTER THAT?
YES. THE NEXT TIME, OR THE TIME AFTER THAT, SHE TOLD ME SHE WAS GOING TO HAVE A BABY.
WAS SHE WORRIED?
WE BOTH WERE.
DID SHE SUGGEST YOU GET MARRIED?
NO. SHE SAID I DIDN'T LOVE HER.
THEN WHAT DID YOU DO?
I GAVE HER SOME MONEY TO KEEP HER GOING - UNTIL SHE REFUSED TO TAKE ANY MORE.

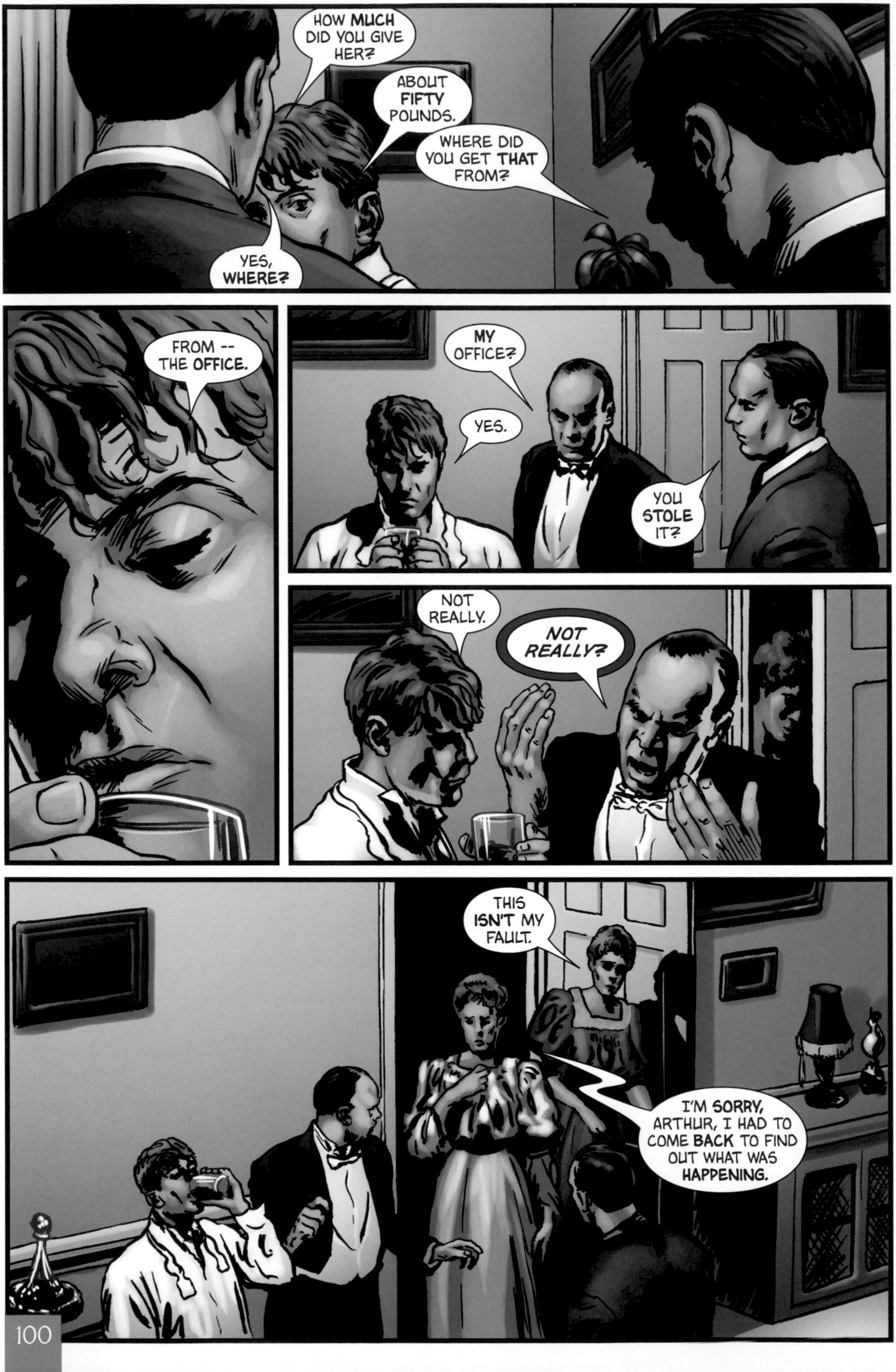
HOW MUCH DID YOU GIVE HER?
ABOUT FIFTY POUNDS.
WHERE DID YOU GET THAT FROM?
YES, WHERE?
FROM -- THE OFFICE.
MY OFFICE?
YES.
YOU STOLE IT?
NOT REALLY.
NOT REALLY?
THIS ISN'T MY FAULT.
I'M SORRY, ARTHUR, I HAD TO COME BACK TO FIND OUT WHAT WAS HAPPENING.

WELL, ERIC HAS **ADMITTED** TO GETTING THE **GIRL** INTO TROUBLE —

AND TO **STEALING** MONEY.

ERIC! YOU STOLE MONEY?

I'LL PAY IT **BACK**.

WE'VE HEARD **THAT** BEFORE.

I **HAD** TO HAVE SOME MONEY —

HOW DID YOU MANAGE TO GET IT?

I COLLECTED **PAYMENTS** FROM CUSTOMERS IN **CASH**.

AND YOU KEPT THE MONEY?

YES.

I'VE GOT TO COVER THIS **UP**.

YOU IDIOT — WHY DIDN'T YOU COME TO **ME**?

BECAUSE **YOU'RE** NOT THE KIND OF FATHER WHO WOULD HELP.

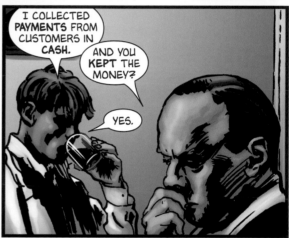

HOW **DARE** YOU!

I HAVEN'T MUCH **TIME**. YOU CAN SORT THIS OUT WHEN I'VE GONE.

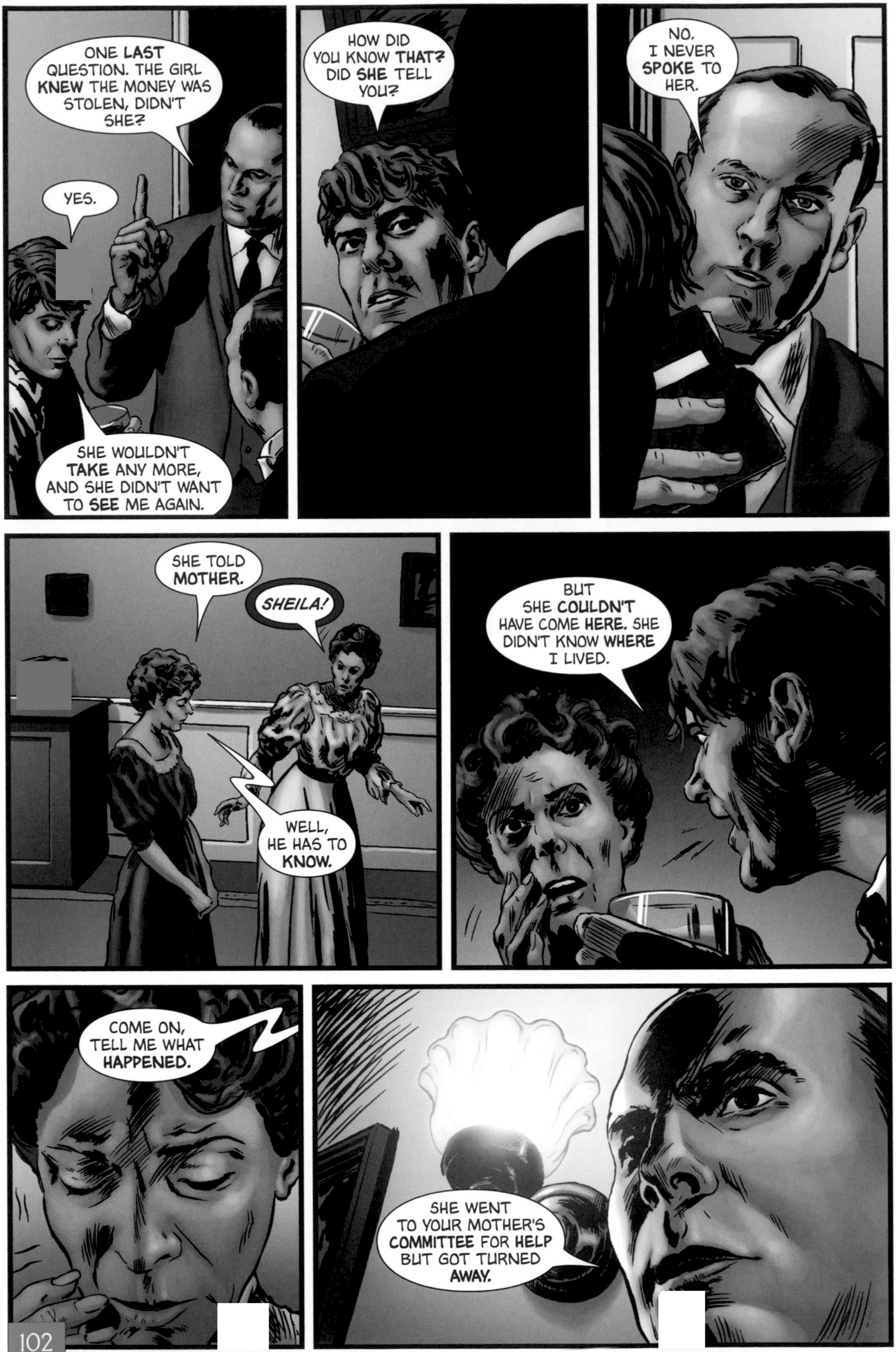

ONE LAST QUESTION. THE GIRL KNEW THE MONEY WAS STOLEN, DIDN'T SHE?
YES.
SHE WOULDN'T TAKE ANY MORE, AND SHE DIDN'T WANT TO SEE ME AGAIN.
HOW DID YOU KNOW THAT? DID SHE TELL YOU?
NO. I NEVER SPOKE TO HER.
SHE TOLD MOTHER.
SHEILA!
WELL, HE HAS TO KNOW.
BUT SHE COULDN'T HAVE COME HERE. SHE DIDN'T KNOW WHERE I LIVED.
COME ON, TELL ME WHAT HAPPENED.
SHE WENT TO YOUR MOTHER'S COMMITTEE FOR HELP BUT GOT TURNED AWAY.

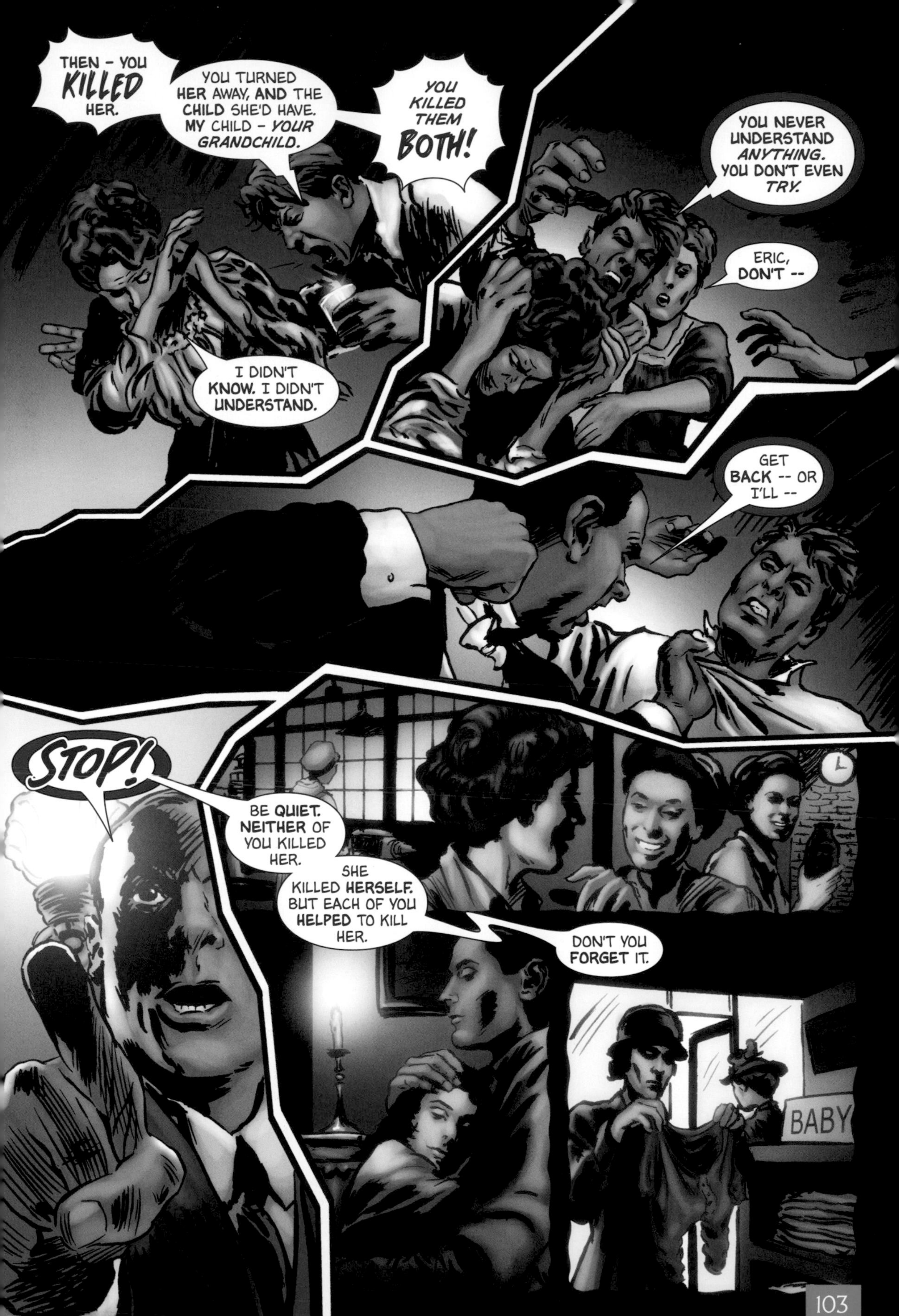
THEN – YOU KILLED HER.
YOU TURNED HER AWAY, AND THE CHILD SHE'D HAVE. MY CHILD – YOUR GRANDCHILD.
YOU KILLED THEM BOTH!
I DIDN'T KNOW. I DIDN'T UNDERSTAND.
YOU NEVER UNDERSTAND ANYTHING. YOU DON'T EVEN TRY.
ERIC, DON'T --
GET BACK -- OR I'LL --
STOP!
BE QUIET. NEITHER OF YOU KILLED HER.
SHE KILLED HERSELF. BUT EACH OF YOU HELPED TO KILL HER.
DON'T YOU FORGET IT.
BABY

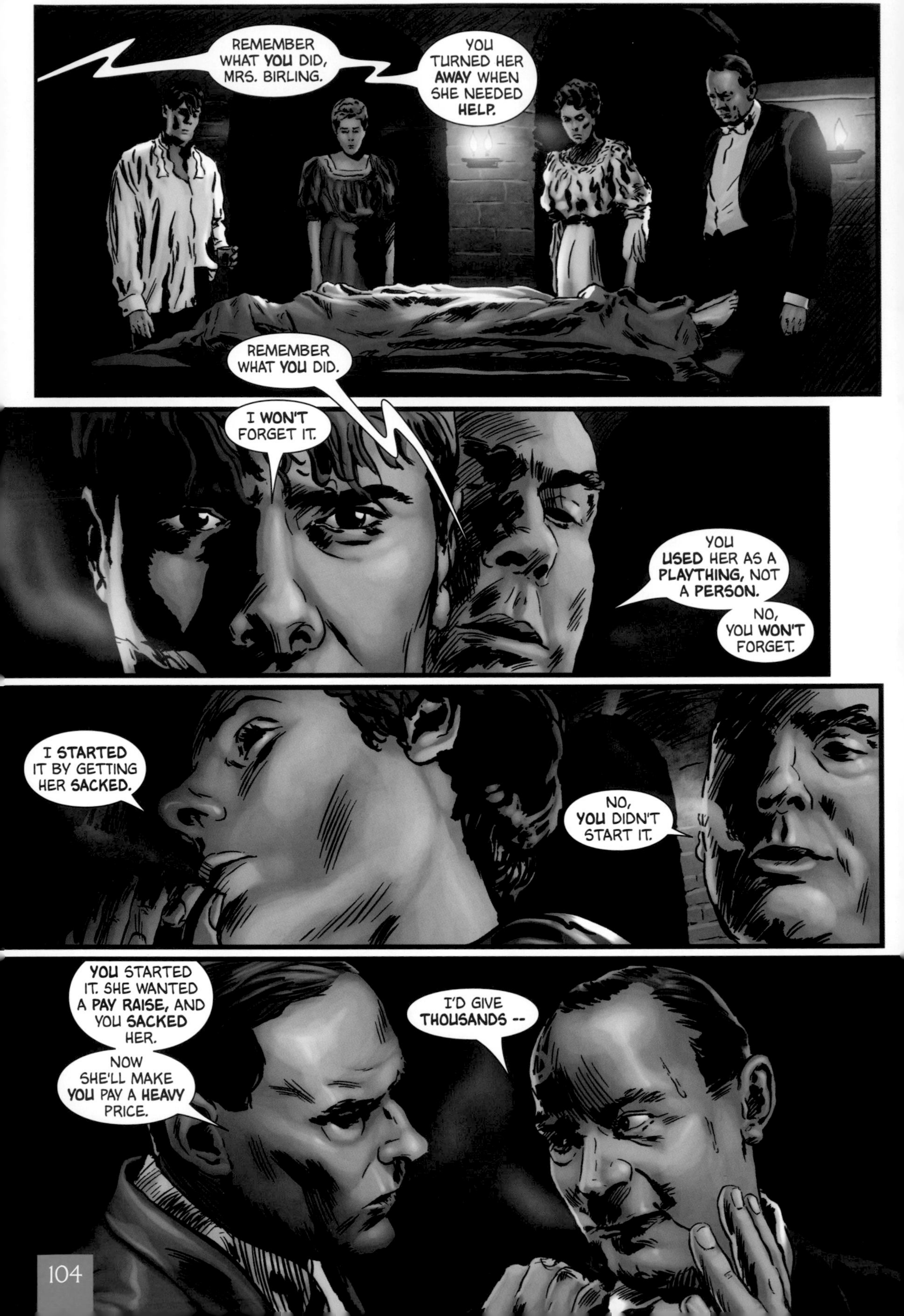
REMEMBER WHAT YOU DID, MRS. BIRLING.
YOU TURNED HER AWAY WHEN SHE NEEDED HELP.
REMEMBER WHAT YOU DID.
I WON'T FORGET IT.
YOU USED HER AS A PLAYTHING, NOT A PERSON.
NO, YOU WON'T FORGET.
I STARTED IT BY GETTING HER SACKED.
NO, YOU DIDN'T START IT.
YOU STARTED IT. SHE WANTED A PAY RAISE, AND YOU SACKED HER.
NOW SHE'LL MAKE YOU PAY A HEAVY PRICE.
I'D GIVE THOUSANDS --

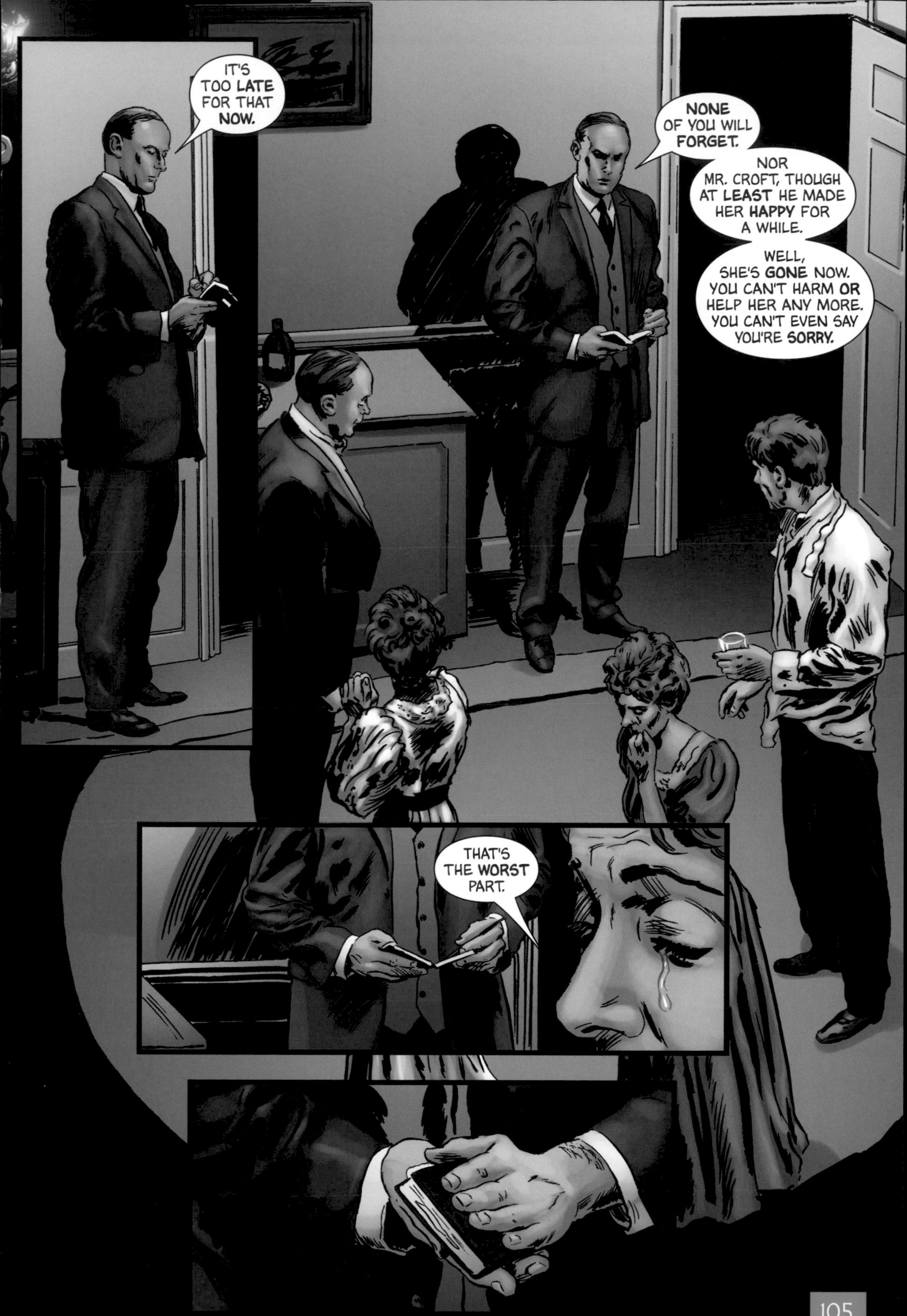
IT'S TOO LATE FOR THAT NOW.
NONE OF YOU WILL FORGET.
NOR MR. CROFT, THOUGH AT LEAST HE MADE HER HAPPY FOR A WHILE.
WELL, SHE'S GONE NOW. YOU CAN'T HARM OR HELP HER ANY MORE. YOU CAN'T EVEN SAY YOU'RE SORRY.
THAT'S THE WORST PART.

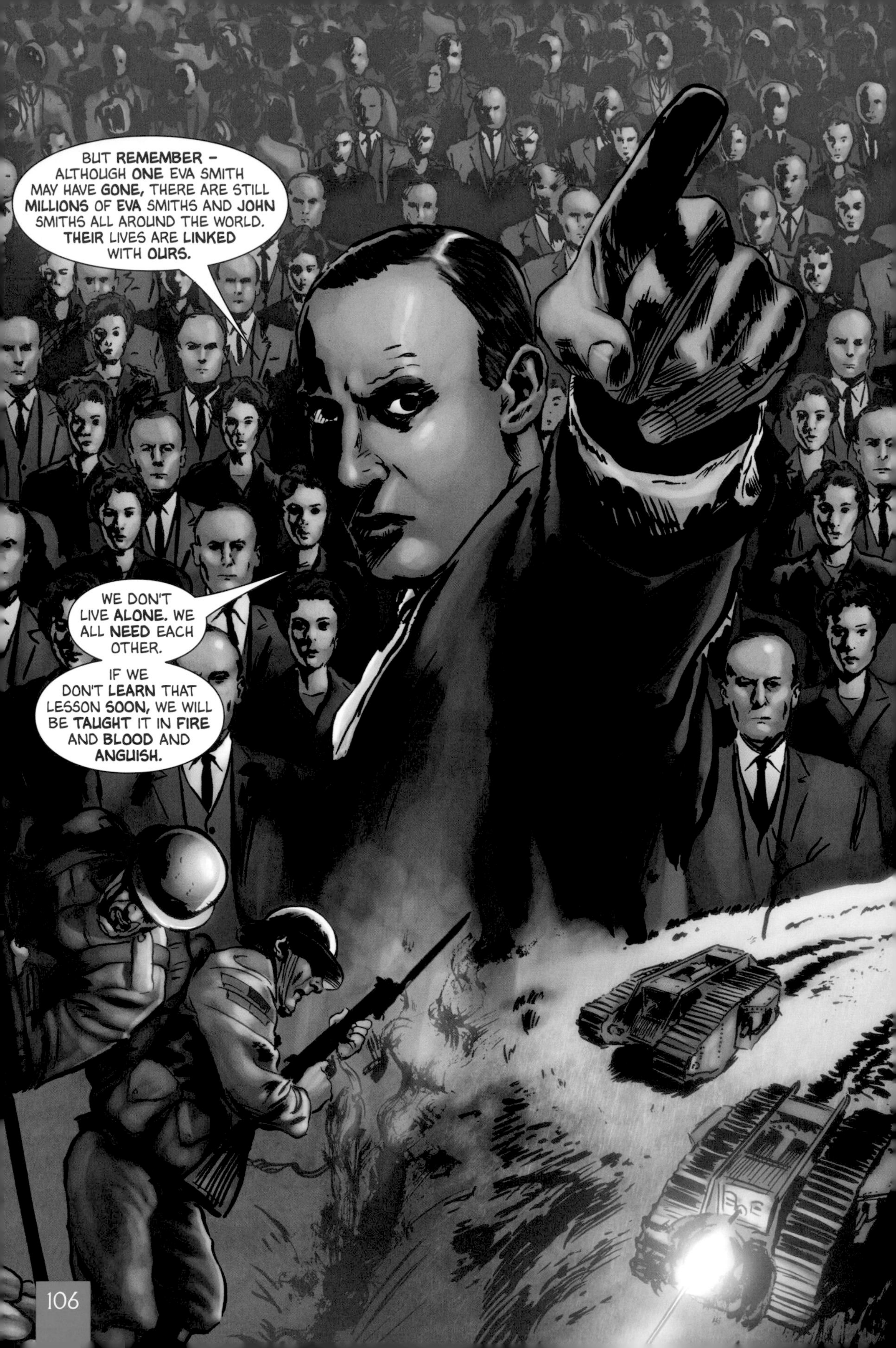
BUT REMEMBER – ALTHOUGH ONE EVA SMITH MAY HAVE GONE, THERE ARE STILL MILLIONS OF EVA SMITHS AND JOHN SMITHS ALL AROUND THE WORLD. THEIR LIVES ARE LINKED WITH OURS.
WE DON'T LIVE ALONE. WE ALL NEED EACH OTHER.
IF WE DON'T LEARN THAT LESSON SOON, WE WILL BE TAUGHT IT IN FIRE AND BLOOD AND ANGUISH.

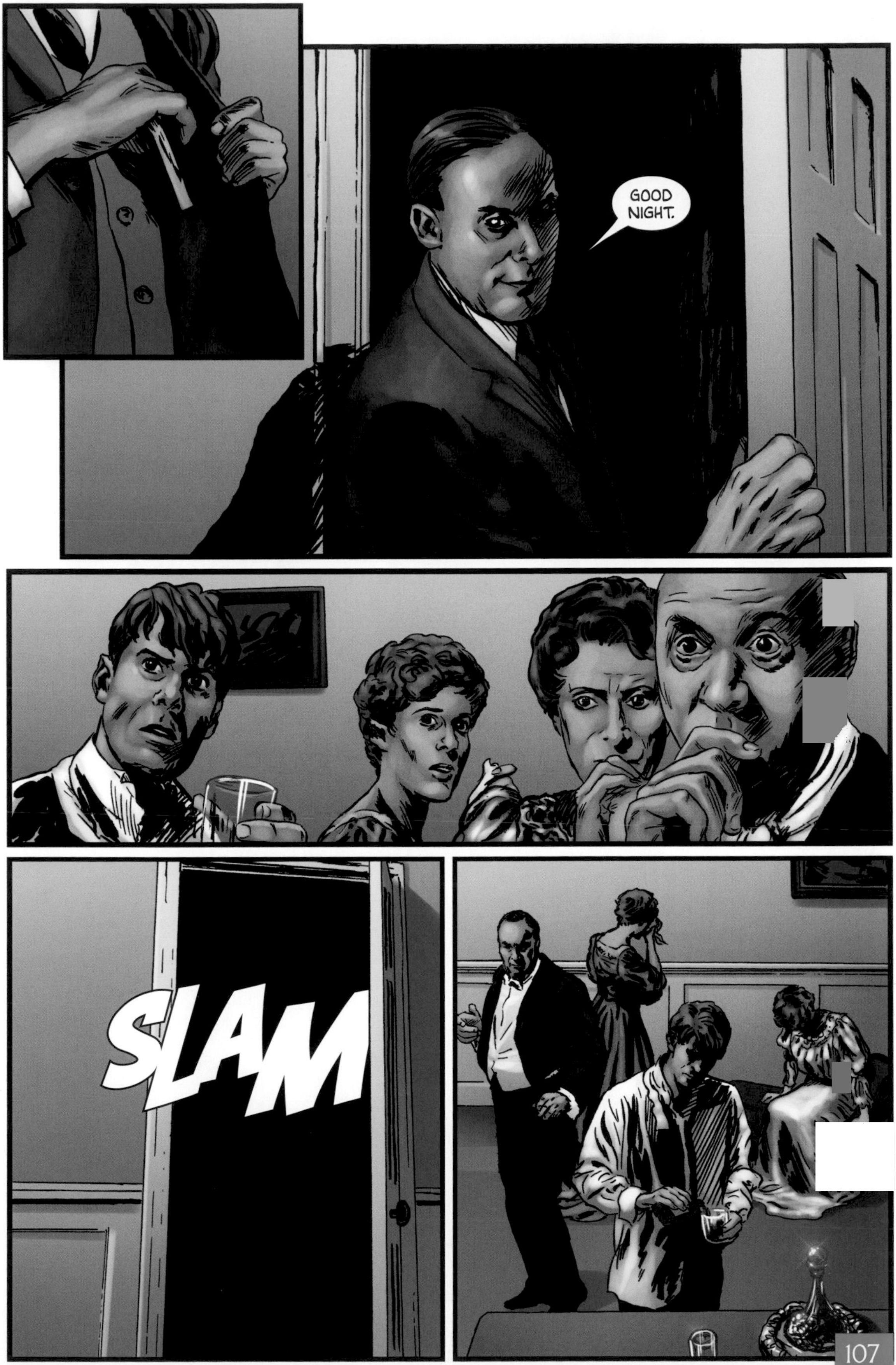
GOOD NIGHT.
SLAM

I BLAME **YOU** FOR THIS.

I BET **YOU** DO.

THERE'LL BE A PUBLIC **SCANDAL**.

I DON'T **CARE** NOW.

WELL **I** CARE. THIS WILL COST ME MY **KNIGHTHOOD**.

HA HA HA!

WHAT DOES A KNIGHTHOOD **MATTER** NOW?

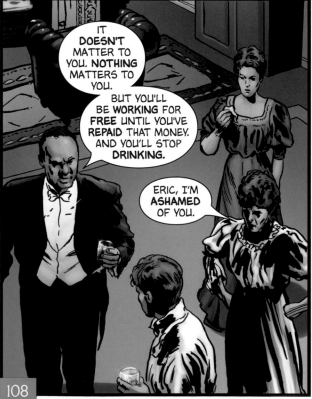

IT **DOESN'T** MATTER TO YOU. **NOTHING** MATTERS TO YOU.

BUT YOU'LL BE **WORKING** FOR **FREE** UNTIL YOU'VE **REPAID** THAT MONEY. AND YOU'LL STOP **DRINKING**.

ERIC, I'M **ASHAMED** OF YOU.

I'M ASHAMED OF **YOU** AS WELL.

BOTH OF YOU.

YOUR MOTHER HAD EVERY **REASON** FOR DOING WHAT SHE **DID**. IT TURNED OUT **BAD**, THAT'S ALL.

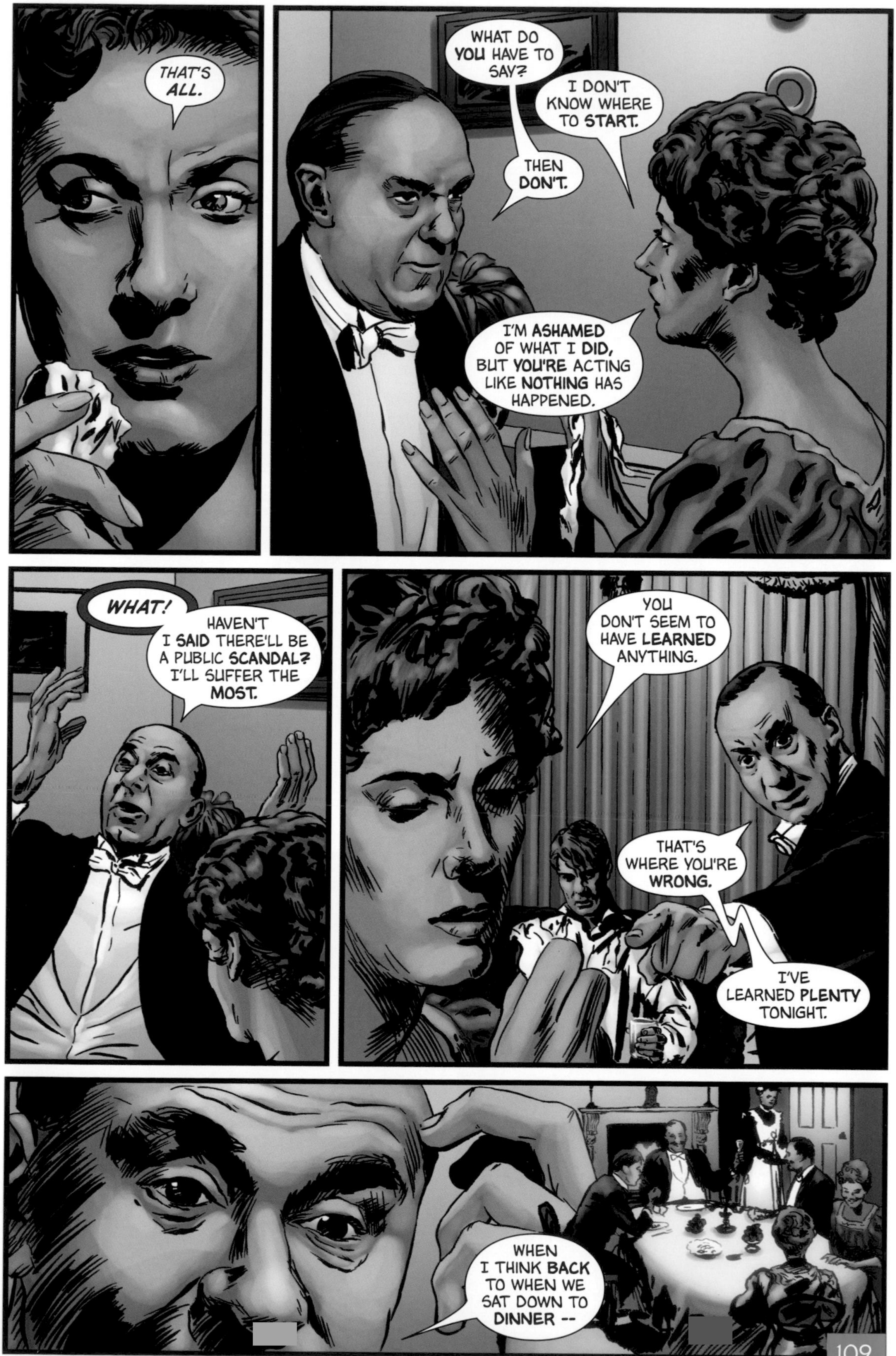
THAT'S ALL.
WHAT DO YOU HAVE TO SAY?
I DON'T KNOW WHERE TO START.
THEN DON'T.
I'M ASHAMED OF WHAT I DID, BUT YOU'RE ACTING LIKE NOTHING HAS HAPPENED.
WHAT!
HAVEN'T I SAID THERE'LL BE A PUBLIC SCANDAL? I'LL SUFFER THE MOST.
YOU DON'T SEEM TO HAVE LEARNED ANYTHING.
THAT'S WHERE YOU'RE WRONG.
I'VE LEARNED PLENTY TONIGHT.
WHEN I THINK BACK TO WHEN WE SAT DOWN TO DINNER --

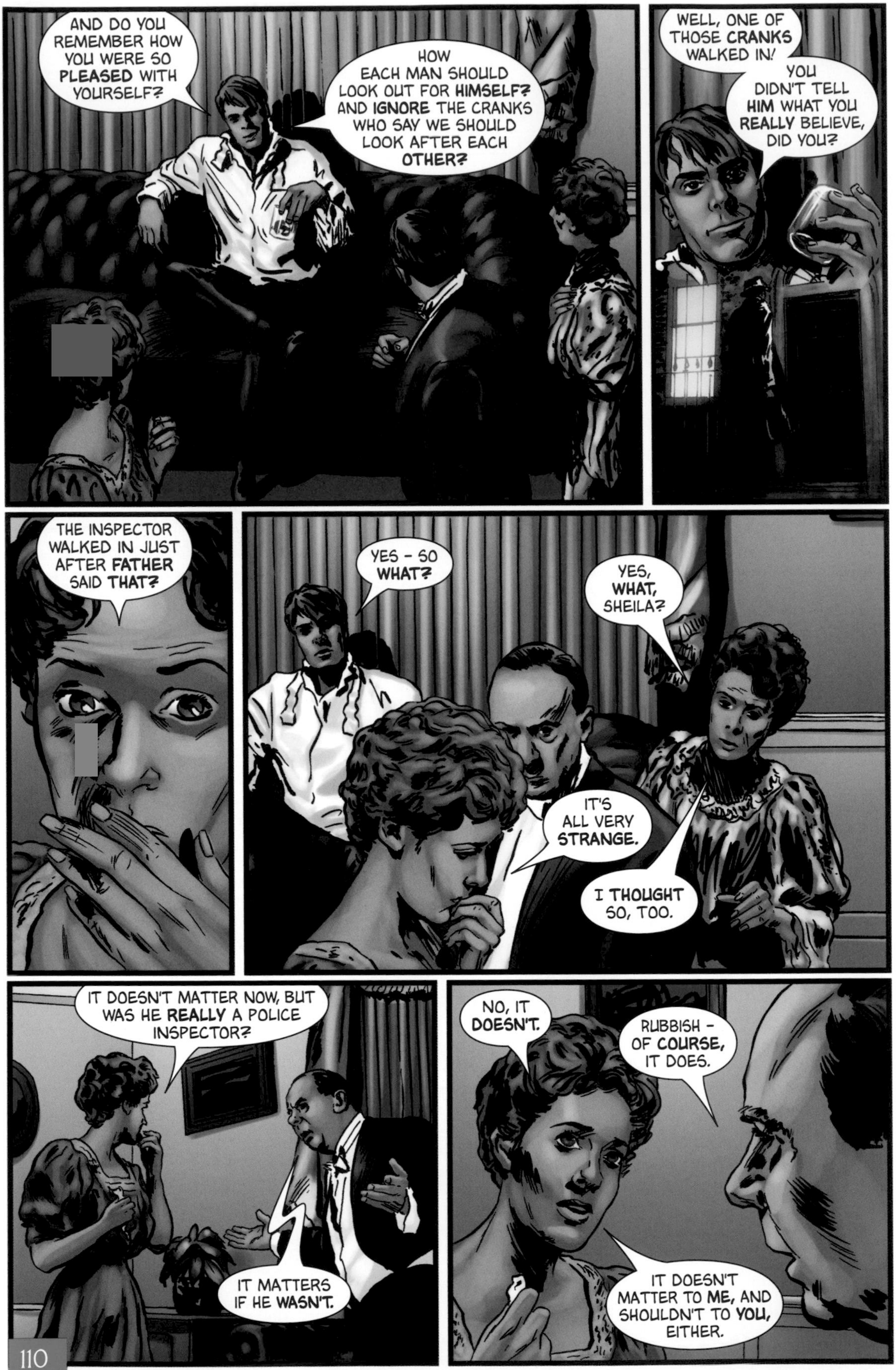
AND DO YOU REMEMBER HOW YOU WERE SO PLEASED WITH YOURSELF?
HOW EACH MAN SHOULD LOOK OUT FOR HIMSELF? AND IGNORE THE CRANKS WHO SAY WE SHOULD LOOK AFTER EACH OTHER?
WELL, ONE OF THOSE CRANKS WALKED IN!
YOU DIDN'T TELL HIM WHAT YOU REALLY BELIEVE, DID YOU?
THE INSPECTOR WALKED IN JUST AFTER FATHER SAID THAT?
YES – SO WHAT?
YES, WHAT, SHEILA?
IT'S ALL VERY STRANGE.
I THOUGHT SO, TOO.
IT DOESN'T MATTER NOW, BUT WAS HE REALLY A POLICE INSPECTOR?
IT MATTERS IF HE WASN'T.
NO, IT DOESN'T.
RUBBISH – OF COURSE, IT DOES.
IT DOESN'T MATTER TO ME, AND SHOULDN'T TO YOU, EITHER.

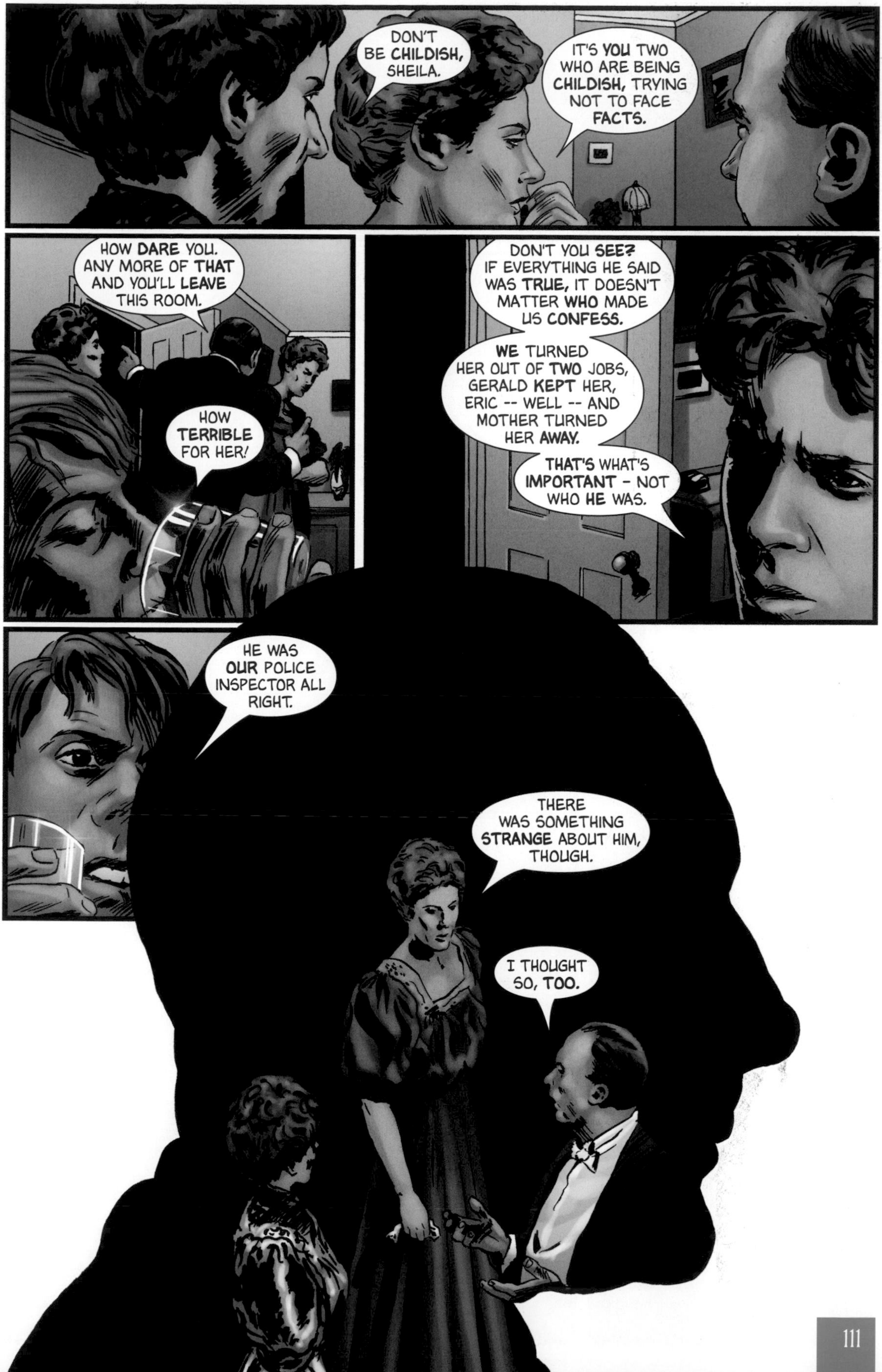
DON'T BE CHILDISH, SHEILA.
IT'S YOU TWO WHO ARE BEING CHILDISH, TRYING NOT TO FACE FACTS.
HOW DARE YOU. ANY MORE OF THAT AND YOU'LL LEAVE THIS ROOM.
HOW TERRIBLE FOR HER!
DON'T YOU SEE? IF EVERYTHING HE SAID WAS TRUE, IT DOESN'T MATTER WHO MADE US CONFESS.
WE TURNED HER OUT OF TWO JOBS, GERALD KEPT HER, ERIC -- WELL -- AND MOTHER TURNED HER AWAY.
THAT'S WHAT'S IMPORTANT - NOT WHO HE WAS.
HE WAS OUR POLICE INSPECTOR ALL RIGHT.
THERE WAS SOMETHING STRANGE ABOUT HIM, THOUGH.
I THOUGHT SO, TOO.

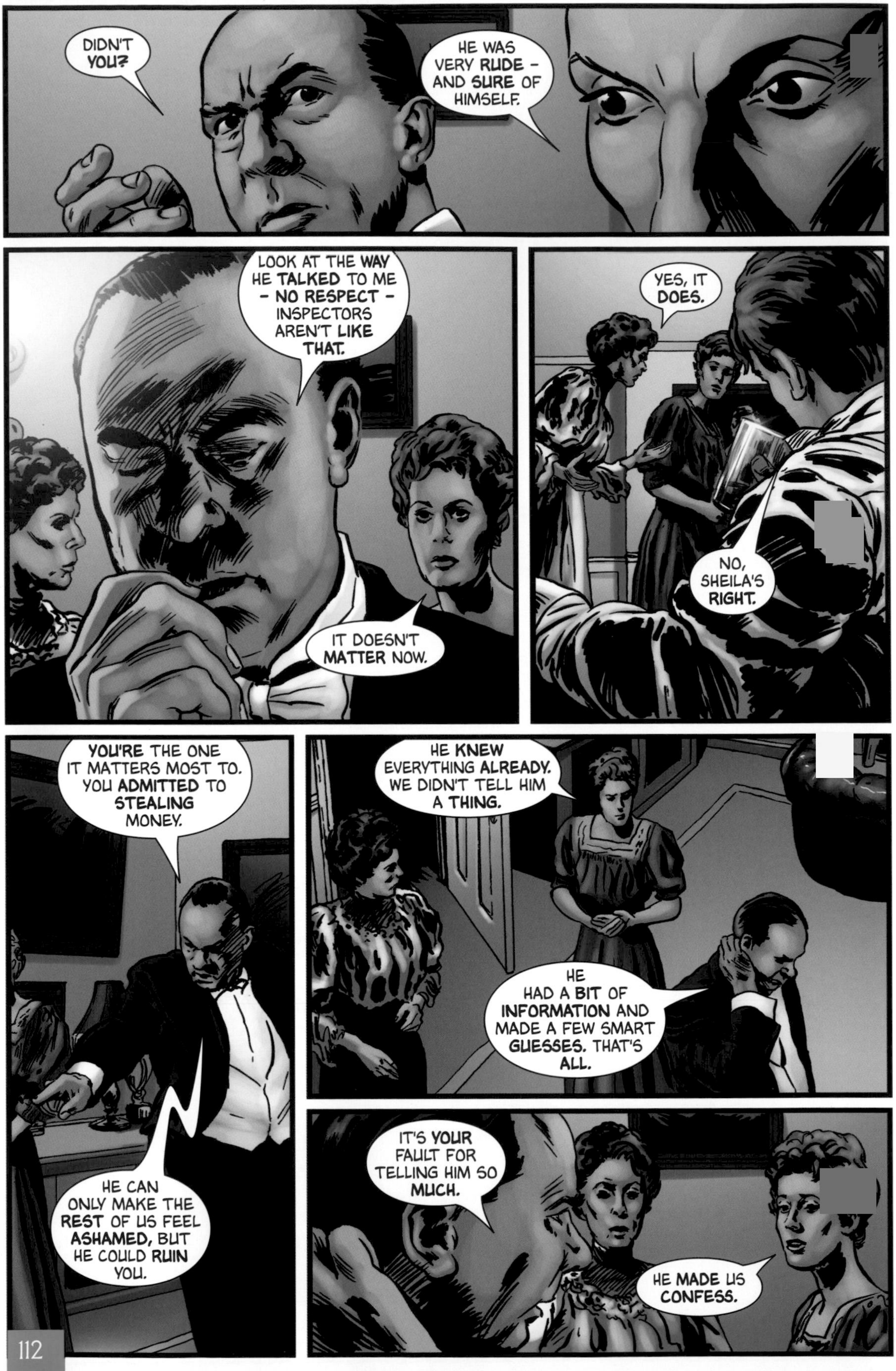
DIDN'T YOU?
HE WAS VERY RUDE – AND SURE OF HIMSELF.
LOOK AT THE WAY HE TALKED TO ME – NO RESPECT – INSPECTORS AREN'T LIKE THAT.
IT DOESN'T MATTER NOW.
YES, IT DOES.
NO, SHEILA'S RIGHT.
YOU'RE THE ONE IT MATTERS MOST TO. YOU ADMITTED TO STEALING MONEY.
HE CAN ONLY MAKE THE REST OF US FEEL ASHAMED, BUT HE COULD RUIN YOU.
HE KNEW EVERYTHING ALREADY. WE DIDN'T TELL HIM A THING.
HE HAD A BIT OF INFORMATION AND MADE A FEW SMART GUESSES. THAT'S ALL.
IT'S YOUR FAULT FOR TELLING HIM SO MUCH.
HE MADE US CONFESS.

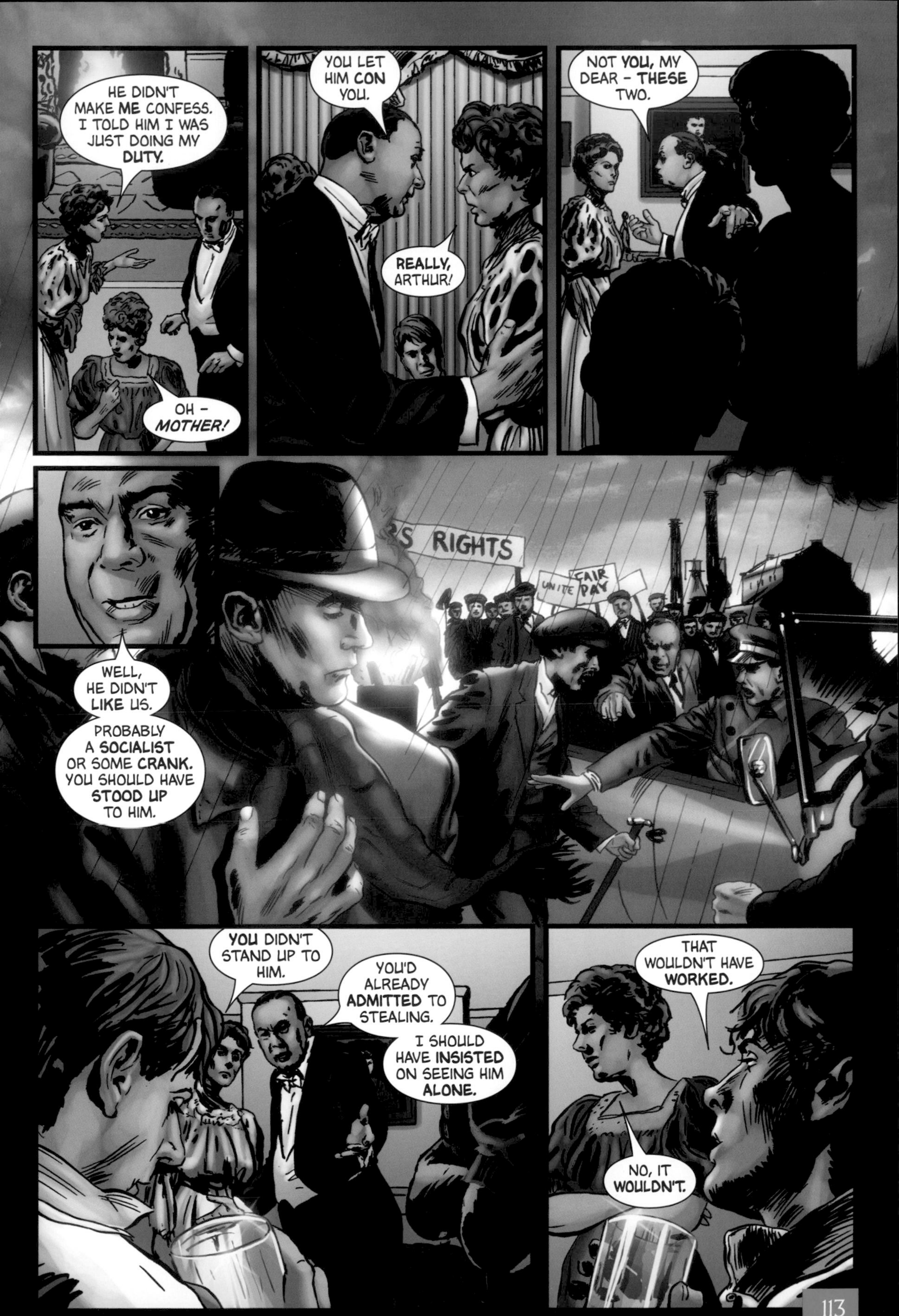
HE DIDN'T MAKE ME CONFESS. I TOLD HIM I WAS JUST DOING MY DUTY.
OH – MOTHER!
YOU LET HIM CON YOU.
REALLY, ARTHUR!
NOT YOU, MY DEAR – THESE TWO.
'S RIGHTS
UNITE
FAIR PAY
WELL, HE DIDN'T LIKE US.
PROBABLY A SOCIALIST OR SOME CRANK. YOU SHOULD HAVE STOOD UP TO HIM.
YOU DIDN'T STAND UP TO HIM.
YOU'D ALREADY ADMITTED TO STEALING.
I SHOULD HAVE INSISTED ON SEEING HIM ALONE.
THAT WOULDN'T HAVE WORKED.
NO, IT WOULDN'T.

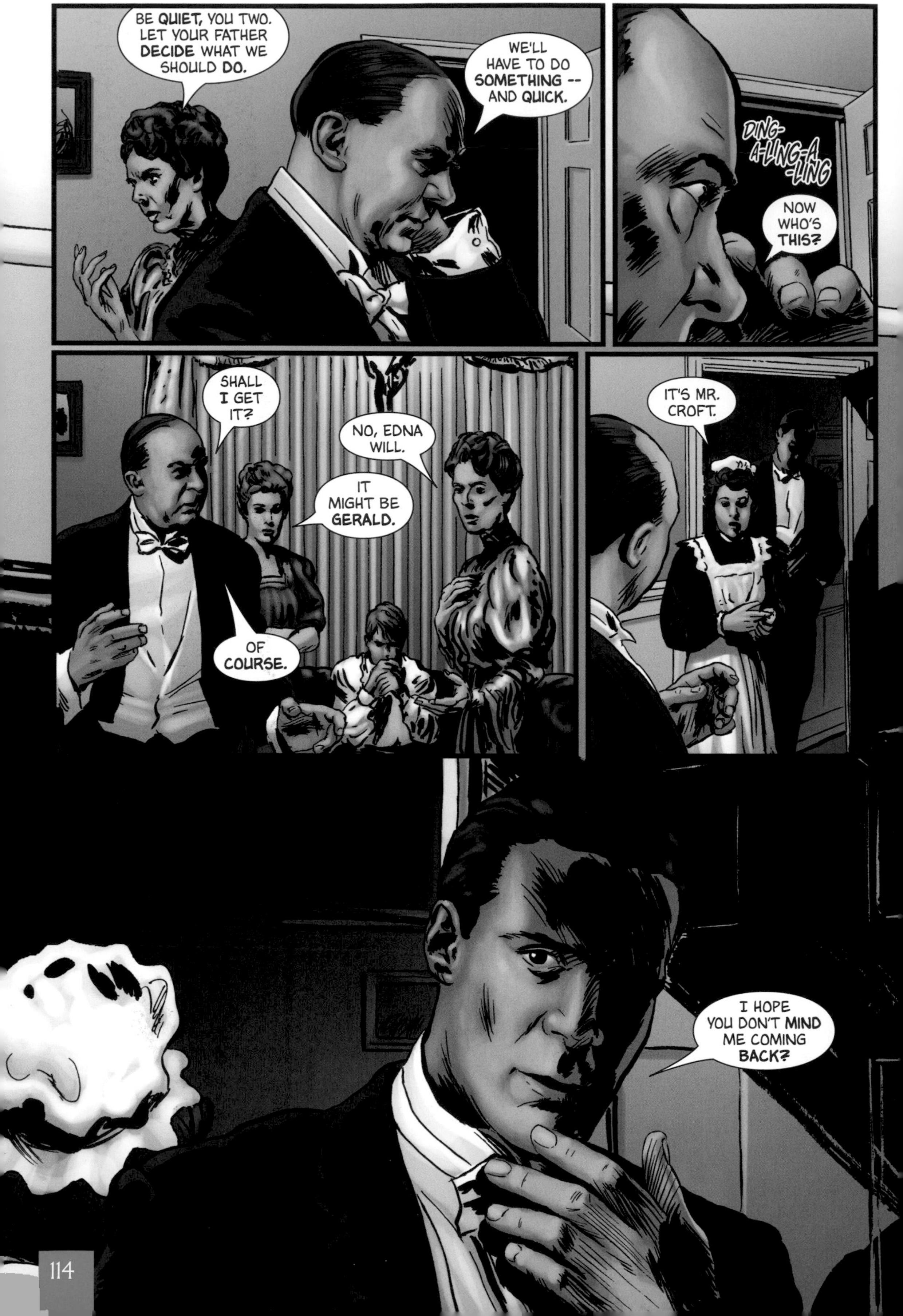
BE QUIET, YOU TWO. LET YOUR FATHER DECIDE WHAT WE SHOULD DO.
WE'LL HAVE TO DO SOMETHING -- AND QUICK.
DING-A-LING-A-LING
NOW WHO'S THIS?
SHALL I GET IT?
NO, EDNA WILL.
IT MIGHT BE GERALD.
OF COURSE.
IT'S MR. CROFT.
I HOPE YOU DON'T MIND ME COMING BACK?

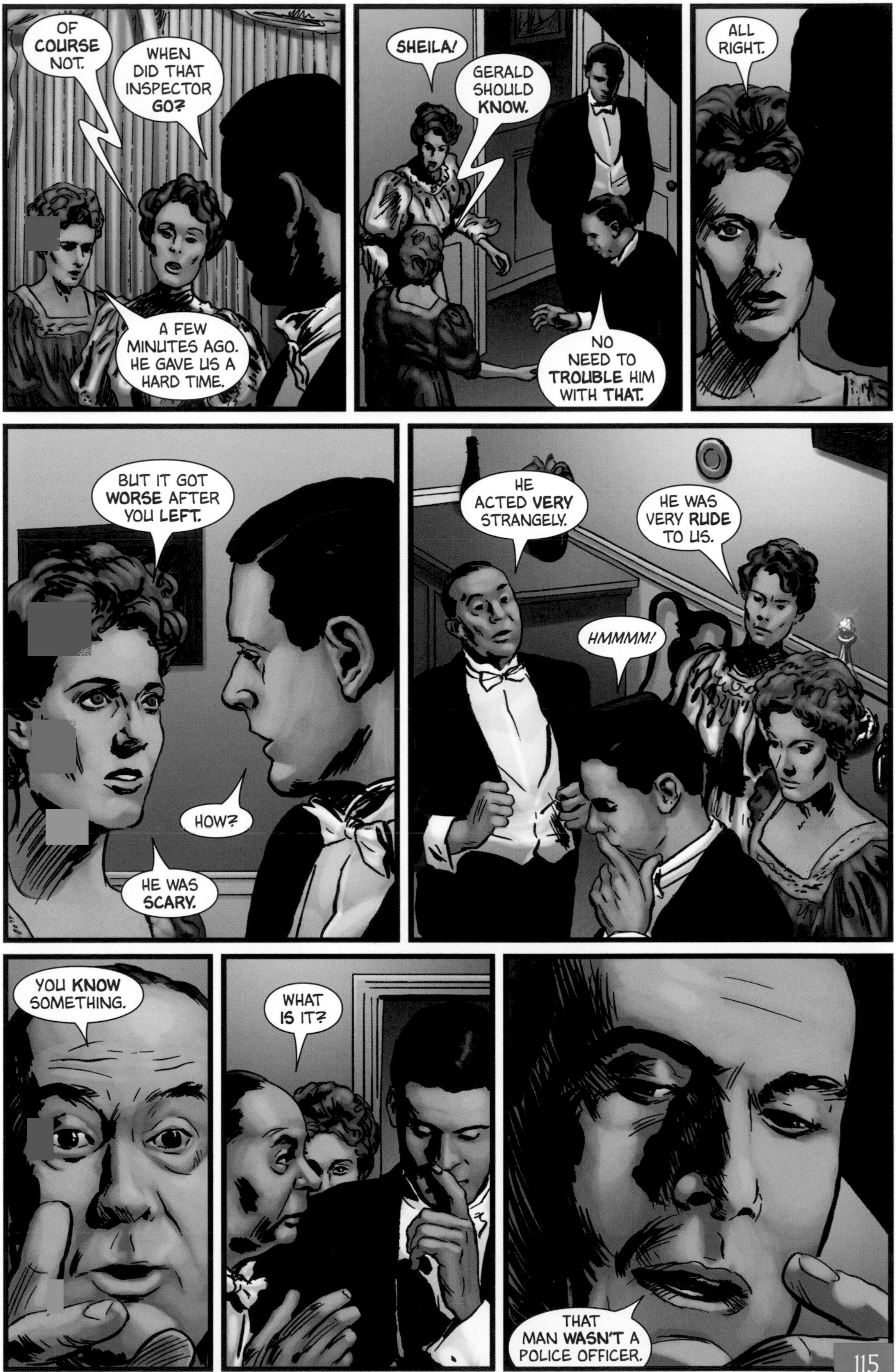
OF COURSE NOT.
WHEN DID THAT INSPECTOR GO?
A FEW MINUTES AGO. HE GAVE US A HARD TIME.
SHEILA!
GERALD SHOULD KNOW.
NO NEED TO TROUBLE HIM WITH THAT.
ALL RIGHT.
BUT IT GOT WORSE AFTER YOU LEFT.
HOW?
HE WAS SCARY.
HE ACTED VERY STRANGELY.
HE WAS VERY RUDE TO US.
HMMMM!
YOU KNOW SOMETHING.
WHAT IS IT?
THAT MAN WASN'T A POLICE OFFICER.

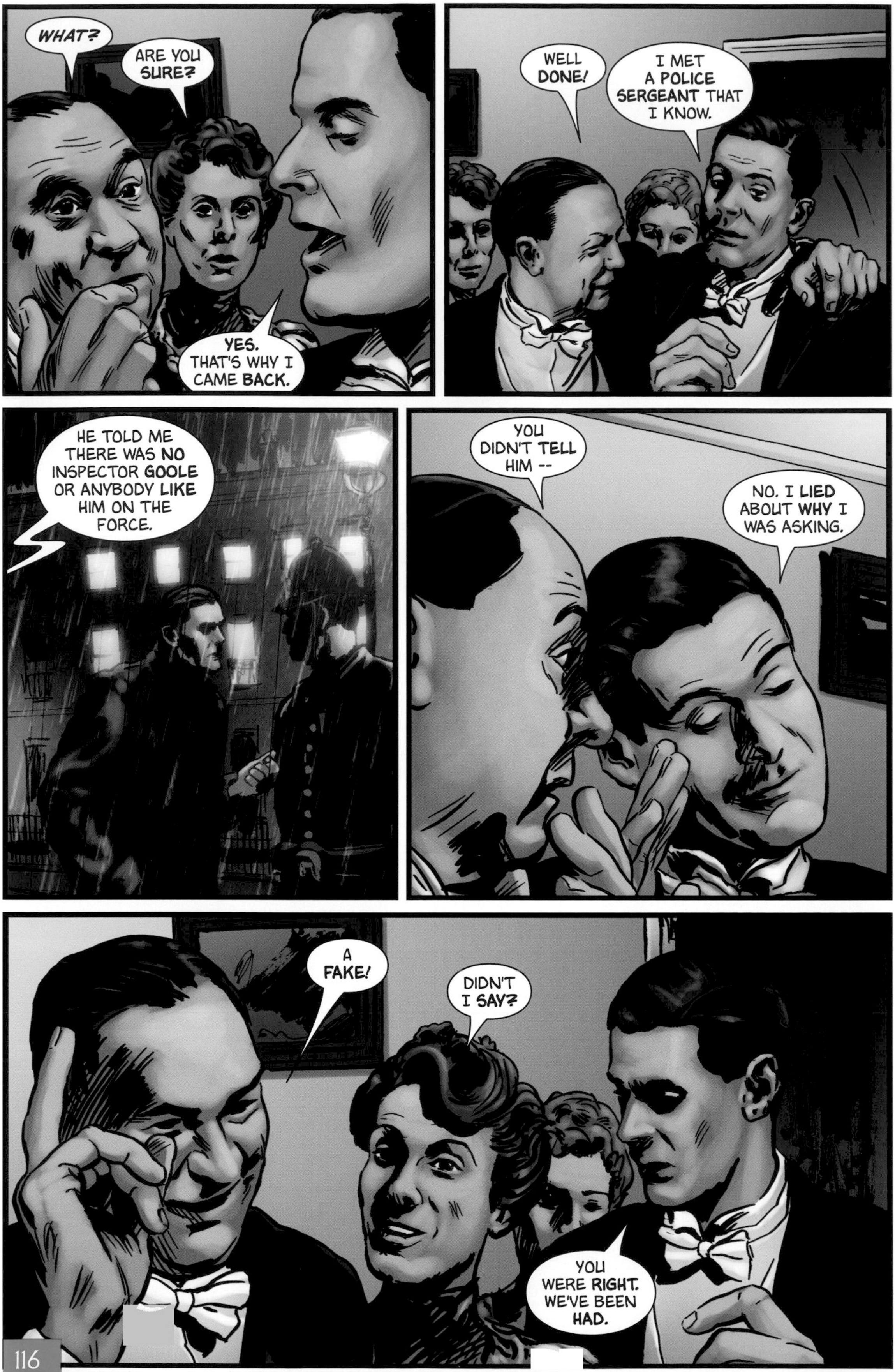
WHAT?
ARE YOU SURE?
YES. THAT'S WHY I CAME BACK.
WELL DONE!
I MET A POLICE SERGEANT THAT I KNOW.
HE TOLD ME THERE WAS NO INSPECTOR GOOLE OR ANYBODY LIKE HIM ON THE FORCE.
YOU DIDN'T TELL HIM --
NO. I LIED ABOUT WHY I WAS ASKING.
A FAKE!
DIDN'T I SAY?
YOU WERE RIGHT. WE'VE BEEN HAD.

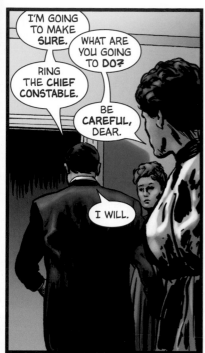

I'M GOING TO MAKE SURE.

WHAT ARE YOU GOING TO DO?

RING THE CHIEF CONSTABLE.

BE CAREFUL, DEAR.

I WILL.

BRUMLEY EIGHT SEVEN FIVE TWO.

I WAS GOING TO DO THIS ANYWAY.

COLONEL ROBERTS, PLEASE. MR. ARTHUR BIRLING HERE...

HELLO ROBERTS. SORRY TO CALL SO LATE, BUT CAN YOU TELL ME IF AN INSPECTOR GOOLE WORKS FOR YOU?

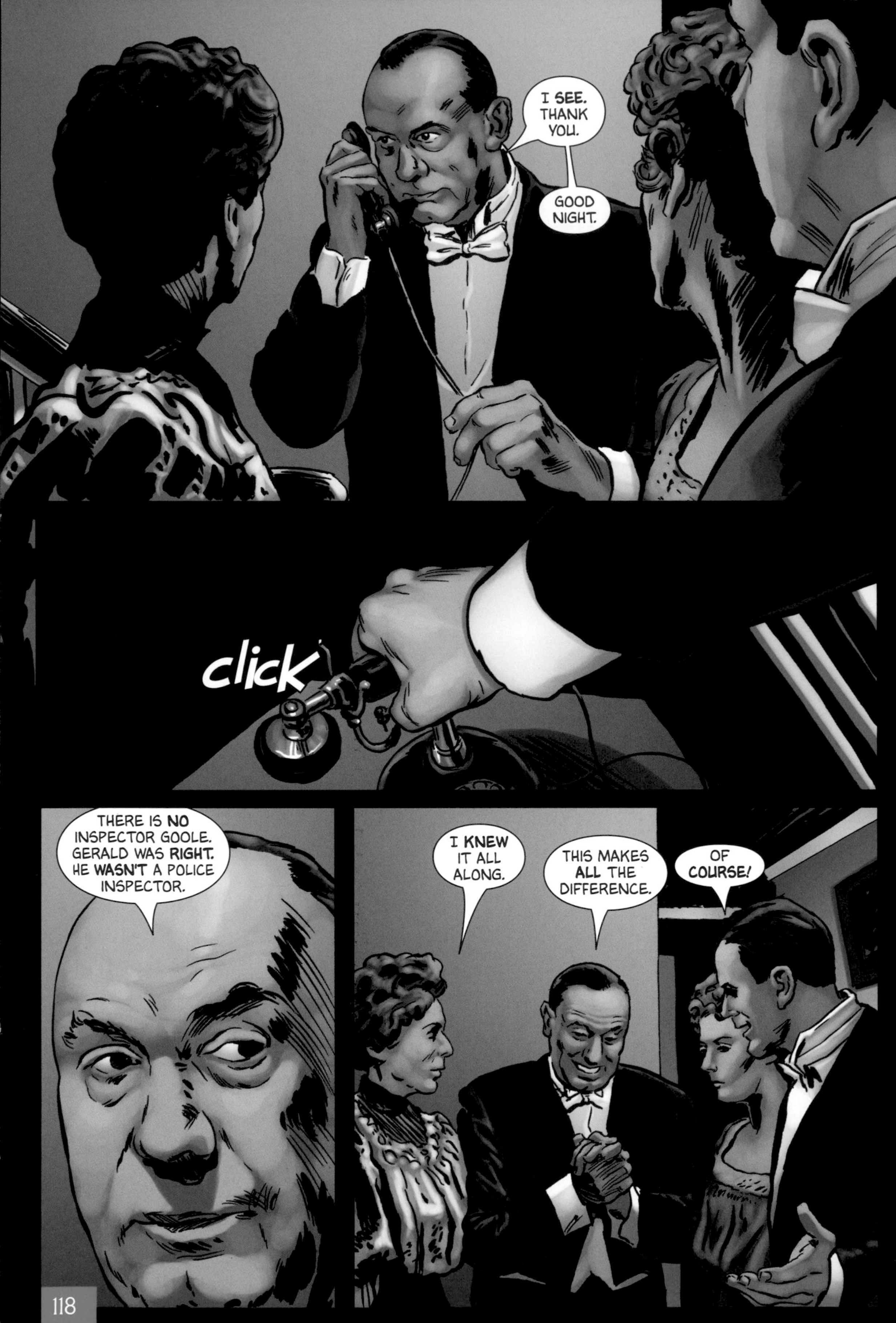
I SEE. THANK YOU.
GOOD NIGHT.
click
THERE IS NO INSPECTOR GOOLE. GERALD WAS RIGHT. HE WASN'T A POLICE INSPECTOR.
I KNEW IT ALL ALONG.
THIS MAKES ALL THE DIFFERENCE.
OF COURSE!

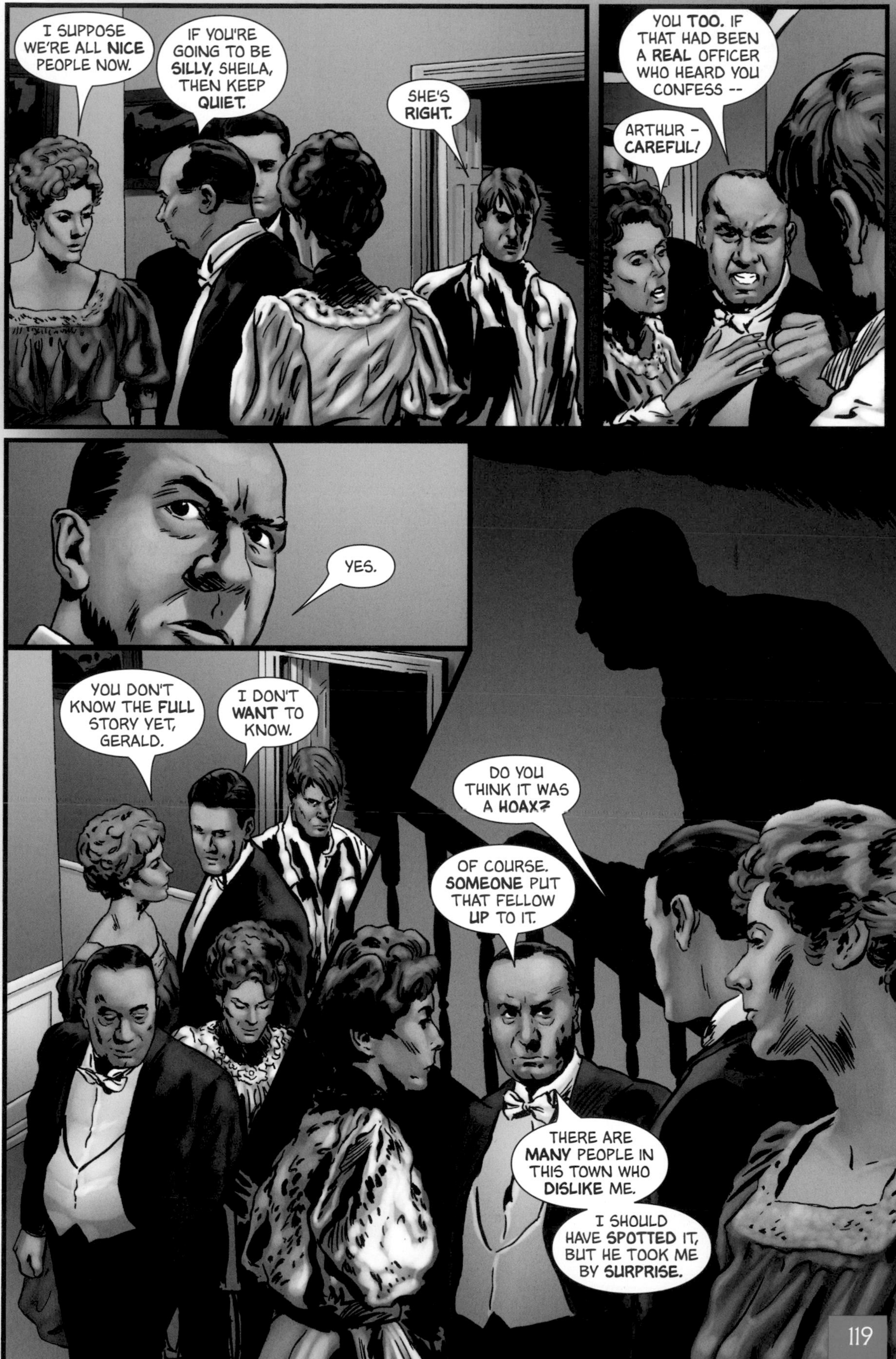
I SUPPOSE WE'RE ALL NICE PEOPLE NOW.
IF YOU'RE GOING TO BE SILLY, SHEILA, THEN KEEP QUIET.
SHE'S RIGHT.
YOU TOO. IF THAT HAD BEEN A REAL OFFICER WHO HEARD YOU CONFESS --
ARTHUR – CAREFUL!
YES.
YOU DON'T KNOW THE FULL STORY YET, GERALD.
I DON'T WANT TO KNOW.
DO YOU THINK IT WAS A HOAX?
OF COURSE. SOMEONE PUT THAT FELLOW UP TO IT.
THERE ARE MANY PEOPLE IN THIS TOWN WHO DISLIKE ME.
I SHOULD HAVE SPOTTED IT, BUT HE TOOK ME BY SURPRISE.

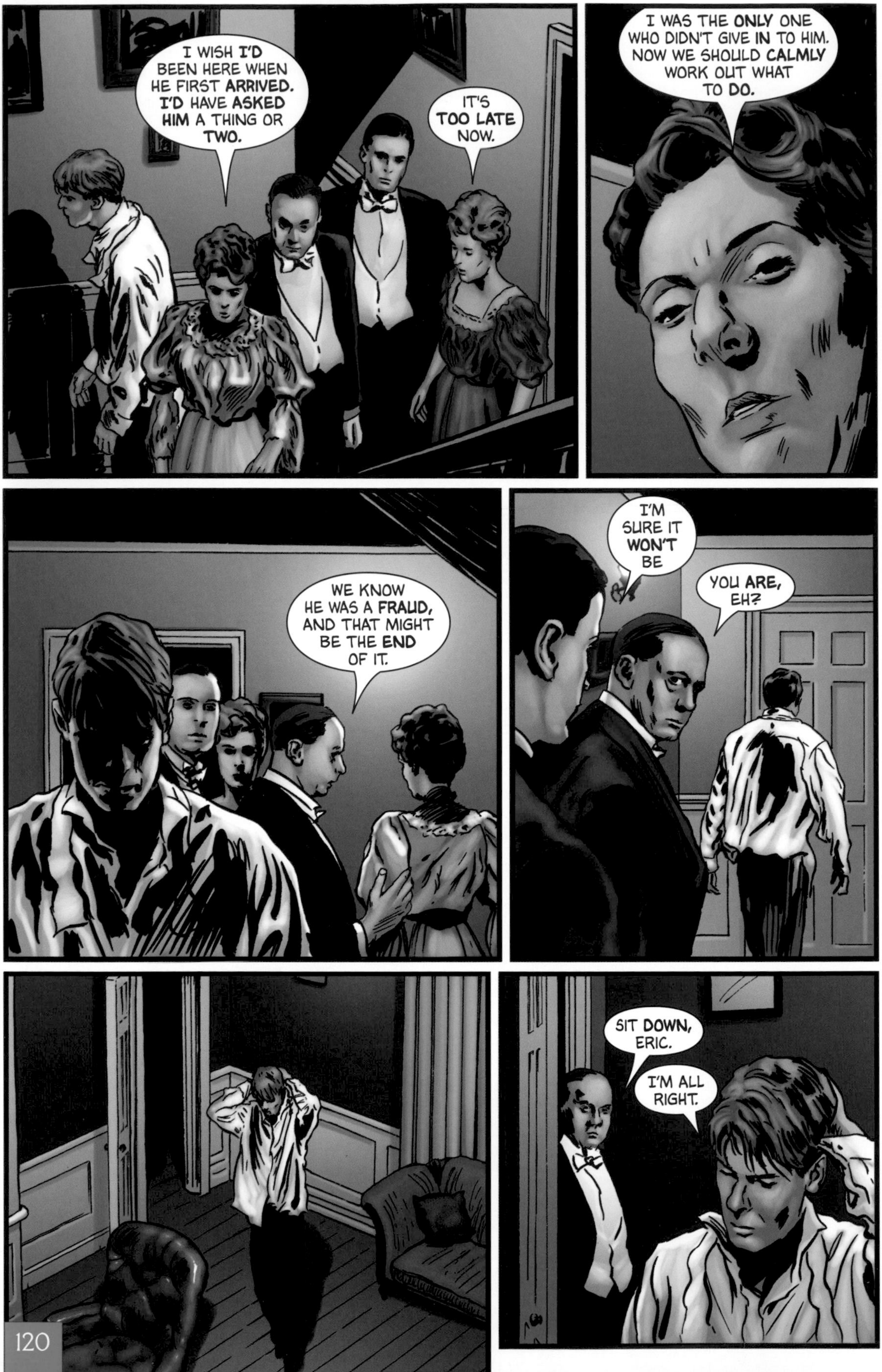
I WISH I'D BEEN HERE WHEN HE FIRST ARRIVED. I'D HAVE ASKED HIM A THING OR TWO.
IT'S TOO LATE NOW.
I WAS THE ONLY ONE WHO DIDN'T GIVE IN TO HIM. NOW WE SHOULD CALMLY WORK OUT WHAT TO DO.
WE KNOW HE WAS A FRAUD, AND THAT MIGHT BE THE END OF IT.
I'M SURE IT WON'T BE
YOU ARE, EH?
SIT DOWN, ERIC.
I'M ALL RIGHT.

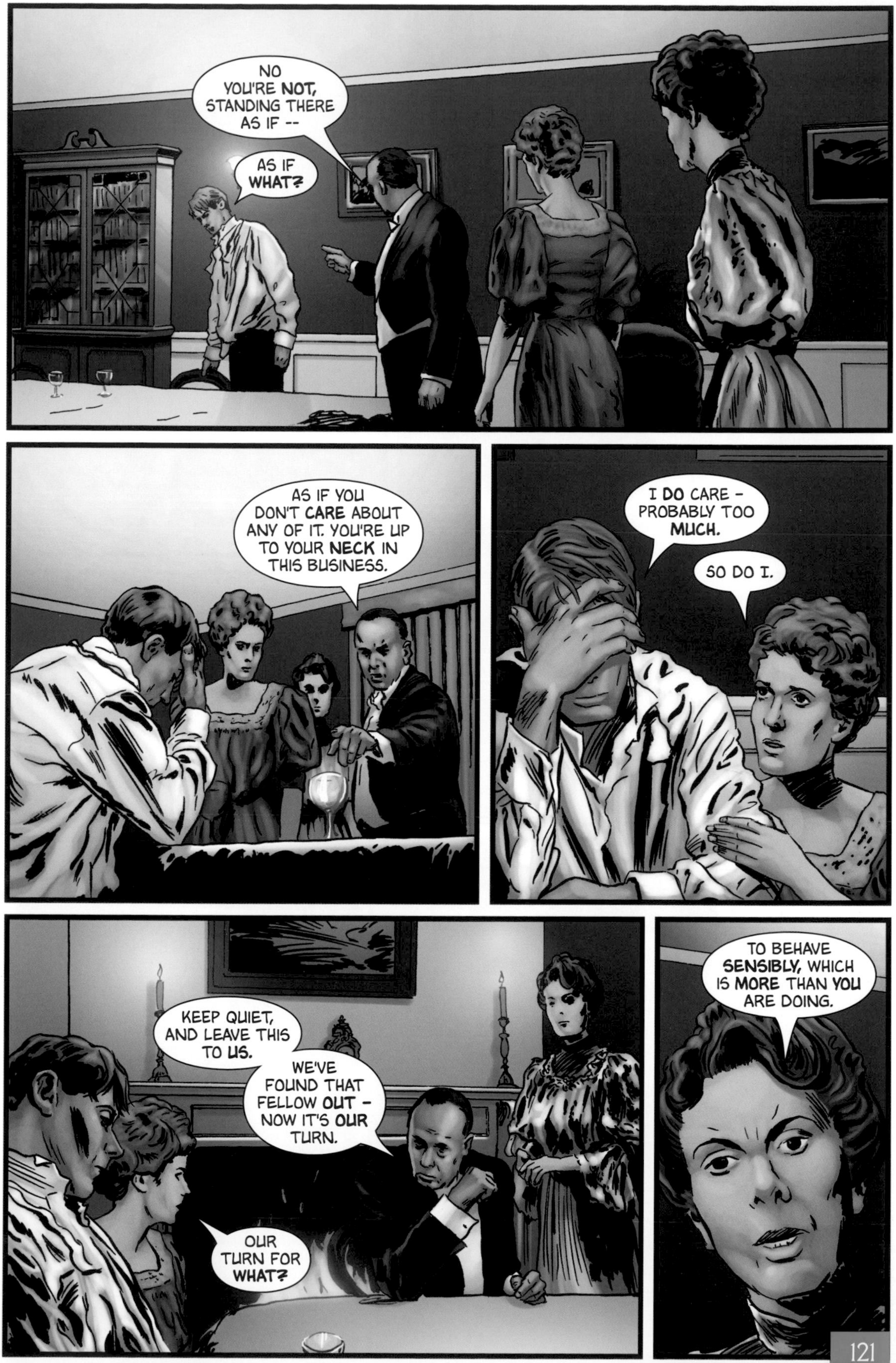
NO YOU'RE NOT, STANDING THERE AS IF --
AS IF WHAT?
AS IF YOU DON'T CARE ABOUT ANY OF IT. YOU'RE UP TO YOUR NECK IN THIS BUSINESS.
I DO CARE - PROBABLY TOO MUCH.
SO DO I.
KEEP QUIET, AND LEAVE THIS TO US.
WE'VE FOUND THAT FELLOW OUT - NOW IT'S OUR TURN.
OUR TURN FOR WHAT?
TO BEHAVE SENSIBLY, WHICH IS MORE THAN YOU ARE DOING.

YOU'RE PRETENDING EVERYTHING IS ALL RIGHT.
BUT THIS GIRL IS STILL DEAD. NOBODY HAS BROUGHT HER BACK TO LIFE.
THAT'S HOW I FEEL, ERIC.
SLAM
WHOEVER HE WAS, WE'RE ALL STILL GUILTY OF WHAT WE DID.
SLAM
I STOLE SOME MONEY, GERALD.
LET HIM KNOW. THE MONEY ISN'T IMPORTANT – IT'S WHAT HAPPENED TO THE GIRL THAT MATTERS.
ERIC'S RIGHT. YOU'RE ALL JUST PRETENDING AGAIN.

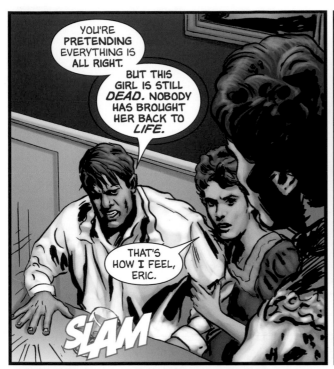

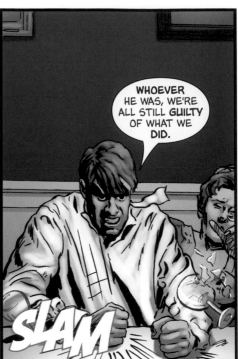

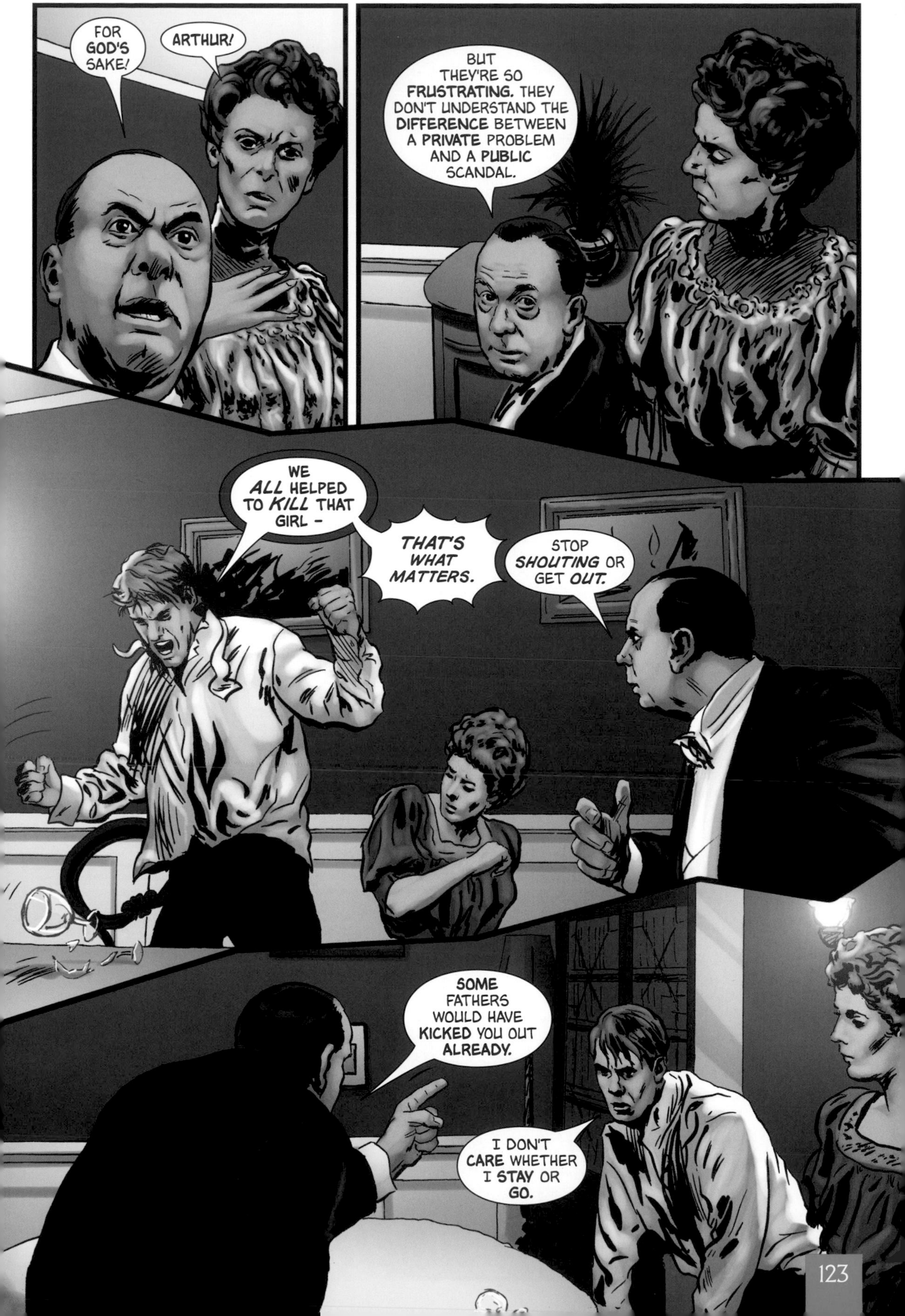
FOR GOD'S SAKE!
ARTHUR!
BUT THEY'RE SO FRUSTRATING. THEY DON'T UNDERSTAND THE DIFFERENCE BETWEEN A PRIVATE PROBLEM AND A PUBLIC SCANDAL.
WE ALL HELPED TO KILL THAT GIRL -
THAT'S WHAT MATTERS.
STOP SHOUTING OR GET OUT.
SOME FATHERS WOULD HAVE KICKED YOU OUT ALREADY.
I DON'T CARE WHETHER I STAY OR GO.

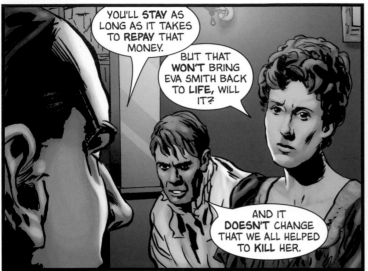

YOU'LL **STAY** AS LONG AS IT TAKES TO **REPAY** THAT MONEY.

BUT THAT **WON'T** BRING EVA SMITH BACK TO **LIFE**, WILL IT?

AND IT **DOESN'T** CHANGE THAT WE ALL HELPED TO **KILL** HER.

DID WE?

OF COURSE.

ARE YOU GOING TO **TELL** ME YOU **DIDN'T** KEEP A GIRL LAST SUMMER?

I ADMIT I **DID** – AND I'M **SORRY**, SHEILA.

WELL, THE INSPECTOR SAID YOU CAME OUT OF THIS **BETTER** THAN THE **REST** OF US.

HE **WASN'T** AN INSPECTOR!

WELL HE INSPECTED **US** ALL RIGHT – AND **BETWEEN** US WE **MADE** THAT GIRL **KILL** HERSELF.

WHO **SAYS** SO? THERE'S NO **EVIDENCE**.

YES THERE IS.

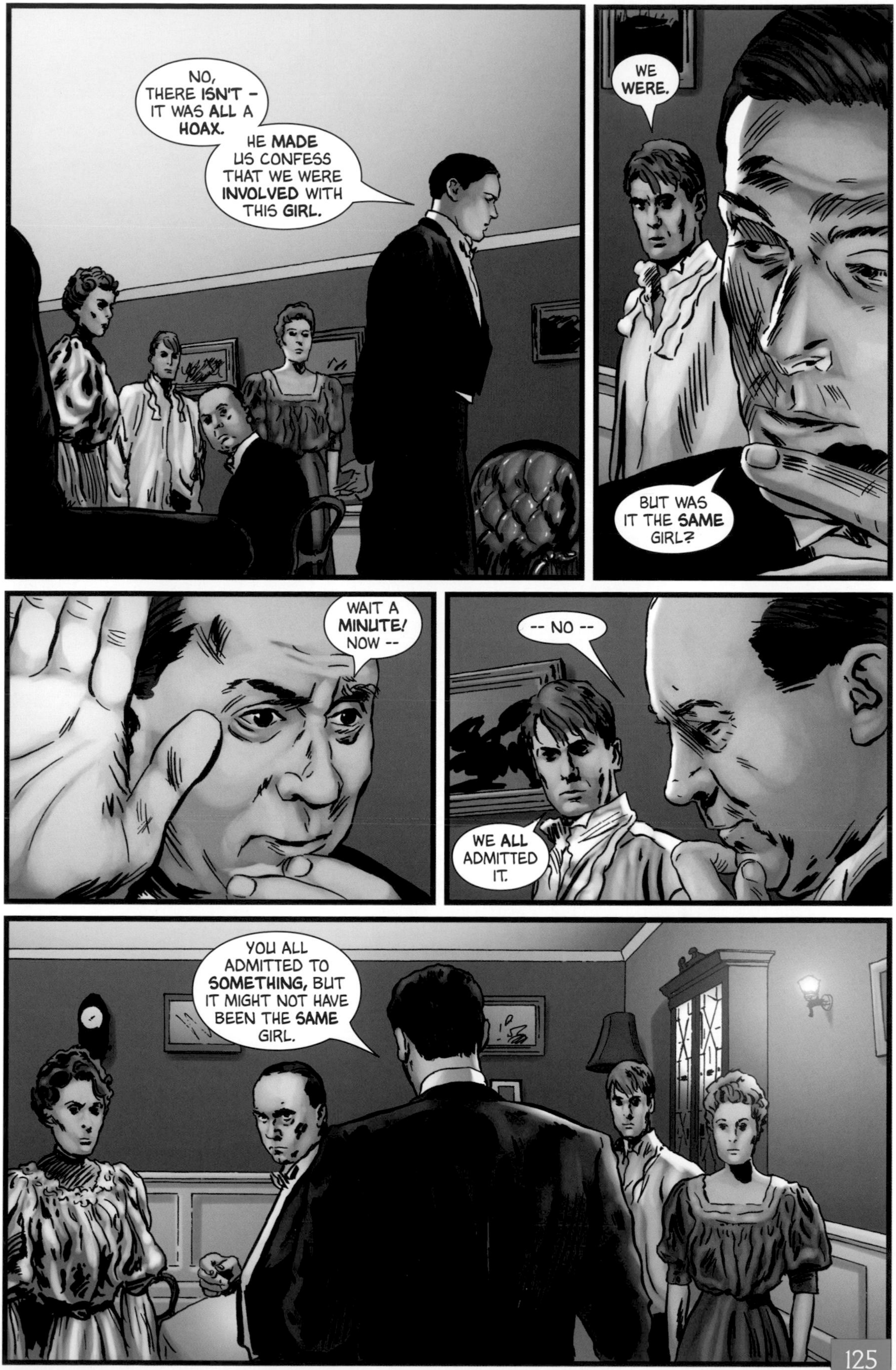
NO, THERE ISN'T - IT WAS ALL A HOAX.
HE MADE US CONFESS THAT WE WERE INVOLVED WITH THIS GIRL.
WE WERE.
BUT WAS IT THE SAME GIRL?
WAIT A MINUTE! NOW --
-- NO --
WE ALL ADMITTED IT.
YOU ALL ADMITTED TO SOMETHING, BUT IT MIGHT NOT HAVE BEEN THE SAME GIRL.

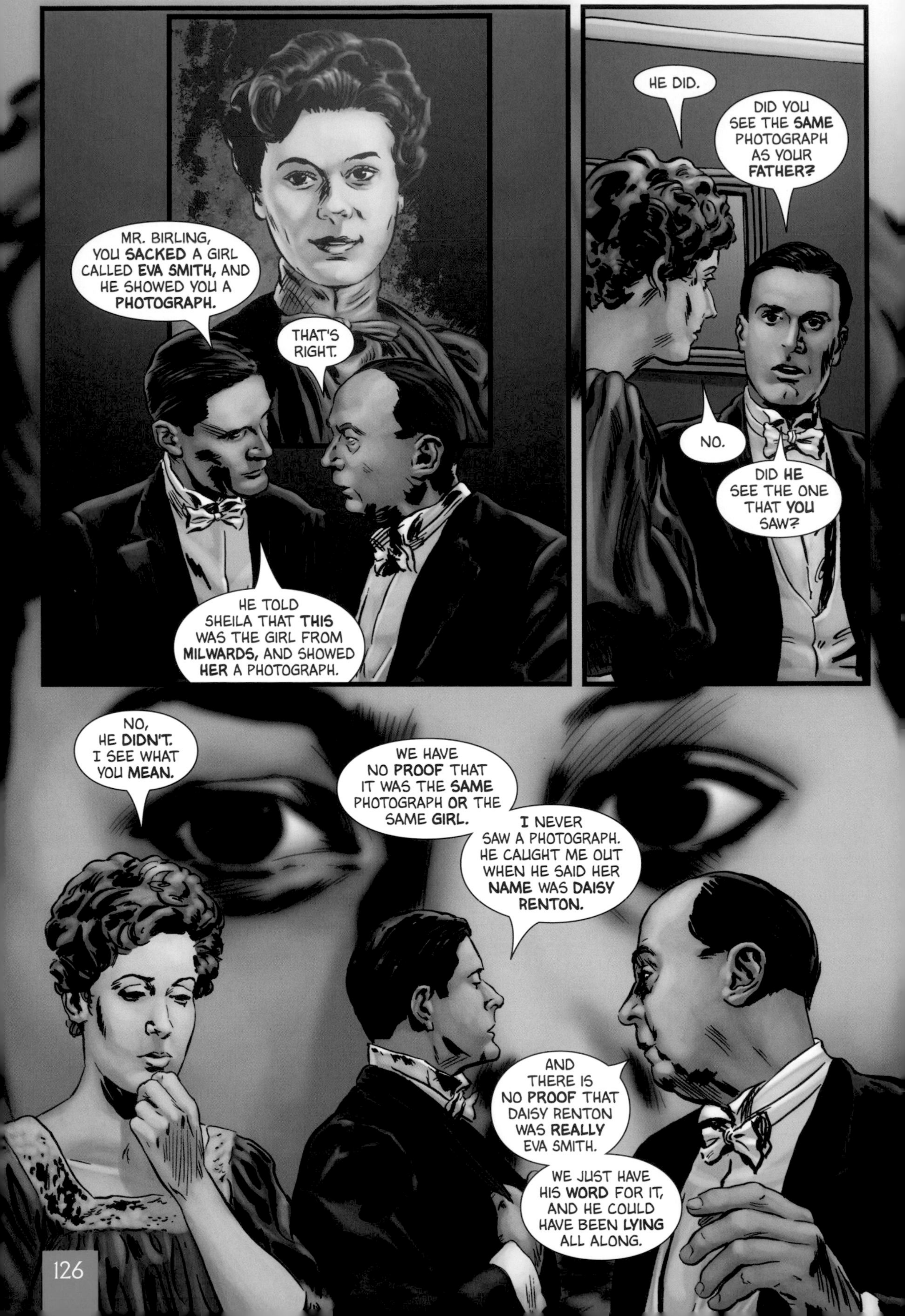
MR. BIRLING, YOU SACKED A GIRL CALLED EVA SMITH, AND HE SHOWED YOU A PHOTOGRAPH.
THAT'S RIGHT.
HE TOLD SHEILA THAT THIS WAS THE GIRL FROM MILWARDS, AND SHOWED HER A PHOTOGRAPH.
HE DID.
DID YOU SEE THE SAME PHOTOGRAPH AS YOUR FATHER?
NO.
DID HE SEE THE ONE THAT YOU SAW?
NO, HE DIDN'T. I SEE WHAT YOU MEAN.
WE HAVE NO PROOF THAT IT WAS THE SAME PHOTOGRAPH OR THE SAME GIRL.
I NEVER SAW A PHOTOGRAPH. HE CAUGHT ME OUT WHEN HE SAID HER NAME WAS DAISY RENTON.
AND THERE IS NO PROOF THAT DAISY RENTON WAS REALLY EVA SMITH.
WE JUST HAVE HIS WORD FOR IT, AND HE COULD HAVE BEEN LYING ALL ALONG.

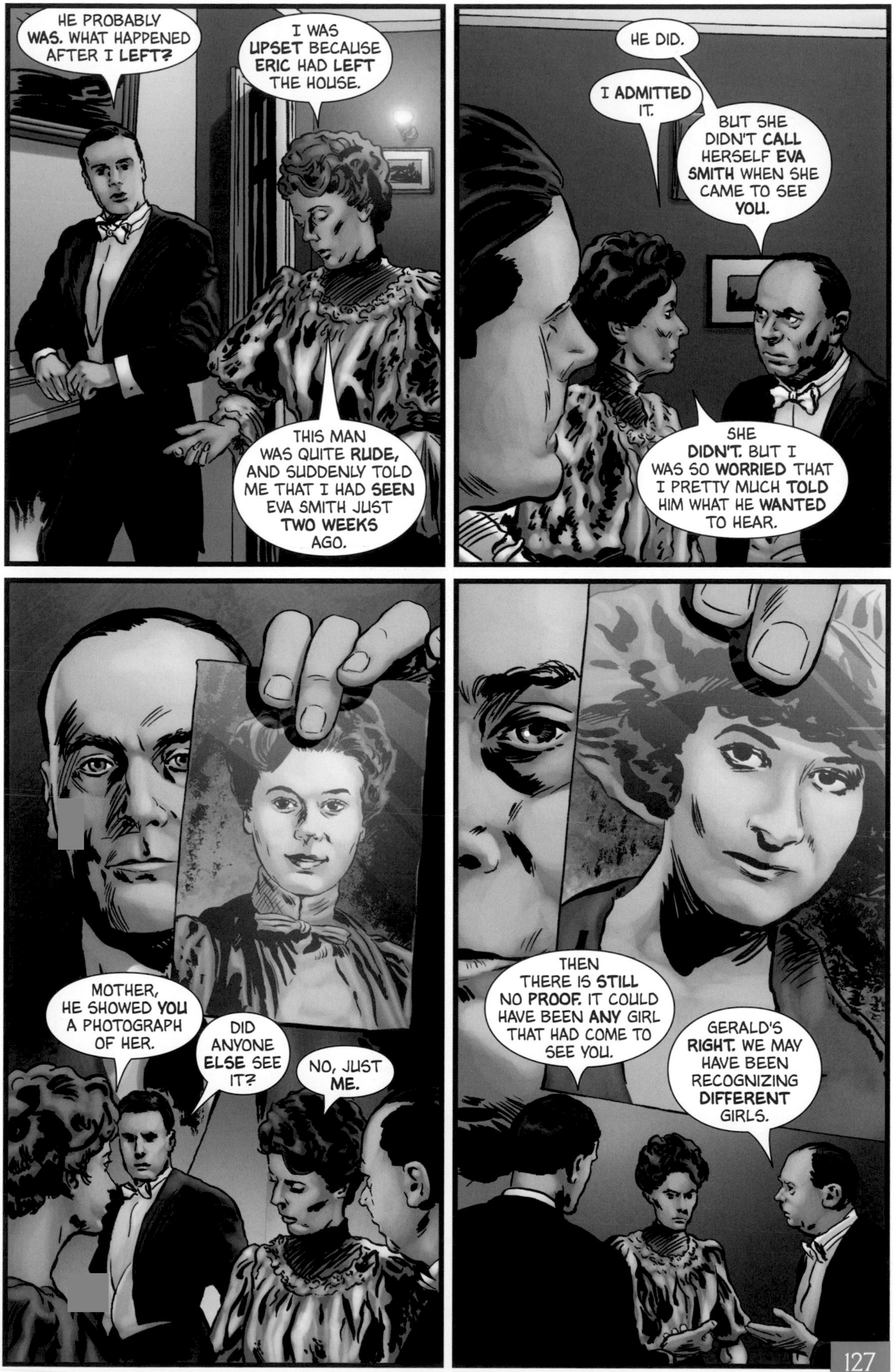
HE PROBABLY WAS. WHAT HAPPENED AFTER I LEFT?
I WAS UPSET BECAUSE ERIC HAD LEFT THE HOUSE.
THIS MAN WAS QUITE RUDE, AND SUDDENLY TOLD ME THAT I HAD SEEN EVA SMITH JUST TWO WEEKS AGO.
HE DID.
I ADMITTED IT.
BUT SHE DIDN'T CALL HERSELF EVA SMITH WHEN SHE CAME TO SEE YOU.
SHE DIDN'T. BUT I WAS SO WORRIED THAT I PRETTY MUCH TOLD HIM WHAT HE WANTED TO HEAR.
MOTHER, HE SHOWED YOU A PHOTOGRAPH OF HER.
DID ANYONE ELSE SEE IT?
NO, JUST ME.
THEN THERE IS STILL NO PROOF. IT COULD HAVE BEEN ANY GIRL THAT HAD COME TO SEE YOU.
GERALD'S RIGHT. WE MAY HAVE BEEN RECOGNIZING DIFFERENT GIRLS.

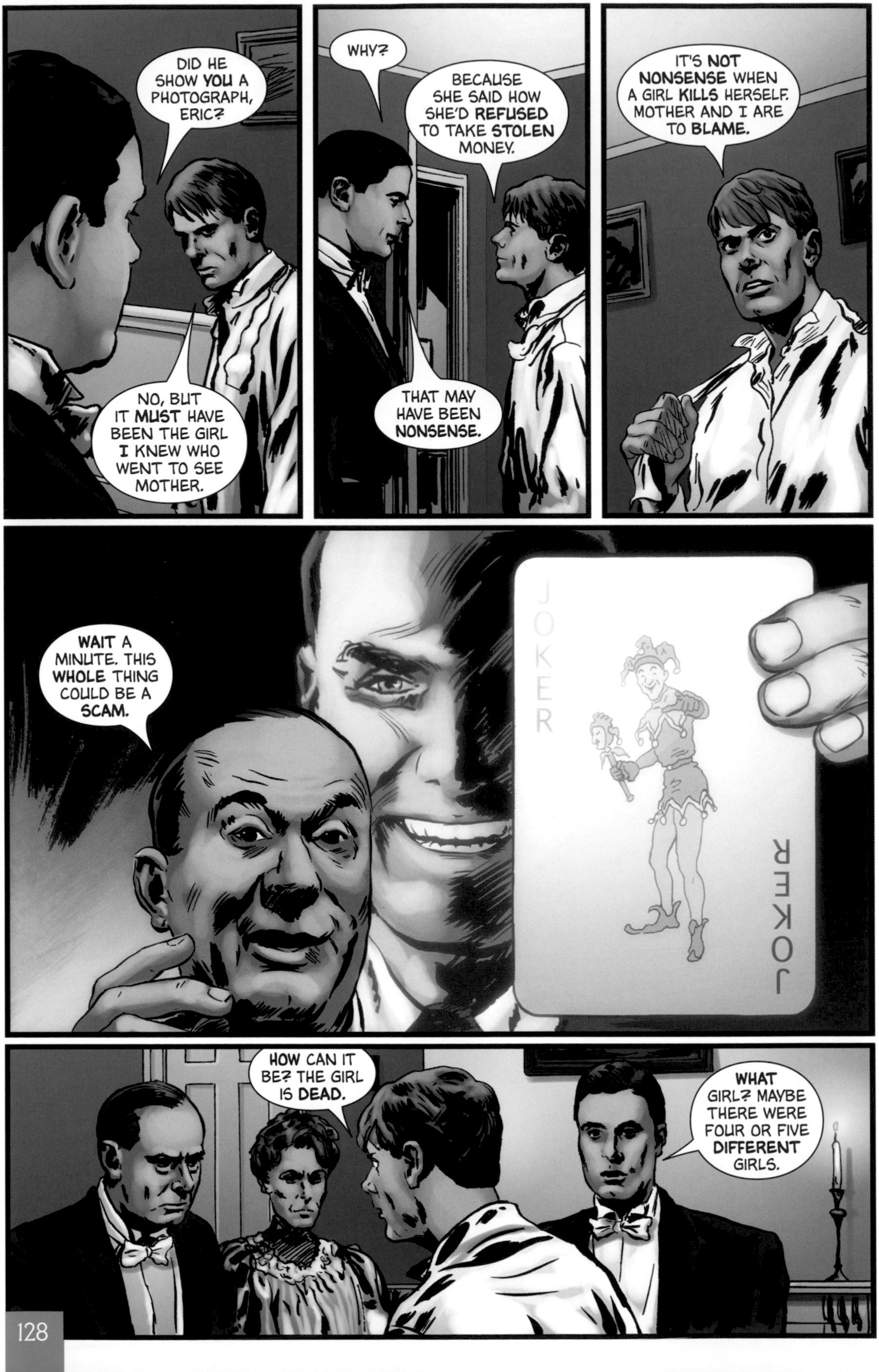
DID HE SHOW YOU A PHOTOGRAPH, ERIC?
NO, BUT IT MUST HAVE BEEN THE GIRL I KNEW WHO WENT TO SEE MOTHER.
WHY?
BECAUSE SHE SAID HOW SHE'D REFUSED TO TAKE STOLEN MONEY.
THAT MAY HAVE BEEN NONSENSE.
IT'S NOT NONSENSE WHEN A GIRL KILLS HERSELF. MOTHER AND I ARE TO BLAME.
WAIT A MINUTE. THIS WHOLE THING COULD BE A SCAM.
JOKER
JOKER
HOW CAN IT BE? THE GIRL IS DEAD.
WHAT GIRL? MAYBE THERE WERE FOUR OR FIVE DIFFERENT GIRLS.

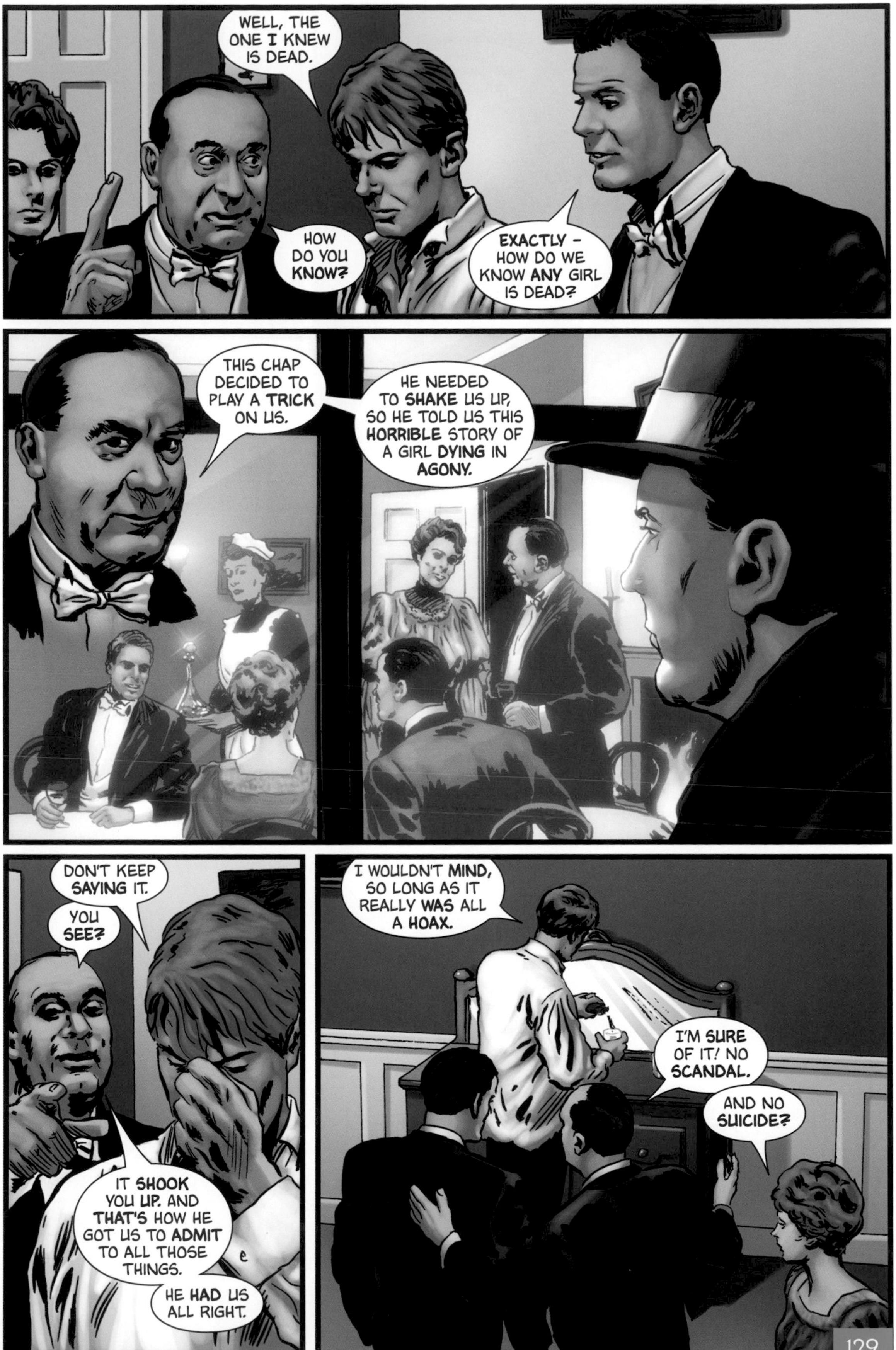
WELL, THE ONE I KNEW IS DEAD.
HOW DO YOU KNOW?
EXACTLY – HOW DO WE KNOW ANY GIRL IS DEAD?
THIS CHAP DECIDED TO PLAY A TRICK ON US.
HE NEEDED TO SHAKE US UP, SO HE TOLD US THIS HORRIBLE STORY OF A GIRL DYING IN AGONY.
DON'T KEEP SAYING IT.
YOU SEE?
IT SHOOK YOU UP. AND THAT'S HOW HE GOT US TO ADMIT TO ALL THOSE THINGS.
HE HAD US ALL RIGHT.
I WOULDN'T MIND, SO LONG AS IT REALLY WAS ALL A HOAX.
I'M SURE OF IT! NO SCANDAL.
AND NO SUICIDE?

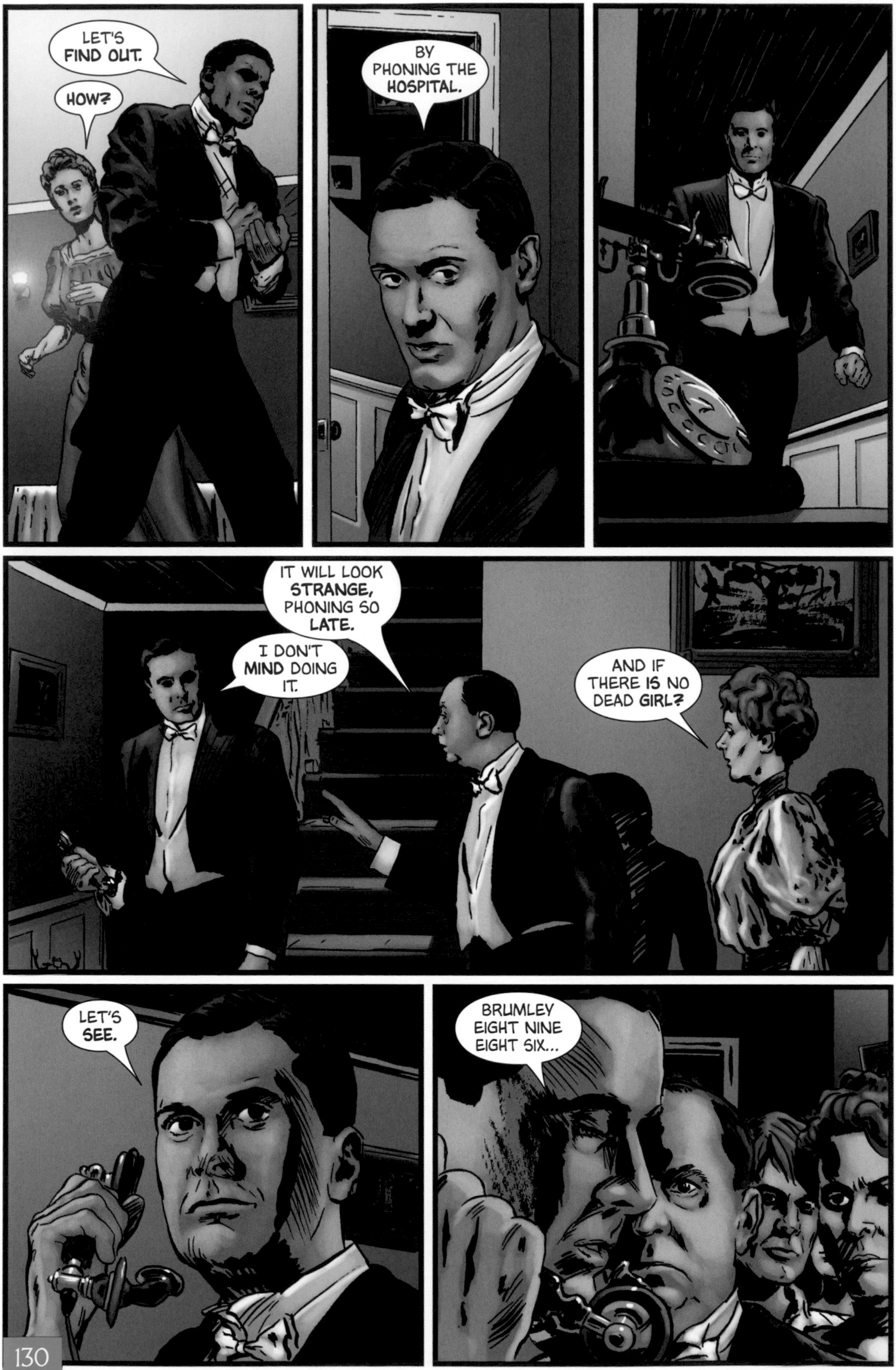
LET'S FIND OUT.
HOW?
BY PHONING THE HOSPITAL.
IT WILL LOOK STRANGE, PHONING SO LATE.
I DON'T MIND DOING IT.
AND IF THERE IS NO DEAD GIRL?
LET'S SEE.
BRUMLEY EIGHT NINE EIGHT SIX...

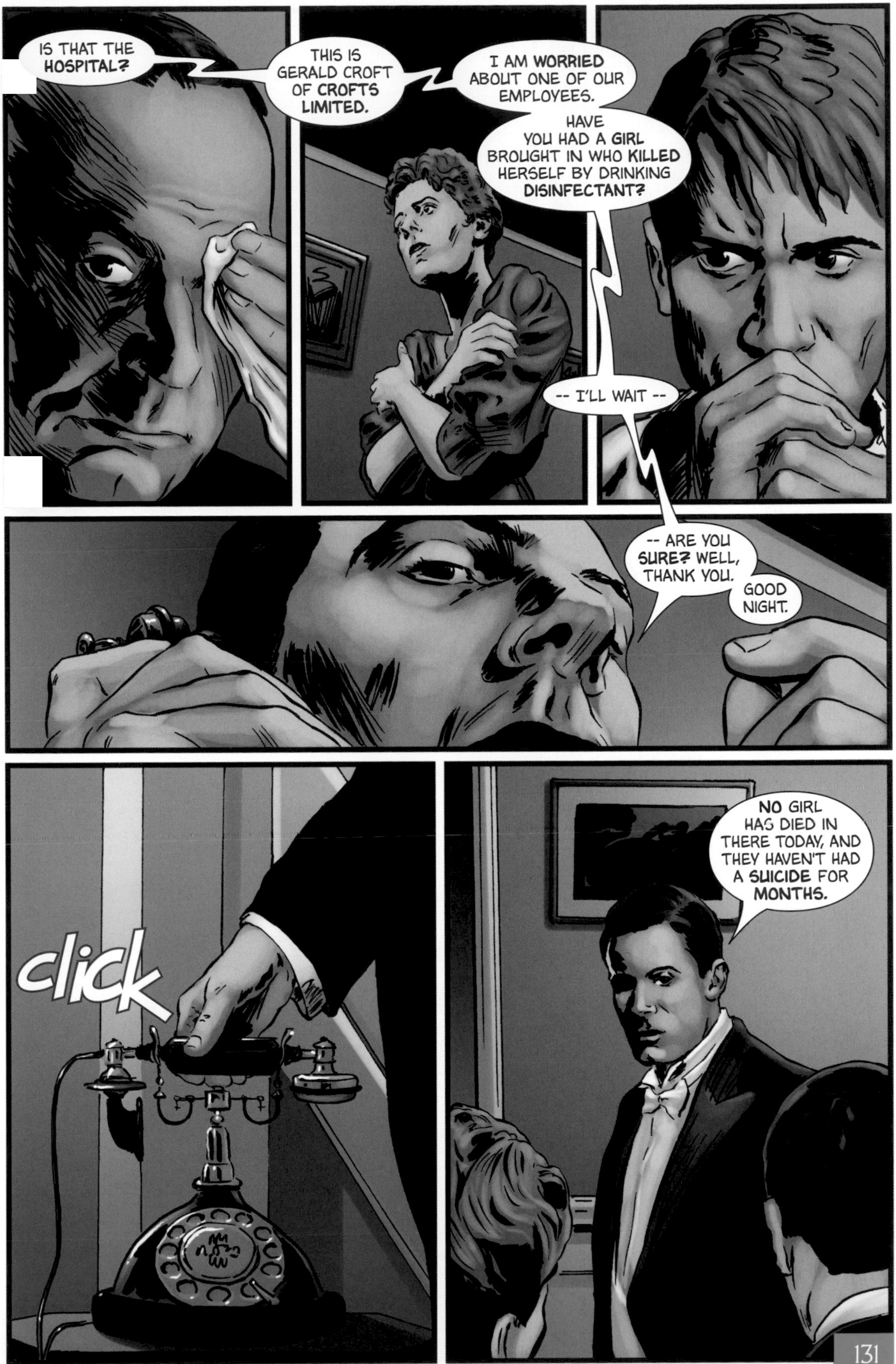
IS THAT THE HOSPITAL?
THIS IS GERALD CROFT OF CROFTS LIMITED.
I AM WORRIED ABOUT ONE OF OUR EMPLOYEES.
HAVE YOU HAD A GIRL BROUGHT IN WHO KILLED HERSELF BY DRINKING DISINFECTANT?
-- I'LL WAIT --
-- ARE YOU SURE? WELL, THANK YOU.
GOOD NIGHT.
click
NO GIRL HAS DIED IN THERE TODAY, AND THEY HAVEN'T HAD A SUICIDE FOR MONTHS.

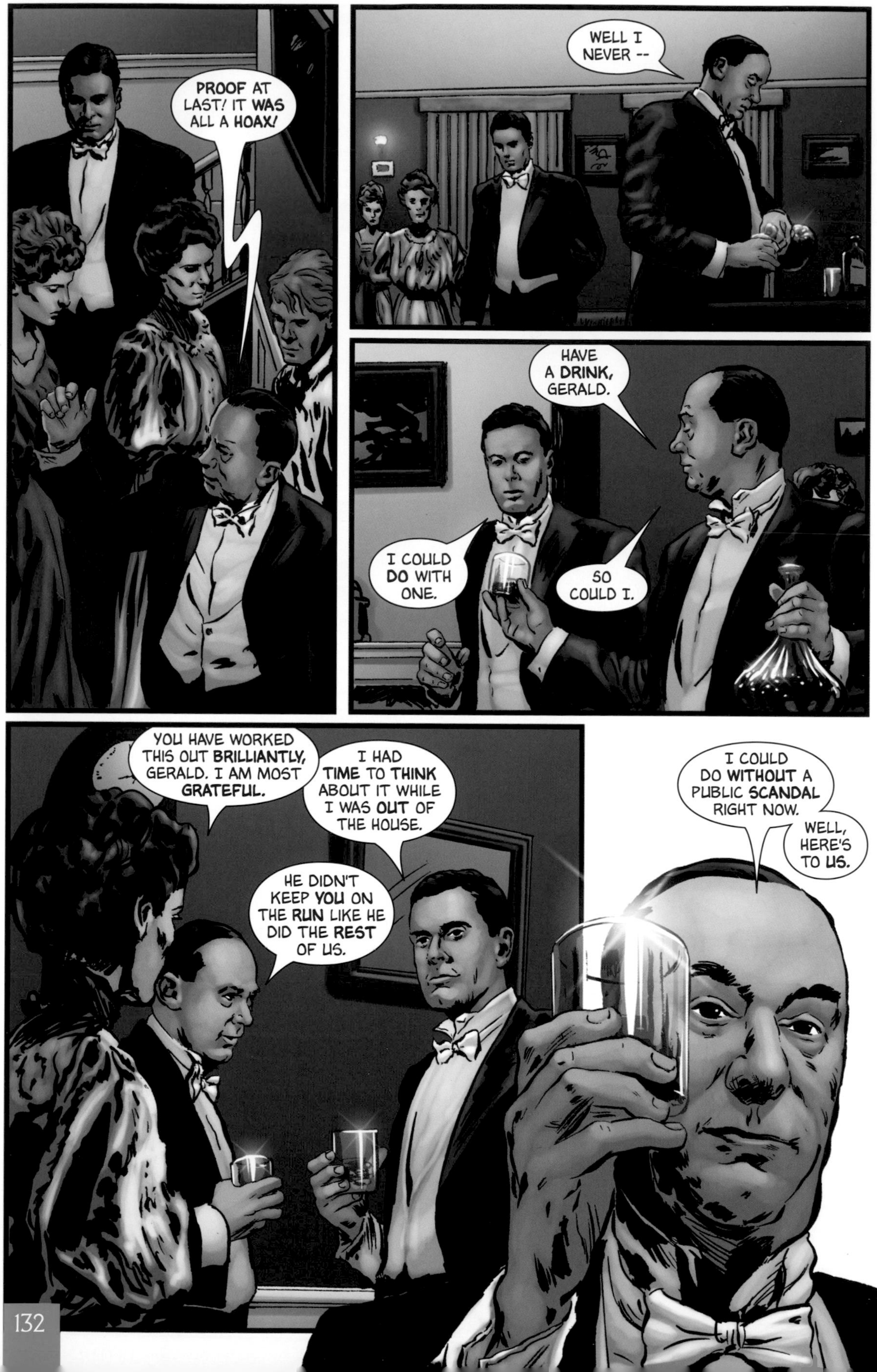
PROOF AT LAST! IT WAS ALL A HOAX!
WELL I NEVER --
HAVE A DRINK, GERALD.
I COULD DO WITH ONE.
SO COULD I.
YOU HAVE WORKED THIS OUT BRILLIANTLY, GERALD. I AM MOST GRATEFUL.
I HAD TIME TO THINK ABOUT IT WHILE I WAS OUT OF THE HOUSE.
HE DIDN'T KEEP YOU ON THE RUN LIKE HE DID THE REST OF US.
I COULD DO WITHOUT A PUBLIC SCANDAL RIGHT NOW.
WELL, HERE'S TO US.

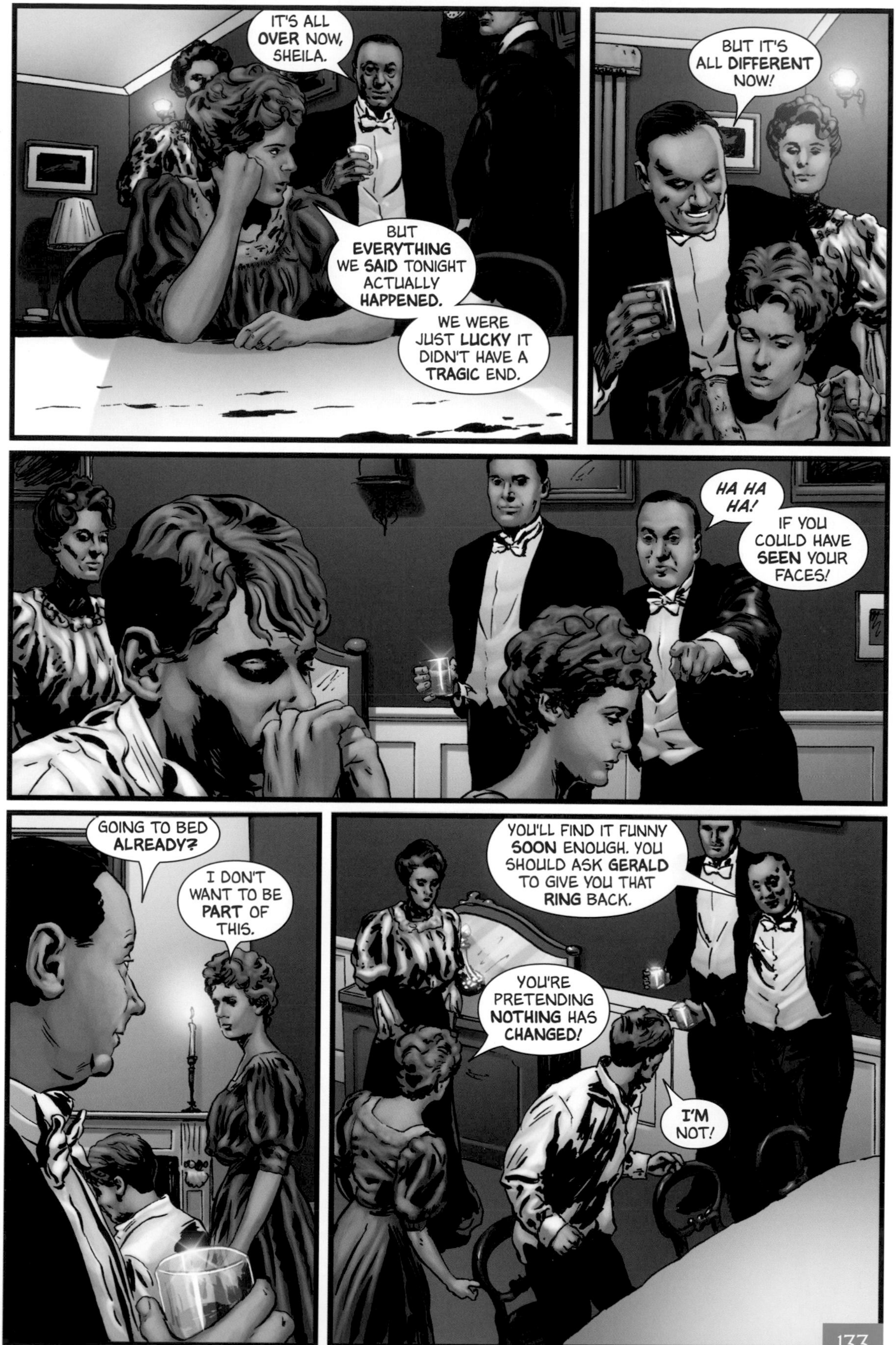
IT'S ALL OVER NOW, SHEILA.
BUT EVERYTHING WE SAID TONIGHT ACTUALLY HAPPENED.
WE WERE JUST LUCKY IT DIDN'T HAVE A TRAGIC END.
BUT IT'S ALL DIFFERENT NOW!
HA HA HA!
IF YOU COULD HAVE SEEN YOUR FACES!
GOING TO BED ALREADY?
I DON'T WANT TO BE PART OF THIS.
YOU'LL FIND IT FUNNY SOON ENOUGH. YOU SHOULD ASK GERALD TO GIVE YOU THAT RING BACK.
YOU'RE PRETENDING NOTHING HAS CHANGED!
I'M NOT!

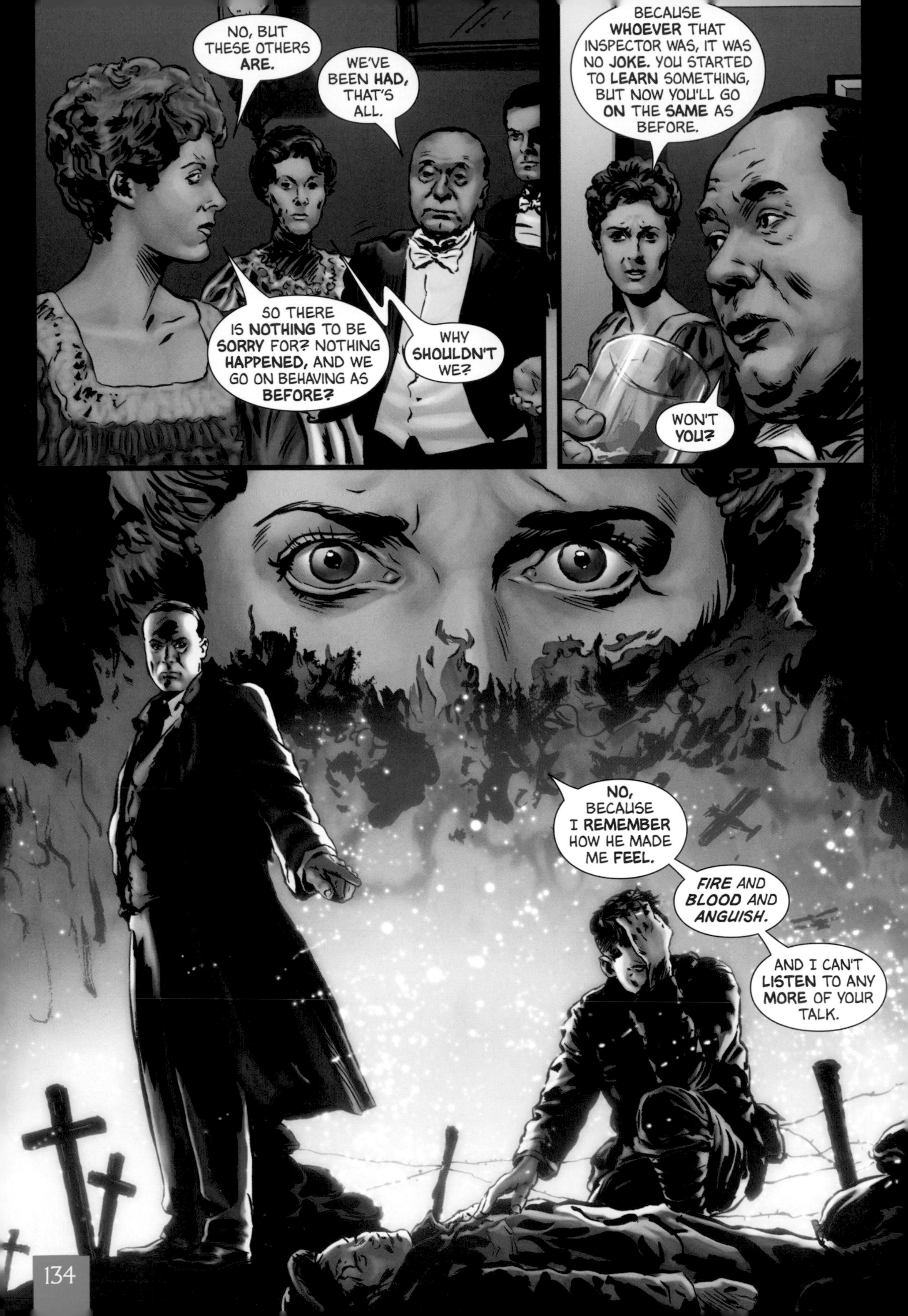
NO, BUT THESE OTHERS ARE.
WE'VE BEEN HAD, THAT'S ALL.
SO THERE IS NOTHING TO BE SORRY FOR? NOTHING HAPPENED, AND WE GO ON BEHAVING AS BEFORE?
WHY SHOULDN'T WE?
BECAUSE WHOEVER THAT INSPECTOR WAS, IT WAS NO JOKE. YOU STARTED TO LEARN SOMETHING, BUT NOW YOU'LL GO ON THE SAME AS BEFORE.
WON'T YOU?
NO, BECAUSE I REMEMBER HOW HE MADE ME FEEL.
FIRE AND BLOOD AND ANGUISH.
AND I CAN'T LISTEN TO ANY MORE OF YOUR TALK.

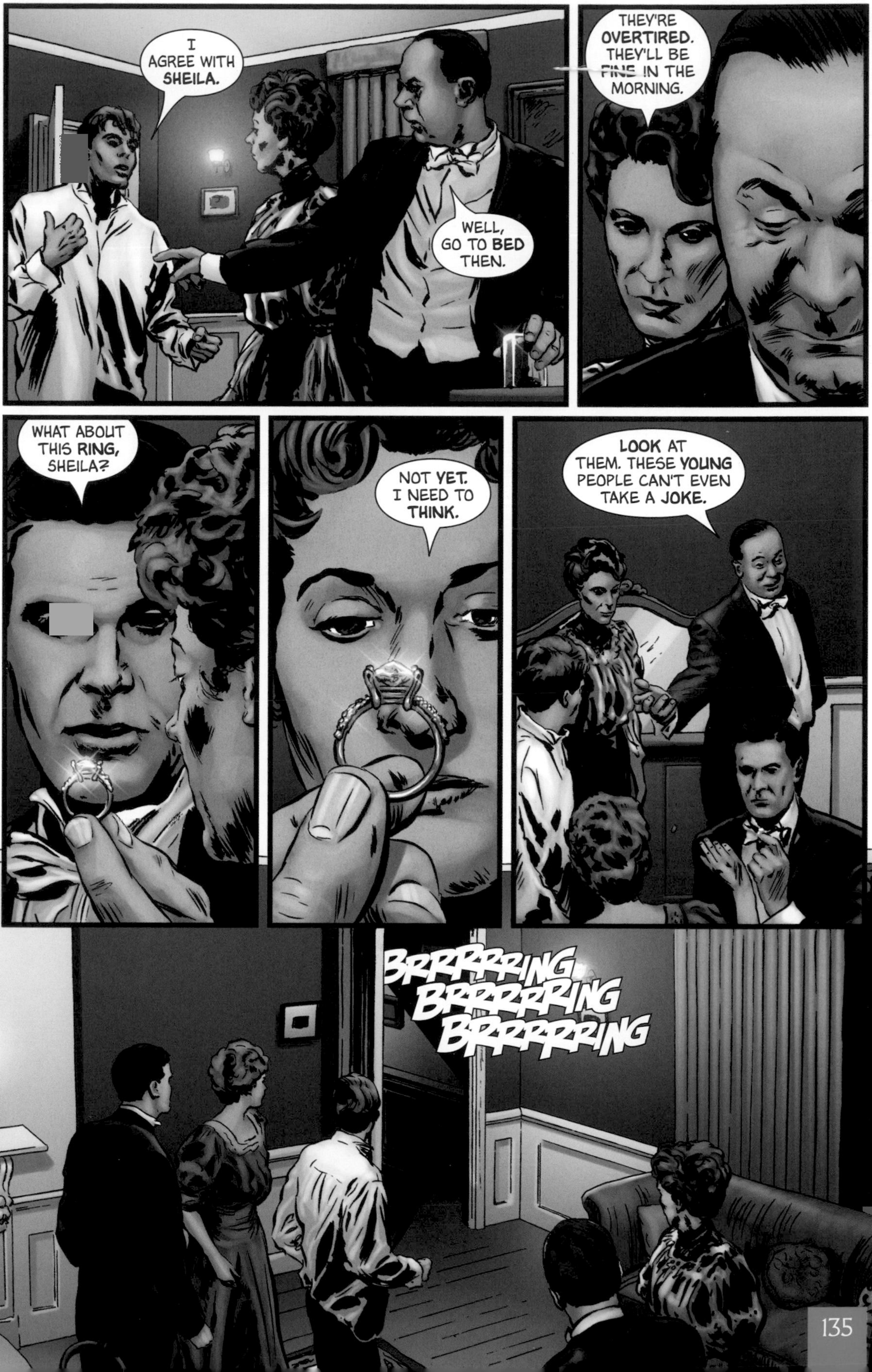
I AGREE WITH SHEILA.
WELL, GO TO BED THEN.
THEY'RE OVERTIRED. THEY'LL BE FINE IN THE MORNING.
WHAT ABOUT THIS RING, SHEILA?
NOT YET. I NEED TO THINK.
LOOK AT THEM. THESE YOUNG PEOPLE CAN'T EVEN TAKE A JOKE.
BRRRRRING
BRRRRRING
BRRRRRING

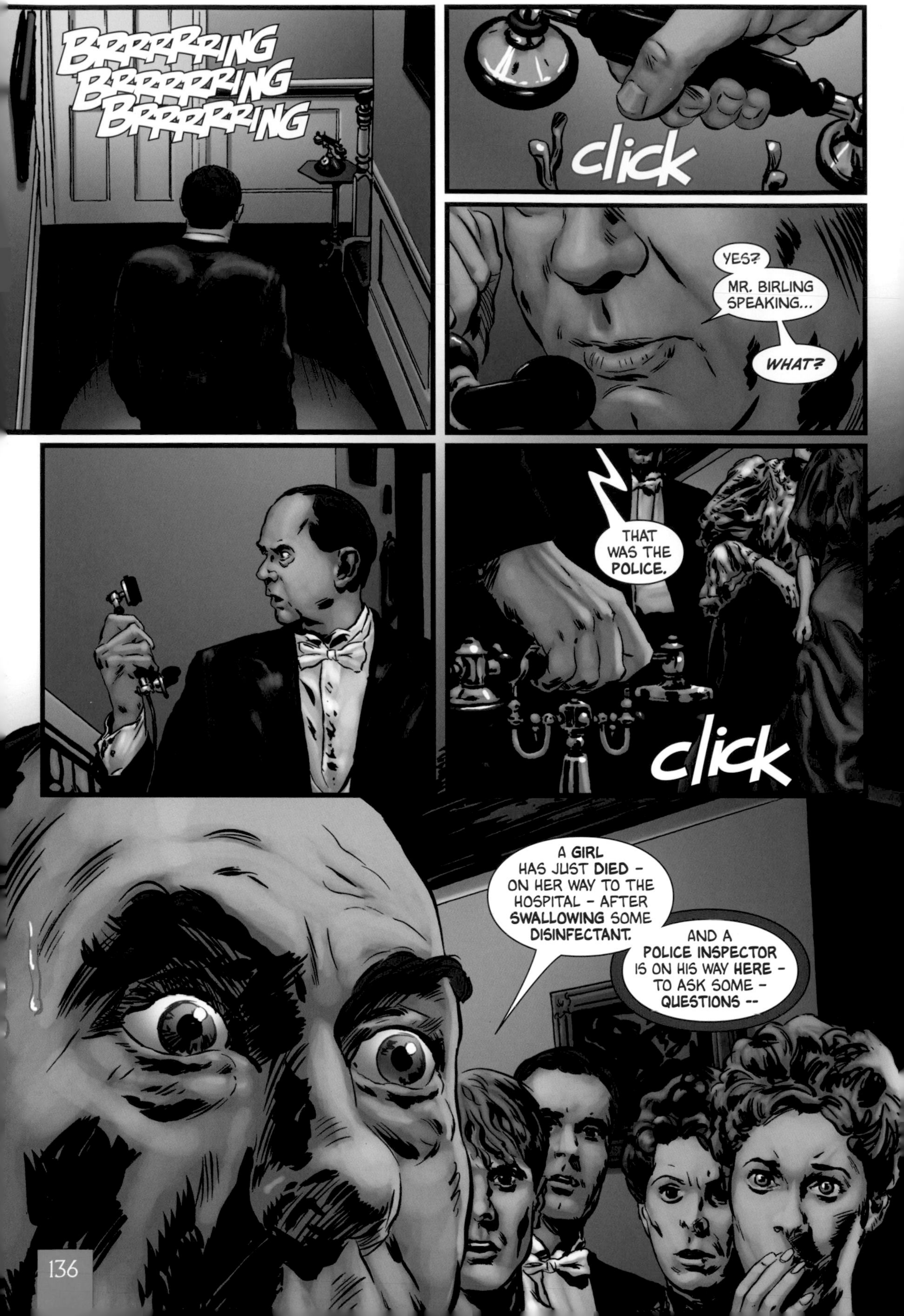
BRRRRRRING
BRRRRRRING
BRRRRRRING
click
YES?
MR. BIRLING SPEAKING...
WHAT?
THAT WAS THE POLICE.
click
A GIRL HAS JUST DIED - ON HER WAY TO THE HOSPITAL - AFTER SWALLOWING SOME DISINFECTANT.
AND A POLICE INSPECTOR IS ON HIS WAY HERE - TO ASK SOME - QUESTIONS --

An Inspector Calls

---◈---

The End

J. B. Priestley

(1894–1984)

John Priestley (he gave himself the middle name of "Boynton" later in life) was born on September 13, 1894 in Bradford, in the north of England. His father, Jonathan Priestley, was a schoolmaster, and his mother, Emma, had worked in a mill. Sadly, Emma died just a few months after giving birth to John, who, after his father remarried four years later, was raised by his kindly stepmother Amy.

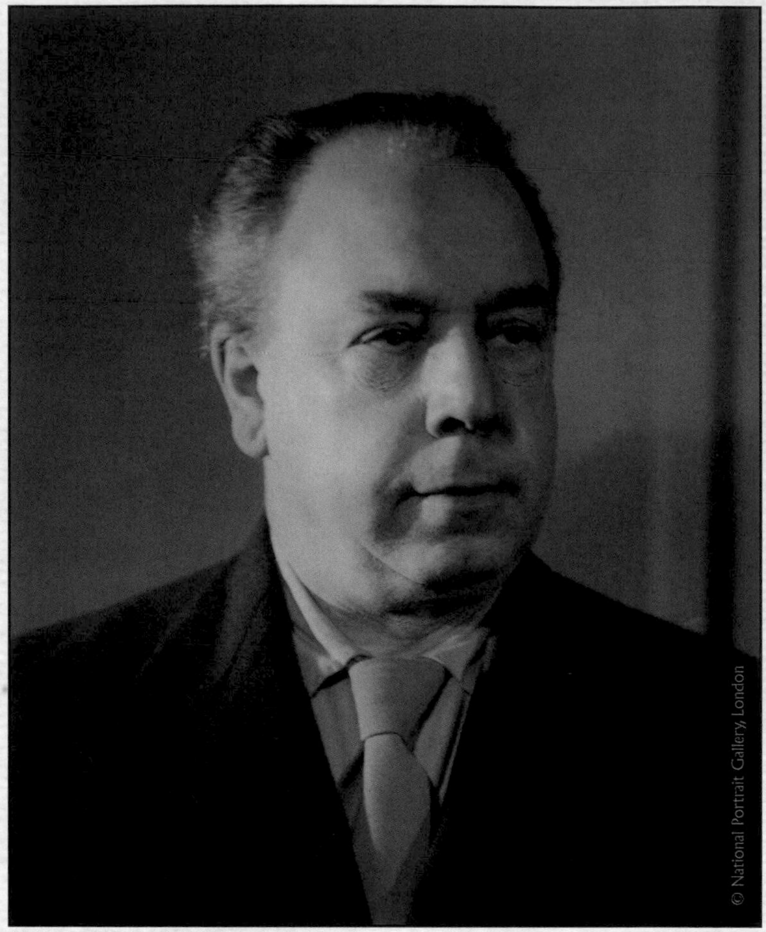

© National Portrait Gallery, London

Priestley attended Belle Vue School in Bradford and soon set his sights on writing. Although a gifted academic, he decided against going on to college, taking instead a modest office job at a local wool firm. He believed that, for a writer, life experience was more important than academic qualifications, and this office job gave him the time and freedom to pursue his literary ambitions. Far from turning his back on learning, however, he surrounded himself with books and used them to continue his education. It was also around this time that, through his father and his father's friends, Priestley became interested in socialism, a philosophy that ingrained themes and beliefs that appear throughout his works, most notably in ***An Inspector Calls.***

When World War I broke out in 1914, Priestley volunteered to join the infantry. He trained for a year in the south of England before being sent to the front line in 1915. Wounded in a mortar attack in 1916, he was sent back to England for treatment and returned to the trenches six months later, only to become a victim of a gas attack. He was left unfit for active duty and transferred to the Entertainers Section of the British Army, where he served until the end of the war.

Priestley held the rank of officer when he left the army in 1919. He received a small grant to attend Cambridge University, where he studied Modern History and Political Science. Although he graduated with a degree, he was never comfortable with the life of an academic and decided to change direction.

In 1921, Priestley married Emily "Pat" Tempest, a librarian from Bradford, and together they began a new life in London. There they had two daughters, Barbara (1923) and Sylvia (1924), while Priestley established himself as a freelance non-fiction writer, completing numerous books and essays around this time. Tragically, Emily died of cancer in 1925, leaving Priestley to raise his daughters. He remarried a year later to Jane Wyndham Lewis, with whom he had two further daughters and a son.

Priestley collaborated with Hugh Walpole on his historical novel *Farthing Hall* in 1929, and its popularity gave him sufficient financial freedom and confidence to attempt his first solo novel. The result was *The Good Companions* which won the James Tait Black Memorial Prize for fiction. It was quickly followed by *Angel Pavement* in 1930, firmly establishing Priestley as a force within the literary world.

Priestley then turned his hand to writing plays. He collaborated on a stage adaptation of *The Good Companions*, and followed that with his first solo-authored play, *Dangerous Corner*, which opened in 1932 and was a great success. Rather than capitalize on this breakthrough, Priestley was soon traveling the country so that he could see first-hand the troubles experienced by industrial Britain during the recession. The result was a non-fiction publication, *English Journey*, which not only established Priestley as a social commentator, but also gave him themes that paved the way for his later works, including *An Inspector Calls*.

Shortly after the start of World War II, Priestley had another career change, becoming a broadcaster for the BBC. Attracting over 16 million listeners, Priestley felt that his broadcasts should try to boost moral during those difficult times by talking about how life would be after the war and by promoting traditional values. Despite his popularity (Priestley's shows had the highest listening figures of any radio program aside from Churchill's speeches), the BBC cancelled his series of "Postscripts" after just a few months because the Ministry of Information believed he was too critical of the government.

Although he was a prolific writer across multiple disciplines, crafting plays, novels, essays, and several volumes of autobiography, Priestley tends to be remembered most for his intense dramas. Through his scripts he was able to couple his political beliefs with his deep interest in time theories, exploring how premonitions enable us to experience events before they occur. The finest example of this combination of themes is his 1945 masterpiece, *An Inspector Calls*. Interestingly, the play was first performed in Moscow, reaching London a year later in October 1946, where it enjoyed a long, successful run.

Priestley continued to balance his writing with his political and social responsibilities. He ran as an independent candidate in the 1945 general election but was not elected as a Member of Parliament, and from 1946-7 he was the British delegate at UNESCO conferences (United Nations Educational, Scientific and Cultural Organization). It was through UNESCO that he met the archaeologist and writer Jacquette Hawkes, whom Priestley married following his divorce from Jane in 1953. Later, spurred on by the nuclear testing of a hydrogen bomb in the Christmas Islands in 1957 (which he argued against in his essay "Britain and the Nuclear Bomb"), he became a founding member of the Campaign for Nuclear Disarmament (CND).

He wrote well into his seventies and remained generally active. The University of Bradford awarded him an honorary doctorate in 1970, and he was granted the freedom of the City of Bradford in 1973. In 1975 he opened the J.B. Priestley Library within the University of Bradford. Because of his strong socialist beliefs, he rejected offers of a knighthood, but in 1977 he accepted the Queen's Order of Merit because the honor had no political connections.

J.B. Priestley died on August 14, 1984, just 30 days before his 90th birthday, at his home in Stratford-upon-Avon, England. Fittingly, the City of Bradford erected a statue in his honor, which stands outside the National Media Museum in the center of what has become the UNESCO City of Film.

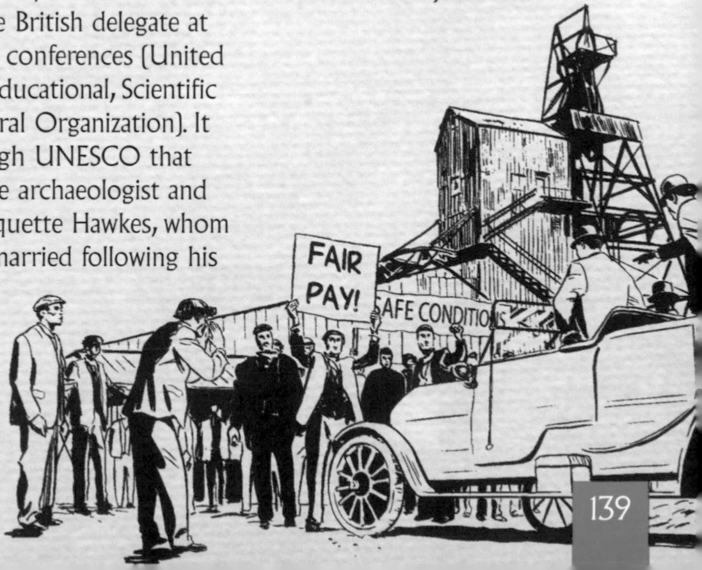
FAIR
PAY!

Page Creation

1. Script

The process starts with the writing of the script. The script describes the artwork for the artist to draw and also details the dialogue, captions and sound effects that will be added by the letterer. There are two editions of *An Inspector Calls*: Original Text and Quick Text. Both use the same artwork but feature different dialogue.

An Inspector Calls by Jason Cobley for Classical Comics

Page 131

Panel 1
We have a row of three small, silent close-ups here, as they wait tensely and nervously for the answer on the other end of the phone. In this panel, Birling is wiping his brow with a handkerchief.

Gerald (off)	is that the infirmary? This is Mr. Gerald Croft – of Crofts Limited… yes… we're rather worried about one of our employees.	Is that the infirmary? This is Gerald Croft of Crofts Limited. I am worried about one of our employees.

Panel 2
Here, we have a close up of Sheila shivering, hugging herself around the upper arms.

Gerald (off)	Have you had a girl brought in this afternoon who committed suicide by drinking disinfectant – or any like suicide?	Have you had a girl brought in who killed herself by drinking disinfectant?

Panel 3
In this last close up of the page, Eric is clasping his hands together nervously, waiting.

Gerald (off)	Yes, I'll wait.	Yes, I'll wait.

Panel 4
This is a close up of Gerald talking on the phone, looking quite impassive, his face giving nothing away.

Gerald	Yes? … You're certain of that… I see. Well, thank you very much… good night.	Are you sure? Well, thank you. Goodnight.

Panel 5
This is a small close up of Gerald's hand replacing the receiver back in the telephone cradle.
Sound FX: Click

Panel 6
His hand just moving away from the telephone, Gerald looks at them all, still tense and nervous, he still expressionless as if the information is almost an anti-climax.

Gerald	**No girl** has died in there today. **Nobody's** been brought in after drinking disinfectant. They haven't had a **suicide** for **months.**	No girl has died in there today, and they haven't had a suicide for months.

A page from the script of *An Inspector Calls* showing the two versions of the text.

2. Character Designs

While the scriptwriter is working on the panel descriptions, the artist can start work on designs for each character. He is striving to find a "look" for each individual that reflects his or her age and personality while making each person distinct to help the reader tell one from another.

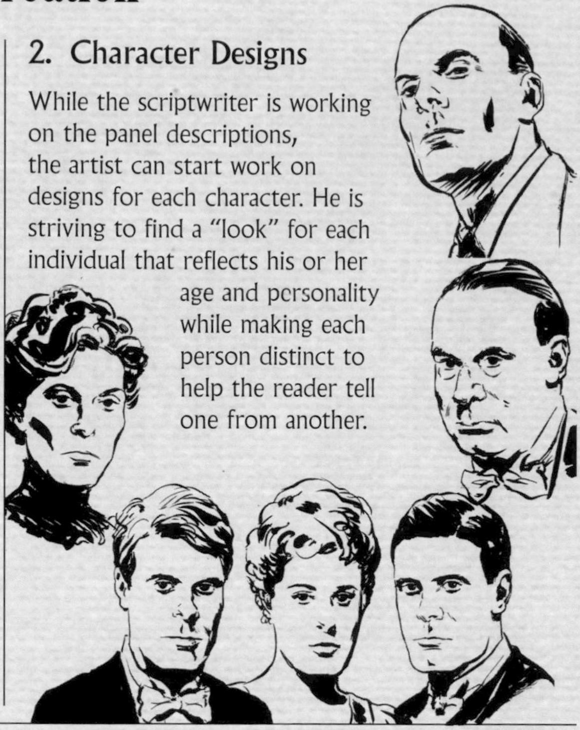

3. Pencils

When creating the artwork for each page, the artist first creates a rough layout to check overall proportions, after which he creates a pencil drawing. He is considering many things during this process, including the pacing of the story, body language, character sizes, perspective, lettering space, texture and lighting. The page below is a superb example of Will capturing mood and tension while also putting over a sense of the passing of time.

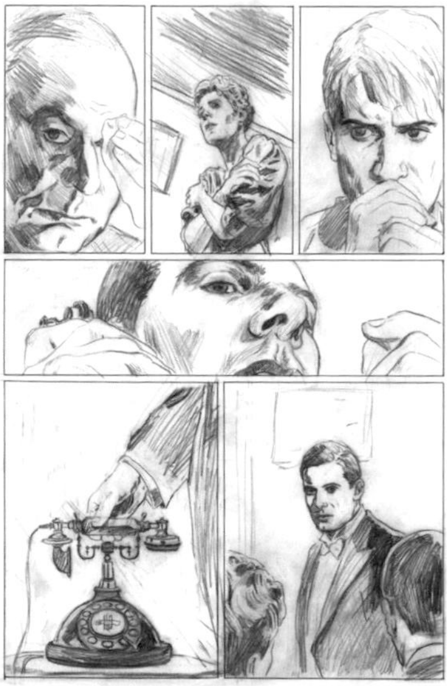

The pencil drawing of page 131

4. Inks

When completed, the pencil sketch is then inked. Inking is not simply tracing over the pencil sketch; it is the process of using black ink to fill in the shaded areas and to add clarity and cohesion to the penciled artwork. Inking also adds texture and drama through shading and lighting, aiming all the time to retain the energy of the expressive pencils.

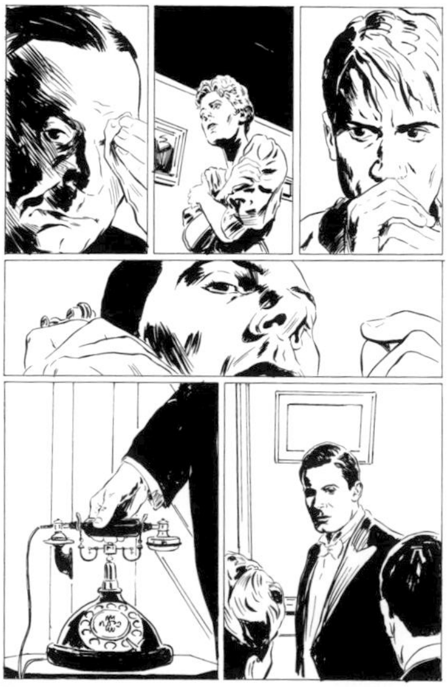

The inked page with pencil drawing removed.

5. Coloring

Adding color really brings the page to life.

The finished artwork before lettering.

There is far more to the coloring stage than just replacing the white areas with color. Some of the linework itself might be replaced with color, also, the light sources are considered for shadows and highlights, and effects are added. Finally, the whole page is color-balanced to match the other pages in the book.

6. Lettering

The final stage is to add the captions, sound effects, and speech bubbles from the script, which are laid on top of each colored page. Two versions of each page are lettered, one for each of the two editions of the book (Original Text and Quick Text).

The lettered pages are then compiled into the finished books, ready for printing.

IS THAT THE HOSPITAL?
THIS IS GERALD CROFT OF CROFTS LIMITED.
I AM WORRIED ABOUT ONE OF OUR EMPLOYEES.
HAVE YOU HAD A GIRL BROUGHT IN WHO KILLED HERSELF BY DRINKING DISINFECTANT?
-- I'LL WAIT --
-- ARE YOU SURE? WELL, THANK YOU.
GOOD NIGHT.
click
NO GIRL HAS DIED IN THERE TODAY, AND THEY HAVEN'T HAD A SUICIDE FOR MONTHS.
131

The finished page 131 with Quick Text lettering.

ORE TITLES AVAILABLE FRO

Classic Literature in a choice of 2 text versions. Simply choose the text version to match your reading level.

Original Text	THE CLASSIC NOVEL BROUGHT TO LIFE IN FULL COLOR!
Quick Text	THE FULL STORY IN QUICK MODERN ENGLISH FOR A FAST-PACED READ!

Jane Eyre: The Graphic Novel (Charlotte Brontë)

• Script Adaptation: Amy Corzine • Artwork: John M. Burns
• Letters: Terry Wiley

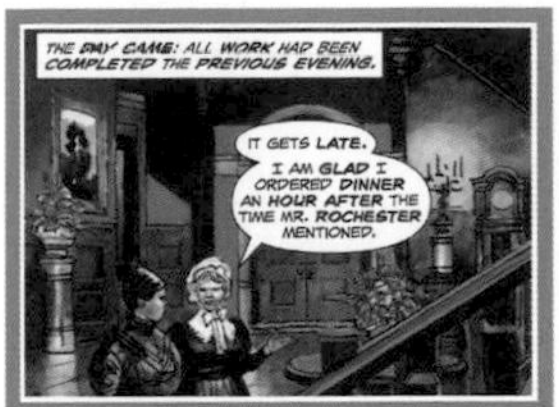
THE DAY CAME: ALL WORK HAD BEEN COMPLETED THE PREVIOUS EVENING.
IT GETS LATE.
I AM GLAD I ORDERED DINNER AN HOUR AFTER THE TIME MR. ROCHESTER MENTIONED.

ISBN: 978-1-906332-47-1

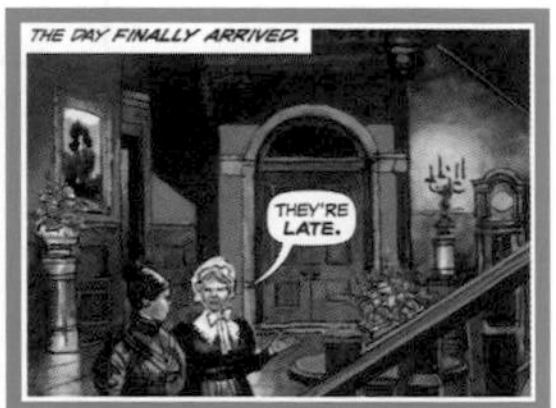
THE DAY FINALLY ARRIVED.
THEY'RE LATE.

ISBN: 978-1-906332-48-8

"I scorn your idea of love and the counterfeit sentiment you offer. And I scorn you when you offer it."

• 144 Pages • $16.95

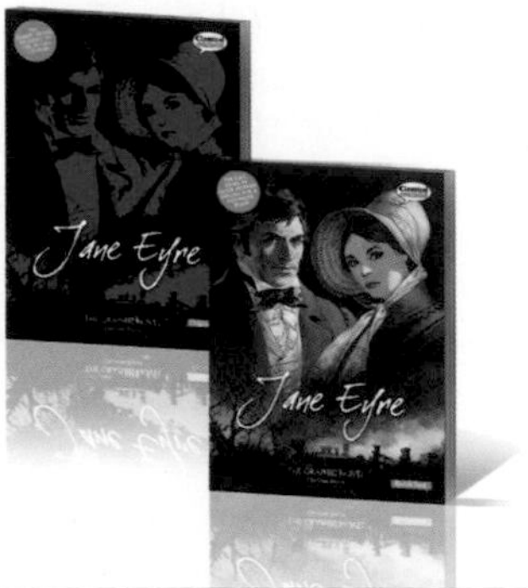

Frankenstein: The Graphic Novel (Mary Shelley)

• Script Adaptation: Jason Cobley • Linework: Declan Shalvey • Art Direction: Jon Haward
• Colors: Jason Cardy & Kat Nicholson • Letters: Terry Wiley

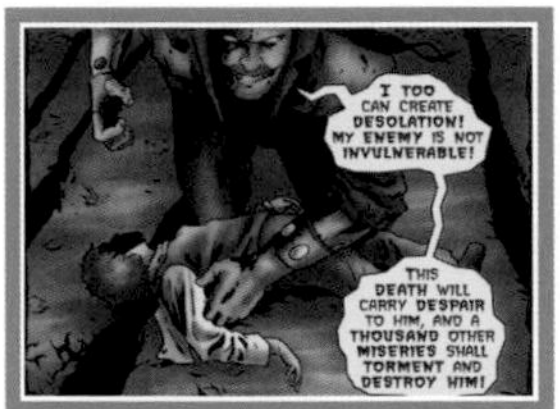
I TOO CAN CREATE DESOLATION! MY ENEMY IS NOT INVULNERABLE!
THIS DEATH WILL CARRY DESPAIR TO HIM, AND A THOUSAND OTHER MISERIES SHALL TORMENT AND DESTROY HIM!

ISBN: 978-1-906332-49-5

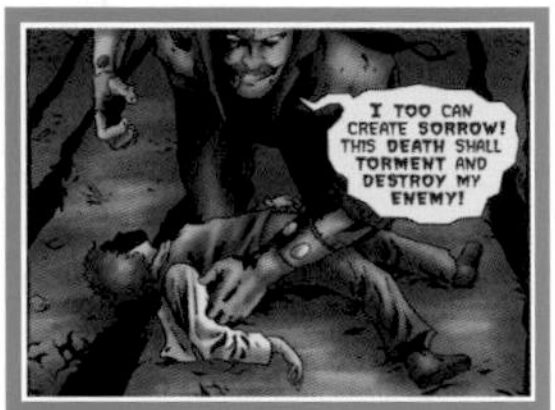
I TOO CAN CREATE SORROW! THIS DEATH SHALL TORMENT AND DESTROY MY ENEMY!

ISBN: 978-1-906332-50-1

"Cursed be the hands that formed you!"

• 144 Pages • $16.95

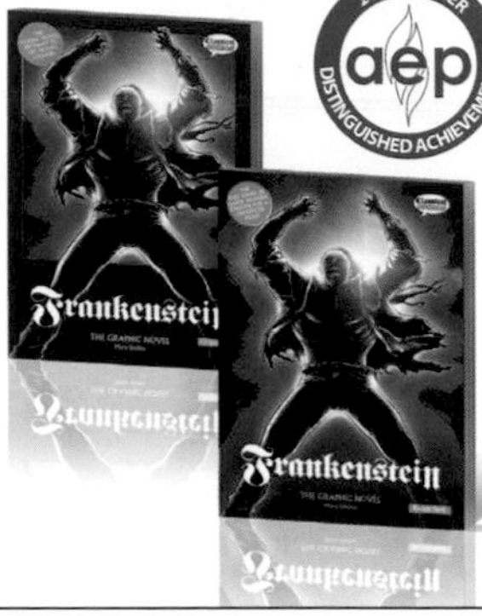

2009 WINNER aep DISTINGUISHED ACHIEVEMENT

A Christmas Carol: The Graphic Novel (Charles Dickens)

• Script Adaptation: Seán Michael Wilson • Pencils: Mike Collins
• Inks: David Roach • Colors: James Offredi • Letters: Terry Wiley

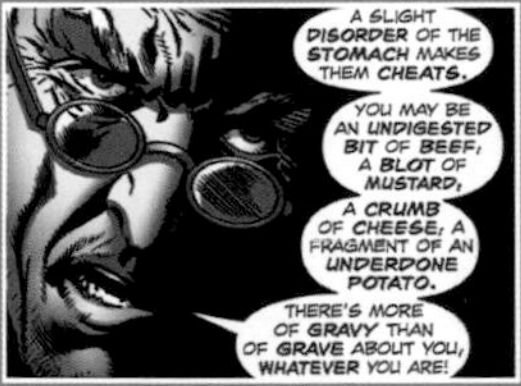
A SLIGHT DISORDER OF THE STOMACH MAKES THEM CHEATS.
YOU MAY BE AN UNDIGESTED BIT OF BEEF, A BLOT OF MUSTARD,
A CRUMB OF CHEESE, A FRAGMENT OF AN UNDERDONE POTATO.
THERE'S MORE OF GRAVY THAN OF GRAVE ABOUT YOU, WHATEVER YOU ARE!

ISBN: 978-1-906332-51-8

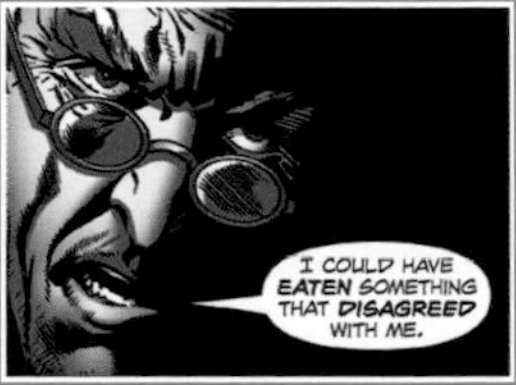
I COULD HAVE EATEN SOMETHING THAT DISAGREED WITH ME.

ISBN: 978-1-906332-52-5

"I will honour Christmas in my heart, and try to keep it all the year. I will live in the Past, the Present, and the Future."

• 160 Pages • $16.95

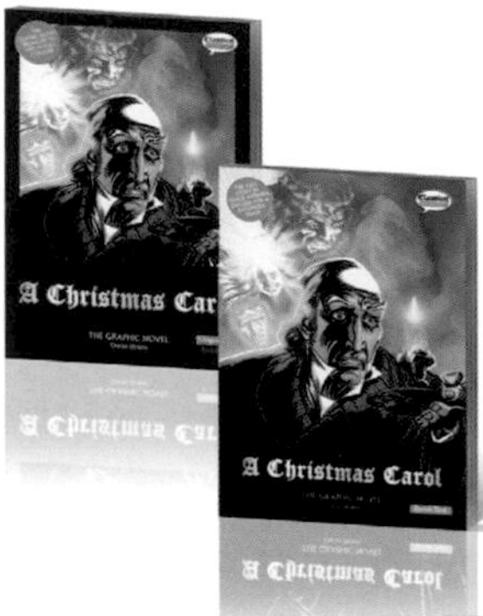

Great Expectations: The Graphic Novel (Charles Dickens)

• Script Adaptation: Jen Green • Linework: John Stokes • Colouring: Digikore Studios Ltd
• Color Finishing: Jason Cardy • Letters: Jim Campbell

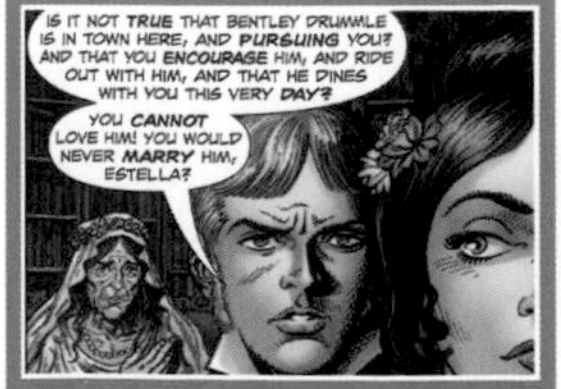
IS IT NOT TRUE THAT BENTLEY DRUMMLE IS IN TOWN HERE, AND PURSUING YOU? AND THAT YOU ENCOURAGE HIM, AND RIDE OUT WITH HIM, AND THAT HE DINES WITH YOU THIS VERY DAY?
YOU CANNOT LOVE HIM! YOU WOULD NEVER MARRY HIM, ESTELLA?

ISBN: 978-1-906332-59-4

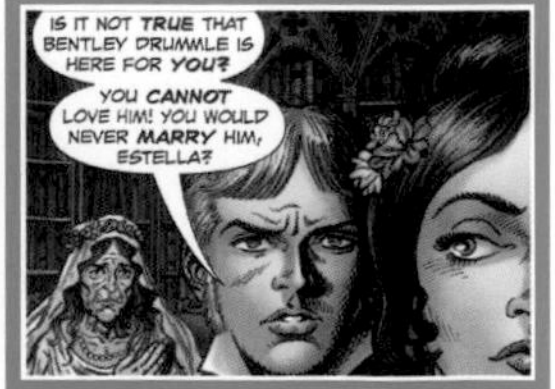
IS IT NOT TRUE THAT BENTLEY DRUMMLE IS HERE FOR YOU?
YOU CANNOT LOVE HIM! YOU WOULD NEVER MARRY HIM, ESTELLA?

ISBN: 978-1-906332-60-0

"I never saw my father or my mother, and never saw any likeness of either of them."

• 160 Pages • $16.95

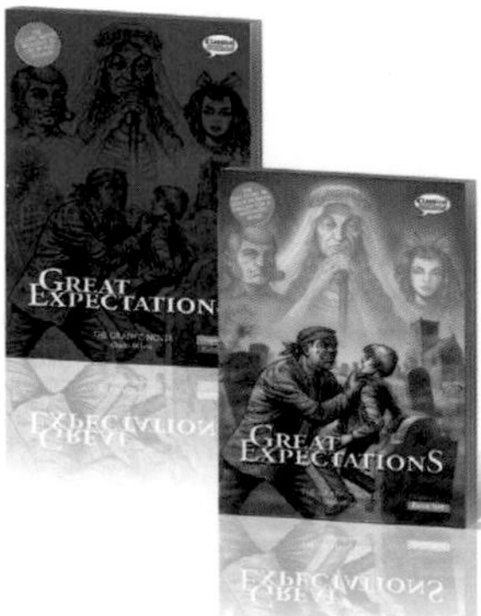

SHAKESPEARE RANGE

Shakespeare's plays in a choice of 3 text versions. Simply choose the text version to match your reading level.

Original Text	THE ENTIRE SHAKESPEARE PLAY - UNABRIDGED!
Plain Text	THE ENTIRE PLAY TRANSLATED INTO PLAIN ENGLISH!
Quick Text	THE ENTIRE PLAY IN QUICK MODERN ENGLISH FOR A FAST-PACED READ!

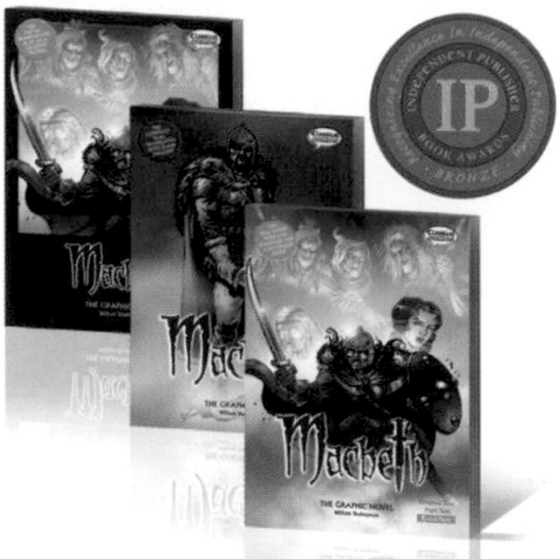

Macbeth: The Graphic Novel (William Shakespeare)

- Script Adaptation: John McDonald • Pencils: & Inks: Jon Haward
- Inking Assistant: Gary Erskine • Colors & Letters: Nigel Dobbyn

144 Pages • $16.95

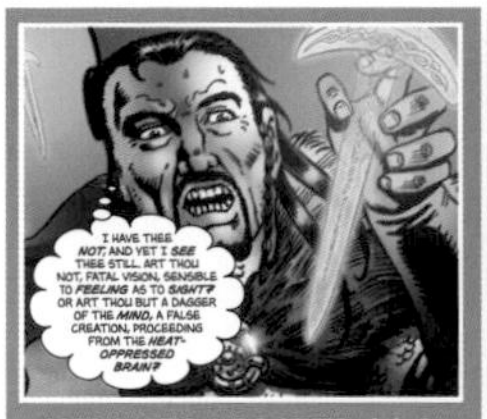
I HAVE THEE NOT, AND YET I SEE THEE STILL. ART THOU NOT, FATAL VISION, SENSIBLE TO FEELING AS TO SIGHT? OR ART THOU BUT A DAGGER OF THE MIND, A FALSE CREATION, PROCEEDING FROM THE HEAT-OPPRESSED BRAIN?

ISBN: 978-1-906332-44-0

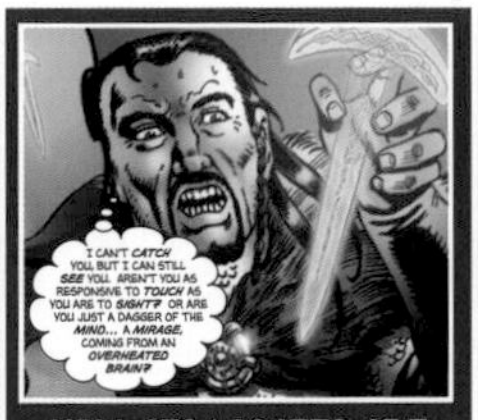
I CAN'T CATCH YOU, BUT I CAN STILL SEE YOU. AREN'T YOU AS RESPONSIVE TO TOUCH AS YOU ARE TO SIGHT? OR ARE YOU JUST A DAGGER OF THE MIND... A MIRAGE, COMING FROM AN OVERHEATED BRAIN?

ISBN: 978-1-906332-45-7

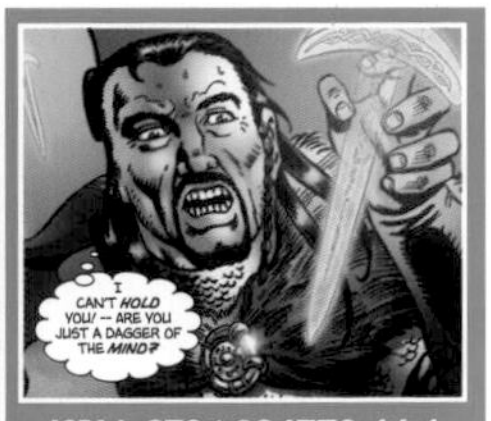
I CAN'T HOLD YOU! -- ARE YOU JUST A DAGGER OF THE MIND?

ISBN: 978-1-906332-46-4

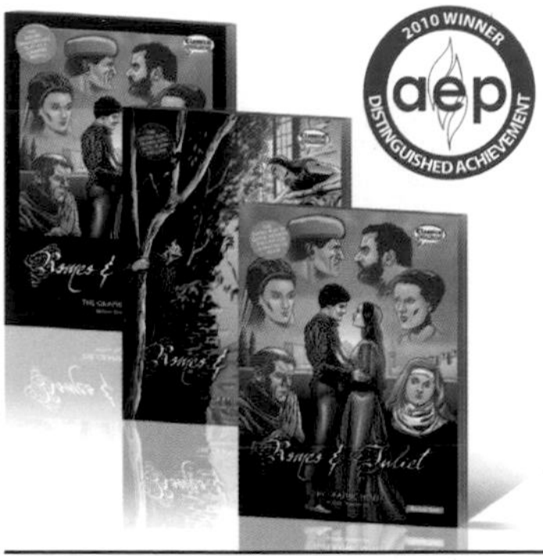

Romeo & Juliet: The Graphic Novel (William Shakespeare)

- Script Adaptation: John McDonald • Linework: Will Volley
- Colors: Jim Devlin • Letters: Jim Campbell

168 Pages • $16.95

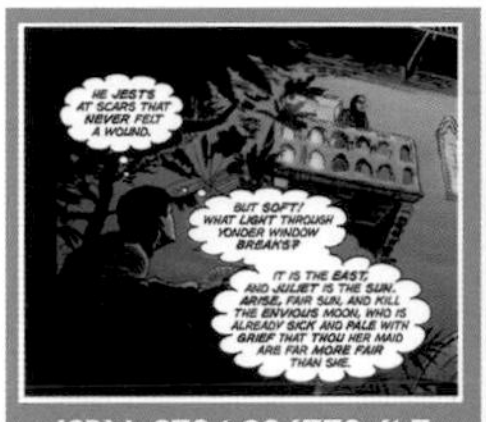
HE JESTS AT SCARS THAT NEVER FELT A WOUND.
BUT SOFT! WHAT LIGHT THROUGH YONDER WINDOW BREAKS?
IT IS THE EAST, AND JULIET IS THE SUN. ARISE, FAIR SUN, AND KILL THE ENVIOUS MOON, WHO IS ALREADY SICK AND PALE WITH GRIEF THAT THOU HER MAID ARE FAR MORE FAIR THAN SHE.

ISBN: 978-1-906332-61-7

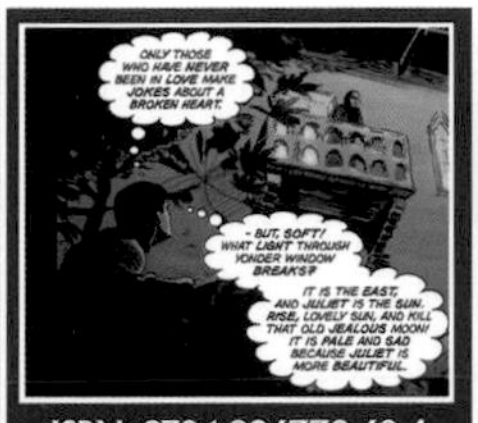
ONLY THOSE WHO HAVE NEVER BEEN IN LOVE MAKE JOKES ABOUT A BROKEN HEART.
- BUT, SOFT! WHAT LIGHT THROUGH YONDER WINDOW BREAKS?
IT IS THE EAST, AND JULIET IS THE SUN. RISE, LOVELY SUN, AND KILL THAT OLD JEALOUS MOON! IT IS PALE AND SAD BECAUSE JULIET IS MORE BEAUTIFUL.

ISBN: 978-1-906332-62-4

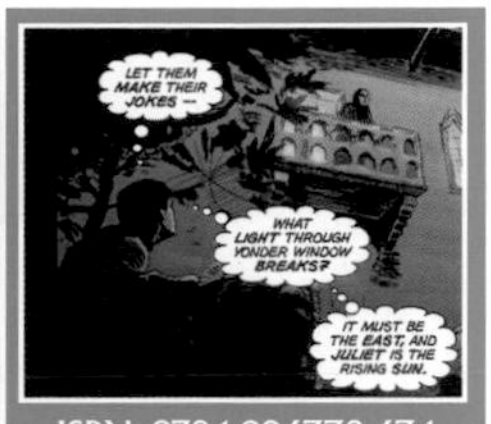
LET THEM MAKE THEIR JOKES --
WHAT LIGHT THROUGH YONDER WINDOW BREAKS?
IT MUST BE THE EAST, AND JULIET IS THE RISING SUN.

ISBN: 978-1-906332-63-1

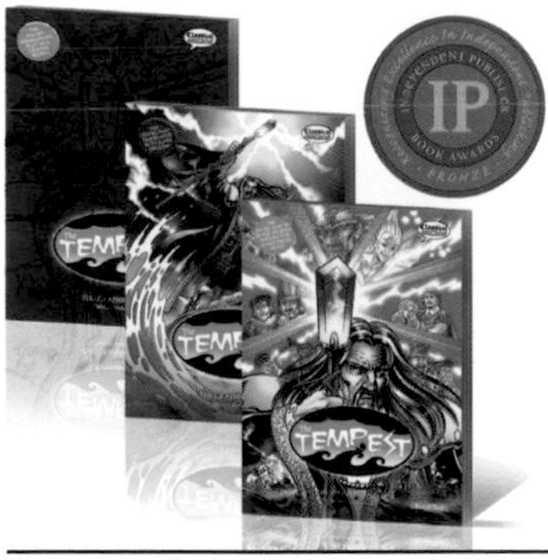

The Tempest: The Graphic Novel (William Shakespeare)

- Script Adaptation: John McDonald • Pencils: Jon Haward
- Inks: Gary Erskine • Colors: & Letters: Nigel Dobbyn

144 Pages • $16.95

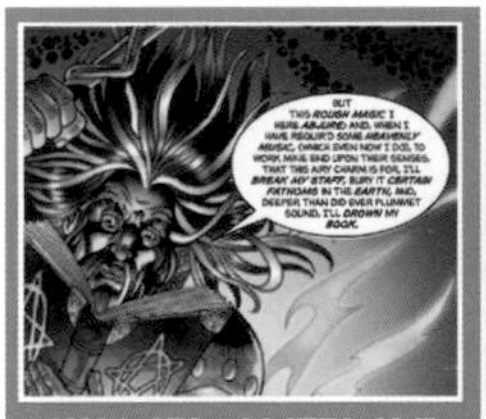
BUT THIS ROUGH MAGIC I HERE ABJURE; AND, WHEN I HAVE REQUIR'D SOME HEAVENLY MUSIC, (WHICH EVEN NOW I DO), TO WORK MINE END UPON THEIR SENSES, THAT THIS AIRY CHARM IS FOR, I'LL BREAK MY STAFF, BURY IT CERTAIN FATHOMS IN THE EARTH, AND, DEEPER THAN DID EVER PLUMMET SOUND, I'LL DROWN MY BOOK.

ISBN: 978-1-906332-69-3

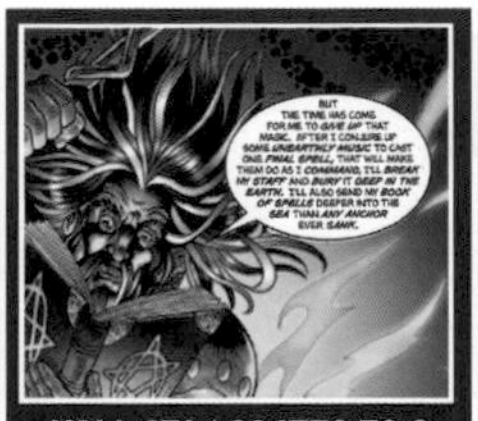
BUT THE TIME HAS COME FOR ME TO GIVE UP THAT MAGIC. AFTER I CONJURE UP SOME UNEARTHLY MUSIC TO CAST ONE FINAL SPELL, THAT WILL MAKE THEM DO AS I COMMAND, I'LL BREAK MY STAFF AND BURY IT DEEP IN THE EARTH. I'LL ALSO SEND MY BOOK OF SPELLS DEEPER INTO THE SEA THAN ANY ANCHOR EVER SANK.

ISBN: 978-1-906332-70-9

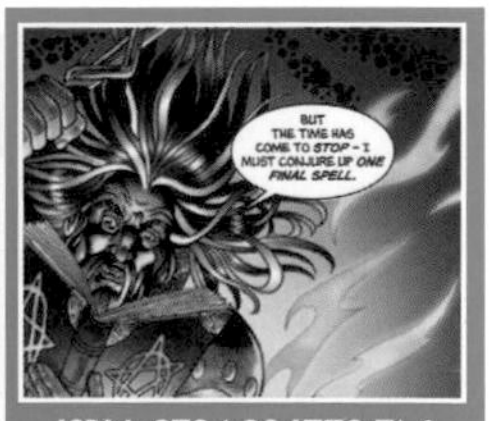
BUT THE TIME HAS COME TO STOP - I MUST CONJURE UP ONE FINAL SPELL.

ISBN: 978-1-906332-71-6

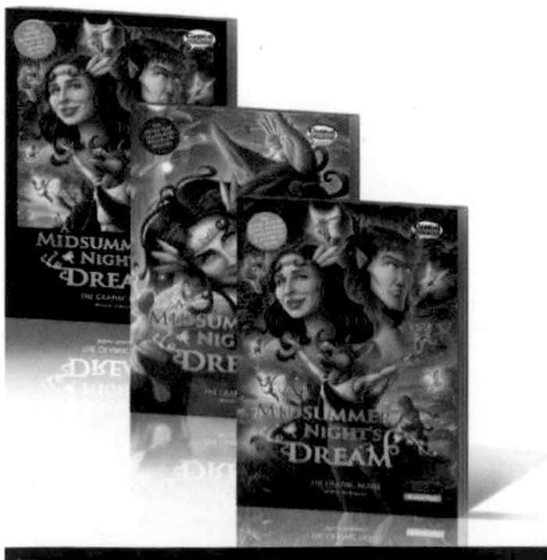

A Midsummer Night's Dream: The Graphic Novel (William Shakespeare)

- Script Adaptation: John McDonald • Characters & Artwork: Kat Nicholson & Jason Cardy
- Letters: Jim Campbell

144 Pages • $16.95

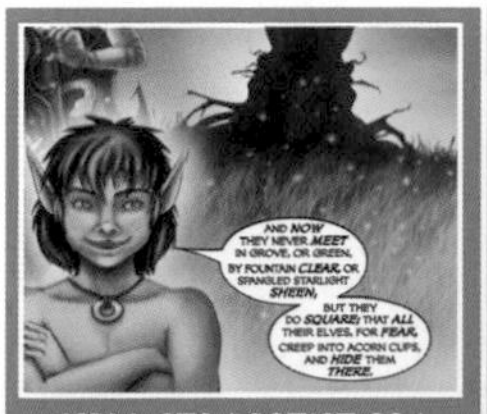
AND NOW THEY NEVER MEET IN GROVE, OR GREEN, BY FOUNTAIN CLEAR, OR SPANGLED STARLIGHT SHEEN,
BUT THEY DO SQUARE; THAT ALL THEIR ELVES, FOR FEAR, CREEP INTO ACORN CUPS, AND HIDE THEM THERE.

ISBN: 978-1-907127-28-1

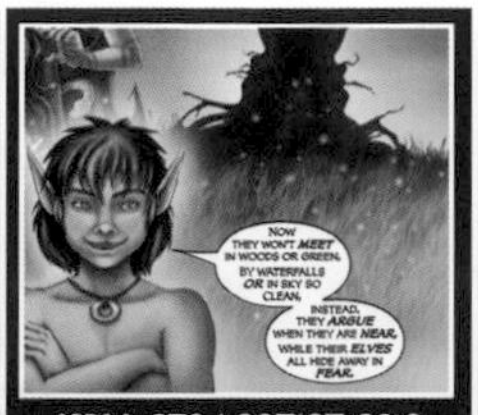
NOW THEY WON'T MEET IN WOODS OR GREEN, BY WATERFALLS OR IN SKY SO CLEAN.
INSTEAD, THEY ARGUE WHEN THEY ARE NEAR, WHILE THEIR ELVES ALL HIDE AWAY IN FEAR.

ISBN: 978-1-907127-29-8

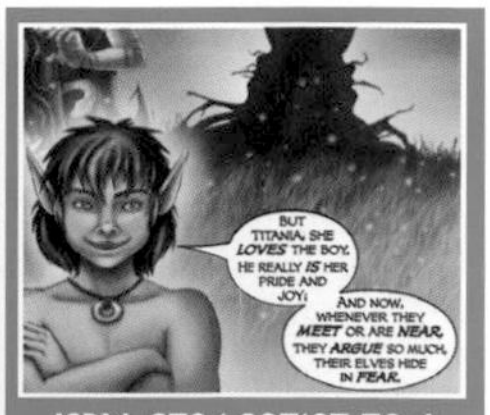
BUT TITANIA, SHE LOVES THE BOY. HE REALLY IS HER PRIDE AND JOY;
AND NOW, WHENEVER THEY MEET OR ARE NEAR, THEY ARGUE SO MUCH, THEIR ELVES HIDE IN FEAR.

ISBN: 978-1-907127-30-4

To see the complete range, and to view samples online, go to www.classicalcomics.com

UR AWARD-WINNING RANGE

"Classical Comics' graphic novels stand out way above others in the genre. The quality of the artwork is exceptional – the detail, relevance to the subject matter and the way they convey the emotions of the books are wonderful. "
Sarah Brew
www.parentsintouch.co.uk

"The students have been really enthusiastic and the teachers have really enjoyed teaching them."
Joanna Adkin, Senior Teacher

"It's capturing the lightning in a different–shaped bottle. Amazing stuff!"
Mike Carey, Novelist & Comic Writer

LOOK WHAT PEOPLE ARE SAYING ABOUT CLASSICAL COMICS.

The Canterville Ghost: The Graphic Novel (Oscar Wilde)

• Script Adaptation: Seán Michael Wilson • Linework: Steve Bryant
• Colors: Jason Millet • Letters: Jim Campbell

WELL, REALLY, WHAT WAS I TO DO? IT IS A VERY DIFFICULT THING TO GET REAL BLOOD NOWADAYS,
AND, AS YOUR BROTHER BEGAN IT ALL WITH HIS PARAGON DETERGENT, I CERTAINLY SAW NO REASON WHY I SHOULD NOT HAVE YOUR PAINTS.
ISBN: 978-1-906332-72-3

WHAT ELSE COULD I DO?
IT IS HARD TO GET REAL BLOOD, AND AS YOUR BROTHER KEPT CLEANING THE SPOT, I SAW NO REASON WHY I SHOULDN'T HAVE YOUR PAINTS.
ISBN: 978-1-906332-73-0

"Quick, quick," cried the Ghost, "or it will be too late."

• 136 Pages • $16.95

The Canterville Ghost
THE GRAPHIC NOVEL

Wuthering Heights: The Graphic Novel (Emily Brontë)

• Script Adaptation: Seán Michael Wilson • Artwork: John M. Burns
• Letters: Jim Campbell

IF I WERE IN HEAVEN, NELLY, I SHOULD BE EXTREMELY MISERABLE. I DREAMT ONCE THAT I WAS THERE.
HEAVEN DID NOT SEEM TO BE MY HOME; AND I BROKE MY HEART WITH WEEPING TO COME BACK TO EARTH; AND THE ANGELS WERE SO ANGRY THAT THEY FLUNG ME OUT INTO THE MIDDLE OF THE HEATH ON THE TOP OF WUTHERING HEIGHTS; WHERE I WOKE SOBBING FOR JOY.
THAT WILL DO TO EXPLAIN MY SECRET, AS WELL AS THE OTHER.
ISBN: 978-1-907127-11-3

I DREAMT THAT I WAS IN HEAVEN, BUT I WAS NOT HAPPY THERE AND I WEPT TO COME BACK TO EARTH.
THE ANGELS WERE SO ANGRY THAT THEY FLUNG ME OUT INTO THE MIDDLE OF THE MOORS, WHERE I WOKE CRYING WITH JOY.
ISBN: 978-1-907127-12-0

"That minx, Catherine Linton, or Earnshaw, or however she was called – wicked little soul!"

• 160 Pages • $16.95

Wuthering Heights
THE GRAPHIC NOVEL

Dracula: The Graphic Novel (Bram Stoker)

• Script Adaptation: Jason Cobley • Linework: Staz Johnson
• Colors: James Offredi • Letters: Jim Campbell

WELCOME TO MY HOUSE! ENTER FREELY AND OF YOUR OWN WILL! COME FREELY. GO SAFELY.
I AM DRACULA, AND I BID YOU WELCOME, MR. HARKER, TO MY HOUSE.
COME IN; THE NIGHT AIR IS CHILL, AND YOU MUST NEED TO EAT AND REST. IT IS LATE, AND MY PEOPLE ARE NOT AVAILABLE.
LET ME SEE TO YOUR COMFORT MYSELF.
ISBN: 978-1-906332-67-9

WELCOME TO MY HOUSE!
I AM DRACULA, AND I BID YOU WELCOME.
YOU MUST NEED TO EAT AND REST. IT IS LATE, AND MY PEOPLE ARE NOT AVAILABLE. LET ME LOOK AFTER YOU.
ISBN: 978-1-906332-68-6

"I went down into the vaults. There lay the Count! He was either dead or asleep, I could not say which."

• 152 Pages • $16.95

DRACULA
THE GRAPHIC NOVEL

Sweeney Todd: The Graphic Novel (Anonymous)

• Script Adaptation: Seán Michael Wilson • Linework: Declan Shalvey
• Colors: Jason Cardy & Kat Nicholson • Letters: Jim Campbell

I'LL CUT YOUR THROAT FROM EAR TO EAR, IF YOU REPEAT ONE WORD OF WHAT PASSES IN THIS SHOP, OR DARE TO MAKE ANY SUPPOSITION, OR DRAW ANY CONCLUSION FROM ANYTHING YOU MAY SEE, OR HEAR, OR FANCY YOU SEE OR HEAR.
I'LL CUT YOUR THROAT FROM EAR TO EAR - DO YOU UNDERSTAND ME?
ISBN: 978-1-907127-09-0

I WILL CUT YOUR THROAT IF YOU TELL ANYONE WHAT GOES ON HERE - DO YOU UNDERSTAND?
ISBN: 978-1-907127-10-6

"Oh! to be sure, he came here, and I shaved him and polished him off."

• 168 Pages • $16.95

SWEENEY TODD
THE DEMON BARBER OF FLEET STREET
THE GRAPHIC NOVEL

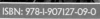